P9-DHQ-127

"We were both drinking," Luke said about his ex. "A lot."

Claire gave him an anxious look.

"One night she went out, with a blood-alcohol reading that was something like three times the legal limit, and plowed into a tree."

"Oh, Luke. Was she hurt? Was anyone else?"

Aside from that night at the ER, he'd never talked about the baby. Not with anyone.

"She wasn't wearing a seat belt, so she was pretty badly banged up. And...she was pregnant, and she lost the baby."

"Oh, my God. Luke, I'm so sorry."

"I accused her of being careless and irresponsible, trying to trap me into marrying her, forcing me to have a baby I didn't want."

Claire snatched her hand away, averting her eyes.

He hated that she pulled away, mostly because he had no clue what it meant. Had he said too much? Sounded too harsh?

"She knew I didn't want a family. There's no way I'll bring another Devlin child into the world and have it grow up the way I did."

"But you're not your father, Luke!"

The Puppy Connection

Lee McKenzie & Pamela Stone

Previously published as *Daddy, Unexpectedly*
and *Second Chance Dad*

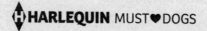

If you purchased this book without a cover you should be aware that this book is stolen property. It was reported as "unsold and destroyed" to the publisher, and neither the author nor the publisher has received any payment for this "stripped book."

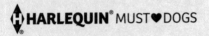

HARLEQUIN® MUST ♥ DOGS

ISBN-13: 978-1-335-00803-9

The Puppy Connection

Copyright © 2020 by Harlequin Books S.A.

Daddy, Unexpectedly
First published in 2013. This edition published in 2020.
Copyright © 2013 by Lee McKenzie McAnally

Second Chance Dad
First published in 2011. This edition published in 2020.
Copyright © 2011 by Pamela Stone

Recycling programs for this product may not exist in your area.

All rights reserved. No part of this book may be used or reproduced in any manner whatsoever without written permission except in the case of brief quotations embodied in critical articles and reviews.

This is a work of fiction. Names, characters, places and incidents are either the product of the author's imagination or are used fictitiously. Any resemblance to actual persons, living or dead, businesses, companies, events or locales is entirely coincidental.

This edition published by arrangement with Harlequin Books S.A.

For questions and comments about the quality of this book, please contact us at CustomerService@Harlequin.com.

Harlequin Enterprises ULC
22 Adelaide St. West, 40th Floor
Toronto, Ontario M5H 4E3, Canada
www.Harlequin.com

Printed in U.S.A.

CONTENTS

From the time she was ten years old and read *Anne of Green Gables* and *Little Women*, **Lee McKenzie** knew she wanted to be a writer. She has written everything from advertising copy to an honors thesis in paleontology, but becoming a four-time Golden Heart® Award finalist and a Harlequin author are among her proudest accomplishments. Lee and her artist/teacher husband live on an island along Canada's west coast, and she loves to spend time with two of her best friends—her grown-up children.

Books by Lee McKenzie

Harlequin Heartwarming

The Parent Trap
To Catch a Wife
His Best Friend's Wife

Harlequin American Romance

The Man for Maggie
With This Ring
Firefighter Daddy
The Wedding Bargain
The Christmas Secret
The Daddy Project
Daddy, Unexpectedly

Visit the Author Profile page
at Harlequin.com for more titles.

DADDY, UNEXPECTEDLY

Lee McKenzie

For my two proudest accomplishments,
Joe and Michaela

Chapter 1

Claire DeAngelo stabbed her fork into the last piece of lettuce on her plate. Two hours ago it was barely appetizing. Now warm and wilted, it was just plain gross. She dumped it into the trash can under the sink and put her lunch dishes in the dishwasher.

"Forget about food. You have more important things to think about." She walked purposefully back to the dining table, sat and opened the calendar on her laptop.

This had been a busy week. She had closed the sale of a home in Seattle's Victory Heights neighborhood and listed two others. She'd lined up three showings tomorrow morning for some prospective home buyers—newlyweds in search of their dream home. She would be tempted to tell them it was all downhill once the honeymoon was over, but she was a real estate agent, not a marriage counsellor.

The company she'd launched several years ago was really taking off and her two business partners were as busy as she was. Busier, given their family commitments. Claire was happy for Samantha and Kristi, she really was, but more than a little envious, too. Since she'd been a little girl, crisscrossing the country from one military base to another, she'd dreamed of a real home with a white picket fence and a big backyard, where she and the man of her dreams could watch their children chase the dog and play with their friends. Technically neither Sam nor Kristi had a white picket fence, but they had everything else Claire wanted.

She stood and walked to the floor-to-ceiling wall of glass that overlooked Puget Sound. She had a pricey penthouse with a million-dollar view, an imperialistic cat who slept most of the time, no children and a soon-to-be-ex husband. She checked her watch. It was two-thirty *and* it was Friday afternoon *and* all her work was done, so why was she feeling so out of sorts?

"Because I'm starving." The salad she'd eaten for lunch had worn off, as had the sense of virtuousness for eating something healthy and almost calorie-free. She went back into the kitchen and looked in the fridge. The makings of another salad, four eggs, a tub of fat-free yogurt and a quart of skim milk. She took out a Tupperware container filled with carrots and celery sticks, then opened a cupboard. A box of breakfast cereal with a measly hundred calories per serving and a package of rice cakes.

What were you thinking? she asked herself.

That you're supposed to be on a diet.

She set the rodent food on the polished granite countertop. Ugh.

"La Cucaracha" started playing on her cell phone. Double ugh. Only one incoming caller was assigned to that ring tone. Her can't-be-ex-soon-enough husband. She'd been hearing it a lot lately, and he was really starting to bug her. She was tempted to let the call go to voice mail, but then he'd leave a long-winded message. And then he'd call back in twenty minutes to find out if she'd listened to it.

"I told you to stop calling me," she said, forgoing the usual pleasantries when she answered.

"This is important."

It always was. "What do you want?"

"My lawyer has drawn up the divorce papers and we're sending them to your lawyer this afternoon for you to sign."

Typical Donald. He assumed she would agree to the terms, just as she had agreed to everything he'd wanted while they were married. They'd bought the luxury condo he'd chosen, postponed having a family because he wasn't ready. Getting divorced would damn well be on her terms.

"I'll discuss them with my lawyer and see what she thinks." She was suddenly overcome by the feeling that lunch had been two days ago instead of two hours, and a carrot stick wasn't going to do it for her. She was craving something rich and sweet and chocolaty. A candy bar, maybe. Or a double-chocolate donut. Or a quart of Ben & Jerry's Chocolate Therapy.

No, make that all three.

"It's a straightforward agreement," he said. "Everything will be divided equally, and we'll split the proceeds from the penthouse…although that can't happen if we don't get it on the market."

Claire picked up one of the rice cakes and pictured a Belgian waffle heaped with fresh strawberries and a mountain of whipped cream, all liberally sprinkled with shaved chocolate. "I still have to find a place to live," she reminded him.

"You own a real estate company, Claire. You've had months to find a new place. It's not that difficult."

It sure hadn't been for him. He had moved out of their home and straight into his new girlfriend's condominium. Deirdre. Claire had never met her, but she imagined the woman was a lot like Cruella de Vil, only meaner.

"My lawyer will call your lawyer," she said.

"One more thing."

With you, there always is. "What?" she asked. She dipped an imaginary spoon into a chocolate-bottomed crème brûlée and pretended to swirl it across her tongue. Heaven.

"We've come up with an equitable division of assets, and I want that book my grandmother gave you."

Claire practically dropped the phone. *We* who? Donald and his lawyer? Donald and Deirdre? "Absolutely not. That was a gift to me, and that makes it mine."

"Doesn't matter," he said. "It was given to you by one of my family members and I want it back."

His mother had given her a butt-ugly red vinyl purse for her birthday last year. Did he want that, too? "It's a children's book," she reminded him. "Why would you want it?" Unless…was Deirdre pregnant? After insisting he wasn't ready to start a family with Claire, that would be the ultimate insult.

"Apparently it's a collector's item and it belonged… *belongs*…to my family."

Of course. This had nothing to do with sentimental feelings about families or children, or even literature. Claire still had all of her favorite books from childhood and over the years she'd added to the collection. When she finally had kids of her own, they would spend many happy hours reading those books together. Donald's grandmother had loved books, too, and had looked forward to a great-grandchild someday. Just before she died, she'd given the book to Claire and made her promise to share it with her children.

Donald probably didn't even remember it was a first edition Beatrix Potter. With him it was only about the money. *Always* about the money. Well, too bad. If he thought he was getting that book, he could think again.

No, he could go straight to hell. In a handbasket.

"It's been a busy week and I have to get back to work. My lawyer will call your lawyer after we've looked at the papers."

He was still blustering when she hung up.

Her hands were shaking and her stomach felt like a deflated balloon. Screw the diet. She dumped the raw veggies and rice cakes into the trash, snagged her purse off the counter and headed for the door. She debated whether to leave her phone at home and quickly ruled it out. The only thing worse than getting another call from the cockroach was missing a call from a client.

On the way back to her building, Claire navigated around a cluster of pylons on the sidewalk. A window-washing platform was suspended a few feet above the ground and a crew of workers was loading equipment onto a truck.

"Claire? Claire DeAngelo? Is that you?"

She whirled around, clutching a paper bag filled with guilty pleasure. Who on earth…?

She looked up at the man on the platform and stopped breathing. She'd recognize that devilish grin anywhere. "Luke!"

He vaulted over the safety railing, landed lightly on his feet in front of her and swept her into an enthusiastic embrace. "I knew it had to be you. What are you doing here?"

"Just taking a break." She waved at the main doors of her condominium complex. "I'm on my way home, and back to work. I mean, I work at home sometimes."

He planted a kiss on her forehead. "How long has it been?"

"I'm not sure. Since college, I guess."

"Wow. Fancy digs," he said. "Good for you. And you look great."

So did he. Back in college he'd had the bluest eyes she'd ever seen and a smile that had melted a lot of girls' hearts. She could see that hadn't changed. The rest of him had. He'd always been athletic but Adonis himself would envy this body. He still had his arms around her and the biceps alone were enough to make a woman feel light-headed. His black T-shirt was streaked with water and dust, and he smelled like hard work and testosterone. When he finally released her, she felt slightly chilled.

"Are you married? Kids?"

She shook her head, still somewhat confounded by this unexpected encounter. "Separated. Almost divorced, actually. No kids. What about you?"

She asked because she felt she had to, but she knew his answer would be negative. Luke Devlin still didn't look like the kind of man who'd ever be caged behind a white picket fence.

"Nope. Single and free as the breeze."

That was Luke, all right. The college friend she'd known and loved, and he could still make her laugh. They had met in first-year American History when they'd been paired up to work on a Civil War assignment. Claire had gone on to major in English literature and Luke had settled for being a major babe magnet. She had occasionally played the role of platonic place-holder, hanging out with him after one of his many breakups, letting the old girlfriend think she was the new one. She had always been surprised they fell for it because, let's face it, serious, studious and slightly over-weight Claire DeAngelo was not Luke's type.

A number of years ago she'd run into one of his old college roommates and he'd told her that Luke had joined the Seattle Police Department. Finding out he'd become a cop had been a shocker but finding him here, working as a window washer, of all things, was a complete bombshell.

"Free as the breeze, huh? Sounds just like the old days," she said.

"Not quite. I had a pretty serious girlfriend for a while, but it didn't work out." His smile faded by a few watts.

What was this? Luke Devlin with a broken heart? Not possible. "Welcome to the club."

"Seriously? Any guy who'd dump you would have to be crazy."

"That's one adjective that works."

Luke grinned at her. "Misery loves company, isn't that what they say? We should grab a bite to eat when

I get off duty. Off work. We can catch up on however many years it's been."

After the insanely busy week she'd had, and especially after that last phone call from her ex, why not? She hadn't been on a date since Donald left, which meant she technically hadn't been on a date since before she got married. Not that a casual, off-the-cuff invitation to "grab a bite" constituted a date, but it would be more fun than sitting down to a salad, alone.

"Dinner would great," she said. "What time?"

"I'm off at five. How does six o'clock sound?"

"Six will work. I'll meet you downstairs at my front door."

He kissed her again, on the cheek this time. As she walked away, she half expected him to swat her rear end the way he used to, but it seemed that even a guy like Luke grew up, at least a little. She looked back when she reached the entrance, but he'd already climbed onto the window-washing platform. That's when she noticed the red lettering on his black T-shirt. Lucky Devil, with three prongs on the tail end of the letter *y*. She was still laughing when she let herself into the lobby and pushed the elevator button. Back in college she would have given almost anything to go on a date with Luke Devlin, even though he'd had a campus-wide reputation for getting lucky. Now she knew better than to give herself to a bad-boy-cop-turned-window-washer, but for the first Friday night in forever, she had dinner plans.

Luke tossed the last couple of pylons into the back of the truck. *I'll be damned,* he thought. After all these years, he kinda sorta had a date with Claire DeAngelo, and he had just enough time to run this load over to the shop and get back here to meet her. Before he climbed into the cab, he reached up and yanked on the ropes to make sure the platform was secure on the roof rack. *Better change your shirt while you're at it.*

He was back at Claire's condominium complex at five minutes to six. He'd made it home in time to take his dog, Rex, out for a run and grab a shower and a change of clothes, and still made it here with enough time to spare to make it look as if he had all the time in the world. He wasn't sure why that was important, but he didn't want to make Claire wait. For one thing, knowing her, she wouldn't.

He leaned against a light standard, arms folded, and while he waited, he kept a watchful eye on everyone who came and went from Claire's building. After his years with the Seattle Police Department, maintaining a keen awareness of his surroundings was deeply ingrained. Claire wouldn't know he was a cop and given his lousy study habits in college, she was probably not surprised to see him washing windows. Just as well. It meant he wouldn't have to tell her he had her building under surveillance, or why.

She took his breath away the instant she stepped through the door. The reticent, sometimes even awkward study-buddy he'd hung out with in college had outgrown her awkwardness and blossomed into a beautiful, confident woman. She had the same soft blue eyes, still wore glasses instead of contacts, still dressed conservatively but with a lot more style.

She smiled when she saw him and raised one hand as if to wave.

"Claire!" The man who called her name was striding toward her.

She froze and her smile faded.

Okay, something wasn't right here. Luke straightened and quickly stepped up beside her.

"Donald, what are you doing here?" she asked.

"You hung up on me. We need to talk about selling the penthouse, Claire. And I want that book."

Ah, yes. The ex. The guy was a little taller than she was, very well dressed and about as intense as they come.

"Not. Now." Keeping her voice calm seemed to require some effort. "I have plans." She glanced up at Luke as though seeking confirmation.

Since Luke didn't like the look of this guy, he was more than happy to play along. He slung an arm across her shoulders and extended a hand to her ex-husband. "Luke Devlin. I don't believe we've met."

Claire's ex looked momentarily confused and then shot Luke a frosty glare. He grudgingly accepted the handshake, though. Luke didn't like his grip any more than he liked him. He was trying way too hard to be firm. For one fleeting second, Luke considered making the guy say uncle.

Don't be a dumb-ass, he chided himself.

"Donald Robinson," the guy said. After he pulled his hand away, he zeroed in on Claire again. "You can't keep putting this off."

This guy wasn't getting the memo.

Luke drew her closer. "Like Claire said, now's really not a good time. We should get going, babe. We don't want to be late."

She looked up at him, lips ever so slightly parted, and gave him the kind of smile that suggested there was actually something going on between them. Since

Donald wouldn't know there wasn't, Luke lowered his head and gave her a light, lingering kiss.

"You are so adorable," he said, purposely making his voice go soft and quiet. "Isn't she adorable?" he asked Donald.

Donald stammered something that sounded more like an excuse than an apology, and backed away. "I'll call you tomorrow," he said to Claire. "I've lined up an appraiser." He looked uncertainly from her to Luke. "Will you…ah…will you be at home tomorrow?"

"I'm not sure," she said. "I guess you'll find out when you call."

For a few seconds Donald looked like he wasn't going to let this drop, but then he threw up his hands and, without saying anything, swung around and walked away. "And I want that book back," he said over his shoulder. "I'm serious."

"Oh, my God," Claire said after her ex disappeared around the corner. She ducked out from under Luke's arm. "I am *so* sorry. And grateful. Thank you. Donald can be…"

An asshole? "Hey, no problem. I probably owed you anyway."

They both laughed at their collective memories from college days, and she seemed to relax a little.

"Any idea where you'd like to eat?" he asked.

She shook her head.

"There's a little Irish pub downtown, not far from the market. Best burgers and fries in town."

"Sure. Sounds wonderful."

He couldn't tell if she meant it or not but jeez, look at her. The powder-blue sweater he'd admired earlier was now topped by a cobalt-colored suede jacket. Both emphasized her dazzling blue eyes. She'd always had a classic style and great taste in clothes, and her taste in food was probably more sophisticated than burgers and beer. His was not and he saw no point in faking it.

"Is this place close enough to walk?"

"Guess it depends how much you like walking," he said. "I've got my bike and a spare helmet." He hoped she'd go for it. If she rode with him, he would have an excuse to bring her back home, and that would give him an opportunity to get inside the building. He was curious about the condo Donald was so determined to unload, but more than that, he wanted to see where she lived in relation to the penthouse they were staking out.

"A bike?" she asked.

"Yeah. Well, a motorcycle." He gestured to where it was parked next to the curb.

She looked decidedly undecided.

Come on, live a little, he was tempted to say. But that would get her back up and then she'd say no. Instead, he casually handed her a helmet as though he assumed she'd done this a hundred times.

Every single one of Claire's instincts—including a few she didn't know she had—screamed at her to say no. But somehow the helmet was in her hands and then she had it on. She must look like a bobblehead, since she definitely felt like one.

"I've never ridden on a Harley-Davidson." She'd never even pedaled a ten-speed.

Luke grinned. "Then I'm happy to uphold that tradition. This isn't a Harley."

"Oh." She gave the black beast a closer look, took in the silver lettering on the side. Ducati. It still looked like the kind of machine a biker would ride, and Luke, with his longish dark hair, well-worn leather jacket and black boots, looked exactly like the kind of guy who would ride it. His jacket wasn't biker-black, though. More the color of espresso. Or dark chocolate. And while Harley-Davidson sounded dangerous and intimidating, Ducati sounded sexy. Like Luke.

He pulled on his helmet and climbed on the bike. "Jump on."

Her heart pounded in her chest. *You are such a wimp,* she scolded. People rode on motorcycles all the time. Luke was a responsible adult. She hoped. She slid one leg over the seat behind him and settled onto the cushy leather, grateful she hadn't changed into a skirt.

"Hang on," he said.

To him? she wondered. Duh. It was him or nothing. She put her hands on his sides, glad for the cool leather between her palms and his rib cage. Every nerve in her body jolted to life when he started the bike, and her pulse roared in her ears. No, that was the rev of the engine. They rolled away from the curb and she flung her arms around him, so tightly she could have counted his ribs through the jacket if she'd wanted to.

The ride to the pub lasted somewhere between five minutes and a lifetime. After he found a parking space and cut the engine, she snatched her hands away from his body and stumbled off the bike. She was both terrified and—oh, God, how could this be happening?—turned on. Being scared, yes, she could understand, but a body all aquiver from clinging to a man on the back of a motorcycle? Who knew such a thing was even possible?

Chapter 2

Luke held Claire's helmet and watched her smooth her tousled hair with shaky hands.

"Your first time?" he asked.

She responded with a silent question in her eyes and a little extra pink in her cheeks.

"On a motorcycle."

"Oh, yes. It was." He liked that the polished, professional grown-up Claire was still college-girl adorable when she got flustered.

"I thought it might have been." He handed the helmet back to her and guided her toward the entrance. "What did you think?"

"Um…" Her color deepened.

Hmm. That good. Here's hoping the ride home had the same effect.

He held the door and followed her inside. The bar

was packed with the usual Friday mix of tourists and the downtown happy hour crowd. He spotted a table for two that was being vacated near the back, and before two other couples could swoop in to grab it, he was holding a chair for Claire.

She sat and slid the helmet underneath. "That was lucky."

Nope. That was experience.

The server stopped and pocketed the change left by the previous customers. "Menus?"

"Sure."

She picked up the empty glasses and put them on her tray, then gave the table a halfhearted swipe with a damp cloth. Claire's reaction had him second-guessing his decision to bring her here, but taking her to a fancier place might have sent the wrong message.

"Do you know what you want to drink?" the server asked.

The way Claire studied the drink list, she could have been cramming for an exam.

"Give us a minute?" he asked.

"Sure thing."

After the woman moved on to another table, he watched Claire suck the ripe fullness of her lower lip between her teeth, release it and slowly run the tip of her tongue across the luscious curve of her upper lip. During their many study sessions back in college, he'd watched her do that a hundred times. And he'd known then, as he did now, that she had no idea how seductive it was. She wasn't trying to tantalize, and that made it even more of a turn-on.

During those study sessions of old he had wanted to kiss that freshly moistened mouth and tease that tongue into coming out to play. But even in those days, when he had been a stereotypical college student with an overactive libido and his party mode in overdrive, he'd had enough sense not to ruin a good thing. The good thing being a study-buddy and a friend. He had never had a female friend who was just a friend, and he'd never had a study partner, period.

Their first kiss had been less than half an hour ago. He had simply wanted to send a message to the jerk of an ex-husband, but now, watching her tongue play with her lips, he wondered if she would let him bookend this date with another kiss when he took her home.

Was this a date? It would be if she let him kiss her again. Was that a good idea? Sure as hell seemed like one from where he was sitting. A kiss was just a kiss, after all. It didn't have to end with them setting the sheets on fire. Besides, he would never use Claire DeAngelo to scratch an itch, and she'd never let him anyway.

The server returned. "Have you decided on drinks?"

"Coffee for me," he said.

"Cream and sugar?"

"Black, thanks."

Over the top of the drink list, surprise registered in Claire's eyes. He couldn't fault her for that.

She set the tattered menu on the table. "I'll have a Diet Coke."

That was no surprise at all.

"Coffee and a Coke. Be right back to take your food order."

"So, Luke Devlin in a bar drinking coffee," Claire said. "That's…different."

"I'm driving."

"Of course. Good point."

"But you could have had something with a little more kick than a diet soft drink."

Something akin to alarm flickered in her eyes and vanished, leaving him wondering if maybe he imagined it. "I'm not much of a drinker."

"Me, neither."

That made her laugh.

Should he tell her the truth? *Step one,* he reminded himself. "I'm serious. I've been sober almost two years."

The amusement drained from her face. "Oh. Luke, I'm sorry I laughed. I shouldn't have."

He leaned closer and touched her hand. "No apology necessary. Sometimes even badasses grow up."

"Not always."

He guessed she was talking about her ex.

"Some of us do," he said. Too bad it sometimes took a disaster to make it happen.

She slowly withdrew her hand. "So, here we are. Ten years out of college and a couple of teetotalers."

"Wow. It's been ten years?"

"It has."

The server set Claire's soft drink and his coffee on the table. "You folks ready to order?" she asked.

Claire gave the menu another quick scan. "What's good here?"

"They have the best burgers in Seattle. The Emerald Isle is my favorite."

She read the description and grimaced. "Two beef patties *and* bacon *and* cheese? I see your appetite hasn't changed."

"I worked hard today. I need the calories."

"And I sat at my desk most of the day, so I definitely

don't. I'll have the O'Chicken burger," she said, smiling at the name as she handed her menu to the server.

"Fries or salad with those?"

"Fries for me," Luke said.

"I should have a salad." Obviously that's not what she wanted.

"Have a salad," he said. "We can share my fries."

The server confirmed their order and drifted away.

"I was surprised to see you this afternoon," she said. "I bumped into one of your old dorm-mates a couple of years ago and he told me you'd joined the Seattle P.D."

So she did know. "Yeah, I got in a couple of years after I graduated college."

"And you're moonlighting as a window washer?"

He didn't want to let her believe that, mostly because it wasn't true. But because of where she lived, and the reason he was working there, he needed to be careful what he did tell her.

"I'm with vice. Sometimes an investigation is easier when the bad guys don't know who we are."

"So you're...what? Working undercover?"

He tipped his head in agreement.

"I thought things like that only happened in the movies."

"If this is a movie, that would make me James Bond."

That made her laugh. "Isn't he a spy?"

"Yeah, but it's a movie, remember? That means I get to be anybody I want. What about you?" he asked, wanting to steer the conversation in a different direction.

"Well, since you get to be Pierce Brosnan—or would that be Daniel Craig?—then I guess I'd be Julia Roberts." She was blushing again. "But more *Mona Lisa Smile* than *Pretty Woman*," she added quickly.

His turn to laugh. "Good to know, but I was talking about the real-life you. You said you work at home."

"I do, some of the time, but nothing movie-star glamorous I'm afraid. I'm a Realtor, and a partner in a business called Ready Set Sold."

He never would have imagined her as a salesperson. Then again she'd be good at anything she decided to do. "Good name for a real estate company."

"We thought so. We're more than just real estate, though. We help people renovate and stage their homes before we put them on the market."

"Good idea. How many business partners do you have?" he asked, hoping she wouldn't say her ex was one of them.

"Two. Samantha Elliott is our carpenter and general handywoman, and Kristi Callahan is an interior decorator. They both do really amazing work, but they're more than business partners. They're my two best friends."

Huh. Three women, best friends, running a business together. He liked the sound of that. "What about Donald? Is he in real estate?" Not that it was any of his business, and he probably shouldn't even bring him up, but something about the guy didn't sit right with him.

Claire plucked a napkin from the dispenser and wiped the table in front of her. "No. He's an investment broker. He did really well at it, which is how we could afford the condo. Things between us started to fall apart right around the time the economy took a downturn, and then I found out he was…"

Luke had a pretty good idea what she was going to say, and he let her get to it without prompting.

"And then I found out he was having an affair."

Bastard. Women like Claire, and his mother, deserved better. His own track record was less than stellar but except for Sherri, he had never been in a relationship long enough to be unfaithful. Even with her, although he'd been tempted a time or two, he'd kept his pants zipped. He might be a chip off the old block in a lot of ways, but his father's infidelity had been the thing he hated most about the man. No way, not even when he'd been drinking heavily, as he had been in those days, would he let himself sink that low.

"Is that when Donald moved out?"

"He didn't have a choice. After I found out, I packed up his stuff and called a moving company."

He felt himself grin. "Hot damn, you're feisty."

He had always liked that Claire was a smart, determined woman. To know she wouldn't put up with any crap from anyone made him admire her even more. Why hadn't his mother kicked his father's ass out of the house a long time ago? Why didn't she do it now?

Claire swirled the straw in her drink. "A lot of men might think that what I did was a bit over-the-top."

"Only the ones who are cheating."

"You mentioned something about a breakup. Were you the heartbreaker or the heartbroken?"

He should have seen this question coming since he'd been the one to bring up exes. "A little of both, I guess. I didn't cheat on her, though."

"Did she? Cheat on you, I mean."

"No. At least not that I know of. We were seriously into partying and then…ah…something happened that made me realize I had a problem. I knew I needed to quit drinking, and it turned out I wasn't much fun to be with when I was sober."

"She actually said that?"

"Not in so many words. And I learned some stuff, too."

"Such as…?"

"Being sober and living with a drunk isn't much fun, either."

"Oh, Luke. I'm sorry. Do you know how she's doing now?"

"No. We sort of lost touch." Which wasn't entirely true. He did know how she was doing. Not good. He didn't want to talk about Sherri or the real reason they'd split up. He never talked about stuff like this with anyone, ever. Why was he opening up with Claire?

A food runner arrived with their order. "The O'Chicken?"

Claire patted the table in front of her, eyes widening as she took in the amount of food on her plate. The kid set the second plate in front of Luke and sidled away as the server appeared. She balanced a tray of drinks on one arm as she pulled a bottle of ketchup from her apron pocket and set it on the table.

"Anything else?" she asked.

He and Claire both shook their heads, and she carried on.

For a few moments there was silence as Luke applied a generous squirt of ketchup to his burger and squeezed another zigzag across his fries. He offered the bottle to Claire but she shook her head. He picked up the top half of his bun—lettuce, tomato, pickle and all—slapped it onto the burger side, and flattened it with his palm. While he watched Claire, he picked it up and took a bite.

She started by rescuing the pickle slice and moving it to the edge of her plate before going to work on the rest of her meal. By the time she'd unwrapped her cutlery, spread the paper napkin on her lap and, with surgical precision, cut her burger in half, he had devoured half of his.

"How is it?" he asked.

"Mmm." She murmured her approval as she swallowed.

"Help yourself to some fries."

She reached across the table, picked one up and dipped it in his ketchup. After biting it in half, she closed her eyes and chewed. "So good," she said when she opened them again. "I haven't had one of these in ages."

"Why not?"

"I've been on a diet." She picked up her fork and stabbed a piece of lettuce.

She looked fine to him. Better than fine. She had curves in all the right places, but if he told her that, she'd probably think he was lying, or coming on to her. He'd been around enough women to know that when they ordered diet drinks instead of regular, salad instead of fries and generally worried about their weight, the smart thing to say was nothing.

So instead he picked up his burger and bit off almost more than he could chew.

A crisp French fry and tangy sweet ketchup were like a perfect marriage, Claire thought. What she didn't know about the latter was made up for by a deep and abiding love of food, the crisper, sweeter and greasier the better. And she had the size fourteen hips to show for it.

"What do you think of the building you live in?" Luke asked after he swallowed a mouthful of burger and washed it down with coffee. His healthy appetite and the rock-hard abs she'd clung to all the way here created an interesting dichotomy.

She twirled the straw as she stared at the surface of her drink for a moment. It sounded as though he was fishing for information, but that didn't make sense. *He's just making conversation,* she decided. They had to talk about something.

"It's not my dream home, but it's okay. We—Donald and I—bought it after we got engaged and we moved in right after the honeymoon."

She bit into her burger. After Donald's phone call that afternoon and his unexpected appearance tonight, she was more annoyed with him than ever. She still couldn't believe he'd shown up at the exact time she was meeting Luke. On the plus side, though, there had been that kiss.

"Does he make a habit of showing up like he did tonight?"

"No, he usually phones. His lawyer sent divorce papers to my lawyer this afternoon. He expects me to agree to whatever is in them."

"What do you want?"

"I guess I still want what I thought I was getting when we got married. To put down roots, have a home and a family."

"Sounds like a wonderful life." The bitter edge to his voice had a bite to it.

She knew he hadn't had the greatest home life growing up, but back in college he had never talked about it. He'd been too busy partying and playing the field. Apparently the partying had stopped, but it was too soon to tell if he'd moved past the seemingly endless string of girlfriends.

"It would be wonderful."

He didn't agree or disagree. "Do you still want that? With him?" he asked instead.

"God, no. But someday, with someone, definitely. But you don't think it's possible."

He shrugged. "I'm not saying it's *im*possible, just that I've never seen it happen."

"Seriously? You don't know anyone who's happily married?" She prided herself in being a realist, but even after her experience with Donald she still believed she had a chance at a long and happy marriage. Without that dream, the future looked awfully grim.

"Well, let's see. My parents have been married for almost forty years. I'm not sure either of them has ever been happy."

Forty years of unhappy would be grimmer than grim. Maybe that's why Luke tended to play the field rather than make a commitment.

"They're still married," she said. "That has to mean something."

Luke shrugged. "Convenience, maybe. My dad can string along his various girlfriends by telling them his wife won't give him a divorce. And I think my mom is so afraid of being on her own that she puts up with all his crap."

Claire thought of her two business partners, Sam and Kristi, who'd both grown up with loser dads and then found men who were loving husbands and devoted fathers. By comparison, she had been raised by parents who were still crazy about each other, even after all these years, yet she had ended up marrying the wrong man. Now she was staring a bleak future square in the eye.

"I'm sorry to hear your mom's had such a rough go of it. Have you talked to her about it?"

Luke pushed his empty plate away, picked up his coffee cup and leaned back in his chair. "Devlin men don't tend to be talkers."

"You're talking to me." She wondered if he would open up about his ex-girlfriend, tell her what happened there. Someday, maybe, but she sensed this wasn't the time to ask.

"True. You always were a good listener. What about your family?"

Was he asking because he was interested, or because he wanted to change the subject? Not that it mattered. She loved to talk about her family.

"My parents are in a retirement community in Arizona. You might remember that my dad spent his entire career in the military so we moved a lot. Now they have a motor home so they're still on the go."

"But that doesn't appeal to you?"

"Not in the least," she said, laughing. "Every time we moved, they did their best to make the new place feel like home for me and my sister. Carmen always fit in right away. It took me longer, and by the time I made friends and started to feel settled, my dad was transferred."

"How did you end up in Seattle?"

"I fell in love with the Pacific Northwest when we were stationed at Whidbey Island, and I decided then that when I grew up, this is where I wanted to live. Now here I am."

"And all grown-up." His voice, deep and quiet all

of a sudden, like the thrum of a bass, reverberated through her.

"All grown-up," she agreed, almost breathless. And she was having some very grown-up thoughts about the man sitting across the table.

Don't be an idiot. Luke Devlin was a man who lived in the moment, always had been and always would be. She was all about the long-term, the white picket fence, the happy ever after.

And how's that working for you? It wasn't. After months of being alone, she was lonely. Would it be so wrong to not be lonely for a change? Even just for one night? To wake up in the morning with a hot guy in her bed and a smug smile of satisfaction on her lips? Heat crept up her neck and she tried to cool her cheeks with her palms.

No, it wouldn't be wrong and she would be tempted, but she still couldn't do it. She couldn't be that woman. Could she?

Chapter 3

Luke waited for her to climb off the bike, then joined her on the sidewalk.

"I'll walk you up."

He'd had to park nearly a block away, it was dark and there was no way he could let her walk on her own. Another man might be tempted to, but not a cop. Never. Besides, he was hoping to be invited in. For the obvious reasons, of course, but also because he welcomed the chance to check out the place from the inside.

"Thank you." She sounded relieved.

On her own she would most likely come and go via the secure underground parking garage, especially at night. Not that anything was ever completely secure, especially given what he knew about the activities of some of the lowlifes who lived here. Tonight he would see her to the front door, maybe farther if he was lucky.

They'd covered about half the distance when prickles of unease shivered up his neck. He knew better than to be obvious, but a couple of casual over-the-shoulder glances revealed nothing. Someone was watching them, most likely just him, and he saw no advantage to tipping off whomever that might be. Had the operation been compromised? His gut told him no. This was about something else.

He sought out the pistol tucked in an inside jacket pocket, curled his fingers reassuringly around the grip as his other arm went out instinctively to draw Claire closer. She glanced up, the obvious question in her eyes.

"Thought you might be cold." It sounded lame, even to him, but she didn't pull away.

"Would you like to come up for coffee?" she asked as she unlocked the front door of her building.

"Sure." Hell, yes. He was glad she'd asked. It saved him the trouble of trying to invite himself in.

Earlier she'd been on edge, possibly due to her ex showing up and giving her a hard time, and he'd thought the evening was headed for disaster. Eventually she had relaxed, and after they got their current relationship status out of the way, they had talked about work, recent movies they'd seen, what some of their old college friends were doing now and even pets. He'd adopted a German shepherd named Rex after the dog failed to meet the K-9 unit's requirements. Claire had a Siamese cat named Cleo. Cleo didn't like dogs, and Rex was afraid of cats. As they left the restaurant and walked to where he'd parked the bike, he'd been hoping that wasn't a metaphor for him and Claire. And then he'd realized that he hadn't used a word like *metaphor* since she'd been his study partner.

Not until they were stepping into the elevator did the hair on the back of his neck fall back into place. Who the hell was out there?

Claire pushed the button for the top floor. Huh. That would put her in one of the penthouses. If hers looked across to the other tower, to the penthouse his team had under surveillance, this evening might hold even more possibilities than he'd hoped it would.

They didn't speak as the numbers ticked by, and then the elevator glided to a stop and the door opened with hardly a whisper. He followed Claire into a spacious and elegantly appointed foyer with a door at either end. His luck held. Keys in hand, she walked foward and opened the door he was hoping was hers.

Inside, his gaze went immediately to the wide, wrap-around sweep of windows, taking in the view of Puget Sound to the west and the complex's twin tower to the north.

Claire set her handbag and keys on the glossy black surface of a long, sleek console table, shrugged out of her jacket and hung it in the closet.

"Can I take your jacket?" she asked.

He shook his head. "I'm good, thanks."

"Make yourself at home."

He took a good look around and thought, *Holy shit. So this is how the other half lives.* He didn't think he'd ever been in a home that was less homey. The space was huge and sprawling, with magazine-worthy living and dining areas, and an open kitchen that would hold half the basement suite he'd rented after he and Sherri split. Aside from the bare essentials, he had yet to furnish the place.

Claire had said the ex's investments had done well.

Either the guy had been filthy rich to start with, or she was the queen of understatement. Or the reality lay someplace in between.

"Impressive," he said, crossing the polished wood floor, ostensibly to take in the view but instead zeroing in on his target in the neighboring tower. Bingo.

"That's what everyone says. The view is what I'll miss most after I...we sell the place."

"I can see why," he said, keeping the conversation moving while he scanned the neighboring penthouse his team had under surveillance.

Blinds obscured the bedroom windows where clients were "entertained," but the main area was wide open. With proper surveillance equipment, he'd be able to see everyone who came and went from the place, including those who "worked" there. Tomorrow, first thing, he would talk to his sergeant. They didn't like to involve civilians if it could be avoided, but this was too fine an opportunity to pass up.

"What kind of coffee would you like?"

He backed away from the window, turned and found himself caught in the green slitty-eyed gaze of a regal-looking Siamese cat. This would be Chloe. She sat on one end of the long, sleek black leather sofa, all four paws tucked out of sight beneath her, tail wrapped snugly around half her body. Suspecting the haughty feline would produce one of those hidden paws and shred his hand if he tried to pet her, he gave her a wide berth as he circled around the island to join Claire in the kitchen.

"What are my choices?"

"You can have anything you like."

"Can I?"

Even the tip of her nose turned pink. "Cappuccino? Latte?"

He studied the elaborate-looking stainless-steel espresso machine on the counter. "Looks complicated. Does it make just plain coffee?"

"Of course." She opened cupboards, reached for cups, took the lid off a canister and scooped out some coffee grounds.

He leaned against the island, while she turned her attention to the machine, and watched her work, admiring the way her blue sweater curved to the contours of her waist and hips. To his surprise, he liked that her invitation to come up for coffee really meant coffee. That hardly ever happened. There was a time he would have nailed a woman the second they stumbled into the apartment, and a time before that when he'd have jumped her in the elevator. Now he was making do with coffee with the one woman he'd always wanted to make out with, because Claire DeAngelo was way too good for a dry hump in a corner of an elevator.

"Here you go." She held out a tall, steaming mug of coffee, smiled up at him and trailed her fingertips across the back of his hand when he took the cup from her.

Was she flirting? Huh. Maybe coffee wasn't just coffee, after all. Before he could figure that out, she picked up her latte cup and saucer, took a sip and smiled as she swiped the foam off her upper lip with the tip of her tongue. Okay, *that* was no accident. He set his coffee on the counter, took hers and placed it next to his and locked gazes with her.

Aw, hell. He'd recognize that smolder anywhere. And yeah, he wanted this, really wanted it, but this had to be her call. Completely. She might not want to make the first move, but she needed to give him another sign if she wanted him to make it.

Her tongue played an encore across her bottom lip.

Did she have any idea how this affected him?

Her smile suggested she did.

He groaned and pulled her into his arms. "You're sure about this?"

She leaned into him, smile gone, eyes even darker.

Please let her say yes.

"I'm sure."

Close enough.

Kissing her to piss off the ex had been little more than a boost to his ego. Kissing her for real jump-started his libido in a way no other kiss had in a very long time. Come to think of it, he hadn't kissed a woman in a very long time. Not since Sherri. Not since he got sober.

Stop thinking, he told himself, *or you'll talk your-self out of this one.*

Claire slipped her hands inside the front of his jacket. He held his breath for a few seconds, hoping she didn't encounter the Glock. He started breathing again when she slid her fingers up his chest, apparently none the wiser. Although she knew he was a cop, she wouldn't like knowing he was armed.

Still doing too damn much thinking.

Claire leaned even closer, her body soft against his. Ordinarily that would have been enough to make him stop using his head, but knowing someone on the street had been watching him still had his senses on height-ened alert, and now he was acutely aware of the wide expanse of windows behind them. Anyone who cared to watch would be able to see them.

"Which way to the bedroom?"

He hated to break the mood, hoped she wouldn't change her mind, but she only tipped her head back and smiled.

"This way." She took him by the hand and led him down a hallway and into a huge master suite.

"Wow." There was a king-size bed, two bureaus, a pair of armchairs separated by a large ottoman and still enough space for a small dance floor. And the drapes were closed.

"I've never done this before," she said.

This being...? he wondered, but didn't dare ask.

"I mean, I've never brought another man here."

Is that right? Now it was up to him to make sure she didn't regret it. He shrugged off his leather jacket, slung it over the back of a chair and slowly closed the short distance between him and Claire. He watched her eyes, looking for any hint of reluctance, any suggestion that she might have changed her mind.

He stopped in front of her but didn't touch her. Without missing a beat, she wrapped her arms around his neck and kissed him.

He would let her set the pace, he decided. Even if it killed him.

He rested his hands on her hips, lightly, relishing the gentle sway as she pressed her mouth to his. Her tongue slid slowly across his lips and his resolve started to wane. For a woman unaccustomed to inviting men to her bedroom, she was damn good at it.

She shoved his T-shirt up his chest, and he made it easy for her by stripping it off and resuming the kiss. Her hands were warm against his bare flesh, and getting hotter by the minute. Time to return the favor. He tugged on her sweater and she let him pull it over her head, exposing a lacy white bra and full shapely breasts that were just…

"Beautiful," he whispered.

He backed her up to the bed, let her go long enough for her to lie down and crawled on next to her, thinking that being horizontal with Claire might be the closest he would ever get to heaven.

"The light," she said, adding a little gasp as his hand explored the lace undergarment.

"What about it?"

"We should turn it out."

"No way." He found the hooks at the back and released them with one hand, first try. Not exactly the sort of thing a guy could put on a resumé, but a damn handy skill to have. "I don't want to miss a thing."

The feel of her and the scent of her skin already had his senses on overload, but he wanted it all. He wanted to hear more of those breathy sighs, taste her and explore every square inch of her. The lights were staying on.

He took one breast into his mouth, marveling at the texture, and how the more he teased, the more it changed. With one hand he explored her belly, hip and thigh, still clad in dark jeans. Finally unable to resist, he slipped his fingers between her legs.

Even through the fabric she was hot and damp, and he was practically delirious with desire. He hardly dared let himself believe that Lucky Devil was about to get lucky with Claire DeAngelo. A momentary flash of uncertainty ripped through him, and he reminded himself that he needed to take this slow. She deserved to be worshipped, not ravished.

Apparently she had other ideas. She tugged at his

belt buckle and when that didn't give way, she ran her hand over the front of his jeans, covering him with her palm. What little willpower he had evaporated.

Next time they would take it slow. Or the time after that, for sure.

He closed his eyes and momentarily gave himself up to her intimate touch, then he undid her jeans, dipped a hand inside her panties and primed her with a couple of quick strokes.

She unzipped his fly and returned the favor.

He stroked her some more, smug in the knowledge that he was here with her, and she was hot for him. Him. He unbuckled his belt and unsnapped his jeans. She had found a way in, but he was desperate to give her full access. And she took full advantage.

This felt so right in so many ways. Sweet, shy Claire, who had always come across as being a little unsure of her womanhood, was moving to the rhythm of his touch, not afraid to show him what she wanted or give him what he needed.

His sense of personal triumph was interrupted by a sound from outside the bedroom. A key in the door? The hair went up on the back of his neck.

The door opened quietly and closed again.

What the hell?

In the space of a heartbeat his instincts shifted from the beautiful woman sprawled beside him to the disturbing awareness they were no longer alone. He put a finger to his lips, indicating she needed to be quiet, ignoring the fleeting second thought brought on by the scent of her.

His gut told him the intruder was the same person who'd been watching him earlier. In one swift silent move he stood, zipped his jeans and retrieved his gun from inside his jacket.

Claire's eyes went wide. *Shh,* he silently cautioned her again.

He moved to the bedroom door, confident that his ability to silently cross the carpet like a cat gave him the advantage. Bad enough someone had picked the lock and broken into the place, but to interrupt him when he was about to have sex for the first time in a really long time? Whoever this was deserved to get shot.

He was halfway down the short hallway when a shadow slanted across the floor ahead of him. He flattened himself against the wall and waited. By the time the shadow-maker appeared, he was ready for him. He slammed the man face-first against the opposite wall and jerked one of his arms behind his back. Air gushed out of the guy's chest with a pleasing *oomph* and the stale scent of whiskey. Luke jabbed the business end of his weapon between a couple of ribs.

"Seattle P.D. Don't move, unless maybe you've got a death wish."

"Police? What the…?"

Luke immediately recognized the voice. Claire's ex. What was this son of a bitch doing here?

"This is break-and-enter." Maybe a pat down would teach Mr. High-and-Mighty to think twice before stalking his ex-wife and breaking into her apartment. Still, some of his tension eased, knowing the intruder wasn't one of the subjects they had under surveillance.

"Luke. Let him go." Claire appeared in the bedroom doorway, and then light flooded the hallway. She had pulled on a dressing gown and folded her arms across the front to keep it closed.

Luke lowered his weapon and reluctantly backed off.

Donald swung away from him, flexing his arm. "How can I break and enter a place if I own it?"

"By not living in it," Luke said. Did this jerk really believe he could come and go from here, from Claire's home, anytime he pleased?

"I thought you were out." Donald spoke to Claire as though Luke wasn't in the room.

Luke took a step toward him. "I don't believe you. You were sitting in your car out front when we got home. You came up here to find out what we were doing."

Donald eyed Luke's bare chest and unbuttoned jeans, then flicked his gaze at Claire. "It's a free country. I can sit anywhere I want, anytime I want."

"A *free* country?" What was this guy? Twelve? "Stalking is against the law. Maybe you'd like to take a trip down to the station and find out how goddamned free you'll be then."

"Luke. I'll handle this."

This no-nonsense Claire was new to him, and he liked her. Liked her a lot. He stood his ground, though, arms loose by his sides, ready to move if Donald decided to stay stupid.

"And you," she said, turning on the ex. "You have no business being here, and you need to leave. Now."

"But what about…"

"There are no buts, Donald. I have nothing to say to you. I told you I'll call my lawyer. My lawyer will call your lawyer. Now get out."

Luke had to hand it to her. A lot of women would have fallen apart under the circumstances, but not Claire. Her demeanor was calm and collected, her voice firm, even a bit forceful. She wasn't backing down, and she wasn't taking no for an answer. Still, he slowly reached around his back to where he'd stashed his gun. The action wasn't lost on Donald, who held up both hands, palms out, and stepped away.

"Okay, okay. I'm going, but this isn't over," he said, backing toward the door, apparently not ballsy enough to turn his back on them. Good call.

"I want this place on the market, Claire. Soon. And I want that book back."

"Out!" Claire's voice was a little sharper.

Donald opened the door, but he didn't leave. "You really a cop?" he asked.

"Yeah, I am."

"You got a badge?"

"It's in my jacket, in the *bedroom*." *You want a pissing contest? Bring it on, buddy.* "Tell you what. You want me to produce my badge, I get to read you your rights."

"That's bullshit." Now that Donald was out of the apartment, he seemed a little less intimidated and a lot more full of himself.

Luke dealt with guys like this all the time. Arrogant, never willing to acknowledge they were in the wrong, always wanting the last word. Short of locking them up, there was only one way to handle them. He shut the door in Donald's face and flipped the dead bolt home with a sharp click. Not that a dead bolt could keep out someone with keys, but Luke was reasonably confident the guy wasn't dumb enough to come back.

"You okay?" he asked, turning to face Claire.

Her bottom lip quivered a little and she shook her head.

"Come here." He drew her into his arms and held her,

happy to offer comfort but feeling like an ass because now he was mostly ticked that Donald's appearance had blown his chances with her. Her breath was warm against his shoulder, her hair soft beneath his hand as he stroked the back of her head.

After a minute or two her body relaxed and she slipped her arms around his waist, letting the robe fall open as she did. He didn't need to look down to know that before she'd put on the robe, she'd shed the bra he'd unfastened earlier.

He hooked her chin with a finger and tipped her face up, needing to get a read on what she wanted from him. He didn't like what he saw.

"I'm so sorry," she said. "He's never done anything like this before."

Luke wasn't so sure. Stalkers usually worked their way up to the kind of brazen behavior they'd seen tonight. If he had to guess, he'd say Donald had been at this for a while.

"You're sure he's never been in here? Maybe when you're not home?"

Her eyes filled with concern. "I...I don't know. I just assumed he wouldn't. None of his things are here."

You're here. While Donald figured there was nothing wrong with hooking up with a new woman, he clearly had an issue with Claire moving on. Probably best not to upset her with that just now.

"I think you should change the lock." He was kind of surprised she hadn't already done that, but she had always wanted to believe the best in people.

"I'll call a locksmith first thing in the morning. Otherwise I'll never get any sleep."

"Speaking of sleep, it's getting late." He brushed her

hair back and lightly kissed her forehead. "You should get some rest. If it'll help, I'll spend the night on the sofa."

"I'd like you to stay," she said, demonstrating that need by sliding her hands over his hips and angling herself against him. "But not out here."

For the second time that evening, she laced her fingers with his and led him into the bedroom. Oh, yeah. He really was a lucky devil. If anyone interrupted them this time, he just might shoot first and ask questions later.

Chapter 4

Claire eased out of a deep sleep, Luke's warm breath on the back of her neck slowly seeping into her consciousness, his body curved snugly behind hers. Early-morning light crept past the edges of the drapes, but according to the clock radio on the nightstand, she had only slept for a couple of hours. It had been a sound sleep, though. The security of having him stay the night, mixed with an exhilarating series of rapid-fire orgasms, had seen to that.

This might never happen again, she reminded herself. And that was okay.

Luke had kept her mind off of Donald's intrusion. Her ex could be annoying, demanding even, but she had never been afraid of him. This morning she didn't know what to think. What had possessed him to let himself in? What would he have done if she hadn't been here?

Better question…what would he have done if she had been here alone? Luke was convinced that Donald had been sitting out front, watching them when they came home from dinner. If so, he knew she was here with another man, and yet he used his key to come in. Why would he do that? Why would he care?

She had been stalling over selling the condo, partly because she hated being rushed into making decisions, but mostly because calling the shots gave her some control over this situation. She could admit that, at least to herself. Now the idea of living here alone, even with the lock changed, creeped her out.

She needed to make a decision and she needed to make it soon, but right now she had better things to do. She was wrapped in Luke's arms, safe and satisfied, and if she didn't wake him, she could lie here a little— maybe a lot—longer.

"You awake?" he asked.

"I am. I thought you were asleep, though."

He nipped her earlobe. "I was faking it."

"You were very convincing."

She shifted onto her back so she could see him, pulling on the sheet to keep her body covered. For a little while last night she'd been a different person, or at least the way Luke had looked at her in the dim light had made her feel different. Instead of being awkward, over-weight Claire, she'd been bold, even a little sexy, and she had done things with him she'd never dreamed of doing with any other man, ever. Not that there'd been many.

But this morning, in the clear, cool light of day, she was back to normal, self-consciously aware of the extra pounds she couldn't shed, not even on a diet of rice cakes and celery sticks.

"I thought about getting up and bringing you coffee in bed." Luke nuzzled the soft spot behind her ear, the way he had last night, but the stubble on his jaw turned it into a brand-new experience. "But I was pretty sure I wouldn't be able to get that coffeemaker to work. Besides…this is nice."

This was heaven, especially now that his tongue was in on the action. Her eyelids drifted shut and she gave herself over to the magic until—

"Oh!" She had loosened her grip on the sheet and Luke whisked it aside. "No, Luke. I'm cold."

"I can fix that." He pulled the sheet back over her, diving beneath it as he did.

He made her laugh, and then he made her suck in her breath, and then she forgot about everything except the thing he was doing that was making her glad she'd decided last night that she could be *that* woman.

An hour later, showered, dressed and feeling more pleased with himself than he had in a long, long time, Luke sat on a stool at the kitchen island, drinking strong, black coffee, just the way he liked it, and watching Claire fix herself a latte. If he could convince her to let him spend some time here and monitor the activity in the building next door—and hang out with her, of course—she would have to show him how to work this contraption. It made one fine cup of coffee.

"Are you working today?" She set her cup on the counter and settled on the stool next to his. "At either of your jobs?"

"Window washers don't do residential work on Saturdays. People tend to be at home and they resent having their privacy invaded."

"Makes sense." She put a container of skim milk back in the fridge. "It seems strange, at least to me, that you actually have to be on their crew. It must be scary, hanging on the side of a building like that."

"It's not as bad as it looks." He didn't mind it, and he only needed to spend a couple of days at it, long enough to get an up close look at the penthouse across the way. "This morning I have a meeting down at the station, though. And some paperwork to catch up on."

There hadn't been a meeting scheduled, but while Claire was in the shower Luke had called his sergeant about this new development, and he had called them in to discuss the pros and cons of adding this vantage point to their stakeout. Providing Luke could find a way to get Claire to go along with it. Could he convince her to do that without letting her in on his real reason for wanting to be here? Sure, he wanted to be with her, and after last night, he figured he had a pretty good shot at spending more time with her. He knew a thing or two about satisfying a woman, and Claire was satisfied. But nobody in their right mind shacked up after one date. But Donald…that jerk just might provide him with the in he needed.

She sipped her drink, and he leaned in to take care of the foam on her lip before her tongue got to it. He liked that he could do that, loved that she would let him.

And there was that smile again. Definitely satisfied. Not that last night had only been about finding a way in here. Last night had been amazing. For the past two years, since getting sober, he'd taken his AA sponsor's advice and avoided relationships, even one-night stands. Last night he'd been more than ready to move forward, and it turned out sober sex was mind-blowing. Huh. Who freakin' knew?

"What about you?" he asked. "Is Saturday a day off?"

"Never. I'm showing condos to some young newly-weds this morning and this afternoon I'm hosting an open house at a property I listed last week." She glanced away. "Before that, I have to call a locksmith."

He touched her arm, her shoulder and finally snagged her chin, turning her to face him. "Let me call someone for you. They usually charge an arm and a leg to come out on weekends, but I have a connection."

"You have a friend who's a locksmith?"

"Not a friend." He pulled his phone out of his back pocket, brought up a number. "A contact I made on the job."

She narrowed her eyes. "Does this guy just keep bad guys out? Or does he help the good guys get in?"

Interesting that she would ask. "Some questions are best left unanswered."

She laughed. "Fair enough. If you can get me a deal and get it done right away, that's all I need to know. That, and what you'd like for breakfast."

"I never turn down a meal. What have you got?"

"Eggs." She got up and opened the fridge. "Green onions, red peppers, mushrooms. I can make an omelet as long as you're okay with no cheese."

"Sounds good to me."

He stood and picked up his coffee, making the call to Marty at Lock 'N' Key as he crossed the living room to the windows. The glass of the opposite building reflected the morning sky, making it impossible to see anything or anyone inside. A good pair of binoculars used from a discreet vantage point would change all that. He needed to make this work.

After making arrangements to have the lock changed, he rejoined Claire in the kitchen. He picked up the knife next to the cutting board and, while she cracked eggs into a bowl and whisked them, he chopped the onions and sliced peppers and mushrooms.

"You're very handy in the kitchen," she said.

"And you thought I was just a pretty face."

She laughed at that.

He tossed a sliver of red pepper into the air and caught it in his mouth. When he offered one to her, she parted her lips so he could slide it inside. He practically groaned out loud.

"I've had lots of practice. With cooking," he added, in case she thought he was talking about something else. "Comes with the territory."

"Confirmed-bachelor territory?"

He couldn't tell if she was baiting him. "Something like that. But even when I was with Sherri, I did most of the cooking. When we ate in, which wasn't often."

Claire set a skillet on the stove and turned on the element. "Do you miss her?"

No one had ever asked him that. "No, I don't. I guess that makes me a bit of a jerk."

"Being in a relationship doesn't mean you'll miss the other person when it's over. I sure don't miss Donald, especially after last night."

"Is that right? I was that good?" It was a smart-ass thing to say, but he couldn't stop himself.

Her face went from flushed to flaming in a matter of seconds, but she was grinning, too. "That's a pretty lethal weapon you have." She plucked a slice of pepper off the cutting board and slid it into his mouth. "I'm sure Donald would agree."

Donald? What the…? *She's talking about the Glock, genius.*

"Getting back to you and Sherri…" She poured olive oil into the pan. "Sorry. I don't have any butter."

He'd caught a glimpse of the inside of her fridge and noticed she didn't have a whole lot of anything. As for him and Sherri, he might as well get that out in the open.

"She's the reason I quit drinking, so I'll always be grateful to her for that. But stuff happened, bad stuff, and there was no getting past it." With the onions and peppers sliced and ready, he started on the mushrooms.

Claire poured the egg mixture into the pan. "I'm listening."

"We were both drinking," he said. "A lot. I used to hide the car keys because once she was into a bottle, there was no stopping her. No matter how hammered she was, she'd get behind the wheel, especially if she ran out of booze."

Between using a spatula to check the underside of the omelet and adding the vegetables to the pan, Claire gave him an anxious look.

"God knows, I'm no saint," he said. "But I got good at juggling the liquor so I was sober when I was on duty. Sherri didn't work so she didn't have that to keep her grounded."

"Do you think a job would have grounded her?" Claire asked.

He leaned against the counter, watching her. "I don't know. Maybe not. Probably not. Anyway, one night she found the keys. Or maybe I forgot to hide them. I'm not sure. She went out, with a blood-alcohol reading that was something like three times the legal limit, and plowed into a tree."

Claire looked up at him then, eyes brimming with concern. "Oh, Luke. Was she hurt? Was anyone else?"

"She was. No one else, though." Which wasn't exactly true, but he didn't know if he should tell her. Aside from that night at the E.R., he'd never talked about the baby. Not with anyone. Not even Sherri.

"That's a good thing, at least. Is she okay now?"

Should he tell her? Did it make sense to tell her? After all this time, here he was. Here. With her. He hadn't known how much he wanted to be with her until she'd invited him into her bedroom last night. He wanted to spend more time with her. Starting tonight, if he could find a way to make it happen.

You know what you need to do.

Step four: Make a searching and fearless moral inventory of ourselves.

Step five: Admit to another human being the exact nature of our wrongs.

Here goes nothing.

"She wasn't wearing a seat belt, so she was pretty badly banged up. Concussion, a bunch of stitches. And…"

Claire sliced through the omelet, slid the two halves onto plates and set them on the counter. "Salt and pepper?" she asked, suddenly very matter-of-fact. Very Claire.

"Sure." He took the stool he'd been sitting on earlier.

She got out cutlery and napkins, took a pair of salt-and-pepper grinders out of a cupboard and sat next to him.

"This is good," he said after swallowing a mouthful.

"Thanks." She picked up her fork. "So you were telling me about the accident."

"When I said no one else was hurt, that wasn't entirely true. She was pregnant, and she lost the baby."

"Oh, my God. Luke, I'm so sorry." She set her fork on her plate and laid a hand on his arm.

He couldn't look at her, not until he finished, because he didn't want sympathy. He wanted to move forward, maybe with her. For that to happen, she needed to know the truth.

"I didn't know about the baby. I don't know if she did, either."

"Really? How far along was she?"

"Two months, maybe a little more."

"And she was drinking all that time?"

"Yeah, a lot. The doctor never came right out and said it, but I got the impression that the miscarriage was probably for the best."

Claire squeezed his arm but stayed quiet, waiting for him to continue.

"Then I said some stuff to Sherri, and she played the victim. She was good at that and I'd always let her get away with it, but not that time. She swore she hadn't been drinking. Just swerved to miss a cat, and then there must've been something wrong with the brakes because she couldn't stop. I called her on it, pointed out that the blood work didn't lie, but she did. About the drinking, the accident, the baby…everything."

"Is that when the two of you broke up, when you decided to stop…?"

"Not quite." She didn't need to know he'd stormed out of the hospital that night, met up with a couple of buddies, got smashed. Two days later he woke up on a friend's couch with a buzz saw carving up his gut, the taste of bile in his throat, a jackhammer pounding on his skull and absolutely no recollection of how he'd spent the past forty-eight hours. If that wasn't rock bottom, if it was possible to feel like a bigger piece of shit than he had that morning, he didn't want to find out.

"I actually went on a bender for a couple of days, sobered up in time to bring her home from the hospital. I accused her of being careless and irresponsible, trying to trap me into marrying her, forcing me to have a baby I didn't want."

Claire snatched her hand away and picked up her fork again, averting her eyes.

He hated that she pulled away, mostly because he had no clue what it meant. Had he said too much? Sounded too harsh?

She refocused on him, this time with intense scrutiny. "But if the circumstances had been different…if the baby had been okay…you'd be a father right now."

That was something he hadn't been able to wrap his head around then, and it didn't get easier with time. "She knew I didn't want a family, and I didn't mean not at that particular time, and I didn't mean just not with her. I meant not ever. There's no way I'll bring another Devlin child into the world and have it grow up the way I did. Sherri knew that."

"But you're not your father, Luke."

Nice of her to say, and he'd sure like to believe it. Truth was, he'd spent most of his adult life being like his father. Getting sober had changed that, he hoped, but it was a daily struggle. Only another alcoholic could understand that and there was no point in trying to explain it to Claire, so he let it drop.

"Sherri and I talked about kids more than once and she always gave the impression we were on the same page. After she lost the baby, I stuck around, tried to work things out, but I knew the only way to fix things was to do it sober. She agreed, but I was the only one who quit drinking. So I joined AA, moved into a place of my own, got a dog and here I am."

"It sounds as though you did what you could, and then you did what you had to do," Claire said.

Nice that she was willing to give him the benefit of the doubt. Or so it seemed. He wouldn't know for sure until she agreed to see him again.

"Speaking of the dog…" He shoveled in the last forkful of omelet, drained his coffee cup. "Rex'll be going squirrelly. I need to take him out for a run sometime this morning or he'll unstuff a piece of furniture."

Claire slid off her stool and cleared away their plates and empty cups. "Why don't you go? I can wait for the locksmith. I still have plenty of time before I meet my clients."

No way. Rex could knock himself out with the arm of the couch that still had some upholstery on it because Luke was not leaving her alone here until Donald's key no longer worked the lock.

"I'll stay. Marty can be a little intimidating." Three hundred pounds and a hundred hours at the tattoo parlor tended to have that effect.

Claire was already dressed for work in tailored navy pants with a matching jacket and crisp white shirt. They had a little time before Marty would get here, and Luke was toying with the idea of unbuttoning the shirt when music started to play.

Was that… "La Cucaracha"?

"It's Donald." She pulled her phone from her jacket pocket. "After last night, he's got a lot of nerve."

Nerve? The guy was either supremely arrogant or completely stupid. Maybe both, and that was always a dangerous combination.

"I'll let it go to voice mail," she said.

"Take it. Otherwise you're giving him the upper hand." He'd like to answer it himself, except that would be adding fuel to this guy's fire, which was already raging out of control. "Act like his showing up here last night never happened."

Claire lowered her eyes as she answered. "Good morning, Donald."

Luke stopped her when she tried to turn away. He couldn't hear what the ex was saying, but he'd be able to read it in her expression.

"I have appointments all day so no, I won't have a chance to talk to my lawyer. I'll call her on Monday." Claire shook her head. "I'm not agreeing to that. The book was a gift and I'm keeping it. Like I said yesterday…"

He could sense the struggle it took to keep her voice steady and not react. He reached for her free hand, stroked his thumb across her palm, wanting her to know she was doing great.

"Yes, I'll call her on Monday morning to set up an appointment, and she'll let your lawyer know what we've decided. Honestly, Donald, it's just a couple of days and I would appreciate it if you would stop calling."

Then she looked at him and he felt her go tense.

"That is none of your business," she said.

He knew what that meant. The son of a bitch was

asking if Luke was still here. He hated this was happening to her, hated to think this jerk would now try to use him as a reason to keep stalking her, even though Luke could tell the harassment had been going on for far too long. Maybe even while they were married. Why did she put up with this?

He was tempted to go down to the lobby and see if he could spot the guy somewhere in front of the building, but this wasn't the time to leave Claire alone. He had ways of finding out what he needed to know about Donald Robinson, and he wouldn't waste any time doing it.

"I have to go. I have appointments and I have to start getting ready."

She ended the call, heaved a huge sigh and set her phone on the counter. "I'm so sorry you're being dragged into this. I don't know why he's doing this."

Luke knew exactly where the guy was coming from. He'd witnessed enough domestic disputes to know there was likely no getting through to Donald, especially since, after being caught at gunpoint last night, he was already hounding her this morning. This guy was trouble, and Luke didn't like what his instincts were telling him.

"Marty should be here anytime, so at least you know Donald can't get back in. What about your open house this afternoon? Will you be there alone?"

Her nod was barely discernible.

"Can you arrange to have someone there with you?" If not, he'd stake out the place himself.

"Do you really think that's necessary?"

"Depends on how comfortable you are with him finding out where you are and showing up."

"I'm not. I'll call my business partners and see if one of them will join me."

"Good plan." He picked up her phone and swiped the screen to bring it to life.

"What are you doing?" she asked.

"Adding my number to your contacts. If you need me for anything, if Donald gives you any grief, I want you to call me."

"I'm sure he won't—"

"Please promise me you'll call."

"All right. If he calls me, I'll call you." She sounded convincing. And then she laughed. "I'll have to find a ring tone for you, so if you call me I'll know who it is."

"Don't need one." He tucked the phone into her jacket pocket, leaned in and caught one soft earlobe between his teeth. "It won't ring when I call. It'll vibrate."

Claire stood in front of the bathroom mirror, brushing her teeth. Luke had just left, she had a new front door key on her ring and this was the first chance she'd had to reflect on the events of the past eighteen hours or so since she'd run into him yesterday afternoon.

She looked perfectly ordinary. Same wavy brown hair, same dark-rimmed glasses, her favorite suit. No one looking at her would ever guess she'd ridden on a motorcycle, brought a man home to spend the night and had a tattooed guy named Marty change her locks.

She rinsed her mouth, then rinsed her toothbrush and returned it to its holder.

"And don't forget seeing your ex held at gunpoint."

Ironic that she and Luke had joked about the movie versions of their lives over dinner last night, and now hers felt every bit like one. But forget *Mona Lisa Smile*. This felt more *Ocean's Eleven*. Or *The Pelican Brief*.

She rolled her eyes at her reflection. "Would you listen to yourself? You're being ridiculous." This was all simply a bizarre series of coincidences that had led to a bizarre series of incidents. In a few minutes she'd be on her way to the office to meet clients, just as she did every Saturday. Her life was perfectly normal, just the way she liked it.

And it was about to get even more normal, because sometime between Donald's intrusion last night and having a tattooed biker change the lock this morning, she had made a decision. It was time to sell the condo, finalize the divorce and move on. If she left for work now, she would get to the office with time to spare. While she waited for her clients to arrive, she could look at real estate listings with her own wish list in mind.

A character home with three bedrooms, hardwood floors, a white picket fence and the world's biggest, deepest, claw-foot tub. The fence was optional because Sam had long ago offered to build one if she found the perfect home minus the white pickets.

Until then, she would keep the Beatrix Potter book in her office. She had already pulled it off the shelf and tucked it in her bag. Donald shouldn't be able to get back in here now that the lock was changed, but she had to give a new key to the building manager and she wouldn't put it past Donald to talk the guy into letting him in. She still didn't know exactly why he wanted in, if he'd been coming here all along or if this was something new, but now that he had a bee in his bonnet about the book, she would keep it locked in her office. The idea of him in here, going through her things, was downright creepy, but so far she hadn't noticed anything missing and she'd like to keep it that way.

She drew in a breath, sucking in her tummy as she buttoned her jacket. She breathed out and watched the pull of the fabric reflected in the mirror. She undid the jacket and let it fall open.

"Why won't you go away?" she asked the muffin top that was discreetly disguised by the extra layers of fabric. Still…

She turned sideways, studied herself in profile, ran both hands down the sides of her body. Luke had insisted on leaving a light on last night, insisting he wanted to see what he touched. She slid her hands back up and lightly over her breasts. *Beautiful.* Not an adjective that had ever come to mind when she looked at herself in the mirror, but that's what he'd whispered, and he sounded as though he meant it. No, if Luke had noticed her weight, he hadn't seemed to mind. Even now, the memory of his careful and deliberate exploration of her body had her heating up all over again.

"Still won't hurt to lose a few more pounds." Ordinarily she went down to the gym every morning and spent twenty minutes on the treadmill, not that it ever seemed to make any difference, but she hadn't wanted to abandon Luke. Besides, she figured the workout he'd given her last night, and again this morning, should have burned at least as many calories as her usual morning routine in the gym, which was one of the building's many amenities. She would miss that when she moved out.

"Who are you kidding?" She hated working out, but she did it anyway. When she no longer lived here, she would join a gym, maybe the one Sam belonged to, or at least buy a treadmill and set it up in one of the empty bedrooms. Otherwise she would turn into a blob.

She washed her hands, towelled them dry and opened a drawer in the vanity where she kept a tube of hand lotion.

She squeezed a small amount of rose-scented lotion into her palm, capped the tube and rubbed her hands together.

Luke had suggested dinner again tonight, said he'd call this afternoon. She got a little warmer, remembering his playful remark about making her phone vibrate. If he did call, that wouldn't be the only thing humming.

She was about to slide the drawer shut after dropping the tube inside when the plastic birth control dispenser caught her attention. She plucked it out, hating the way her chest went tight.

Had she missed a dose? Yes. Last night, for sure. And maybe the night before that? She closed her eyes and drew a couple of long, steadying breaths before she let herself look.

Oh. God.

She tossed the plastic disk into the drawer and slammed it shut. She hadn't taken one in nearly a week.

Chapter 5

Claire sat on the edge of the bathtub and let her face fall into her hands. This could not be happening. Luke had asked her about birth control last night, and she had assured him that she had it covered. At the time she'd been tumbling down the deliciously slippery slope of Luke-induced preorgasmic ecstasy when he'd asked the question. She remembered gasping yes because she was all but brainless and no other answer would have worked. And then he'd been inside her and sealed the deal on that orgasm.

But now, what if…?

She'd wanted a baby since she and Donald were first married, but she'd never missed a pill because he had wanted to wait. Now that she was single, she'd thought about stopping birth control altogether. Why bother if it wasn't necessary? But to let herself be so careless last night. How could she have let that happen?

Over breakfast Luke had shared his deep and lingering resentment over being lied to and tricked into parenthood, and at the same time he'd made his feelings known to Claire, too.

She knew I didn't want a family, and I didn't mean not at that particular time, and I didn't just mean not with her. I meant not ever. There's no way I'll bring another Devlin child into the world and have it grow up the way I did.

It hadn't been his only reason for breaking things off with Sherri, but it had been one of them. Would Claire be able to convince him that she hadn't lied? That she'd just made a mistake? And if she couldn't make him believe her, could she live with his anger and mistrust, no matter how well justified they were?

"Stop! Listen to yourself. You don't even know that you are pregnant."

She had been on the Pill for a long time, so missing a few probably didn't even matter. There was really only one way to find out. She dug her phone out of her pocket and called the clinic, relieved they had a last-minute opening that fit right between her morning clients and her afternoon open house.

Years ago she'd seen the doctor, albeit under different circumstances, and that time she'd been given the morning-after pill. But she'd been a freshman then, young and inexperienced. This was different. She was a responsible adult, and she wanted a baby. Last night she'd been with the man she had fantasized about for four years while they were in college, and a few more after they lost touch. So okay, she *was* the woman who slept with a man on a first date. But the woman who tricked a man into having a baby he didn't want? No way. *Claire DeAngelo was not* that *woman.* If she was pregnant, she would figure out a way to deal with it on her own. If Luke didn't want to be a father, he didn't have to be one.

On the elevator to the parking garage, and for the first time since she and Donald had moved in here, Claire felt nervous, and it was because of him. She pressed the unlock button on the key fob as she crossed the parking lot, then slid behind the wheel and locked the door as soon as she was inside.

With her resolve stronger than ever, she called Sam and after she had her on the line, connected them to Kristi.

"Good morning. What's up?" Sam asked.

"I was wondering the same thing," Kristi said.

"I've made a decision," Claire told them. "I'm selling the condo."

"Finally!"

"It's about time!"

"Wow," she said. "I didn't realize you both felt so strongly about this."

"Sweetie," Kristi said, "it's a big decision and it's none of my business so I would never offer advice on something like this, but that place is so not you."

"Not to mention that it's time to wrap things up with Donald. Clean break, fresh start and all that." Trust Sam to be so direct.

"You're right," Claire said. "I'm kind of kicking myself for dragging my heels over this." Although if she hadn't been taking her time, chances were she wouldn't have run into Luke. One night with him had made putting up with Donald's phone calls worthwhile.

"Did something happen to bring this on all of a sudden?" Kristi asked.

"I was wondering the same thing," Sam said.

"You could say that." How much should she tell them? Would it be better to wait until they met in person?

"I just poured myself a cup of tea, Nate's taken the twins to their gymnastics class and Jenna's still sleeping," Kristi said. "I have all the time in the world."

"Me, too," Sam chimed in. "Our housekeeper just made a fresh pot of coffee, and AJ and Will have taken the dog to the park. I'm all ears."

Claire took a long, deep breath and plunged in. "I ran in to an old friend yesterday. He suggested we go out for dinner and it was…nice."

Sam laughed. "Okay, so you hook up with a guy, start making major life decisions within twelve hours and it was *nice?* That would make you queen of the understatement."

"Who is this mystery man? How long have you known him?" Kristi asked.

"We were friends in college. We never dated or anything, mostly we just studied together. Anyway, he's a detective with the Seattle P.D., he's working on some undercover assignment, and I bumped into him yesterday afternoon and—"

"Did you bring him back to your place after dinner?"

"Kristi! I'm not going to answer that."

"Sweetie, you just did."

"And now for the obvious question…" Sam said. "Did he get under *your* cover?"

Kristi laughed.

"Is it that obvious?" Claire asked. It was as if these two had suddenly become clairvoyant.

"You phone us out of the blue on Saturday morning and announce that you're selling your condo."

"And then you tell us your decision is based on dinner with an old friend."

Put that way, she supposed it was obvious.

"Okay, fine. Yes to both questions."

Her business partners squealed and giggled like a pair of teenage girls at a sleepover, and repeated what they'd said when she told them she planned to put the condo on the market.

"Finally!"

"It's about time!"

"Have you told Donald?"

Jeez, maybe these two really were psychic. The truth was, she couldn't wait to tell them about Donald's unexpected appearance last night, and Luke's *very* unexpected response to it, but that would have to wait. When she did tell them, she wanted to actually see the looks on their faces.

"I'm doing my best not to talk to Donald about anything. I see my lawyer on Monday, and I'll let her tell his lawyer."

"Good plan," Kristi said. "Will you handle the listing yourself?"

"I can't. It's a conflict of interest."

"Makes sense. Do you have someone in mind?" Sam asked.

"I do. Remember Brenda Billings? She's been selling higher-end properties in the city for years and she seems to have no problem finding buyers."

"Anything we can do to help?" Sam asked.

Claire was hoping they'd ask. "I'd love it if you'd both come over and do a walk-through with me before I list it. I don't think it needs a lot, but it's always great to have fresh eyes."

"Are you kidding?" Kristi asked. "After everything you've done to help me find my dream home—"

"Not to mention your dream guy," Sam added.

"That, too. Of course we'll help you."

"And when you start to look for a new place, I'll do an inspection for you. Check out the roof, plumbing, electrical."

The residual weight of the second thoughts she was having lifted and drifted away, replaced by the exciting possibility of finding a home that was right for her. An old character home and plenty of room for the family she hoped to have someday. *But not too soon,* she thought, experiencing another anxious twinge.

"And I'll help with color schemes, draperies and any other decorating you might want to do. It'll be fun," Kristi said.

"Have I told you guys lately how much I love you?"

"Are you kidding? You're the glue that holds this company together. You name it, we'll do it for you."

Sam's generous statement was flattering, but not even remotely true. The three of them made a solid team, and not a day went by that Claire didn't thank her lucky stars for putting the three of them at the same meeting of a group of Seattle businesswomen a number of years ago. They had met and clicked, and within a matter of weeks, Ready Set Sold had been born.

"When can we get started?" Kristi asked.

"I have some time tomorrow afternoon," Sam said. "Sundays are always quiet at my house."

"Me, too," Kristi said. "How 'bout we drop by and go through your condo, and if you've found any listings for places you like, you can show us those, too."

"That'll be great. What time?" Claire asked. If Luke spent the night again, she would need to have him gone before the girls arrived. It wasn't that she didn't want them to meet him. She wasn't ready to share him yet.

Sam was the first to answer. "How about right after lunch? We'll have Will down for a nap by then, and my mom always rests in the afternoon, too."

"That's good for me, too," Kristi said. "One o'clock?"

"Perfect. I'll see you both then." That would give her all morning with Luke. If there was going to be a morning with Luke. And if there was, she would have to add grocery shopping to her growing list of things to do today. "Right now I've got to run. I need to stop by the office, then I'm showing properties for the rest of the morning. Wish me luck?"

She desperately wanted to ask for luck during her visit to the clinic, but that would mean admitting that she'd been stupid and irresponsible. Since her business partners thought she was the glue that held them together, she couldn't bring herself to tell them that last night she'd let herself come completely unglued. Besides, there was a very good chance she had nothing to worry about. She started the car and left the parking garage.

Nothing to worry about. Hold that thought, she told herself. *Hold. That. Thought.*

On his way into the precinct, Luke stopped at the front desk, happy to see Kate Bradshaw on duty. She was a rookie, smart as whip, cute as a button and had a serious hate-on for male stalkers after a close friend

so Cam's out there going through footage taken by airport security cameras."

Derek shut his laptop and joined the conversation. "He's known to be one of Phong's bodyguards. The suspicion is that he's arriving ahead of his boss to scope out the situation, determine the security needs."

"Could be the break we've been waiting for," Luke said. They could have executed a search warrant weeks ago, after the first prostitute died from a drug overdose, but that would only net them a couple of Phong's underlings and a handful of sex trade workers, most of whom had been smuggled into the country illegally. That would put an end to this setup, but it would also force Phong and his associates underground for at least six months. Been there, done that, more than once. This time they were waiting him out.

Patsy tucked her phone into her shoulder bag. "So, Luke. Jason tells us you might have a new vantage point for us."

"I do, if I can get it to work. Turns out a…um… friend of mine has a penthouse in the next tower and it faces our target. If I can get in there with some good surveillance equipment, we should be able to see everyone who comes and goes."

"Nice to have friends in high places," Derek quipped.

"Tell us about your friend," Jason said.

"Her name's Claire DeAngelo." Watching his sergeant jot her name in his notebook caused Luke a moment of regret. Claire would hate to know she was being talked about, checked out, but it had to be done. "I knew her in college. She's a real estate agent, lives there alone. Ran into her yesterday, got myself invited up and liked what I saw."

Jason set his pen down and gave Luke a long, steady look. "You sleeping with her?"

He probably should have seen that coming. If he had, maybe he wouldn't be blushing like a schoolgirl right now.

Derek laughed. "Lucky, you dog, you."

Jason picked up his pen. "That could work to our advantage. I don't like to involve civilians if it can be avoided, but if there's any chance you can get yourself moved in there…?"

It was an open-ended question that only Luke could answer. "I'll see what I can do."

"If you work it out, call me. I'll line up the equipment you'll need."

"I can't be too obvious about this," Luke said. "Otherwise she'll be asking questions." And giving him the boot, unless he could convince her that his main reason for being there was to be with her. Which was partly true, although no one in their right mind moved in together this early in a…whatever this was. It was way too soon to call it a relationship. Besides, he disliked the *R*-word almost as much as the one that started with *L*.

"We'll make sure you're the soul of discretion," Jason replied. Then he finally cracked a smile. "At least as far as surveillance goes."

Still, Luke's mind was filled with second thoughts. He genuinely wanted to spend time with Claire. Daytime, nighttime…the more time, the better. So it wasn't like he was using her, right? He was making the most of a good opportunity. Not to mention that if she let him stay, he'd be there if loser Donald made an encore appearance. So why did he suddenly feel like a piece of crap?

Because you're not being up-front with her, asshole. He hated when people did that to him. That's how he and Sherri had been with each other, it's the way his parents operated, but it didn't have to be that way with Claire. He could be open about plenty of other stuff, so that when it came time to explain about the undercover op, she would understand. He hoped.

"Everyone have today's assignment?" Jason asked.

"Sure do," Patsy said. "I'm heading downtown, looking for a couple of girls who used to work for Phong and managed to get out."

"I was wondering what that getup was all about," Derek said.

"You got something against fishnets and platform shoes?"

"Not a thing. What does your boyfriend think of them?"

"Better not to go there," she replied. "I'll see if I can get these girls to open up, tell me how things work on the inside, who delivers the drugs."

"Now that these girls are on the outside, they might not be willing to talk. They might think it's a setup," Derek said.

Patsy batted her heavily mascaraed eyelashes at him, then grinned at Jason and Luke. "Apparently the man's not aware of my powers of persuasion."

Luke returned the smile. He'd been thinking the same thing. "I'm technically off duty today. I'm running a check on someone, shouldn't take long. Unrelated to the undercover," he added quickly. "Then it looks like I'll be cooking dinner tonight."

"Lucky lady," Jason said.

"Derek, what about you?" Luke asked.

"I'll take over from Dex this afternoon. She'll pull the utility van out of there and I'll bring in the motor home, make it look like I'm there for the night. Actually I will be there for the night."

Luke's radar went off. "Was someone from the team there last night?"

"No," Jason said. "This is our first shot at watching who comes and goes from that building. Why?"

"No reason. Just keeping abreast." And getting closer to confirming it was Donald who'd been watching him and Claire last night. They needed to nip that in the bud. If Luke was going to spend as much time there as he hoped, having that jerk hanging around could complicate things. Luke hated complications. He hoped Kate had been able to dig up something on him.

"So if we're done here..." He'd stop by the front desk on his way out, then he needed to come up with a plan to convince Claire to let him stay. Dinner was a good start, then he figured a repeat of last night's performance in the bedroom just might seal the deal.

Nice work if you can get it.

Yeah, and it's that kind of thinking that will get you into serious trouble with Claire.

He had two objectives here, and if he was going to be successful, he needed to watch his step on both counts. He'd always liked her, a lot, but things were different now. There was a chance he might actually be worthy of her. Now he had to prove he was no longer the party animal she'd known in college, the guy who coasted through with mediocre grades and a perpetual hangover, and had a hard time keeping his pants zipped. Much as he wanted to believe he was no longer that man, he wanted Claire to believe it more.

Luke stopped by the front desk on his way out of the precinct. Kate was on the phone but she held up a finger to indicate she'd be a minute.

"Find anything?" he asked when she ended the call.

She tore a strip off a memo pad and handed it to him. "The guy drives a Lexus LS. Nice set of wheels. I gave you the plate number."

"Anything else?" Luke asked.

"A couple of traffic violations, otherwise nothing noteworthy. I've been busy, though, so I'll keep digging."

"Appreciate it." As he left the precinct and climbed onto his bike, he turned off his thoughts about the undercover operation and the business with Donald and pondered dinner. Something simple, he decided. He'd have to hit a grocery store, since Claire's fridge was virtually empty, and he'd also give his dog a good run because, with any luck, Rex would be spending another night on his own.

Chapter 6

The two-hour open house felt more like ten. Claire had just listed this home in East Queen Anne, not far from where Sam lived, and she liked to host an open house as soon as possible—it was an excellent way to get a sense of what buyers liked about the home and what didn't work for them. Today her heart wasn't in it, and her scattered thoughts were everywhere but on the job at hand.

That morning she'd shown several properties to her new clients and they'd liked one in particular, but wanted to sleep on it before deciding whether or not to make an offer. Fair enough.

Then she'd gone to the clinic, and she hadn't liked what she'd heard. After a mini lecture on why birth control only worked when taken regularly, she'd left with a diaphragm and instructions on how to use it. The doctor had suggested using condoms until the pregnancy scare was over, but she couldn't imagine how that would work. Last night Luke had told her he'd been tested for STDs after breaking up with Sherri, since he really had no idea whether or not she'd been with another man, and Claire had gone for the same test after learning about Donald's infidelity. Since they were both clean and she was on the Pill, a condom hadn't been a consideration. How could she ask him to use one now without telling him she had totally messed up? She couldn't, and she wouldn't. This was her problem, not his.

She was about to pack up her briefcase when her phone vibrated. The rest of her started to hum, too, much as it had when she'd ridden behind him on his motorcycle. As she answered, it dawned on her that "La Cucaracha" hadn't played all day, at least not since that morning. Maybe Donald was finally getting the message.

"Hi, Luke."

"Hey, you. Are you at home?"

"Not yet. I'm just leaving the open house, but I'll be there in about twenty minutes. Why?"

"Do you have plans for dinner?"

"Not so far."

"Good. What do you say I grab a few groceries and drop by, fix some for both of us?"

"You're offering to cook for me?" Another first for her.

He laughed. "Sure am. Nothing fancy, mind you, but I can manage the basics."

"You don't have to shop, though. I can pick up some groceries on my way home."

"Tell you what." His voice dropped an octave. "You

go home, slip into something…comfortable. I'll look after the rest."

"Oh." The hum upgraded to a serious throb. "Sure."

"I can be there in an hour," he said. "Does that work for you?"

Yes! "Sure. Yes, of course." *Could you maybe think of something intelligent to say?* "You're sure there's nothing I can do?"

Normally she would offer to pick up a bottle of wine. If there was one semi-useful thing she'd learned from living with Donald, it was how to choose the right wine, even though she seldom drank any herself. Under the circumstances, anything with alcohol was completely inappropriate, and besides, there were still quite a few bottles in the wine rack.

"You've been working all day," he said. "Go home, put your feet up, and I'll see you in a while. Do you have a barbecue?"

"Yes, there's one on the terrace. I've never used it, though."

"And we're going to maintain that tradition."

All she could think was…wow. Luke Devlin had already proven that he knew what a woman wanted in the bedroom. But to know his way around the kitchen, too… That was just…wow. It could be that he was simply looking for an excuse to get back into her bed, which was fine by her. Being wined and dined—figuratively, at least—was a brand-new experience, and she liked it. When she and Donald had entertained, mostly his business associates, he'd loved to stand out at the barbecue and make a show of doing the cooking…after she had done the shopping and food preparation.

"I'll see you soon," she said, feeling a little breathless. If she hurried, she would have time for a quick shower before she got comfortable.

Luke decided to leave the Ducati at home and loaded the groceries into his old truck instead. He was glad Claire had agreed to dinner because he'd already shopped for the things he needed to make it. After he talked to her on the phone, he'd taken Rex for a run and showered, and now he was ready for a night out. The whole night.

When he got to her place, he drove slowly up the street, scanning the vehicles parked on both sides. Sure enough, there was the Lexus. He didn't like the weight that settled in his gut, not one bit. What the hell was with this guy?

Luke noted the driver sitting behind the wheel, then he circled the block and parked a few cars back. After five minutes, Donald didn't move, so Luke got out and, with one arm wrapped around his bag of groceries, walked up the row of cars, and rapped on the driver's side window.

Startled, Donald jumped and swung sideways. In an instant his expression went from wary to defensive.

Luke indicated he should lower the window. Donald shook his head. Luke stood his ground. Finally the window slid open a couple of inches.

"What do you want?" Donald asked.

"Here's a funny thing," Luke replied. "I was going to ask you the same question." He waited for the jerk to respond with a statement about it being a free country, but the guy seemed to think better of it.

"I need to talk to my—"

If he was going to say *wife,* he thought better of it.

"I need to talk to Claire. She hasn't answered my calls so I was going to buzz her, see if she'll let me in."

Total load of crap. "You've been sitting here awhile."

Donald narrowed his eyes but didn't respond.

"I'm just on my way up," Luke said, keeping his tone conversational. "She takes my calls. I can give her a ring right now, see if she's got a few minutes."

Donald shook his head. No surprise there. "This is private," he said. "Between me and Claire."

"Pretty sure she said her lawyer'd be in touch with yours. Monday, wasn't it?"

"This can't wait."

Luke wasn't buying that, not for a minute, and he was done listening to this guy's lame-assed excuses.

"I don't believe you. All these calls to Claire amount to harassment. Hanging around here is stalking. Letting yourself into her apartment is break-and-enter." He leaned in close to the window.

Donald pulled himself back from the window.

"Unless you want to get slapped with a restraining order, I suggest you get yourself out of here. Don't call. Don't even think about coming back or calling. If Claire said her lawyer will be in touch, then her lawyer will be in touch."

A string of obscenities was muted by the car window sliding shut and the sound of the Lexus's engine springing to life. Luke stepped aside as Donald swung away from the curb and sped away. He watched until the swanky car and its sleazy driver disappeared around the corner, then made his way to the building's entrance and buzzed Claire to let him in.

On the elevator ride up, he debated how best to tell her about the run-in with Donald. He hated to alarm her, but she seemed to think her ex was annoying but not dangerous. Women who knew they were being stalked had a damned tough time protecting themselves. Claire couldn't keep herself safe if she didn't know what her ex was up to, or what he might be capable of doing.

Luke was willing to bet that Donald had let himself into the building after she'd gone out today, finding that his key no longer worked in the door to the apartment. If changing the lock after last night's encounter at gunpoint wasn't a deterrent, this guy truly could be dangerous.

He stepped off the elevator and all was momentarily forgotten when Claire opened the door for him and took his breath away. No need to say hello, he decided. Instead he slid his free hand into the hair at the nape of her neck and pulled her in for a kiss.

A girl could get used to this, Claire decided. Luke knew his way around a kitchen, and he was making himself right at home in hers. He had insisted she leave dinner entirely up to him, so she'd sat at the island sipping a virgin Bloody Mary—he had even salted the rim of the glass—while he whipped up a steak marinade, chopped vegetables for a salad and scrubbed a couple of baking potatoes.

The whole time their conversation had flowed easily. He'd had a meeting at the police station that morning, and she had shared a few anecdotes about her time spent with new clients that morning and the open house that afternoon, while carefully avoiding the details of where she'd spent her lunch hour. Then he'd told her about his run with Rex that afternoon, and had surprised her by producing a catnip mouse.

Smart man. She would have to remember to do something similar for his dog, if she ever had an opportunity to meet him.

It usually took Chloe a long time to warm up to anyone, especially men, but they had both laughed while the cat, usually so dignified and composed, had rolled on the floor with the felt toy before tossing it around and pretending to stalk it. Finally, while he stood at the counter preparing food, Chloe had made a show of rubbing herself against Luke's legs.

Quite the little hussy, Claire thought. *I guess that makes two of us.*

The kiss Luke had given her when he arrived had hinted at dessert before dinner, but then he'd shrugged out of his jacket, slung it over the back of a kitchen stool and emptied the bag of groceries he'd brought with him. She'd then sat on that same stool, sipping her drink and occasionally fingering the smooth, supple leather, wondering if his gun was tucked inside, finding the prospect strangely stimulating.

Watching a man who was this comfortable in the kitchen was a new experience. Come to think of it, the past twenty-four hours had been filled with firsts.

Spending the night with a man after their first date.

Seeing her ex held at gunpoint. She smiled.

Realizing there was a chance she could be pregnant. That wiped away the smile.

Her doctor had offered emergency contraception earlier that day, and Claire had declined without even having to think about it. She had used it once before, years ago, and it had been absolutely the right thing to do under those circumstances. As for the guy responsible for that scare, there was no question she'd been a terrible judge of character. By comparison, Donald had seemed safe, albeit a little boring, and she'd been wrong again.

This time the possibility of being pregnant was different. Not because she believed she and Luke had a chance at a relationship—there was no way this would stick and he'd already made it more than clear that he didn't want a family—but because she had loved him once, could maybe love him again. If they had created a baby together, she would love it more than life itself. She drew in a long, shaky breath and forced her thoughts back to the present, and a very nice present it was, with every woman's dream of a man here in her kitchen, making dinner for her, and clearly intending to spend the night.

The sun was setting and the air was getting cool by the time Luke carried the marinated steaks out to the barbecue on the terrace.

"How do you like yours?" he asked.

"I don't mind a little pink."

"Good to know. I'll put yours on first."

"Let me guess. You like yours rare."

"Good guess," he said with a shrug and a wink.

Claire joined him outside and after she set the table for two, she lit a couple of candles and turned on the overhead heater. She leaned on the railing for a moment, taking in the pink-hued streaks across the darkening sky and their reflection in Puget Sound. This was the one thing she would miss about this place.

Luke came up behind, put his arms around her. "Dinner won't be long."

She leaned against him, liking the feel of his body

behind hers, and folded her arms over his. "This is very sweet of you. Thanks for doing this."

"My pleasure," he said. "Nice view, too."

She angled her head so she could see him. He was looking down at her. "You're not looking at the view."

"Yes, I am."

"Oh, that's smooth." She laughed, though. She'd always liked that he was so laid-back and relaxed around women, and really liked that she was now the recipient of his easygoing attention. This was fun. He made her— serious, list-making, by-the-book Claire DeAngelo— feel sexy, a little playful, even. He also made her wish this could be something more than two friends who'd figured out that being friends had certain—dare she say it?—benefits.

She could stay like this forever, but he had other ideas. Instead of becoming more intimate, he brushed her cheek with his lips and backed away. "I'll just toss my steak on the grill and then we'll be ready to eat in a few minutes."

"A few minutes?" She laughed. "That's pretty rare."

He winked again as he flipped her steak, placed his next to it and lowered the lid of the barbecue. "Be right back with the salad and baked potatoes."

She turned and leaned on the rail so she could watch him when he came back outside. And he was a sight to behold, with a salad bowl nestled in the crook of an arm, a pair of baked potatoes in one oven-mitted hand and an assortment of condiments in his other hand.

She stepped forward and took the sour cream and bacon bits from him, then the salad, and set them on the table. "You should have asked me to give you a hand."

"No way. This is your night, remember."

Her night. She liked the sound of that.

He tossed the potatoes into the air, caught one with the mitt and the other with his bare hand, and dropped them on the plates. "Hot."

"If you get tired of moonlighting as a window washer, you can get a job as a waiter."

"Very funny." He held out her chair for her. "Sit. I'll be right back with another round of drinks, and then those steaks should be ready."

As he waited on her, it struck her that she'd never met a man who was this confident without being arrogant, this gorgeous without thinking he was God's gift. Admittedly, she didn't have a whole lot of experience in this area. She hadn't dated much in high school, and after a devastating incident in her freshman year that she did her damnedest not to think about, she hadn't dated much in college, either. Hanging out with Luke had been fun and surprisingly safe, but after graduation they'd lost touch.

A few years later she'd met Donald, and while he hadn't exactly swept her off her feet, he had been charming and attentive. It wasn't until after they were married that his charm waned and his attention wandered. Since they'd separated, his behavior had become unpredictable and, frankly, unacceptable. She had stalled selling the condo, partly as a way to get even for his infidelity, so she supposed she was partly responsible, but all that should change once they had the place on the market.

Luke set two more drinks on the table. "Be right back with those steaks."

A minute later he was, and the steak, with its perfect grill lines and a hint of garlic and rosemary, had her mouth watering.

He took the chair across the table, added a generous serving of salad to his plate and carved into his baked potato. She followed suit, and for once didn't worry about how many calories were in the salad dressing, sour cream and bacon bits. She was pretty sure she'd be working them off later.

She picked up her glass.

Luke lifted his and touched the rim to hers. "I noticed you have a well-stocked wine rack," he said. "You should feel free to open a bottle if you'd like to have some with your dinner."

She sipped her virgin Bloody Mary and fluttered her lashes at Luke. "Trying to get me drunk, Devlin?"

He looked taken aback. "No, jeez—"

"I was kidding. Relax. And no, I don't want wine with dinner." A girl could only work off so many calories in one night. "I'm not much of a drinker. Come to think of it, I haven't opened a single bottle since Donald, um, moved out."

Luke stabbed his fork into a piece of steak. "I remember that from college. You were not much of a partier, not the way a lot of us were."

Claire dropped her gaze to her plate, remembering those days all too well, especially her reason for becoming *not much of a partier.*

Luke reached across the table and touched her hand. "I meant that as a compliment."

She looked at him, tried to smile. "I know. It's just… it's nothing."

"I know nothing when I see it and whatever this is, it's not nothing."

ties I showed them. They're going to sleep on it and call me tomorrow."

"And your open house?"

She suspected he was only interested in knowing if she'd found someone to be there with her. "That went well, too. I took your advice and asked one of my business partners to go with me."

"Glad to hear it. Has Donald called again?"

"Not since this morning."

Luke went quiet for a moment, as though carefully considering his next words, and it made her uneasy.

"No sign of him hanging around the open house this afternoon?" he asked.

"No." What did he mean by *hanging around?* "What makes you think he would do something like that?"

"I hate to tell you this, but he was parked out front when I got here a while ago."

Claire's chest went tight. She set her fork down, knowing she wouldn't be able to swallow anything anyway. "Donald was here? Where, exactly?"

"He was parked across the street."

"He was in his car? Are you sure it was him?"

"I'm sure." His gaze connected with hers and didn't waver. "I'm going to tell you something, and I'm not going to apologize for it."

"Did you pull your gun on him again?" she asked, not able to hold back a nervous laugh.

Luke laughed for real. "No, that'd be pushing my luck. I looked up his vehicle registration so I would recognize his car if I saw it."

"You can do that?"

A slight nod indicated he could.

"And you did it because...?"

"Because I was concerned he might be stalking you. Turns out, he is."

Stalking? Donald was stalking her? "That doesn't make sense. He's the one who cheated and moved on."

"It doesn't have to make sense to anyone but him. And when I asked why he was here, he didn't have a good reason. Or any reason."

She picked up her napkin and noticed her hands were shaking. "You talked to him?"

"I did."

Luke stood, came around to her side of the table, pulled her to her feet and into his arms. She went willingly, wanting to draw on his strength, letting his warmth seep into her suddenly chilled body.

"I'm sorry, Claire. I hate having to tell you about this, but you need to know. You can't keep yourself safe if you don't."

"What did he say?" she whispered. "When you talked to him?"

"Said he needed to talk to you but you weren't answering his calls, so he was going to ring the buzzer."

Not answering his calls? That made no sense, either. "Other than that one time this morning, he hasn't called today. The way he's been lately, that's kind of unusual but I figured..." Truth was she'd been feeling rather smug about it, assuming now that Donald knew she was seeing someone, he was backing off.

"I don't think he had any intention of buzzing. He knew you were here, though. I'm sure of that. He was waiting to see if I showed up."

"Are you sure? Maybe there's some other explanation—" She desperately wanted there to be. The thought of her ex-husband sitting out there in his car, watching the building, knowing when she was out and when she was home…

Her gaze darted to the railing and beyond. The terrace wasn't visible from the street. From here they couldn't even be seen from the complex's other tower. Silly to worry, to feel exposed out here, but still she shuddered.

Luke must have felt it, too, because he drew her even closer. He didn't say anything, though. He just held her. She would never have guessed he could be like this. Gentle, comforting, and in a nonsexual way. She didn't know why that surprised her, but it did. She wrapped her arms around his waist, nestled closer and pressed her face against his shoulder. This felt so good, so right. There was nothing she could do about Donald right now, but there was something she could do about this.

"Let's go inside."

"You've had enough to eat?"

"Mmm-hmm. Now I'm ready for the next course." She tipped her head back and he lowered his at the same time. The kiss they shared was filled with give-and-take, and for maybe the first time in her life, she wasn't afraid to show a man that, yes, she wanted him, but she also needed to feel safe, secure, sheltered from the world, at least for tonight. Tomorrow would take care of itself.

Chapter 7

Dessert always had been Luke's favorite course. They'd finished dinner several hours ago. Now, just minutes shy of midnight, he lay next to Claire, spent and relaxed, satisfied the same was true for her, and certain there was no sweeter way to end dinner with a beautiful woman. With her back against his chest and his arm limp across her waist, he could feel her breathing slowly grow shallow and even.

Years ago his knack for charming the ladies had earned him the nickname Lucky. Truth was, he'd been careless and irresponsible, and if he had one regret, it was that he couldn't turn back the clock and undo all the moronic things he'd done while he was drinking. Getting sober had kick-started his conscience, though. At first he'd tried to justify all of it by using the booze as an excuse, but over time he'd come to realize there was no was excuse. He'd done a lot of shitty things, he needed to own them, and when he could, he had to try to make amends for them.

Being here with Claire felt right in just about every way possible, starting with the fact that she was one of the few women—hell, maybe the only woman—who had somehow looked past his flaws and been friends with him anyway. He had wanted to make love to her during their days of being study-buddies, but something had held him back. Maybe because he'd always been sober, more or less, for their study sessions and had enough sense to know he didn't deserve to have her. Claire wasn't a one-night stand, and other than Sherri, those one-night stands were what he'd done best.

With the tip of a finger he slowly, lightly drew circles around her navel and thanked his lucky stars he'd never screwed things up with her.

Something had happened in her past, though. Over dinner he'd made an off-the-cuff comment about her not being much of a partier. He hadn't anticipated her reaction, but it was one he'd seen before. Sadly, it was one that every cop saw way too often. Victims of domestic violence, sexual assault, rape—no matter who they were or what the circumstance, they had one thing in common. It was *that* reaction, and it was always *nothing*.

Oh, shit.

What if he…?

Had he ever…?

Shit.

Claire shifted against him. "Is something wrong?"

"No. Why do you ask?"

"You got tense all of a sudden. Did you hear something?"

"Everything's fine," he whispered against her hair. Except it wasn't, not by a long shot, and he needed to clear the air.

"Earlier, when I asked you if something had happened, you said it was nothing. I didn't buy it, and then I got to thinking about all the stupid stuff I used to do. All the partying and drinking. And that got me wondering, when we were in college, did I—?"

Claire rolled over, and in the dim light cast by a single bedside lamp, he tried to read the reaction in those midnight-blue eyes.

He kept an arm around her because he was sure that no matter how she answered his next question, the truth would be in her physical response.

"Was it me? Did I ever come on to you or…" God, this was hard. "Or something worse?"

For a split second her eyes went wide, then softened along with the rest of her. She touched a hand to the side of his face, kissed him lightly on the lips. "Never." Then she smiled. "I used to wish you'd ask me out…."

That was a surprise. He'd had no idea.

"But you never did," she said. "You didn't do anything else, either. What made you ask?"

"I was a jerk back then. Young, stupid. Drank too much too often, woke up some mornings with no memory of what I'd done the night before. I'd hate to think I ever did anything to hurt you."

"Of course you didn't. We were just friends."

He drew her closer and returned the kiss she'd given him. "So what happened to you?"

"I… What makes you think anything happened?"

"I'm a cop. I see women's reactions to certain things.

Yours was textbook." He still wasn't sure she would tell him, though, until he heard her sigh.

"It was a long time ago, freshman year to be exact. FYI, I didn't even know you then. I went to a party in one of the dorms. To say I wasn't used to drinking would be the understatement of the century, but there was this boy and I wanted him to think I was cool.

"I woke up the next morning with the hangover from hell. I didn't know whose room I was in, but I was alone. My underwear was on the floor and I had no idea if he used any kind of protection. When I got back to my dorm, my roommate dragged me off to the campus clinic. And after that—" She gave a nervous laugh. "As you said, I've never been much of partier."

"Did you remember what happened?"

She shook her head. "Vaguely."

Sounded like maybe she'd been roofied. "Did you press charges?"

"No. At the time I believed it was as much my fault as his. We were both drunk. Maybe if I hadn't had so much to drink—"

"It wasn't your fault." He hated that women believed that.

"I know that now. But then I was young, naive, and I think I was more upset about losing my dignity and self-respect than my virginity."

Anger rumbled through him. There'd been plenty of girls in college who were willing to jump into bed with a guy. Hell, he'd made out with plenty of inebriated girls at parties, sometimes went all the way with them, but he had never crossed that line, never forced a girl to give it up against her will.

Not that you can remember, anyway. What about all

those morning-afters when he had no memory of what the hell he'd done the night before? And who was to say that wasn't a selective memory? Anger was suddenly overcome by guilt.

"I feel like I should apologize for the entire male species. We can be idiots." Maybe apologizing to her was a way to make good for his past indiscretions.

She snuggled closer, laughing softly. "Sorry, that's one apology I can't accept."

"Why not?"

"Because you're not responsible for half the human race. Besides, I'm okay. I learned that I needed to look out for myself, that it was up to me to keep myself safe."

Her comment shifted his thoughts to Donald, and he suspected hers went there, too. Tonight he had planned to discuss moving in here, but an opportunity hadn't presented itself and now wasn't the right time. He'd wait until tomorrow, over breakfast, maybe. If he had to, he'd create an opportunity.

"I hope you don't mind me saying this," Claire said. "But this is something Donald and I never did together."

Luke and Claire had done a lot of things since they'd stumbled into the bedroom tonight. He wasn't sure which of them she meant. "I'm afraid you'll have to be more specific." He stroked the hair back from her forehead and tucked it behind her ear.

"Pillow talk."

He was already acutely aware that another man had shared this bed with her. Now the periodic pangs of jealousy that'd been elbowing him in the gut were chased away by a smug sense of superiority. No question he'd satisfied her sexually, but emotionally? As far as he knew, that was a first. The old Luke would have been scared witless by that, but this new-and-improved—or so he hoped—version of himself liked the idea. A lot. There might be some depth to his character, after all.

"Pillow talk, huh? That's what you call this?"

Somehow, without him noticing, she'd slipped a hand around him and now it was slowly exploring the contours of his backside.

"What would you call it?" she asked.

For the briefest of instances, surely no more than a millisecond, the *L*-word flashed through his brain. No freaking way was he calling it that. That would be crazy. Make that insane.

"Pillow talk works for me."

"Good." That hand of hers got a little bolder. "What about this? Does this work?"

With his arms around her, he flipped onto his back and rolled her on top of him. "I was thinking we should get some sleep."

"Really?" She smiled down at him. "You don't *feel* sleepy."

She definitely knew how to keep a guy awake. "Are you saying you've had enough pillow talk for one night?"

"That's what I'm saying."

He took her face in his hands and kissed her, long and deep. There'd be plenty of time for talking. Tomorrow.

Claire was clearing away their breakfast dishes, although it was close to noon, when "La Cucaracha" blared from her phone. *Now what?* she wondered as she picked it up. Luke was out on the terrace gathering up last night's dishes but he must have heard it, too, because he appeared immediately.

"What do you want, Donald?"

"I wanted to find out what time you're meeting with your lawyer tomorrow."

That was the best excuse he could come up with? Talk about lame. "I don't have an appointment yet," she said, trying to keep her tone pleasant. Given his behavior of late, there was no sense in antagonizing him. "I'll call her office first thing in the morning and set something up."

Luke came up behind her and quietly set a stack of dishes on the counter.

"Why didn't you do that on Friday?" Donald asked.

"I was busy." Which wasn't exactly true. She'd run into Luke and everything else had completely slipped her mind.

"We need to get the condo listed, Claire. It could take months to find a buyer."

"I'm working on it."

There was a long pause before Donald spoke. "Really? I know someone—"

"I already have an agent in mind. If I'm going to do this, I want someone I can—" She almost said *trust,* but that would really get Donald riled. "I want someone I know."

This could be tricky. Having a lockbox with a key would make it easier for Donald to get in, and just the thought of it had her feeling queasy. They would have to make the showings by appointment only.

"Fine," he said. "At this point I don't even care. I want to get my money out of that place."

A car horn blared in the background, and Claire

could have sworn it echoed the same piercing sound that rose up from the street and through the terrace doors. She pointed outside, silently mouthing to Luke that she thought her ex was down there.

He strode through the apartment, across the terrace to the railing and scanned the street below.

"Claire? Are you still there?"

"Yes. Yes, I'm here. Sorry, I got distracted."

Luke turned to face her, gave a single nod. His mouth, with those magic lips, usually so expressive, so ready with the quirky smile, was pressed into a grim line.

"Um, listen, I really should go. Sam and Kristi are coming over for coffee and I need to get ready for them."

"So you're alone right now?"

How to answer that? If she said she was alone, he might want to come up. If he knew Luke was here…

Who was she kidding? Donald had been out there when Luke got here yesterday. For all she knew, he'd spent the night out there, waiting to see if he'd left. Would he do that? Sit there all night? Why? Why did he care? And what about Deirdre? Luke was right. Something wasn't right and for the first time in her life, Claire was truly afraid. Make that terrified.

"Claire! I asked you if—"

"I have to go, Donald." She ended the call without answering his question and as her shaky fingers let her phone clatter to the counter, she sagged into Luke's arms.

Luke had been waiting for a window of opportunity to appear, and that crazy son of a bitch had just flung it wide open.

"Why is he doing this?" Even muffled against his chest, there was no mistaking the panic in Claire's voice.

He held her close, hoped she wasn't going to cry. He'd never been good with crying women. "I don't know. He probably doesn't know, either, although I guarantee he's cooked up a story to justify what he's doing."

"What should I do? Get a restraining order?"

"It's not that easy." He smoothed her hair, hoping she found it comforting. "To do that, you would have to provide evidence that he's threatened you or that he poses a threat in some way."

"What about my phone records? That would show how often he's been calling. And then there's the other night, when he came in here."

"The phone calls won't be enough. He could say those were necessary."

Claire pulled back and looked up at him. "Necessary?"

"I'm not saying they were, but he could argue they were about the divorce, the property settlement and that you've been stalling."

"Hey, whose side are you on here?" She tried to pull away.

He kept her close. "Yours, of course, but I'm being realistic."

"It's not helping."

"I might have a solution."

"Really? What it is it?"

He hesitated, hoping she wouldn't be offended, or think he was trying to take advantage of the situation to make a move on her.

"I'm all ears, Luke."

"I could stay here for a bit, at least until you talk to

your lawyer and real estate agent and get all that stuff sorted out. Maybe that's all it'll take to get Donald to back off."

"You want to move in?"

"When you put it like that, it sounds awfully—"

"Fast?"

"Yeah, fast." Speed-of-light fast.

She was smiling. "What would we tell people? That we're a couple? Or that you're my bodyguard?"

She was messing with him. He hoped. And exactly which people was she referring to? "Do we need to tell them anything?"

"I guess not. Unless they ask, and then maybe we should have our stories straight."

The plan wasn't five minutes old and already it was complicated. He hated complicated. He wanted to monitor the activity in the neighboring penthouse, he wanted to be with her and he wanted to keep her safe.

Right. That didn't sound complicated at all.

"Do we need a story? Maybe we just say we're seeing each other and let people draw their own conclusions. It's not like I'll be moving all my stuff in."

"And are we 'seeing each other'? I mean, it's been less than forty-eight hours since we bumped into each other."

And they'd bumped into each other a lot since then.

"What about your dog?"

He hadn't factored Rex into the equation. "My landlady will look after him for however long this takes, and I can still swing by and take him for a run. His nose'll be out of joint, but he'll get over it."

"You could bring him here."

"I don't know. He's a big dog. And what about

Chloe?" He'd won her over with a catnip mouse. He had a feeling it would take a lot more than that to get her to warm up to an eighty-pound German shepherd with a mild inferiority complex.

"It'll be good for her. After I move into a place of my own, I'd like to get a dog. Having Rex here would help her get used to having one around."

"I guess it can't hurt to give it a try." He could always take Rex back to his place if it didn't work out.

"I work from home some of the time, so I could take him for walks."

"Rex would like that." And this could have a plus side. Being nabbed at gunpoint hadn't discouraged Donald. Maybe the idea of a canine takedown would make him think twice. But the biggest plus was that she'd agreed to let Luke stay. He was in, she had agreed to it without hesitation and she didn't seem to suspect he had any other motivation for wanting to be here. Not that being with her and keeping her safe weren't important; they were. But would those things alone have been enough to prompt him to take such a big step, and so soon? Not a chance.

Now, looking down into Claire's smiling blue eyes, seeing the trust she had in him, gave a little more edge to the already sharp guilt pangs he was feeling. How would she react if she found out he'd deceived her? She'd boot his ass out of there so fast, he wouldn't even it see it coming.

"I should finish cleaning up the kitchen." She slipped out of his arms and opened the dishwasher. "Sam and Kristi, my business partners, are coming over. They're going to help me get the condo ready to put on the market."

The place already looked like a show home, and he found it hard to imagine how they would improve on that.

"I have stuff I need to do, too, so I'll clear out and leave you ladies to do your thing. I won't leave until they get here, though."

"I appreciate that. I'm not quite ready to be here on my own just yet."

He hadn't wanted to mention Donald again so he was glad they were on the same page. "I'll bring in the rest of the dishes from the terrace."

"Thanks." She was already rinsing plates and cutlery.

Outside, Luke loaded glasses, napkins and several other items onto the tray Claire had left on the polished tile counter next to the built-in barbecue. This outdoor kitchen was better equipped than most indoor kitchens. It even had a sink and running water. He'd never seen anything like it. And while this wasn't the sort of place he'd have pictured Claire living in, it was a reminder that they were from different worlds. He had never really considered buying a place of his own, but if he did, this sure wouldn't be it. Not on a cop's salary.

After checking to be sure Claire was occupied, he glanced over the rail at the street below. The Lexus was gone. He'd known it was Donald's car because the guy had been standing on the sidewalk next to it while he was on the phone harassing Claire. Luke had another meeting with Wong and the rest of the team early that afternoon, and he'd definitely check with Kate Bradshaw again to see if she'd dug up any more dirt on this guy. For Claire's sake, he hoped they didn't find anything, but it sure wouldn't surprise him if they did.

Claire's phone went off as he carried the tray inside and set it on the counter. Not the cockroach, thank God.

"That's Sam and Kristi," Claire said. "They're just texting to let me know they're almost here." She took the tray from him. "I know you have things to do, so you don't need to hang around. I'll be fine for a few minutes on my own until they get here."

This was an interesting development. "So, you don't want me to meet your friends? Or you don't want them to meet me?"

"Of course I want them to meet you." She set the tray on the counter, put her arms around his neck, did her best to give him a seductive little smile. "Eventually. I'm just not ready to share you yet."

She stopped talking and he watched her face turn pink. Adorable.

"You're a pretty little liar," he said. "Did you know you blush when you're not telling the truth? It's cute."

The pink turned to red. "Okay, fine. It's just that this—us—it's so new, and you don't know those two." She rolled her eyes. "Of course you don't know them. You haven't met them. What I mean is, they're both in relationships, really solid ones, and if they meet you now, here, on Sunday morning, they'll assume you spent the night here—"

"I did spend the night here." He probably shouldn't be enjoying this as much as he was.

"They don't need to know that. They'll jump to all sorts of conclusions and I'll never hear the end of it."

"So you're worried they'll take one look at me and tell you to make a run for it?"

She laughed. "You really can be a devil, Luke Devlin. You know perfectly well what women think when they see you."

He shouldn't tease her, but who could resist? He lowered his head and brushed her lips with his. "Listen, darling. If one of your friends makes a pass at me, I promise I'll let her down easy."

He loved hearing her laugh. "You're hopeless," she said. "But you can stay, as long as you promise to behave."

He took her hand in his and drew a cross over his heart. "Oh, I'll be good. I promise."

The buzzer announced her friends' arrival. Saved by the bell. Initially he had only wanted to stay until they got here so he could be sure Donald wouldn't have an opportunity to get to her while she was alone. Now he was curious to meet these women, and yes, he would be on his best behavior because suddenly it was important that he make a good impression.

Chapter 8

Claire opened the door to her two best friends and an enormous bouquet. Kristi, holding the flowers, gave her a one-armed hug. Sam, with her trusty clipboard in hand, hugged her with both arms. Then Kristi thrust the flowers into her hands.

"Oh, my goodness. These are beautiful. I love roses. But what have I done to deserve flowers?"

"Think of them as an early housewarming present," Kristi said.

"And an overdue good-riddance-to-Donald gift." Just like Sam to shoot straight from the hip.

Kristi jabbed her with an elbow. "Be nice."

Sam grinned. "I am. You'd know that if you heard what I really wanted to say."

As always, these two were a breath of fresh air, and their visit was exactly what she needed right now. Usually the steady one, she now needed someone else to keep her grounded.

"Come in. Luke's here, just leaving, actually, but I'd like you to meet him." Then she dropped her voice to a whisper. "And be nice…both of you."

"Oooh." Sam and Kristi bumped shoulders and exchanged looks.

"Of course we'll be nice."

"We're always nice."

Luke had his jacket on and was leaning against the island when Claire led them into the kitchen. Chloe had jumped onto the counter and was brushing the side of her face on his shoulder. The little flirt.

The smile he gave Claire would have had her shedding some clothes if they were alone.

"Luke." She was having difficulty breathing, as if she'd just run up a flight or two of stairs. Or ten. "These are my friends and co-owners of Ready Set Sold. Sam is our carpenter, and Kristi is the interior decorator."

The smile he gave them was disarming but in a completely different way. The handshake he shared with Sam was brief and businesslike, a little reserved, even. Claire could see she was quietly assessing the man.

With a nod, Sam stepped back. "Good to meet you."

Claire took a quick breath, unaware she'd been holding it.

Kristi was all smiles. She shook Luke's hand for far too long to be strictly professional but not long enough to send the wrong message. "Very nice," she said. "To meet you. Very nice to meet you."

"Pleasure's all mine," he said. "I wish I could stay but I understand you ladies have work to do, and I have a meeting this afternoon myself."

Kristi all but giggled, and even Sam was getting soft around the edges.

"I'll walk you out." Claire shooed the cat off the counter and reached for his sleeve.

He caught her hand in his, briefly held both it and her gaze hostage, then slipped his arm around her. "Good plan. Sam, Kristi," he said over his shoulder. "I hope I see you again soon."

"Oh, yes."

"Absolutely."

"For sure."

"Soon."

Like a pair of silly schoolgirls. And who could blame them?

At the door, Luke turned her into his arms. "Your friends are watching," he said, low enough that only she could hear.

"I figured they would be."

"Okay, just as long as you know." And with one hand on the back of her head and the other on her butt, he drew her into an intimate embrace and a kiss that really wasn't meant to go public.

"I'll call you about dinner," he said after he lifted his head. "And…" He glanced up at their audience and smiled. "And that other thing we talked about."

He let himself out, and left Claire with lots of explaining to do.

Sam and Kristi both rushed into the foyer, grabbed her by the arms and hauled her back to the kitchen.

"Oh. My. God." Kristi sounded very much like Jenna, her fourteen-year-old daughter. "I… I'm…"

"I think what she's trying to say is, wow," Sam said.

"Holy handsome hunk of wow," Kristi added.

Claire knew she was sporting a foolish grin and she didn't care. Kristi's description summed him up just about perfectly.

Sam urged her onto a stool and stepped back to look at her. "That was some kiss."

"Those were some abs," Kristi said. "And pecs, and—"

"He was wearing a jacket," Claire reminded her. "And a shirt. You did not see abs and pecs."

"Didn't have to. That man's got it all…abs, pecs, biceps. Don't even think about telling us otherwise. We won't believe you."

"I wouldn't dream of it." She couldn't have kept the smug out of that reply if she'd tried. He was pretty much perfect in every possible way.

Kristi slid onto the next stool. "Now let's have it, and don't you dare spare a detail."

"No way. You know the Ready Set Sold rules. Business first, chitchat later."

"Evil taskmaster." Sam set her clipboard on the counter, leaned on her elbows and groaned. "I think we can make an exception, just this once."

"I agree," Kristi said. "This is just too delicious to postpone."

Claire gave them a firm head-shake. "No way. We never made that exception for either of you. Not when we found out you and AJ were long-lost lovers," she said to Sam. "Not when Kristi told us she and Nate were fake dating, either, and we're not breaking the rule for me."

"Fine." Kristi pretended to pout. "But if I have to work, I'm going to need a cup of tea."

"Of course." Claire slid off her stool and walked

around to the kitchen side of the island. "Sam, I'll make you some coffee."

"Oh, um, no thanks. Unless you have decaf."

Sam drinking decaf? That never happened. Claire eyed her suspiciously as she filled the kettle, and noticed Kristi was doing the same.

"What's up with you?" Kristi asked.

"Nothing." Sam shrugged to support her claim, but her cheeks turning pink suggested otherwise.

"Oh. My. God." Kristi clapped her hands together. "You're pregnant!"

Still feigning innocence, Sam eyed the package on the counter. "Are those bagels?"

Claire switched on the kettle. "Sam? Are you?"

Now completely red in the face, Sam grinned. "We are. AJ and I decided to keep it to ourselves until we were through the first trimester, just in case—"

Claire and Kristi rushed at her from both sides and then they were group-hugging and shedding happy tears.

"I can't believe you kept this from us!"

"When did you find out?"

"How far along are you?"

"Three months," Sam said, laughing and crying at the same time. "We just told Will this morning that he's going to have a baby brother or sister."

"How did he take it?"

"Is he excited?"

"He asked if we were getting another dog, too. He says the baby should have a puppy of its own, but we really think he just wants another dog."

"That is too funny," Kristi said. "And I am so, so happy for you."

"Me, too. AJ must be thrilled."

"Beyond thrilled," Sam said. "He's been to all my doctor's appointments with me, and he was there for the sonogram last week. Oh, that reminds me. I have it with me." She retrieved it from under the sheets of paper on her clipboard.

Kristi went misty-eyed. "Oh, I want one," she said as she gazed at the mottled grey image.

"Have you and Nate talked about it?" Sam asked.

"We have, and we've decided to wait. We've just blended our two families and it's going really well. Jenna's crazy about her new little sisters and the twins absolutely adore her, but it's still a big adjustment so we'll hold off a bit before we add a baby to the mix."

Somewhat reluctantly, Claire accepted the photograph when Kristi handed it to her. She had been trying not to think about her own predicament, but Sam's news brought it all back in a rush. Now, suddenly feeling a little light-headed, a little queasy, even, she backed herself onto a stool and sat down. *It's just nerves,* she told herself. This was way too soon for morning sickness, or so the doctor said.

The boiling kettle snapped her back to the present. "Teatime," she said. "I'll make you a decaf, Sam. And a latte for myself." *Better make that a decaf latte,* she thought. *Just in case.*

"I still have my eye on one of those bagels," Sam said. "You won't believe the appetite I have these days."

"Help yourself. There's cream cheese in the fridge."

There was no missing the looks exchanged by her friends.

"Bagels and cream cheese?"

"In *this* kitchen?"

"Do you think we've somehow stumbled into a parallel universe?" Sam asked Kristi.

"Knock it off, you two. Luke brought them."

"Makes sense. You can't expect a man with a body like that to live on rabbit food."

"I'll have you know I've lost two pounds." She'd gone into the bathroom and weighed herself that morning while Luke was still in bed, and she was practically giddy about it.

"Good for you."

She opened a cupboard, took out mugs and plates. "To be honest, I'm not sure how it happened. I've been starving for weeks and haven't lost an ounce. This weekend I totally fell off the wagon, haven't been watching what I've been eating, and I'm down two pounds. Two point two, to be precise."

Sam and Kristi traded another knowing glance.

"Don't start, you two," she warned. "Don't even think about it."

Sam feigned surprise, Kristi sealed her lips with an imaginary key and tossed it over her shoulder, and they grinned at each other again.

But Claire couldn't help thinking about it. Even though it was just a couple of pounds, she felt different. Not thinner, but she did feel... *Okay, go ahead, let yourself think it. Sexy.*

She made a decaf Americano for Sam and a skinny decaf latte for herself—just in case—while the kettle boiled for tea. When the drinks were ready, she set them on a tray. "Let's sit at the dining room table."

The dining room was not so much a room as an area defined as such by the presence of a large, sleek table and eight high-backed parsons' chairs. It was bordered on one side by the back of the leather sofa in the living area, and on another by the floor-to-ceiling windows overlooking Puget Sound.

Kristi picked up her tea. "I do love this view."

"It's a major selling feature," Sam said. "Not really my thing, though. I love the view of Lake Union from our place, but at the same time we still have a lot of privacy. Having that other tower right there, wondering who's behind those windows and whether or not they can see us…" To make her point, she gave a little shudder. "It's kind of creepy."

Until a few days ago, Claire hadn't given it much thought. Now, knowing that Donald was hanging around, possibly even coming inside the apartment when she wasn't here, she was creeped out, too, but for different reasons. It was time to move on.

She had noticed that Luke seemed interested in the view, especially from the windows that faced the next tower. That's where she'd seen him with the window-washing crew, so it might have something to do with that. He hadn't said anything more about looking into that company and since it was part of a police investigation he probably couldn't, but she assumed he'd be back there on Monday. At least he wouldn't have far to go to work, she thought.

"All right, let's get started." Kristi's laptop was open and ready.

Claire sipped her latte. "First I need a timeline. After I talk to my lawyer tomorrow, I'll call my friend Brenda about listing the condo for me."

Sam tapped the eraser end of her pencil against the page on her clipboard. "Will Donald agree to using her?"

"He won't have a choice. We're co-owners, but this is my home and I want total control over how it's being shown. I trust Brenda, so Donald will have to trust her, too."

Kristi dug her calendar out of her bag and flipped it open. "Sam and I should finish up at the Fletcher house tomorrow, and I have an appointment with a prospective client on Thursday morning, otherwise my week is clear."

"I'm going to a demolition site on Wednesday to salvage some oak flooring and anything else that looks promising. Other than that, I'm all yours."

"I appreciate this so much," Claire said. "I don't think there's much we need to do here."

"I agree. Your home always looks like a magazine spread," Sam said.

Kristi looked around and gave a little sigh. "No toys, no stray items of clothing, no dog hair all over everything."

And no character, Claire thought. None whatsoever. Starting tomorrow there might be a dog, though. Maybe a baby in nine months. Her pulse sped up. She shouldn't even be thinking about that possibility, and this wasn't the time to distract her friends with those tidbits.

"And you both know how much I envy you."

"Your turn will come," Sam said.

"And when it does, you're going to be an awesome mom. And dog owner," Kristi said, because everyone knew Claire wanted one. "Now, about that timeline…"

"Right. Lawyer and real estate agent tomorrow. Our calendars are all clear on Tuesday, so we can start in here. Sam, I don't think we need much in terms of renovations, but I've always thought I could make more of the terrace."

"I agree. I'll take some measurements out there today and see what I can come up with. Right away I'm thinking cedar planters and some bench seating that includes built-in storage. Those are easy to build on-site, especially if I have the boards precut, and they can be left to age naturally."

"That's a great idea," Kristi said. "Inside I'll want to unify the look. You have some lovely folk art pieces—the welcome wreath on the door, the painted milk can you use for umbrellas. They're very homey and totally you, but the contrast between those things and the modern interior is too...contrasty."

Claire knew that, but she loved those things because to her they gave the place a cosier feel. "I'll pack them up and put them in my storage locker," she said as she typed it into her task list. "What else?"

Kristi gazed around the space. "The decor is very monochromatic. That adds to the ultramodern feel of the space, but it also feels generic so I think you should layer in some colour. We'll look for a few simple pieces that will work here and that you'll be able to take to your new place."

"And now we're talking colors." Sam stood and unclipped a measuring tape from her belt. "That's my cue to go out and take a look at the terrace. Just promise me there won't be any wallpaper."

"No wallpaper, I promise!" Claire laughed and gave her a wave. "Go do your thing. We'll come get you when we've finished in here."

Luke was the first to arrive for the meeting at the precinct. He paced across the room and back, twice, and was debating whether to stay put or go look for Kate Bradshaw to see if she'd dug up anything on Donald when Jason Wong strode into the room.

"Afternoon, Sarge."

"Luke. Glad you could make it. Where's everyone else?"

"Don't know. Maybe finishing their Sunday brunch and cursing the boss who called them before noon on a Sunday and told them to get down here for a meeting?"

Jason laughed. "Yeah, I'm a real ogre. There've been a couple new developments, including information on Phong's whereabouts. Could be the break we've been waiting for."

It was about time. "I'm sure everyone's on their way. In fact, here's one now," he said as Cam Ferguson walked into the room.

"Jason, Luke. How's it going?"

They both agreed it was going well.

"Thanks for coming in. I know you haven't had a lot of sleep."

Luke hadn't, either, but at least he'd spent the night in a bed. After Cam had finished up at the airport yesterday, he'd taken over for Lindi in one of the surveillance vans.

Cam ran a hand over the stubble on his chin and glanced at the clock on the wall behind Jason's desk. "Couple hours."

"It shows," Luke said, knowing his colleague could take a little good-natured ribbing, no matter how sleep-deprived he was.

"Unlike Detective Smithe-with-an-*e*," Wong said as Patsy strolled in, a Starbucks cup in one hand, her phone in the other, calm, cool and collected as always.

"What can I say? A girl needs her sleep," she quipped.

Unlike Cam, Luke figured she'd look this good on no sleep.

"Where's Derek and Dex?" Patsy asked.

Jason checked his watch. "On their way."

"I'm here, I'm here," Derek said, rushing in. "Had to drop one of the boys at the soccer field. I'd've asked the wife to do it, only she took the other one to the pool for swimming practice."

A few days ago Luke would've felt sorry for the poor guy and congratulated himself on being footloose and free of family obligations. Now as he watched Derek settle onto a chair, looking a little harried, he didn't feel so smug. From the few things Derek had said about his family, Luke got the sense that he and his wife shared household and child-raising responsibilities. They were a team. There was a time when he'd have considered this couple to be just plain lucky to have found a pattern that worked, but now he knew it was more than good fortune. Derek worked at it, so did Jason. And while Luke hadn't grown up with any kind of role model for being a husband and a father, he was surrounded by them now.

"Where's Dex?" Derek asked.

"Right behind you." Lindi Dexter stood in the doorway in paint-spattered jeans and an old sweatshirt, ponytail pulled through the back of her ball cap.

"Good of you to join us," Cam said.

Lindi grinned and flipped him the bird. "Hey, I was painting my kid's bedroom. It's my day off." She was a single mom with two teenage daughters. Luke had no idea how she managed to hold it all together, but she did. Women were way better at that than most men, or so it seemed to him.

"Now that we're all here and the pleasantries are out of the way," Jason said, wasting no time getting down to business, "we have new information on Phong. A security guard spotted him at Sea-Tac last night, coming off a red-eye from Miami. We weren't even sure he was in the country, now he's right here in our backyard."

Derek rubbed his hands together. "He's as good as ours."

"Was he alone?" Patsy asked. "Or did he bring more girls with him?"

"He's too careful for that," Jason said. "He has other people doing drug drops and smuggling the girls into the country. We've been picking up communications, though. Text messages and emails with instructions for his lackeys. Cam's been able to unencrypt them, and he figures it's Phong who's sending them."

Luke gave him a congratulatory slap on the shoulder. "Nice work."

"Thanks. The messages are coming from a cell phone, and there's good reason to believe it's Phong's. The guy's extremely careful, though, and the challenge—if and when we ever do pick him up—will be to make sure he has the phone on him. If it isn't, then he'll deny he ever had one and claim he's just a victim of circumstances, in the wrong place at the wrong time."

"Yada, yada," Patsy chimed in. "Meanwhile he's smuggling girls, and by girls I mean children, into the States and forcing them into the sex trade. We need to get this guy."

"We're close," Jason said. "And getting closer by the hour. That's why I needed you all here for a face-to-face. If we're going to pull this off, we need a unified effort. Luke has a new development, and I'll start by letting him fill you in on that."

"As you know, a friend of mine lives in that condominium complex," Luke said, choosing his words carefully. Wong was aware of what was happening with him and Claire, but no one else had to.

"Fancy digs," Lindi said.

"And you say she's a friend?" Cam smirked. "That's not your usual modus operandi."

Funny. "I've known her since college. She has some personal stuff happening right now and I'm going to be staying with her a bit." He'd filled in their sergeant on all the pertinent details, including Donald's behavior, and he'd been honest and up-front when Wong asked if he was sleeping with her. The others could speculate all they wanted, but they didn't need the same level of detail. "This gives us the perfect opportunity to set up surveillance on the interior of the Phong condo. We can see everyone who comes and goes, and if he shows up, we'll know it. If we're lucky enough to see him with his phone, we go in."

"Once he's there, we won't need luck," Cam said. "I'm already set up to route some communication to his phone through a server in Vietnam. If he responds, we've got him."

"We've managed to get into an empty suite two floors down," Jason told them. "We'll have Derek and Patsy there along with a couple guys from SWAT at all times. They'll make sure we get access to the penthouse when we need it."

"So Luke's friend," Patsy said. "You've brought her in on this? Are you sure that's a good idea?"

"No, we haven't," Jason said. "Luke and I talked it

over and decided against it. He's moving in this afternoon and setting up a telescope on a tripod. Pretty standard for a lot of those places. People like to check out the boats in the sound, do a little whale watching. The telescope can be swivelled around to look at anything. The camera's built into the tripod itself, so it'll be stationary and aimed at the penthouse twenty-four-seven. Cam's got his IT guys working on it right now."

Derek grinned. "Watch out, bad guys."

"We are good," Lindi said. "I could use something like that to keep an eye on my girls when I'm not around."

"See me after the meeting," Cam said to her. "I'll get you set up."

That got a laugh from everyone.

As always, Jason allowed them a moment of good-natured camaraderie before reining them in. "To summarize, we'll have Luke in the penthouse, Lindi and Cam monitoring the footage we get from the camera, and Derek and Patsy ready to move in. There's a good possibility that some of Phong's girls don't speak much English, if any. It'll be good to have a woman in there, especially one who can communicate with them. The plan is to have everything and everyone in place by early this evening. Let's hope our guy doesn't keep us waiting."

"So Luke doesn't get to swing from the side of the building on the window-washing platform?" Lindi asked.

The question had Jason grinning. "'Fraid not. Now that we have a better option in place, it's too risky. Right now, at least as far as we know, we're flying under their radar and we want to keep it that way. Phong and his boys might think it's more than a coincidence that we have a crew gawking through their windows, so I've pulled the window-washing crew off the site."

"Damn." Cam smacked his palms together. "I was looking forward to seeing him up there."

"Maybe next time," Luke said. "Or maybe you'll draw that straw."

"Me and heights?" Cam said. "No way. I can't even stand on a stepladder to change a lightbulb."

"But you're okay with it being me."

"Oh, I have no problem with that."

Luke laughed along with the others. Cam liked to give everyone a hard time but when push came to shove, he had everyone's back. Luke hadn't actually minded the assignment. After all, it's what had reconnected him with Claire. Now he had an even better vantage point, not to mention a nice big bed and a beautiful woman to share it with. Call it fate or karma or just plain luck, things could not have worked out better.

As soon as the meeting broke up, Luke assured his boss he'd be back to pick up the surveillance equipment, then excused himself and made his way out to the front desk, hoping Kate Bradshaw would be there.

His luck was holding.

"Hey, Luke. Good you're here. I have something to show you."

"Am I going to like it?" he asked.

"Not even a little bit." She opened a drawer, pulled out a folder and handed it to him.

Luke flipped it open and scanned the sheet. A couple of speeding tickets, one DUI, for which some fancy lawyer got him an acquittal, and… Shit. A restraining order filed by a former girlfriend, and one charge of sexual misconduct, brought about by an employee who later dropped the charges. Luke usually liked knowing his instincts were bang on, but this was different. If it was just Donald, yeah, he'd be smug as hell. But this was about Claire, and given the guy's behavior, any self-righteousness Luke might have indulged in was eroded by concern. The guy was a piece of work, and he'd bet anything that Claire wasn't aware of any of this.

"Thanks, Kate. I owe you one."

She grinned. "I'll add it to your tab."

"So how's it going?" he asked, figuring he owed her a little small talk after all she'd done for him. She had been paired up with him right after she graduated the academy, and they'd hit it off. He'd even toyed with the idea of asking her out, and he'd been pretty sure she would have said yes. In the end he'd decided it best not to complicate things, and now thanked his lucky stars he'd had the good sense and good judgment to keep things professional.

"Everything's going great," she said. "This is my last shift on the desk. After my days off, I'll be back on the street."

Good cops hated paperwork, so it was a positive sign that she didn't like working the desk. "Give me a shout when you're back on the job. If our investigation is still ongoing—" Although he hoped to God it would be wrapped by then. He was ready for something new, and he hated the idea of deceiving Claire any longer than absolutely necessary. "If it is, I'll talk to Wong about finding a place for you. If not on this op, then maybe the next."

Her eyes brightened, exactly the reaction he was looking for. "Really? Thanks, Luke. That'd be great."

"Happy to do it." He folded the report she'd printed for him, stuck it in his back pocket and handed the file folder back to her. "Thanks again for this."

He didn't like most of what was in it, but he was more certain than ever that being at Claire's was the right place to be. He'd be a happy man once the investigation wrapped up and he could come clean about one of his reasons for wanting to be there. Meanwhile they would deal with Donald. And maybe, just maybe, Luke and Claire would figure out where this thing between them was going. He still didn't know exactly how he felt about her, but he damn sure wanted to stick around and figure it out.

Chapter 9

It took Claire and Kristi less than half an hour to do a quick tour of the apartment, take photographs and make notes. They decided to use a vibrant shade of cranberry for their accent color, and settled on a time on Tuesday afternoon to shop for accessories.

"A few pillows, a vase, some nice tall tapers in those silver candlesticks," Kristi said. "It'll be perfect."

"It will," Claire agreed. "Thank you for this. I'm so bad at this sort of thing."

"That's why you have me." Kristi gave her a hug. "Let's go see what Sam's up to. I'm ready to wrap up the work portion of the program and get on to the fun stuff."

Claire had to admit that she was looking forward to it, too. She passed around bottled water from the fridge after they regrouped around the table, took a seat and turned her iPad back on.

"I know you have a bunch of questions about Luke." They would no doubt have some questionable suggestions, too. "But first I have something to show you. Yesterday morning, before I met my new clients, I spent some time at the office searching the listings, and I think I found a house."

"Claire! You've been holding out on us!"

"Let's see it!"

She brought it up on the screen. "Here it is." She gazed at the listing, even more certain than the last time she looked at it, that this was it. This was home. She held her breath as she angled the screen so her friends could see it.

Kristi's eyes lit up. "Oh, sweetie. It's adorable. It even has a white picket fence, and I love the bay window. Is that the living room?"

"It must be, at least I hope it is. I've always wanted a living room with a bay window. It'll be perfect for a Christmas tree. And the house is bigger than it looks from the street. There are three bedrooms, plus it has an eat-in kitchen as well as a formal dining room."

"Have you looked at it already?"

"Not yet. I was hoping the two of you would look at it with me."

Kristi clapped her hands excitedly.

Claire turned to Sam, who had yet to say anything. "What do you think?"

"I think it's perfect for you. I was planning to build you a white picket fence for a housewarming present. Now I'll have to come up with something else."

"That's so sweet. I have to confess that I did a drive-by on my way home yesterday and the fence looks as though it could use some work and a fresh coat of paint."

"Consider it done. Does it have a second story or is this upper window in the attic?"

"The listing says it's one floor with a crawlspace, so I guess it must be an attic."

"I'll take a stepladder when we go to see it. I'd like to take a look up there. The roof appears to be in good shape, but we still want to be sure the attic's dry and insulated."

"And I'll take lots of interior photos so we can work on the design."

"If I decide to put in an offer." Was this crazy? Was she crazy? She hated change. She never did anything without making a list, setting up a spreadsheet, looking at all the angles, weighing all the pros and cons.

And look at you now.

In fewer than forty-eight hours she had decided to go ahead with the divorce and sell the condo. She had rushed into an affair with a man who was, by his own admission, not relationship material. At least, not as far as she was concerned. He didn't want a family, *not ever,* and she wanted one more than anything. She'd had sex without taking the proper precautions and there was a chance she could be pregnant. Now she was seriously thinking about putting an offer on a house she hadn't even seen, and she was already daydreaming about turning one of the bedrooms into a nursery.

"Oh, no," Kristi said. "No, no, no, no. Don't start, don't you dare."

"What?"

"You're having second thoughts."

"No, I'm not."

"Yes, you are." Sam leaned across the table and

grabbed her hand. "You've got your I'm-having-serious-second-thoughts face on, and it isn't pretty."

Kristi took her other hand and squeezed. "Sam's right. You have to do this for yourself, hon. Dive in headfirst without thinking about it."

She'd already done more than her share of leaping without looking this weekend, but they were right. This was something she had to do for herself. Not because Donald was demanding she do it, and definitely not because she secretly hoped there could be a future in this thing, whatever it was, with Luke.

"I know, and I will. I probably should have done this a long time ago."

"You needed to do it when you were ready," Sam said.

"And now that you are," Kristi said, "we're with you, every step of the way."

"Thanks, guys. I don't know what I'd do without you." She was the steady one, the one with both feet firmly planted, the giver of advice. Being on the receiving end was new, and she had a feeling she'd better get used to it.

"Soo," Kristi said. "You and Luke. I can't believe you never told us about him."

"Or how, after someone like him, you somehow ended up with Donald."

"Sam!" Kristi's admonishment was quick, and unconvincing.

"I'm sorry. I never liked him, and there's no sense pretending I did."

"It's okay, Sam. I don't like him anymore, either. But Luke and I were never...you know. We were just friends."

"Right. Just *friends*." Kristi laughed. "In case you're wondering," she said, winking at Sam, "that's what we called it when we were in college."

"I see. I went to trade school. We didn't have any fancy euphemisms for hooking up."

"No, we really were just friends, and we did not hook up. Believe it or not, we used to study together."

"Seriously? If I'd had a study partner like him, I never would have been able to concentrate. I would have flunked out for sure."

Claire had been too much of a Goody Two-shoes to let anything like that happen, but she had surreptitiously studied Luke over the top of a textbook on plenty of occasions, and yes, she'd been distracted more than once.

"We don't really care about the past anyway," Sam said. "Not when the present is so much more..." She paused and feigned a dreamy-eyed pose.

"Yummy," Kristi said, filling in the blank. "Where did you run in to him?"

"Just down the street, in front of the next building. He was—" Best not to mention the window-washing thing, she decided. "I'm not sure what he was doing. Some sort of police work, I guess."

"Oooh, was he in uniform?" Kristi's expression matched Sam's.

"No. He's a detective, undercover and all that, so he doesn't seem to wear one."

"And then he got under your covers," Sam said, waggling her eyebrows.

"Seriously?" Claire asked. "You couldn't let that one go this time?"

"Not a chance, not even a slim one." Sam, pencil

tucked behind one ear, sipped some water from her bottle.

"Where do you think this is going?" Kristi asked. "Or is it too soon to tell?"

Definitely not too soon to know it was going nowhere. Luke had made it clear that he wasn't relationship material and he really wasn't daddy material. He had been completely up-front about it, and for her, for now, that was okay.

"Not too soon at all. He's not a family man, and right now I'm not looking for one. I'm still trying to undo one mistake and I'm not about to make another. Luke is fun to be with—"

"I'll bet he is." Sam grinned, and there went those eyebrows again.

Kristi put an arm around Claire's shoulders, gave them an affectionate squeeze. "If anyone deserves to have some fun, it's you. What about Donald? How's he taking this?"

Claire shrugged. "I'm sure he doesn't care, but he is getting on my case about the divorce, and about selling the condo, and about getting his hands on the book his grandmother gave me."

"I can understand why he'd want to get his money out of the condo. I'm not saying that justifies him harassing you," Kristi was quick to add. "Just that I get it. What I don't get is why he'd want an old children's book. That seems totally out of character."

Claire had thought so, too. "I agree, or at least I did until I went online and did a little research. I took the book to the office yesterday, in case Donald decides to come here to look for it."

Sam's eyes widened. "I never thought of that. You need to change the locks."

"I did." She just didn't want to explain what had prompted that. "Anyway, I did a quick search for the book his grandmother gave me. It's an old edition of Beatrix Potter's *The Tale of Peter Rabbit,* and it turns out to be worth a lot of money."

"A kid's book?" Sam asked.

"How much is a lot?" Kristi asked.

"Thousands of dollars."

"Wow!"

"Really?"

"I was surprised, too, but that explains why Donald wants it."

"I thought he was loaded," Sam said.

Claire shrugged. "He earns a good salary but he likes to spend money as much as he likes to make it, and if his investments aren't doing well, he could be having some cash-flow problems."

"I can't tell you how relieved I am to know you've changed the lock," Kristi said. "We've both been worried about you. It was a good idea to have Sam at your open house yesterday, too, and I want you to promise to keep us in the loop. If he's harassing you or, God forbid, worse, you need to tell us."

"And tell Luke," Sam added. "Donald hasn't got the balls to mess with him."

She was so right, Claire thought. Recalling the look on Donald's face after his unexpected appearance on Friday night, and Luke's very unexpected reaction, still made her want to giggle.

Sam checked her watch and jumped up. "I have to

get going. The nanny is off today and AJ's holding down the fort."

Kristi did the same. "Me, too. Nate took the girls to the mall, and in exchange I told him I'd walk the dogs when I get home. You'll let us know when you'd like to look at the house?"

"Of course."

"And you'll call if Donald gives you any more grief?"

"I'll call, I promise."

Before they left, she hugged them both and again congratulated Sam on the baby news. She felt guilty for not being completely open and honest with them about Donald's recent antics, but nothing would be gained by it and they would worry unnecessarily.

She closed the door, locked it and leaned against it. Donald was Donald. He could be a jerk, but he wasn't dangerous. Was he?

Luke dropped his duffel bag to the floor outside Claire's door, leaned the case containing the telescope against the wall and studied the Home Sweet Home wreath that made, now that he thought about it, an odd statement about the reality on the other side of the door. More like wishful thinking on Claire's part. He wanted to see her, had looked forward to this moment since he'd left for his meeting late that morning, but he couldn't bring himself to slide the key into the lock. He hated to deceive her, not tell her that he had more than one reason for wanting to be with her.

Given his track record with women, that realization caught him off guard. Had he ever been completely open with a woman? Or been willing to acknowledge the true depth of his feelings? No. But then he'd never felt like this before, and he didn't know why. Could be that in the past the booze had taken the edge off his conscience. Or it could have something to do with the woman waiting for him on the other side of this door. Easier to believe this was about being sober than it was to sort out his feelings for Claire. Whatever it was, he couldn't stand here all night, holding on to a piece of brass he was reluctant to use.

"What do you think, Rex? Ready to go inside?"

The dog had been waiting patiently next to the duffel bag since Luke had given him the command to sit. He remained sitting, although his tail wagged in response to the question.

"You might not be so chipper after you meet Chloe."

Rex cocked his head to one side.

"Did I forget to mention her?"

The dog's head tipped to the other side.

"Sorry, buddy." He stuck the key in the lock and turned it. "You'll figure out a way to get along with her. Besides, we can't stand out here all night."

The scent of something cooking greeted him as he opened the door. Garlic, oregano…pasta sauce would be his guess. He hadn't realized how hungry he was. And then Claire joined him in the foyer and suddenly he was a different kind of hungry.

Without hesitation she glided up to him, slid an arm around his waist, tipped her head back for a kiss. Her lips were soft and inviting, the kiss full of promise. Too bad his hands were already full, or he'd be tempted to explore the shapely curves of the black dress that was primly covered by a red-and-white checked apron.

"Something smells good. Besides you, that is."

"Lasagna."

"Homemade?"

"Mmm-hmm." She pulled him in for one more kiss. "It's one of my favorite things."

"Mine, too."

"Do you need a hand with—" She stepped back and her eyes lit up. "Rex! I was hoping you'd bring him. What a handsome boy you are." She petted the top of Rex's head, and he opened his mouth and started to pant.

"I bought dog biscuits for him. Is it okay to give him one now?"

"Sure."

"I was hoping you'd say yes." She pulled a treat from her apron pocket.

"Sit," Luke said.

Knowing what was in store, Rex readily complied.

"Good dog." Claire offered the biscuit and Rex gingerly took it. "He's a beautiful dog, Luke. I'm glad you brought him with you. Do you need a hand with the rest of your things?"

"Thanks, I can manage." He set his duffel bag on the foyer floor and reached back into the hallway for the telescope.

"That's everything?" Claire asked.

"This is it. For now. I can always run back to my place if I need anything."

"What about Rex's food?"

He toed the duffel. "It's in here."

"And the box?"

"Oh, ah, that's a telescope. I hope you don't mind. Since you have such a great view, I thought I'd set up it over there." He indicated the long stretch of windows in the living room. "Check out the harbor, that kind of thing."

Claire smiled. "Good idea. Donald used to keep binoculars in there, but a telescope sounds even better. For now, why don't you put the dog food in the kitchen and take your things down to the bedroom while I finish dinner?"

"Sure thing."

It was all very domestic, and yet it no longer felt right. Jason Wong had emphasized the importance of not letting Claire in on Luke's reason for being here. And much as he tried to tell himself that he was there for her, to make sure Donald didn't give her any more grief, there was no denying that his primary reason for moving in was to follow through with this investigation. To do that, he had to deceive her. There was no getting around it, and there was no denying it.

The cat was curled up asleep on the end of the bed. She got up, stretched, yawned and blinked at him when he came into the room, and responded favorably when he scratched the back of her neck.

"You might not like me so much when you see who I've brought with me."

He left the cat licking her paws and grooming her ears and went to join Claire and Rex in the kitchen. The dog sat on the floor next to her, hoping for another treat.

"Rex. Over here." Luke pointed to a floor mat.

The dog slunk over and sprawled on it.

"Good boy. Stay."

Claire was standing at the island, tossing a salad. "He sure is well-behaved."

"He was well-trained when I got him. The trick is

to not let up with it. He knows the limits, and he lives for the rewards."

"Like dog biscuits?"

"Mostly it's going for a run every day, fetching his rope toy, hanging out at the dog park."

"Nice life, Rex," Claire said with a smile. "It's a little cooler tonight so I thought we'd eat inside. Is that okay with you?"

"Sounds good. I'll set up my telescope, unless you'd like help with dinner?"

"Go ahead. I have everything under control."

The setup for the telescope/webcam was every bit as easy as the techies had assured him it would be. And for several minutes, since Claire was watching from the kitchen, he made a pretext of actually looking at a couple of boats anchored out in the sound. He would have to remember to do that from time to time so she didn't get suspicious.

Finally he settled on a stool across the counter from her, which was really where he wanted to be.

"I have sparkling water if you'd like some."

"Sure."

"Ice?" she asked. "Lime?"

"Both, thanks."

From a black lacquered tray at the end of the island, she scooped cubes from a silver ice bucket into tall glasses, filled them and slid a slice of lime onto the rim of each glass.

She passed one across to him and started on a salad dressing, measuring olive oil, balsamic and herbs into a bowl, whisking them together.

"I figured you didn't like to cook." He added the lime to the water in his glass and took a long drink.

"Seriously? What made you think that?"

"There wasn't much in your fridge that first morning."

She set the salad dressing aside and reached for her glass. "The only thing I like more than cooking is eating. I've been trying to diet, so having a lot of food around is way too tempting."

Again, he wanted to say she didn't need to worry about her weight, and once more decided against it. "I know all about temptation," he said instead.

"I know you do."

He liked that when the subject of alcohol came up, she didn't pussyfoot around.

"For me it's dessert, especially anything chocolate. The darker and richer, the better. Although…" She hesitated, as though not sure she wanted to expand on that. "I've also been known to sit and watch a movie and polish off an entire bag of cookies."

Somehow that didn't sound as bad as an evening spent with a bottle of whiskey, even though she seemed to think it did. "Everything in moderation is never as easy as it sounds."

"Tell me about it. Anyway, I do love to cook, and it was fun to shop this afternoon after Sam and Kristi left, knowing there'd be someone here to cook for."

"You went out after your meeting this afternoon?" He wanted it to sound like a casual question, but the police report Kate had given him earlier was still burning a hole in his back pocket.

The look she gave him was easily just as scorching. "Yes, I did. I can't hide, always have someone here with me, never go out on my own. Yes, Donald's making a nuisance of himself, and yes, I wish he would stop, but he won't hurt me."

Let it go. Sharing the details of that report with her now would ruin their evening. In the morning he'd find a way to bring up Donald's checkered past without letting her know he'd actually seen the report. Bringing it here had been a dumb move. He should have left it at his apartment when he'd picked up Rex.

"How'd the meeting go with your business partners?" he asked.

The timer went, and as she pulled a pan of lasagna from the oven and served it onto plates, she excitedly shared the details for staging her condo before putting it on the market, and the plan to look at a new place on Tuesday.

He carried the plates to the dining table that was already set with candles, cutlery and cloth napkins, and Claire followed with the salad.

Rex stood up, as though expecting an invitation to join them.

"Stay."

Rex's disappointment was palpable.

"Would he like to go out on the terrace?" Claire asked. "It's not quite the same as having a backyard, but it might be more interesting for him than sitting on a mat."

Before either of them could get up to open the double doors, Claire's cat strolled into the room. She took one look at the dog and arched herself into a pose perfect for Halloween, ears back, hackles raised. Rex dropped to the floor, flattened himself on the mat and crossed his paws over his nose.

"That is too funny," Claire said, laughing at the pair

of them. "In spite of Chloe's hissy fits every time she sees a dog, I don't think she'd ever actually go near one. And poor Rex doesn't seem to realize he's way bigger and tougher than she is."

"That's why he didn't make the K-9 unit. He's a good tracker but every time he sees a cat, he drops like a rock."

"I wonder why."

"We figure he must've had a run-in with a cat when he was a pup, but no one knows for sure. He's a good dog, otherwise. Smart, dependable, fearless, except when it comes to cats."

Claire got up from the table and opened the terrace doors. "Want to go outside, Rex? She won't bother you out there."

"Go," Luke said.

Rex leapt to his feet and made a run for it.

"Chloe doesn't go outside?" Luke asked.

Claire came back to the table and sat down. "Not a chance. She's pretty much afraid of her own shadow. Her reaction to dogs is purely a defense mechanism."

Luke picked up his fork and sampled the lasagna. "Wow, this is really good."

"Thank you."

"Seriously, this is probably the best I've ever tasted. Where'd you learn to cook like this?"

"From my Nonna DeAngelo. My sister and I used to spend summer vacations with her in Chicago. She's an amazing cook, and lasagna is one of her specialties. I like to think mine is almost as good as hers."

"Hard to imagine anything better than this," he said after downing another mouthful.

Claire wagged a finger at him. "If you ever meet my nonna, it'll be best not to mention that."

He had just been starting to relax, getting used to the idea of being here with Claire, but the thought of meeting her family brought back the guilt he'd been feeling while he stood outside her door a while ago. He wanted to be here with her, regretted that he had to deceive her, hated to think how she'd react when she found out.

Maybe she didn't need to find out.

That was always a possibility, one the old Luke would have welcomed and taken full advantage of. The man he was now, the man he wanted to be with Claire, couldn't do it. He needed to prove to her that he was honest, reliable and here for her, so that by the time they busted the brothel and, hopefully, had Phong in custody, she wouldn't feel she'd been taken advantage of.

He'd start by cleaning up the kitchen. And then he'd take her down the hall and remind her again why she really needed him here.

Chapter 10

Driving home from the office late Friday afternoon gave Claire a chance to reflect on all the changes in her life since she had run into Luke. So many changes that it was nearly impossible to believe it had only been a week ago. The days since Luke moved in had flown by in a flurry of appointments with her lawyer, her real estate agent and her business partners. Those were interspersed with moments spent with him, some stolen, others planned, all like a dream that had unexpectedly yet almost magically come true.

His dog and her cat had grudgingly reached a truce, although Rex was still on the defensive whenever Chloe got too close. Claire loved taking Rex for a walk, and one afternoon she had even gone for a run with him and Luke. Just as suspected, she'd had a hard time keeping up.

Twice Luke had taken her out on the Ducati, and

she'd decided that living dangerously had some serious advantages. The only thing better than riding on the bike, with her arms around him and her body on fire, happened in the bedroom.

What struck her most, though, was how much he had changed over the years. Sitting astride the bike in his leather jacket, he still looked very much like the devilish Luke Devlin she'd crushed on in college, but the reality was very much the opposite. He was thoughtful about how he adapted to her routine, interested in her ideas and opinions on everything, helpful around the house. A gentleman in every sense of the word. Every woman's fantasy. The bedroom was another matter. Her fantasy was no match for the reality, and he wanted to be with her, Claire DeAngelo, in spite of the extra pounds.

On Monday she'd met with her lawyer and gone over the divorce papers, and they had pretty much agreed with everything. There would be a fifty-fifty split of the proceeds of the condominium after it sold. To her relief, Donald wasn't asking for anything from her business, which meant she couldn't go after any of his investments, either. Since she wanted nothing of his, that was not a problem. The only sticking point was the Beatrix Potter book, and now that she knew its value and that he would sell it the first chance he got, she had dug in her heels and flatly refused to hand it over.

Still tucked inside the book was the card his grandmother had written when she had given the book to her.

Dearest Claire,

Because you share my love of books, I'm giving this one to you. It's my hope that someday you'll share *The Tale of Peter Rabbit* with your children, and so they learn the importance of always listening to their mother.

With much love,
Hettie Robinson

She had shown the card to her lawyer, who agreed that the book had undisputedly been a gift to Claire, not to Claire and Donald. She was confident that, if necessary, a judge would agree, so the book was removed from the property settlement and for now remained locked in the safe at the Ready Set Sold office. On Kristi's suggestion, as they staged the condo, the rest of Claire's collection of children's books had been packed into boxes, three of them, and hauled down to the storage room.

Luke had helped her, and he had been surprised by how many she had and how old some of them were. Many had been hers since childhood—several even contained her name awkwardly printed in crayon. Others she'd acquired over the years at bookstores, flea markets and garage sales, and a few had been gifts from close friends who knew about her passion for children's books.

Luke had also seemed taken aback by her fondness for them. She hadn't wanted to ask why, but she could guess. To him they likely represented the things he didn't want, including a family.

With everything that had happened this week, Claire had pushed the possibility of a pregnancy to the back of her mind. Now, driving home at the end of a busy week and looking forward to some free time this weekend, all the what-ifs and the flutter of anxiety that accompanied them were back.

Don't think about it. It was probably still too soon for a home pregnancy test to give reliable results, and she wasn't sure she wanted to know anyway. Right now, by not knowing, she didn't owe Luke any kind of explanation. If she was pregnant, she would have to tell him, and she didn't know how he would react.

Yes, you do.

He would react to her news the same way he reacted to Sherri's. Badly. He'd feel duped and angry, and who could blame him? She'd told him she was on the Pill, and he'd had sex with her, believing she had everything taken care of. She'd gone into this knowing it wasn't a forever thing but she was happy right now, maybe happier than she had ever been, and she wasn't ready for it to end.

She debated whether or not to stop and pick up groceries, and decided against it. She was in a celebratory mood, and she and Luke deserved a night out. Yesterday she'd put the condominium on the market, and this morning she had put an offer on the little yellow house with the white picket fence. It was a good offer, and her agent expected a response from the sellers by this evening. The house was perfect, and she had her fingers crossed she would get the response she was hoping for. As soon as she got home, she would call to make a reservation at her favorite Italian restaurant, then she'd run a nice hot bubble bath. If Luke was home, maybe he'd join her.

Her body was already humming with anticipation as she turned the corner onto her street and saw the police barricade at the end of the block, in front of her building.

No, it was the building next door.

That's where Luke had been doing some sort of undercover work with a window-washing company, although, come to think of it, he hadn't mentioned it again and she hadn't seen them there this week.

A uniformed officer waved her around the corner, which meant she couldn't access the underground parking garage. She rolled down her car window.

"Hi," she said to the man in the middle of the intersection. "I live in this building."

"Sorry, ma'am. The street's closed due to a police incident. I can't let anyone through."

"You mean I can't get into my apartment?"

"I'm afraid not."

"Do you know what this is about, or how long it's going to last?" It was obviously something pretty serious, but she couldn't help feeling a little resentful. There was a bubble bath up there that had her name on it.

"Sorry," he said. An unintelligible voice crackled over his radio, although apparently he understood it because he gave a clipped response before turning his attention back to her. "Ma'am, I have to ask you to move along. We need to keep this area clear for emergency vehicles."

This was getting her nowhere. Better to find a place to park and call Luke. Maybe he could get her inside.

Two blocks away she pulled into a parking space, dug her phone out of her bag and pulled up Luke's number. The call went to voice mail, so she gathered her handbag and briefcase from the passenger seat and walked the two blocks downhill to her building. Since this was a police matter, Luke had to be here. If she could find him, he could tell her what was going on, maybe even get her inside.

The police officer she'd spoken to earlier was occupied with more motorists wanting to know what was going on. Beyond the barricade were numerous police cars with lights flashing, two ambulances and dozens of people milling around on the sidewalk across the street. On the corner, a news reporter she recognized from a local television station faced a camera and spoke into a microphone, but Claire couldn't get close enough to hear what she was saying.

She scanned the crowd, looking for Luke and hoping she didn't find Donald. After they'd listed the condo and her lawyer had sent the amended divorce papers to his lawyer, he had backed off this week. Now would not be a good time for him to show up.

What on earth was going on here? she wondered as she continued her search for Luke. And then there he was, lean and solid, dark hair curling over the collar of his leather jacket. She'd recognize that jacket anywhere. He stood with his back to her, talking with two other men, Rex sitting at his side. They were almost as tall as Luke. The one facing her had sandy-blond hair and was wearing a grey Seahawks hooded sweatshirt. The other had jet-black hair and a faded jean jacket. Both were undercover cops like Luke, she was sure of it. Whatever this was, it must be big.

After a quick backward glance to see that the officer on the street was still distracted by onlookers and passersby, she slipped past the barricade, dodging other people as she made her way toward him. She was within earshot when the blond guy in the grey hoodie reached out and gave Luke a playful jab in the shoulder.

"Nice work, Luke. If you hadn't sweet-talked that chick upstairs into letting you move in and set up surveillance, we'd've never have nailed this guy."

"And you managed to keep her in the dark all this time?" the dark-haired guy asked.

Luke nodded and laughed. "She doesn't have a clue."

Several seconds ticked by before she realized they were talking about her, and then her shoes might as well have been glued to the pavement. Luke had laughed. Called her…

"Clueless?" She must have said it out loud because three heads swung her way.

Luke's cocky grin faded as the color literally drained from his face.

She had let herself be taken in by his looks, his charms, all that phoney vulnerability. What had seemed too good to be true was, well, too good to be true. She had acted like a fool, and he had played her as one.

"You smug son of a bitch. You *sweet-talked* me into this? You think I'm *clueless?*"

"Shit. Claire, listen—"

"No, *you* listen. As soon as this three-ring circus is cleared up, I want you and your crap out of my apartment."

"I can explain—"

"Explain what? That you still treat women the way you always did, sweet-talking them into giving you whatever you want? Save your breath. I get it. You haven't changed at all."

The touch of Rex's cool, damp nose against her hand tugged at her heartstrings, but not enough to calm her down. She should be furious, but right now the humiliation left no room for anger. She had nothing to say, and she'd be stupid to stand here and let him make this even worse, so she did the only thing that made sense. She swung away from him and ran.

After no more than ten steps he caught up and grabbed her by the arm. "Claire, wait."

"No!" She pulled away. "Don't touch me."

He let go immediately. "I know how that sounded but if you'd let me explain—"

No way. "I might be naive, but I'm not stupid." Aware of the people around them, that his friends were watching, she struggled to keep calm. "The sweet talk is over, Luke. We're done." She turned away again and this time he let her go.

She hurried past the barricade and up the hill to her car. After the first block, she stopped to catch her breath and glanced back to be sure he wasn't following her. He wasn't.

She trudged up the second block, cursing men for being heartless, heartbreaking jerks, cursing Seattle's steep hills, wondering what she should do when she did get to her car. Call one of her friends? Kristi, she decided. She was good in a crisis.

Once in her car, she locked the doors and pulled a bottle of water out of her bag. Her hands shook so bad, it was all she could do to unscrew the cap and hold the bottle to her lips long enough to take a few sips. After she put it away and drew a couple of deep breaths, she got out her phone and called Kristi.

"Oh, sweetie. I'm so sorry," her friend said after Claire spilled the details. "You need to come straight to my place, as long as you're okay to drive. I can pick you up if you'd like."

"I'm okay." Or at least better than she'd been a few minutes ago. "Thanks, Kristi."

"Don't even mention it. I'm pretty sure I owe you one anyway. I'll call Sam and see if she's free. She'll either join us, or go hunt Luke down and kick his ass."

That made Claire laugh. "See, this is why I love you guys."

"Right back at you. Now get yourself over here."

"I'm on my way." She tossed the phone into her bag and pulled on her sunglasses. She hoped Kristi would let her stay the night. She had no idea when she could get back into her building, and she wouldn't go back, anyway. Not until she was sure Luke had cleared out of her apartment and out of her life, this time for good.

Luke wanted to punch something. Of all the crappy bad luck that had come his way, this was the crappiest.

"Look, man." Cam Ferguson wore the concerned look of a man who figured he could end up on the receiving end of somebody's fist. "I am so sorry. I had no idea that was your woman."

"Not your fault." Much as Luke would like it to be. He'd been trying to play it cool, not wanting to let on to anyone that he had feelings for Claire, and it had backfired. Big-time.

"You want to go after her?" Jason asked. "We're winding down here. Patsy's already got the girls in the van. She's taking them to a safe house for questioning. And here's Derek now."

"Thanks, but I'm not sure that's a good idea."

Instead he turned his attention to the main entrance

and watched Derek escort Phong, hands cuffed behind him, into the back of a waiting police car. The moment they'd all been working and waiting for, and now it was a total anticlimax. Behind them, uniformed officers led three more men out of the building. One was Phong's pimp/drug dealer. The other two were a couple of johns who had the dirty rotten luck of being in the wrong place at the wrong time.

He could relate. Before Claire showed up, he'd been about to take Rex back upstairs to the condo. Instead he'd stuck around, not wanting to miss this, and now he'd screwed up everything.

He knew Claire well enough to know that when she told him to get out, she meant it. And who could blame her? He had hurt her and he hated himself for it. Now it was up to him to find a way back in. If he wanted any kind of a shot at fixing this, he had to give her some space, a chance to calm down. It would be better to call her. Not that she would answer, but he could leave a message, apologize, explain why he couldn't be honest with her, and why he hadn't been honest with his colleagues. Could he convince her that using her place for surveillance wasn't his only reason for wanting to be with her? Or would she always believe he was still the same smug son of a bitch she'd known in college? Time would tell. All he could do now was hope for the best.

Still hiding behind her sunglasses, Claire rang the doorbell at Kristi and Nate's place. She hoped her friend would answer the door and not her husband, her teenage daughter or her twin stepdaughters. Claire couldn't face anyone else right now. Bad enough that Kristi had to be the one to witness her meltdown. Luckily it was

Kristi who opened the door because *meltdown* was a little bit of an understatement.

"Oh, sweetie. I'm so sorry." Kristi hugged her. "Come in, come in."

Claire pulled off her sunglasses and dabbed at her eyes with a tissue. It would be easy to let herself have a good cry, but she was still too furious for that.

"Come with me." Kristi led her down to the bathroom, got out fresh towels and a washcloth. "Take your time, wash your face, I'll go find you something comfortable to put on. Oh, Sam's on her way. She should be here any minute."

"What about your family...?"

"Not to worry. Jenna's at a sleepover at a friend's place, and Nate took the twins and the dogs over to his mom and dad's for the evening. We have the place all to ourselves."

That was something of a relief. It was one thing to let her two best friends see her like this, but she couldn't cope with anyone else right now.

She splashed some water on her face, ran a comb through her hair and changed into a pair of sweatpants and a T-shirt that Kristi had produced. There was no way Kristi's clothes would fit her so these must be Nate's, but she was beyond caring.

In the family room, she found that Sam had arrived.

"Come sit here," she said, patting the sofa seat cushion next to her.

"I'll go fix us some drinks." Kristi urged her to take a seat. "Be right back."

Claire sat and sank into Sam's embrace, and Sam plucked a tissue from the box and pressed it into her hand.

"Thanks." She had never been a crier, though. It

didn't solve anything anyway. It was just that this hurt so darned much.

"Kristi gave me the *Reader's Digest* version of what happened with Luke. I had already seen the TV news coverage about the place they busted and the arrests, but I never put two and two together to come up with Luke using your place for whatever kind of surveillance they were doing."

Surveillance. That's what Luke was doing, using her place, using *her*. "I honestly had no idea." She was that big a fool.

Sam filled her in on the sordid details of the young women who'd been smuggled into the country and forced into the sex trade, the drugs and how it had been the overdose and death of one of the young women several weeks ago that tipped off the police and launched the investigation.

"So it was…what? A brothel? Seriously? In my condominium complex?" Claire groaned. "And just after I've listed it. Who's going to buy it now?"

Her life was turning into a vortex and she was watching it all being sucked down the sewer. What else could go wrong?

Her phone rang. "La Cucaracha" played.

Sam snatched the phone out of her hand. "No freaking way is that loser getting to you now. Just ignore him."

"He's probably heard the news and I'll bet he's thinking the same I am, that between this and the current state of the real estate market, we'll never a find a buyer."

"Too bad," Sam said. "There's not a damn thing you

can do about any of it, but he'll try to pin it all on you anyway."

That did sound like Donald. *At least he's predictable.* Luke had been full of surprises since the moment they'd met, and she'd had enough surprises to last a lifetime.

Kristi returned with a tray of drinks. "Sam, that's decaf coffee for you. Claire, I was going to make you a latte, then I decided something stronger was in order. Have a few sips of this," she said, pressing a glass into Claire's hand.

Absently Claire gazed at the amber-colored fluid in the cut-crystal old-fashioned glass, heard the clink of ice as she raised it to her lips. She quickly lowered it when the sharp, peaty scent filled her nose.

"What is this?"

"Scotch, on the rocks. It'll take the edge off."

Claire set the glass on the coffee table. "I can't drink that."

Sam picked up her coffee cup. "We know you're not much of a drinker, but this is one of those times when you can make an exception."

"No, I mean I *really* can't drink that." Her current reality was all but forgotten in the face of Luke's betrayal. A simple glass of Scotch had it rushing back.

"Why not?"

"There's no harm in one little drink."

Claire felt herself smile, and then she started to laugh. *This is so not funny,* she told herself.

"Okay, now she's getting hysterical," Sam said. "What do we do?"

"I'm not." She took a long, slow breath to calm herself. "Honest. I don't know why I'm laughing. I'm not hysterical. I'm not. But I… There's a chance I could be pregnant."

Chapter 11

"Pregnant?" Sam and Kristi chorused.

"Are you sure?" Kristi swept the glass of Scotch off the table and set it on the tray.

"Is it Luke's?" Sam asked.

"No, I'm not sure. And, yes! If I'm having a baby, of course it's his. How many men do you think I've been sleeping with?"

"Sorry, sorry, sorry." Sam was obviously chagrined. "That was a stupid question. It's just… Oh, my God, I was not expecting this."

"How did this happen?" Kristi asked. "I mean, I know how it happened, but I thought you were still on the Pill."

"I am, or I was, but I missed a few, quite a few, actually." She told them how she had messed up and about the birth control her doctor had recommended until she knew for sure.

"Have you taken a pregnancy test?"

"Not yet. It's only been a week and—" This was the hardest part of her confession. "Things were going so well with Luke and I didn't want to spoil it. Even before what happened this afternoon, I knew this wasn't a forever thing. He doesn't want a family, isn't interested in settling down, and he was completely up-front about that." But she never would have suspected he was using her. The old Luke, sure, but this Luke? Never.

"Claire, this doesn't sound like you." Kristi's narrow-eyed scrutiny made her squirm. "Did you just plan to end things at some point and have his baby without telling him?"

"Of course not! I would never do anything like that. The thing is, even though I knew he doesn't want a family, I did believe he wanted to be with me."

He had been very convincing, and she had fallen for it. Thud. Knowing how gullible she'd been, how easy it had been for him to manipulate her, hurt every bit as much as his betrayal.

"I guess I was secretly hoping his feelings were strong enough that he would change his mind. Now that I know that's not true, I'm not sure how I'll handle it." If anything needed to be handled.

"I don't know that I agree," Sam said. "When we met Luke last Sunday afternoon, I saw how he looked at you. Seriously, the guy could not take his eyes off you. It's damn hard to fake that kind of thing. Most men aren't good enough actors to pull it off."

Claire laughed, and even to her own ears it had a bitter edge to it. "Trust me, he's had a lot of practice. He had a string of girlfriends in college, and they all believed he was crazy about them…until they found out he wasn't."

"There's a difference between reality and wishful thinking," Kristi said. "I know what Sam means. The way Luke looked at you—"

Claire stopped her. "Please, stop. You both mean well and you don't want to see me hurting…I love you for that…but the thing Luke and I had, whatever it was, it's over."

"Okay, fair enough." But Sam's concession was short-lived. "I have no trouble believing the guy was a player. I'll bet girls have been throwing themselves at him since he hit puberty. But the baby…that's a whole different matter. I'll go out on a limb here and predict he has a change of heart after you tell him."

Of course Sam would believe that. Her husband would move heaven and earth to be with his kids.

"I want to believe that as much as you do, sweetie, but I'm afraid it's not going to happen. That first morning over breakfast, Luke told me about his ex, how he'd only found out she was having his baby after she was in a car accident and had a miscarriage."

"What did he do?"

"He ended the relationship."

Sam and Kristi exchanged a look.

"Can I ask one more question?" Kristi asked.

"Of course."

"Are you in love with him?"

Claire inhaled slowly, then exhaled with a whoosh. She had doubts about a lot of things right now, but she was absolutely certain about this. "Totally, madly, head-over-heels."

"You should tell him," Sam said.

"Right. Because I haven't been humiliated enough already."

"No. Because if I'm right and he is as crazy about you as I think he is, then—"

Claire's phone went off again, this time vibrating on the coffee table where Sam had set it. Speak of the devil…

Sam picked it up, read the display name and grinned at Kristi.

"Don't answer it!" Claire said.

"It says…" Sam paused. "Lucky Devil?"

"Luke put that in my phone. I can't talk to him. Not right now." She didn't bother trying to hide the bitterness. "He's had that stupid nickname since college. It's what his buddies called him, given his way with women." He even had the T-shirt to prove it, she thought, remembering the day she'd run in to him. At the time she'd found it funny. Now the joke was on her.

Before either of her friends could respond, her phone rang again.

"Oh, my God," Sam said. "You need to turn this thing off." Sam read the call display again. "This one's from Brenda Billings. Isn't she your…?"

"My Realtor." Claire grabbed the phone. "I do have to take this call. We put an offer on the house this morning—"

She jumped up and crossed the room to the sliding doors that overlooked Kristi's patio. "Brenda, hi. Thanks for calling. Any news?"

"Yes, I have, and it's good news. They accepted your offer, including all the conditions. They're moving out of the city at the end of the month, so they've even agreed to the early possession date you asked for."

"Oh, um, wow. That's good. Really good." A few hours ago she had wanted this so much it hurt. Now she wanted to feel happy about it, and couldn't. It was all too much. Being with Luke, the maybe baby and now a new home.

"Claire? Is everything okay?"

She whipped off her glasses and dabbed the corners of her eyes with her sleeve. "Fine. Everything's fine. I'm right in the middle of something, though. Can we meet, tomorrow maybe, to go over the details?"

"Of course we can. How's ten? Or is that too early?"

"No, that'll be perfect."

"Would you like me to come to your place?"

"Um, no. I have to run errands first thing. Can we meet at my office instead?" Since Brenda hadn't asked, Claire assumed she hadn't seen the evening news, and she didn't know if she could get back into her building tomorrow morning.

"Your office tomorrow at ten. See you then. And Claire…?"

"Mmm-hmm?"

"Congratulations! You just bought a house."

"Thanks."

She turned back to Kristi and Sam, who looked as though they were waiting to pounce.

"I got the house."

Then they were on their feet, she was sandwiched in a group hug, and they took turns assuring her that she was doing the right thing.

"So happy for you."

"It's a perfect house for you."

"A chance for a fresh new start."

"We're going to throw the most awesome house-warming party."

A housewarming party. That would be fun. But not as much fun as a baby shower. With that thought, she gave in to the tears, although she couldn't have said if they were happy or sad.

The sky was turning from dusk to dark when Luke left Claire's condo. The patrol cars, barricades and crime scene tape were gone and the street was quiet as he led Rex out the front door and onto the sidewalk. Everything back to normal. And then the hair on his neck went up.

Donald? Had to be, he decided, making a show of looking around as he hitched his duffel bag onto his shoulder and unclipped Rex's lead. *Bring it on, asshole.*

He spotted the Lexus halfway down the block. In this light the driver's side appeared empty, but he couldn't be sure. He'd parked his truck on the next block so he had to walk past Donald's car anyway. Not that he needed an excuse, and the mood he was in right now, it would be best for Claire's ex if he was inside the car. With the doors locked.

His first instinct was right. The car was unoccupied, but Donald was there. He stepped out of a recessed doorway as Luke approached.

Luke stopped walking. "Rex, watch." The dog immediately halted and fixed his sights on Donald. "Good dog."

"Nice night to walk your dog."

"What do you want, Robinson?"

"I want to know what the hell went on here this afternoon. Claire isn't answering her phone and I wanted to make sure she's okay."

"Claire's fine." Although he doubted that was any more true for her than it was for him.

"What about the police raid?"

"What about it?" He was in no mood for questions, even less so for small talk. "If you saw the news, then you know what went down. Nothing more I can tell you."

"Bull." Donald shifted, giving the appearance that he was stepping forward.

Rex flattened his ears and growled.

Donald took a step back instead. "What's with your dog?"

"I don't think he likes you."

"He should be on a leash."

And you should be in a jail cell. "Rex won't move... unless I tell him to."

Donald fished his keys out of his jacket pocket. "I have to get going."

"Good plan."

"If you see Claire, tell her—" Whatever the message, he seemed to decide against having Luke relay it.

"I'll tell her I ran into you."

Donald got into his car and made a show of peeling away from the curb. The jerk.

"Good boy." Rex followed him to the truck, hopped in when Luke opened the passenger door for him.

Luke tossed his duffel bag in the back and then, behind the wheel, it was all he could do to resist squealing his own tires as he slammed the truck into gear and drove away from what was, without a doubt, the best thing that had ever happened to him.

Twenty minutes later, after he'd dropped Rex and the rest of his stuff at his place and swapped the truck for the Ducati, he stood on the sidewalk in front of a downtown liquor store.

In the two years since he'd quit drinking, this was hands down the stupidest thing he'd ever done. Hell, he hadn't even done anything yet, but he was on the precipice of a long, slippery slope.

Let yourself slide and you might never make it back up.

You don't know that, not for sure. Maybe one night, one slip off the wagon wouldn't be so bad.

Listen to yourself. Is this what you want?

No. He wanted Claire. But right now he wanted this more. He wanted to wallow in self-pity and guilt awhile, until the booze let him talk himself into believing that none of this was his fault, and then finally have it wrap its silky tentacles around his consciousness until he no longer felt anything.

He pulled out his phone to see if he'd missed a call from Claire. He hadn't. Then he scrolled through the numbers in his contact list, paused at hers before he kept going, not even sure what he was looking for until he found it.

Norman G. His AA sponsor.

We admitted we were powerless over alcohol—that our lives had become unmanageable.

After two years, after all the work he'd done, how the hell had he ended up back at step one? He hit the call button, listened as Norm's phone rang, felt his heart do a dip in his chest when it went to voice mail.

"Norm. It's Luke D. I'm…"

What? What could he say? *I'm this close to throw-ing the past two years down the toilet?*

"I'm taking it one day at a time. Some shit went down today, but I'm okay. I'm not going to hit the bottle." He'd hit the road instead.

Helmet on, he revved the Ducati, roared away from the curb and headed for the exit to the I-5. Where to go? North? Canada, maybe? South to Oregon? The lack of a passport in his pocket made it an easy decision. After he eased the Ducati onto the freeway, he opened her up and gave himself up to the ride. It was the only other way he knew to get numb.

Claire woke in Kristi's daughter's room, vacant be-cause Jenna had been at a sleepover. The rest of the house, judging by the commotion, was wide-awake. Water running, footsteps racing down the hallway, dogs barking and Kristi shushing everyone.

Grateful as she was that she hadn't had to go home last night to an empty apartment and the risk of run-ning into Luke, she now needed to be alone. Quietly she slipped out of bed and into the bathroom down the hall, which was mercifully free. After a quick shower she put on the clothes she'd worn yesterday, brushed her hair and dabbed on some lip gloss, which was the only thing she could find in her handbag.

Kristi was coming down the hallway with a cup of coffee when she emerged from the bathroom. "Good morning. How'd you sleep?"

"Not bad." Better than she'd expected.

"I thought you might like some coffee. It's decaf." Kristi winked. "Just in case."

"Thanks, but you didn't have to. I should go."

"I know. I assumed you'd want to avoid the Callahan-McTavish household's Saturday-morning madness, and I thought you might like to have something while you get ready but it looks like you already are."

"I hope you don't mind."

"Of course not! You have a busy day ahead, what with buying a new house and all. A good thing, given everything that's happened." Kristi set the coffee cup on a hall table and hugged her. "Have you listened to Luke's message yet?"

"No." She'd been tempted to last night after she'd crawled into bed, but was afraid to trust her reaction to hearing his voice. She had avoided it again this morning for the same reason. "I'll wait until I'm home."

"I completely understand. Will you call me after you've sealed the deal on the house?"

"I will." In spite of her momentary panic last night, she knew it was the right thing to do. The house was exactly what she'd dreamed of, practically perfect, really, and the few things that weren't quite right could easily be made so, especially with Sam and Kristi's help.

"And you'll call after you listen to Luke's message?"

That actually made Claire laugh. "You really want a report on that?"

"Sweetie, I'm thrilled about the house, you know that, but I'm dying to hear what Luke has to say. And you need to give him a chance to explain, especially under these circumstances." She gave Claire's belly a playful pat.

"Okay, okay, I'll call. Just don't hold your breath."

"Come on, I'll walk you out to your car."

You really do have the best friends in the world, Claire told herself as she backed out of Kristi's driveway. She was leaving a lot of things behind, mostly unpleasant ones, and heading into a future filled with equal parts excitement and uncertainty. Knowing her friends wouldn't let her go it alone made all the difference.

Luke woke that morning with a clear head, a heavy conscience and a dog who was ready for a run.

"First things first." He pulled on the jeans and T-shirt he'd stripped off and tossed on the floor a few hours ago, brushed his teeth and went into the kitchen.

He pulled open the fridge, snagged the milk carton and opened the spout. He checked the expiration date before he took a swig and poured the contents down the sink. Good thing he took his coffee black, he thought as he filled a pot with water, turned on the stove and snagged a jar of instant out of the cupboard. Just a week, and he'd already become accustomed to all the fancy gadgets in Claire's kitchen.

Mostly, though, he missed her. Missed waking up to the warm body next to his, the mind-blowing morning sex, the cozying up for coffee afterward. He'd screwed up, and other than apologizing he didn't know how to fix it. Maybe he couldn't. Or maybe he shouldn't even try.

He spooned coffee crystals into a mug while he waited for the water to boil. He'd been close to having a drink last night. Somehow he'd found enough inner strength to talk himself out of it, but next time he might not be so lucky. And there would always be a next time. What if he couldn't stop himself?

One day at a time, they said. At least he'd figured it out last night. But then he'd hit the highway and lost himself in the adrenaline rush of high speed on the open road. That had been stupid, and completely irresponsible.

Claire didn't deserve that. He didn't deserve her. He needed to apologize to her, even try to explain why he'd let his team believe he had "sweet-talked" her into letting him stay with her, and why, for the sake of the investigation but also for her own safety, he hadn't been able to tell her what and who they had under surveillance.

Be willing to make amends. Huh. Back to step eight already. More like back to step eight *again*.

He found his phone in his jacket pocket, checked it for messages. A voice mail from Wong saying there was a meeting at one o'clock. Another from his sponsor, offering to meet for coffee that morning. And a text from Cam, apologizing for the screwup. Nothing from Claire. No surprise there.

How was he supposed to handle this? He had more experience with effing things up than fixing them. He had already left her a message. Now he needed a Plan B because if he kept calling, he'd be as bad as Donald. She didn't need any more of that kind of crap in her life.

Send her flowers? Right, because this was just like a birthday.

He still had the key to her condo—he'd needed to lock the dead bolt on the way out. Would she let him give it back in person? That might be his best, and only, shot. Now to figure out the timing. Best to give her twenty-four hours to respond to the message he'd left yesterday. Then, if he didn't hear from her, he would send her a text message about the key, and he'd make a point of letting her know he had no intention of using it.

Rex jabbed Luke's leg with his snout. "I know, buddy. We both need to let off some steam."

He'd change into sweats, pound the pavement for half an hour. Then he'd grab coffee and get a pep talk from Norman, go to his meeting. After that, if he still hadn't heard from Claire, he'd move on to Plan B.

Chapter 12

Two weeks after sealing the deal on her new home, Claire stood in the middle of her kitchen and surveyed the stacks of cardboard boxes, all neatly taped shut and labelled with their contents. The movers would be here in the morning and tonight would be her last night in the penthouse condo that had never quite felt like home.

Chloe sat hunched on a stool, eyeing the piles with disdain.

"You're going to love our new home." Claire stroked the soft fur on the top of her head. "I know you don't believe that now, but you'll see. The dining room has a big window with a window seat that looks out onto the back garden, and you can sit there and watch the birds."

She had always wanted a window seat, and it was just one of the many things about the house that made it so right for her. By some miracle—and she didn't even believe in miracles but she couldn't think of a better way to describe it—Brenda Billings, her Realtor, had found a buyer for the condo, despite its hefty price tag and the fact that a mere two weeks ago the police had raided a brothel in the next building. She still had difficulty wrapping her head around that one. The owners weren't taking possession for two months, but Donald had agreed to the sale in spite of his now obvious financial woes.

The divorce papers had been signed, and although the Beatrix Potter book had stayed in Claire's possession, Donald still called or sent a text message about it every day, sometimes both and often more than once. She deleted them as they came in and did her best to ignore them, and would have found it laughable that a grown man was fixated on a children's book if he wasn't so darned annoying.

After she'd finalized the purchase on the house, she had listened to Luke's first phone message. He had apologized, offered an explanation about wanting to protect her, which was why he hadn't told her about doing surveillance and hadn't told his colleagues about their relationship. A truckload of manure as far as she was concerned. She had already known he was working undercover, and what possible difference could their relationship make to a handful of other police officers? The truth was obvious. He hadn't mentioned the surveillance to her in case she said no, and he hadn't mentioned the relationship to his colleagues because there was no relationship. He'd only let her believe it was about the two of them. And about making sure Donald left her alone, so make that two truckloads.

The day after Luke left that message, he had texted her with an offer to come by or meet her someplace to return the key. She had sidestepped that by telling him to drop it off at the Ready Set Sold office. He had done as she'd asked and she had made a point of not being there, although she'd been given an earful by their office manager. Marlie had called her the instant he'd left, gushing about what a "gorgeous hunk of manhood" he was and admonishing Claire for letting him get away.

But Claire hadn't let him go, she'd sent him packing, and it had been the right thing to do. Somewhat to her surprise, he hadn't given up. Every day he'd sent a text message, always in the evening after she'd finished doing some packing and was getting settled for the night. At first they were short and to the point.

Left the key with your secretary.

The next day he'd written, *I get that you don't want to see me. If you change your mind, can I buy you a latte?*

After she ignored those, the messages became less serious.

Rex would like to know if Chloe misses him.

Rex wants to know if there are any dog biscuits left.

Since he hasn't heard from Chloe, Rex wonders if he's in the doghouse, too.

His pattern had become predictable, and she found herself looking forward to the message. It was schoolgirl silly, but it was true.

Sam and Kristi insisted the messages meant he was genuinely sorry for what he'd done, that he wanted a second chance, and that Claire should give him one. But she couldn't let herself do that. Not yet.

She still needed to take a pregnancy test, but she had decided to wait until she was in her new home. If she was having Luke's baby, and in her heart she hoped she was, then she wanted that news to be connected to her new home, not the condo. She had too many negative associations with this place. The house represented a fresh start, a new chapter in her life. If that included the baby she had dreamed about for so long, she was ready for it. And fully prepared to raise a child on her own, since she knew Luke didn't want to be part of a fresh start with her.

And that's why she couldn't reply to his messages. Not until she knew for sure, one way or the other. It had been three weeks since the first night they'd slept together, she still hadn't had a period, and she'd felt queasy when she got up that morning. Those things could be due to stress, or they could mean she was having a baby.

The pregnancy test she'd bought that morning had been tucked away in her handbag, and tomorrow the waiting would be over. After that she would have to answer one of the two big questions.

If she wasn't pregnant, should she respond to Luke's messages? Consider letting him back into her life? The part of her that had recklessly become *that woman* a couple of weeks ago screamed *yes!* But her sensible side reminded her there was no future with a man who couldn't commit to a family.

If she was expecting, then she needed to figure out how to tell Luke, and when. Claire was inclined to wait, but Sam was emphatic that he needed to know right away. She had made a similar mistake, not telling her husband, AJ, about their son, Will, and they had lost three precious years of being together as a family.

There was no danger of Luke wanting a family, he

had already made it perfectly clear he didn't, but of course he had a right to know. And Claire always did the right thing. She just needed to work on the timing.

"La Cucaracha" blaring on her phone dragged her back to the present. This time it was a text message.

Doesn't make sense to have so much money tied up in an old book. Willing to split the $$ when we sell it. Call me.

"Oh. My. God." She deleted the message, wishing she hadn't read it at all. "We're not discussing this, ever, and *we* are not divvying up any money because *I* am not selling the book." What part of this did he not understand?

The book was still locked in the safe at the office, and she had already decided to keep it there until Donald got his share from the sale of the condo. He and Deirdre were obviously having financial problems, but Claire hoped he would forget about the book once he received his share from the sale of the condo.

She ran a hand over her belly. "Maybe I'll have someone to read it to." Maybe.

A month ago she would never have believed she could be hoping and praying to be pregnant. Now the prospect of raising a child on her own held none of the worry it would have then, and she knew why. She couldn't have the man she loved, but if she could have his baby, she would love their child with all her heart.

If there was a baby.

She scooped Chloe into her arms and held her close in spite of the animal's loud and vigorous protest. "Please let there be a baby," she whispered. "Please."

* * *

Luke slowed the truck to a crawl and scanned both sides of the street as he drove past Claire's condominium complex. No sign of the Lexus. Either Donald had backed off, or he was being more discreet now that he knew Luke was onto him.

Every day since Claire had told him to get out, Luke had driven by, sometimes more than once. He hated that he did it, but he wasn't looking for Claire. Or so he kept telling himself. He was keeping an eye on Donald.

He had also sent her a text message every day, and although she had only responded to the first one, with instructions for returning her key, he was sure she read them. He wanted to do more, but aside from making sure Donald wasn't hanging around, there wasn't much else he could do.

He already knew what he'd say in tonight's text message, though.

Should he send her a housewarming gift, too? Or would that be too much?

Probably too much. He wouldn't know what to give her, anyway.

Another children's book? She had so many already, he wouldn't have a clue where to start. Still not a bad idea, though. He'd file that one away for future reference.

This would be the last time he needed to come here. The day he'd dropped off her key, he had found out from the woman who worked in her office that she had purchased the house she'd been so excited about and would be moving at the end of the month. The woman, who had introduced herself as Marlie, probably would have spilled more information if he had asked. But she also would have told her boss, he had no doubt of that. She had referred to Claire as one of her angels—she called the three women Marlie's angels—which suggested they had a close bond and a good working relationship. He wouldn't expect anything less of Claire.

The only thing he couldn't figure out was how she'd ended up with a jerk like Donald Robinson. She was beautiful, smart and sexy as hell, and she was a good person. Hardworking, honest—not exactly the first things to come to mind with a real estate agent, but no doubt it was those qualities that made her so successful at it.

It killed him to think she'd been date-raped back in college, but he hated the idea of her being with Donald almost as much. That sick son of a bitch's hands on that knockout body was pure torture, the long drawn-out kind that started as a slow burn deep in his gut. The hotter it got, the further it spread, until it cut off his breath. Like it was doing right now.

Claire believed that selling the condo and moving into a place of her own would put an end to any further communication from Donald. Luke doubted it would, but for her sake he hoped she was right.

Luke cruised past her building and sure enough, there was a moving van parked in front, back doors open, and a man was pushing a dolly loaded with boxes up the ramp.

Did Donald know she was moving today? Most likely, but the better question was did he know where she was moving? When she'd shown Luke the real estate listing, he had made a mental note of the address and had already scoped out the neighborhood. Unlike the busy streets downtown, if Donald hung around Claire's new place in that fancy car of his, he'd stick out like a snowman in July. Did the guy have enough smarts to realize that? Hard to say, but in case he didn't, Luke intended to keep an eye on him.

The move went off without a hitch. For the past two weeks, Claire had spent practically every waking moment organizing and packing. It had paid off today, and it had also helped her keep her mind off Luke. Having the support of the two best friends in the world was also a help. Make that a godsend.

"Have I told you how much I love this house?" Kristi was unpacking table linens into the bottom drawer of the vintage sideboard Claire had found online.

Claire unwrapped the silverware chest Nonna DeAngelo had given her and set it on top of the sideboard. "Once or twice."

"Or ten," Sam added.

Kristi made a face at her.

Sam responded with one of her own. "Hey, I love it, too. I just don't wear my heart on my sleeve."

They made Claire laugh, and she loved them for it. They had been waiting here when the moving van pulled up, had already helped her unpack and organize the kitchen. They intended to stay until Claire took the pregnancy test, and she wouldn't have it any other way.

Sam finished replacing the switch plate cover, stuck her screwdriver in her back pocket and tested the dimmer switch she'd just installed.

"It works," Claire said.

"Of course it works."

"That's such a pretty chandelier," Kristi said, closing the drawer. "And that's the last box we had to unpack in here."

"Good. It's time we took a break." Claire went into the kitchen and returned with three chilled bottles of water and a vegetable tray and dip she'd picked up at the deli. "Let's sit," she said, setting them on the dining room table.

Sam unscrewed the top of her bottle and took a long drink as she settled onto one of the chairs. "Ah. I needed that."

"Me, too." Kristi joined her. "Mmm, nice and cold. Sit," she said to Claire, patting the chair next to her.

She could use a break but she was antsy and on edge, partly energized by the exciting newness of all this, but mostly anxious about the pregnancy test. She was all but convinced she was pregnant, and she would be disappointed—no, devastated—if she wasn't.

She took the chair next to Kristi, though, and sipped some water.

"This might be a good time to show you the plans I've been working on for your attic." Sam dipped a celery stick and crunched. "You might not want to do the work right away, but it's something to consider."

"Let's see what you've got." She and Kristi leaned in to look at Sam's drawings.

"The access hatch to the attic is in the hallway so that's a perfect place to put in the pull-down stairs. There's enough clearance to install a ceiling down the center of the attic, under the peak of the roof, then follow the slope down to sidewalls that would be about four feet high."

"My kids would love a space like that," Kristi said. "It would make a great playroom."

The idea of a child's playroom caught Claire's imagination, too. And triggered a memory. "You know, it reminds me of a house we rented near one of the air force bases where my dad was stationed. I'm not sure where, we moved so many times, but I remember my sister and I loved the pull-down staircase. My mom helped me and my sister set it up as our own little hideaway, complete with bean bag chairs and Bon Jovi and Madonna posters. It's been years since I've thought about that."

"Wow, you had a cool mom." Sam, who'd been raised by a mother who struggled with mental illness, looked a little wistful. She slid the drawings off her clipboard and gave them to Claire. "I wrote up a supply list and cost estimate, too. You have plenty of room in this house, but you can think about it for the future. And opening up more space always adds value."

"I'll definitely think about it for down the road. And it's not like you'll be able to do any major construction right now, not until after the baby is born."

Sam laughed and shook her head. "Now you sound like AJ. He'd have me on bed rest, if he could, but my doctor says I'm in great shape. I'm still running, just not as hard and not as far as I used to, and I should be able to keep working right up until the baby's born."

"That may be the case, but I still think you should think about hiring an assistant," Claire said. "At least a helper who can do all the heavy lifting for you."

Kristi munched on a carrot. "I totally agree."

"I've been thinking the same thing," Sam said. "And I'd like both of you to be in on the interviews when I do. And whoever we hire will have to have a good range of skills, not just be 'helper.' I'll want to take some time off after the baby's born, so the person we hire will have to be a good fit for all of us."

"That's a really good idea." Claire swiped a broccoli floret through the dip, popped it into her mouth and wiped her fingers on a paper napkin. She hadn't eaten since breakfast, hadn't even thought of food, which was unlike her, and she hadn't realized how hungry she was.

"Speaking of babies," Kristi said. "You do know Sam and I aren't leaving until you put us out of our misery and take that pregnancy test."

Claire knew exactly how they felt. "I know, and I'm not sure why I keep putting it off. I guess I want everything here to be done and perfect, so when I find out that I am...*if* I'm pregnant, then I won't have to think about anything else."

"You really are hoping it's positive, aren't you?"

"I am. Is that crazy? Am I crazy?"

"No!"

"Definitely not."

"I've always had this romantic vision of me living in a house with a white picket fence and having a cat and a dog and a family."

"You're halfway there," Sam said.

"At one time I believed I'd have all those things with Donald." She caught her friends exchanging a look. "I know, what was I thinking? So I gave up on the dream, but then Luke came along and..."

"And you really do love him, don't you?" Kristi asked.

She fought the lump forming in her throat. "I do."

"Are you still getting text messages from him?"

Claire smiled. She couldn't help herself. "I am."

"Have you replied to any of them?"

"Not yet. I mean, what's the point? If I'm pregnant, he will freak out. And if I'm not—"

"You'll freak out," Kristi said.

"Funny. I was going to say that if I'm not, do I want to be involved with someone who isn't interested in having a relationship?"

Sam grinned. "When that someone looks like he does? Um…yeah, you do."

"All these what-ifs are making me crazy." Kristi snagged another carrot and stood up. "If this place has to be perfect before we can find out if you're having a baby, then we need to get back to work. What's next?" she asked.

Claire reached for her iPad and brought up her checklist. "The kitchen, dining room and my bedroom are done. Everything's in place in the living room, I just need to figure out where I want to hang pictures. And the boxes of stuff for the bathroom and linen closet still need to be unpacked."

Kristi picked up her water bottle. "I'll look after the bathroom while the two of you finish up in the living room."

"Good plan." Sam got up and reached for her toolbox.

"And when we're finished, I'll order pizza for dinner."

Sam grabbed her by the arm and steered her into the living room. "No way. When we're finished, we'll find out if you're having a baby. *Then* you can order pizza."

Chapter 13

"Please tell me we're done," Sam said an hour later. "Everything's unpacked, Kristi flattened all the boxes and put them in the garage, I even fixed that loose floorboard on the veranda. If you find another excuse to keep us in suspense, you might as well just shoot me."

"There's just one more thing," Kristi said. "Sorry, Sam! I'm anxious, too, but we forgot about Claire's housewarming present. It's out in my van."

"Right." Sam carried her toolbox outside. "I'll put this away in my truck while you get the gift."

"You've both done so much already, a gift isn't necessary," Claire said.

Kristi dug her camera out of her bag and looped the strap around her neck. "Come on," she said, taking Claire's arm. "We need you outside, too."

Curious, Claire stood on the veranda and waited until

her friends returned with a large, flat package wrapped in brown paper and tied up with raffia.

"Sam and I worked on it together, so it's one of a kind."

Claire slipped off the wrapping and managed to catch a glimpse of a wreath for her front door before her tears blurred her eyes. Happy tears. She took off her glasses, wiped her eyes, took a closer look at the gift.

"It's beautiful, and it's exactly right." It was made of wood, with a miniature cutout of the actual house in the center, painted yellow with a red door, a white picket fence in front and *Home Sweet Home* spelled out in painted wooden letters around the outside.

"Oh, you guys. Thank you. I love it." She hugged them both at the same time. "Everything really is perfect now." She had left the wreath on the door at the condo, deciding this house deserved something a little more special. And now it had it.

Sam took the wreath from her and hung it on the door, on a hook she must have installed while she was out here nailing down floorboards.

Kristi folded the paper wrapping and took the lens cap off her camera, and Sam joined her on the sidewalk in front of the house. "Picture time. I want to take one of you on the veranda, right there by the front door, next to the wreath."

"I'm a mess!" Claire said. She was wearing old jeans and a baggy sweatshirt and hadn't combed her hair in hours.

"You're not, you look gorgeous, and this is not a portrait. This is one of those special moments that needs to be recorded."

Knowing Kristi was right, that this was a photograph

she would cherish forever, she went along with them. And then she joined her friends on the sidewalk, gazed back at the house with the newly adorned red door and started to cry all over again.

"All these tears," Sam said, linking arms with her. "You must be pregnant."

Kristi took her other arm. "Let's find out."

They went inside and led her down the hall to the bathroom.

"In you go," Sam said. "We'll be right outside the door."

Kristi gave her a gentle shove through the doorway. "I put the box on the counter."

Sam tapped her wrist. "Let us know as soon as you've, you know, done your thing, and I'll set my stopwatch."

"This might not work," Claire said, feeling she needed to warn them, and caution herself. "It says it's best to do it first thing in the morning."

"Enough with the excuses already." Sam laughed. "You're killing me here."

"If it's negative, we'll come back in the morning and do another one," Kristi said, pulling the door closed.

Feeling light-headed and a little giddy, Claire opened the package. She had already read the instructions at least a dozen times, so she "did her thing" and opened the door.

Sam set her watch.

"The instructions say it takes—"

"Oh, I know how long it takes. Did one of these myself a couple of months ago."

Kristi took the stick from Claire and held it behind her back. "Was AJ in on it, too?"

"Of course. We didn't get to do any of these things together when I was expecting Will. This time he doesn't want to miss a thing."

Not Luke, Claire thought. He hadn't taken their relationship seriously in the first place, and he didn't want kids at all. Would there be a time when he regretted not being part of this baby's beginning, if there was a baby? She would always regret that he wasn't here.

Kristi sighed. "I still think you and AJ, reconnecting after all that time, finding out he's the one who adopted Will…it's like a modern-day fairy tale."

Sam rolled her eyes. "Or a soap opera."

"No way. When have you ever seen a happily-ever-after in one of the soaps? Yours is definitely a fairy tale."

Sam's stopwatch beeped.

"Ready?" Kristi asked.

More than ready. "I've been ready forever."

Sam took one hand and squeezed.

Please, please, please…

Kristi took her other hand, pulled the stick around so she could read it. Her eyes filled with tears. "Girl, you're having a baby."

One of them screamed, or maybe all of them did, and then Claire found herself in the most exuberant group hug ever. Together they laughed and cried and jumped up and down.

Sam gushed about how much fun they would have shopping for baby clothes, planning their nurseries, comparing baby bumps.

Kristi insisted that, even though she wasn't pregnant…yet…she be included, and especially that she be consulted on designing their nurseries. "This is going to be so much fun!"

Finally they made their way to the kitchen, and Claire realized she was starving. "I really need to have something to eat, and I did promise you pizza."

"Pizza? To celebrate this kind of news? No way," Sam said. "We need to go out and do this up right."

"I agree," Kristi said, ponytail bobbing. "Someplace fancy because we have two babies to celebrate."

Claire couldn't say why exactly but she was reluctant to go out. Maybe it was the newness of her new home, or maybe it was the baby news. One she wasn't ready to leave, and the other she wasn't ready to share with the world.

"Look at us," she said. "Grungy work clothes, not to mention my hair's a mess and I'm not wearing any makeup." She hadn't put any on that morning because she had suspected it would be an emotional day, filled with happy tears, and she had been right.

"True," Kristi said, looking down at her cropped yoga pants and bright yellow sneakers. "And it would take forever for me and Sam to go home, shower and change, and get back here."

"You're right. Pizza it is, but we need to plan a special night out, sometime this week."

Relieved that her friends weren't disappointed, Claire hunted down her phone and did a search for pizza places in the neighborhood.

"They'll be here in twenty minutes." She set her phone down and gripped the edge of the kitchen counter, suddenly feeling faint.

"Whoa, you're looking a little shaky." Sam grabbed

her shoulders and held on. "How much have you had to eat today?"

"Not much, I'm afraid."

Kristi slipped an arm around her waist. "Come on. We'll go sit in the living room, get you comfy and wait for the pizza. And no more dieting," she added. "You're eating for two now."

Dieting had been the last thing on her mind today. She usually thought about food way more often than she should, but today she'd been too busy, too excited. And now she was even more light-headed than she'd felt in the bathroom, and something in her stomach was doing cartwheels.

Sam turned on the gas fireplace and Kristi got her settled in the armchair next to it. Aside from the little break they'd taken earlier, she hadn't sat down all day. Kristi was right. She really would have to take better care of herself.

Her friends brought in plates, napkins and bottled water from the kitchen, and after the pizzas arrived they flipped open the boxes and dug in. Silence reigned for several minutes and then, somewhat satisfied after the first few bites, they chatted and laughed and shared pregnancy and baby stories. Claire soaked up the warmth of her new living room with its beautiful bay window and brick fireplace with a wide mantel. Then she turned her attention to her two best friends, laughed at their baby stories and decided she had to be the luckiest woman in world. She might not have the man she loved, but she had a lot…a lot more than most…and she was surrounded by people she loved and who loved her.

"Either I was really, really hungry or that was the

best pizza I've ever tasted." Sam crumpled her napkin into a ball and tossed it into an empty box.

"I think it was both." Kristi flopped back on the sofa and patted her stomach. "I'm stuffed now, though. And we should probably get going and let you get some rest. But before we go, we have one more present for you."

"Another one?" After the wreath they'd given her, she couldn't imagine a single thing she needed.

"This one's not for the house, though. It's for you." Kristi pulled a gift bag out of the enormous tote bag she always carried around with her. "We didn't give it to you sooner because this is for you and the baby."

Inside the bag were two books, one filled with baby names, another that claimed to contain everything a woman needed to know about pregnancy. Once again Claire's eyes filled with tears, and she decided this had to be hormonal because she'd been weepier today than she'd been in years. She got to her feet and there was more hugging and even more tears as she thanked them. Then they cleared away the pizza boxes and she walked with them to the door.

After Sam and Kristi left, she locked the front door. It was silly to still be worried about Donald. He hadn't come back to the condo, at least not as far as she knew, and since she'd changed the locks, he couldn't get in anyway. He might keep calling but he wouldn't come here. Would he? No. To her knowledge, he didn't know where she'd moved. Luke had been worried about him, but then his motives weren't so pure, either.

Just to reassure herself, she went through the kitchen and made sure the back door was locked, too. Then she returned to the living room and settled back into the armchair by the fireplace and swung her feet onto the ottoman. Chloe, who'd been hiding under the bed since they'd arrived in the morning, stalked into the room and gave a cautious look around. Apparently now that the house was quiet, she was feeling braver, or at least less freaked out by all the changes.

Claire patted her lap and the cat jumped up to join her. "Good girl," she said, enjoying the company.

For a few moments she simply gazed at the fire. As happy as she was, today held a bittersweetness that wouldn't to go away anytime soon. Luke had never been hers to lose, but not having him in her life left a hole that was never likely to be filled. Still, there was much to be grateful for, she thought, as once again she took in her new surroundings. She had this cozy new home, she had friends who would always be here for her and best of all she was having a baby.

"Don't get too set in your ways too soon," she whispered to the cat. "The changes haven't stopped yet."

On the side table next to her chair, her phone vibrated. She picked it up and read the message.

Home sweet home?

Yes, Luke. Home sweet home.

Luke hit the send button on his phone, tossed it onto a pile of newspapers on the coffee table and picked up the TV remote. No sense waiting for Claire to reply. He knew she wouldn't.

Was it a mistake to let her know that he knew she had moved today? He hoped not. Besides, her secretary would have told her about their conversation, he was sure of that. He'd like to know what she thought of the messages he'd been sending every day. Did she read them? He was pretty sure she did. He was kind of disappointed she didn't reply, but on the bright side she hadn't told him to get lost.

He surfed through a dozen channels while he debated whether to stay in or go out. Better stay home. If he went out this late, he would either drive past Claire's new place or he would drive by a liquor store, and he had no business doing either. Staying sober these past couple of weeks had been harder than any other time in the past two years.

At least work had kept him busy. Phong remained in custody, bail denied. The team had wrapped up the interview with Phong's girls, mostly with the help of translators, and written up their statements. Then there was all the forensic work on the apartment itself, which was still a crime scene, and the inventory of all the drugs and cash that had been confiscated. Most of the reports should be wrapped in the coming week, and then he'd have a little more free time.

He and the team had worked toward this bust for months and he hated that he wasn't more stoked about the outcome, and he only had himself to blame. He couldn't seem to move past this screwup with Claire, and he didn't know why. He should probably stop communicating with her. He sent a message at the same time every evening, when he knew she was winding down after a long, busy day, likely getting ready to go to bed. If she said she didn't miss him, he'd believe her. Their rhythms had been in perfect sync, though, and if she said she didn't miss the intimacy, she'd be lying. Until he found a way to pick up where they left off, he figured that reminding her of those shared intimacies right before she went to bed was his best shot at keeping himself on her radar.

He got up off the couch, laughing at Rex, who stretched his hind legs over the spot he'd just vacated. After one last futile check for messages, he headed for the bedroom.

"'Night, Rex. Maybe we'll hear from her tomorrow."

The dog's one-eyed examination suggested he didn't believe it any more than Luke did. It really was time to come up with a better plan.

Three days after she'd moved into her new house, Claire was stuck in traffic on her way home from the office. The route she'd tried yesterday had been slow. Today she was at a standstill. She had plenty of time, though, and this gave her a chance to think about what to wear tonight because, true to their word, Sam and Kristi made a reservation at one of their favorite downtown restaurants.

"We're going totally glam," Kristi had insisted. "While you and Sam can still fit into your glamorous clothes."

Claire smiled at that, trying to think of the last time she'd seen Sam in anything other than jeans and a work shirt. Probably not since her wedding, which had been a small, intimate affair with only family and a handful of friends. Sam had worn a sleeveless, cream-colored satin shift, knee-length, with matching pumps and the stunning ruby pendant earrings that had been AJ's wedding gift to his beautiful bride. It turned out that Sam, understated and elegant that day, had been hiding a knockout figure under those work duds of hers, and the groom hadn't been able to take his eyes off her.

Claire accelerated slowly as traffic started to move again.

Of the three of them, Kristi was, without question, the girliest. Knowing her, she'd probably sat down at her sewing machine last night and whipped up something brand-new, one-of-a-kind and totally eye-popping.

Claire still had no idea what she would wear tonight. She had several basic black dresses in her wardrobe and each of them had been a very safe choice. Black was classic, it worked for any occasion, and it was slimming. In theory, at least. Ever since that week with Luke, she'd been wishing she had something sexier in her closet. She had actually splurged on some new lingerie but that had been the day of the raid on her condominium complex, and she hadn't had a chance to test-drive it.

She would dig it out and wear it tonight. There was no law that said a girl couldn't feel good about herself, even though she was just having dinner with friends. She was still pondering what to wear over the lingerie as she turned onto her street. The sight of two police cruisers parked halfway down the block had her braking and flashing back to a couple of weeks ago when she'd come home to find the condominium complex surrounded by police vehicles.

Déjà vu I can live with, but please don't let this have anything to do with my house. Or, God forbid, Luke.

Her dread increased, though, as she drove slowly down the street. The police cars with their lights flashing were parked right in front of her place and a police officer stood in her front yard, talking on a radio. Several neighbors she hadn't even met yet were clustered across the street.

Great introduction to the neighborhood, she thought

as she pulled up and jumped out of her car. "Is there a problem here?" she asked, walking through the open gate.

"Ma'am." The guy tipped his hat. "Is this your home?"

"Yes, it is. I just moved in on the weekend."

"I'm afraid to tell you that you've had an intruder. One of your neighbors called it in."

Someone was in her house? Her first thought was for Chloe. "My cat—" She started for the front door.

The officer stepped in front of her. "Sorry, ma'am. I have to ask you to wait here until the house is clear. Two officers are inside right now."

"Inside? How?"

"Seems the intruder climbed in through an unsecured window."

An unsecured window? She was pretty sure she hadn't even opened any of the windows, it wasn't warm enough. But had she checked to make sure they were locked? No, she was sure she hadn't. What was she thinking? Someone could have broken in while she was there, sleeping even. To wake up and know someone was in her home…her skin crawled.

A voice crackled from the officer's radio, but Claire couldn't make out what was being said.

"The intruder has been apprehended," he said. "They're bringing him out now. Would you rather wait in your car, ma'am? They'll be taking him down to the station, and then we can go inside with you, make sure everything's as it should be."

It had to be a random break-and-enter, so did she want the intruder to see her? No, not at all, so waiting in the car was probably a good idea.

She had her hand on the door handle when two more

officers appeared from the side of the house, escorting a man…

Was that…

"Donald?" Not thinking clearly and not caring one little bit, she rushed toward them. The officers had Donald by both arms and… Ha! His hands were cuffed behind his back, and for once he actually looked cowed.

"You broke into my house?" Anger and disgust bubbled up inside her. "How do you even know where I live? Have you been following me?"

The officer who'd been standing on the lawn quickly stepped up and took her arm, preventing her from getting any closer. "You know this man?"

"Unfortunately, I do. He's my ex-husband." At least that part was fortunate. "Emphasis on *ex*," she said, watching them secure the loser in the backseat of one of the cruisers. One officer got behind the wheel, the other, a woman, walked toward Claire.

"Alex, can you go with Vern, take this guy downtown and get him processed? I'll stay here and go through the house with the owner."

She extended her hand. Claire, still seething and inexplicably relieved that it was the woman staying behind, accepted the handshake.

"I'm Officer Kate Bradshaw."

"I'm Claire DeAngelo. This is my home, and that—" She waved at the car pulling away. "That scumbag is my ex-husband."

"He told us his name is Donald Robinson."

"That's right. Have you…I don't know…arrested him?"

She didn't answer the question. "He told us he doesn't live here. That would make this break-and-enter."

Break-and-enter. The exact words Luke had used that night when Donald came to the condo. The man she had once been married to, thought she had been in love with, had become a stranger. And a criminal.

"I hope you lock him up and throw away the key."

A hint of a smile twitched on Officer Bradshaw's lips. "Is it okay if I go back inside with you so we can go through the place together? He wasn't in there for long, but I'd like you to make sure everything is where it should be, that nothing's missing. And I'll need to get a little more information from you."

"Of course. Come in."

Kate Bradshaw followed her up the steps and waited while she unlocked the front door.

"Nice place," the woman said after she followed Claire inside. "Have you lived here long?"

That was an odd question. "No. Just a few days, actually."

"So it's your place. Mr. Robinson has never lived here with you?"

"No." The second question made the first one sound a little more appropriate. "He has never lived here, and he's not welcome here."

Kate Bradshaw jotted notes. She was maybe five-foot-five, slender but solid-looking, and very, very pretty. Claire wondered if she had pulled her gun on Donald before she'd handcuffed him. It would serve him right. Maybe this time he'd learn his lesson.

"Do you know if Mr. Robinson has ever had any prior criminal charges or convictions?"

"He never mentioned anything like that."

"And where did you live before you moved here?"

Another odd question. Claire gave her the address and watched her write it down.

"How long have you and Mr. Robinson lived apart?"

"Almost a year."

"I see." She flipped her notebook shut. "Let's take a look around. You can let me know me know if you notice anything's missing. And we'll check your windows, make sure they're locked."

"The other officer said that's how he got in—"

"That's right. A bedroom window at the back of the house, the room that's empty."

The baby's room. Claire thought she might throw up. They spent nearly half an hour going through the house, made sure the windows were locked and as far as Claire could see, nothing was missing. But Donald was only after one thing, the Beatrix Potter book, and it was still locked in the safe at her office.

"I can tell you why he broke in. His grandmother gave me an extremely rare edition of an old book. It turns out that it's quite valuable and now that we're divorced, he wants it back." That had to be it. How hard up for money was he? He had tracked her down, broken into her house to look for the book and what…? Was he going to steal it from her? For Donald to do something this stupid, he had to be in serious, *deeply* serious financial trouble.

"I see." Kate Bradshaw flipped open her notebook, made some more notes. "And you can prove the book belongs to you?"

"Yes, I still have the gift card that came with the book. My lawyer has seen it and she's confident that if it ever became a legal issue—" and how ironic that it had "—the card proves that it belongs to me."

"I see. So this book has already been an issue?"

"Yes, and it was settled, or at least I thought it had been."

"And there's nothing else he might have been looking for? Jewelry? Rings?"

Did she mean wedding and engagement rings? Claire had given those back with the rest of his things when she'd sent him packing, but this woman didn't need to know that so Claire simply shook her head.

"I need to get down to the precinct with this information. Here's my card," she said, pulling one from her pocket and handing it to Claire. "Please call me if you think of anything else that might be pertinent, or if you notice anything missing. And I'll keep you up-to-date with any developments concerning Mr. Robinson."

"Thank you, I appreciate that."

"And be sure to keep those doors and windows locked."

"Oh, I will." And first thing in the morning she would arrange to have a security system installed.

Kate hesitated, hand on the doorknob. "I hope you don't mind me asking you one more question."

"Go ahead."

"Do you happen to know Luke Devlin?"

Hmm. The earlier questions that had seemed odd were now a little less…odd. "I do. Why do you ask?"

She shrugged. "No particular reason. Your former address looks familiar. Luke was involved in a situation at that complex a couple of weeks ago. He mentioned that he knew someone who lived there, and I thought your name sounded familiar."

"I take it you know Luke, too?"

"We work together."

I'll bet you do. "Luke and I used to be friends. We went to college together."

She hoped it sounded casual, off the cuff, since anything she said was sure to get back to him. Then it dawned on her that he would hear about the break-in, as well.

Kate opened the door and stepped out. "Things like this can be unnerving. Maybe you have a friend or family member who can come stay with you for a bit?"

"I do." They were probably at the restaurant already. "Thanks."

"Take care."

She shut the door, locked it and went to get her phone. Sam and Kristi would be getting worried, and the last thing Claire felt like doing right now was getting glammed up for a night out on the town.

Chapter 14

Luke watched Norman dump sugar into a cup of coffee, peel open three little creamers and pour those in and stir. They'd been meeting in this little greasy spoon since Norm, nineteen years sober, had taken Luke under his wing at the first AA meeting he'd ever attended. They'd increased these get-togethers since Luke's close call at the liquor store a couple of weeks ago.

Norm sipped his coffee, sighed appreciatively and leaned back in his chair, giving his ample girth some breathing space. "So…how've you been?"

"Good. More or less."

"How 'bout we start with the less?"

Luke had grown up with a father who was absent much of the time and three sheets to wind all of the time. They had never talked, not really, unless he counted his father's negative and often vulgar criticism.

A man who asked straight up how he was feeling, how he was doing and zeroed right in on the problem areas, was an anomaly that had taken some getting used to. His initial instinct was still to gloss over, even cover up what he was really feeling. Norm, God love him, cut through his bullshit like a hot knife through butter.

"I miss her."

"Have you been in touch?"

"Not yet." She ignored his text messages so there'd been no point in calling. Now he realized he shouldn't have left it so long, should have tried to see her in person and get her to hear him out.

"The longer you leave it, the harder it gets." Norm drank some more of his coffee. "Ah, that hits the spot."

Luke gulped his black brew, which, after a week of drinking Claire's coffee, now tasted cheap and bitter. "I shouldn't have left it, but I figured she needed space. She was dealing with her divorce, moving into her new place."

"And now?"

And now he worried it might be too late. "I don't know."

"Does thinking about this make you feel like having a drink?"

Luke stared into his cup. "Yeah." Hell yeah.

"Does being with her make you feel like having a drink?"

Luke looked up, connected with his friend's intense scrutiny. "When I was with her, no. It was the furthest thing from my mind."

"Then I guess you know where you need to be." Norm's deep laugh accompanied that bit of wisdom. "See how easy that was?"

What Norm said made total sense, and sounded a lot easier than it was. Claire's forgiveness would be hard won, if he managed to win it at all. And yes, she was good for him, she always had been. He wouldn't have made it through college without her help. But what did he have to offer her? She was smart, sexy, damn successful in her own right. Any man would be lucky to have her, but she sure as hell didn't need one to look after her.

"You're already overthinking this," Norm said. "Sometimes a man's gotta shut that off and just do what he's gotta do."

"You're a wise man, Norm." Luke drained his cup.

Norm reached for his wallet, but Luke held up a hand, tossed a couple of bills on the table. "My treat. Cheaper than seeing a shrink."

The man's expansive chest heaved with laughter. "You're a good kid, Luke. Don't sell yourself short."

They stood, gave each other a one-armed hug that ended with a pat on the back.

"See you at a meeting soon?" Norm asked.

"You bet." Luke pulled his ringing phone from his jacket pocket. The call was from Kate Bradshaw's cell. "It's work," he said. "I have to take this."

He slid back into the booth, watching Norm leave the coffee shop as he answered. "Hey, Kate. What's up?"

"Remember that guy you asked about a couple weeks ago? Donald Robinson?"

The name alone had the hair up on the back of his neck. "Yeah. What about him?"

"We just booked him for break-and-enter."

"Son of a bitch. What'd he break into?" he asked, although he already knew the answer.

"His ex-wife's place. She's a friend of yours?"

"Claire DeAngelo. Yes, she's a friend." Was a friend. "Is she okay?" If that guy touched her…

"She's fine. She wasn't home at the time, but she pulled up just after we arrested him, probably on her way home from work."

Thank God for that. "How did he get in?"

"Through a bedroom window. One of the neighbors saw him."

"What time?" Luke was on his feet and heading for the door.

"Just before five this afternoon."

In broad daylight? Talk about stupid. Luke's initial assessment of the guy was bang on.

"How's she doing? Did she seem okay?"

"Pretty shaken. I stayed with her for a bit, went through the house, made sure everything was secure. Suggested she might want to call someone to come and stay with her a while."

He got up and left the coffee shop. He knew exactly who she would call. Sam and Kristi. "Did you wait until someone showed up?"

"No. I took her statement and we went through the house to see if anything was missing, then I came back to the precinct. Vern and Alex already had him booked."

"Is he still there?" He crossed the street and climbed into his truck.

"You bet he is."

"How long can you keep him?"

"I'm pretty sure we can stall long enough to keep him overnight."

"Good stuff. I owe you one."

"You already owe me one."

"Okay, I owe you two. Thanks for letting me know about this, Kate. I appreciate it."

"No problem. I had a hunch she was someone special."

She was that, all right. "You'll let me know when Robinson's back on the street?"

"You bet."

He ended the call, shoved the phone into his pocket and revved the engine. Norm was right, he thought as he swerved out of the parking lot. Sometimes a man knew what he had to do, and right now Luke knew he had to go to Claire. He hated to think how rattled she must be, but this might be what it took for him to get his foot in the door. Besides, if he didn't go see her, he'd go down to the precinct to see Donald, and that wouldn't end well for either of them.

It was just after dusk and Claire's lights were on, including the porch light, when Luke pulled up in front of her place. A good sign. He wondered if her friends were here with her, and then he wondered how things might play out for him if they were. Had they already formed a united front against him? Or would Claire be reluctant to call him a "smug son of a bitch" in front of her friends? Time would tell.

He took several minutes to sit and study the house. He'd driven by before so he'd seen it, but he'd mostly been on the lookout for her ex so he hadn't given it a really good look. She'd said buying the condo had been mostly Donald's idea and it hadn't suited her. Too stark, way too pretentious. Some of the furniture had looked like it belonged there, while other pieces, the ones that were hers, had been decidedly out of place. Not here, though. He'd bet she and her things fit this house, snug as a glove.

He got out of the truck, let the door quietly click shut and walked through the gate. He climbed the steps as lightly as he could, not wanting to frighten her if she was alone, and rang the bell before he lost his nerve.

There were voices, which meant she wasn't alone, then footsteps, and the door opened. It was her friend Kristi, dressed to kill in a dark red cocktail dress.

"Um, hi. Is Claire here? I was wondering—"

"Come in." She gave him a light-up-the-room kind of smile, not at all what he expected, and swung the door open. "Claire's right here, in the living room."

He stepped into a small foyer and closed the door. So far, so good.

"Kristi? Who is it?" Claire asked.

He'd even missed the sound of her voice.

"Follow me," she said. "It's Luke."

He entered the living room behind Kristi, vaguely aware that the other friend, Sam, sat curled on the sofa, also wearing some kind of fancy dress, but his real attention was on Claire.

He could tell she'd been sitting in an armchair next to the fire, but she was on her feet by the time he entered the room. She looked ghostly pale, but he supposed that was to be expected.

"What are you doing here?"

"I heard about what happened, wanted to make sure you're okay."

"I'm fine. My friends are here, so you should go."

"Actually," Sam said, getting up from the sofa, "would you look at the time? I need to get home before my son goes to bed."

"Me, too." Kristi already had one arm in her coat. "Jenna will be wanting help with homework, and it's nearly the twins' bedtime, too."

Claire glared daggers at them, clearly not wanting to be left alone with him, while their haste to clear out was an obvious ploy to ensure that's exactly what happened. Interesting. They were her friends, but he recognized allies when he saw them. These two were on his side. Good to know.

"Are you sure you can't stay a little longer?" Claire asked.

Sam winked as she slipped past him on her way to the door. "Sorry. I'll call you in the morning."

"We'll let ourselves out. Lock up behind us?" she asked him.

He followed them out, half expecting one or the other to give him a hint about what he needed to do next, but they couldn't get out the door fast enough. He locked it and went back to the living room.

Claire was back in the armchair, feet tucked up beside her, arms folded. "You shouldn't have come here."

"I was worried about you. I wanted to make sure you're okay," he repeated.

He wanted to pull her into his arms, touch her, taste her, tell her everything would be all right. Instead he sat on the sofa, uninvited but at least she hadn't told him to get out.

"I'm fine."

"Claire, look—"

"No, you look. I'm sure your girlfriend couldn't wait to call and tell you what happened, but she shouldn't have bothered.

His…who? "What are you talking about? I don't have a girlfriend."

The look she gave him suggested she knew otherwise.

What the hell? Did she think…? "Are you talking about Kate?"

"Yes."

"She's not my girlfriend." And now he was really glad he'd never asked her out. That would just be one more thing to explain.

"Then why was she asking weird questions?"

"What kind of weird questions?"

"About me and you, about Donald, about how you used my condo—"

"She said that?" He found it hard to believe Kate would be that loose-lipped.

"Not exactly."

"Then what did she say?"

Claire shrugged and drew her arms around herself even tighter. He hated that the warm, wonderful woman he'd known had shut herself off from him, and hated even more that it was his fault.

"It's not so much what she said as how she said it."

He leaned forward, forearms on his knees. "Kate and I worked together her first year on the force. She's a good cop, and yes, she's easy on the eyes, but I'd just got sober and I knew I shouldn't…so I didn't. Kate and I are just colleagues. And friends, I hope.

"If her questions sounded a little unusual, it's because I asked her to see what she could dig up on Donald. It was right after that first night, when he came into your place and we were…"

The memory of that night stirred something in him,

and it must've had a similar effect on her because she regained a little of her color.

"And she found something?"

He nodded. "Just allegations. No convictions. I couldn't give you specifics, and I wasn't sure how you'd react to my checking up on him. And then you let me stay, and I figured it didn't matter because if he did try something, I'd be there to—"

"Protect me? What about being honest? I hate being lied to, even it's just lying by omission."

"I know. I'm sorry." How many other ways were there to say it?

"I don't care anymore."

He winced at that.

"You hinted that Donald might do something, that's why you wanted to move in, but that was really just one lie to cover up another. You let me think you were interested in me when all you wanted was a place to stake out that other apartment."

He was on his feet, across the room and sitting on the ottoman in front of her chair before she had a chance to react.

"Do you honestly believe that?" He pulled her hands into his. "The time we spent together, that was amazing. But I also had to walk a fine line between keeping you completely out of the picture, for your own protection, and not jeopardizing the investigation."

"So you lied, I get it, but you didn't lie to the people you work with. I heard what that guy said, Luke. That you 'sweet-talked that chick upstairs' into letting you move in." She snatched her hands out of his, crossed her arms and tucked her hands out of sight. "And you laughed. You *laughed* and said I didn't have a clue. I heard you."

He knew exactly what he'd said. In the past several weeks he'd relived the regret more times than he could count.

"Claire, I didn't mean any of it."

"You need to move away from me. Go back and sit over there."

He moved, reluctantly. It hurt, a lot, to know she couldn't stand to be close to him, but he also knew he wouldn't get another chance to change her mind. Hard as it was for him to open up about these things, he had to spill his guts.

"I've done a lot of things I'm not proud of. The drinking, the screwing around. Yes, I had a reputation, and I'd be lying if I said I wasn't proud of it. Some of that was my father's influence, some of it was the booze, but most of it was me being an egotistical jerk. Or a 'smug son of a bitch,' as some have said."

The flicker in her eyes told him she recognized those words as her own.

"Even with Sherri, and I have to tell you, those were some of my darkest days, I never let on to anybody that I had feelings for her."

He still didn't know what those feelings were, but they weren't the same as the ones he felt for Claire now, or even what he'd felt for her back in college. Those old feelings and these new ones weren't the same, either. Good God, why did this have to be so complicated? Way more complicated sober than drunk. So much for having a clear head.

Claire sat across the room, calm and quiet and still

strangely pale, apparently unwilling to throw him a line. So he pressed on.

"I never told Sherri I cared about her. It's never been easy for me to do that, and I always blamed it on the way I was brought up. My father criticized my mother and yelled at me, and for the most part she ignored both of us. I grew up hearing a lot of 'I can't stand you' and 'I hate you,' but none of the other…stuff." Stuff? He still had trouble saying the *L*-word, even in a general way.

"I never once heard anyone in my family say 'I love you' to anybody." There. He'd said it, and it shocked the hell out of him. He had never said it to anyone, and not once, not even when he was a kid, had anyone ever said it to him.

Claire was leaning forward in her chair now, with the makings of tears in her eyes.

"Look, don't get me wrong. I'm not asking for sympathy, it's just the only way I know how to make you understand where I was coming from. I couldn't tell you how I felt about you, so I sure as hell wasn't telling anyone else."

"Are you going to tell me now?" she asked, her voice so quiet he barely heard the question.

"I would, if I knew what it was. I liked you a lot when we studied together. You were smart and funny, you were different from the other girls I knew, in a good way, and to be honest…you kinda scared me."

Her lips had just enough smile to give him hope. "I was a mousy, overweight overachiever. Pretty scary, all right."

He would never understand where those ideas came from but if she'd let him, he would do everything he could to dispel them. "We need to get you a different mirror. You were never any of those things, not on the outside. I thought you were perfect. Too perfect for me, that's for sure."

He tried to ignore the tear that slid down her cheek. He had to because he wasn't finished yet.

"When I saw you a couple of weeks ago, I couldn't believe you agreed to have dinner with me. And then you invited me up and…wow. You didn't scare me, that's for sure."

She laughed and wiped away the tears. "I've never done anything like that, not on a first date. I've always played it safe, and look where that got me. So that night I assumed you wanted something casual and I told myself I was okay with that, so I threw caution to the wind. But when I overheard your conversation, I realized you weren't the only one lying to me. I was lying to myself."

He wanted to go to her and kiss her senseless, but she still looked so vulnerable. Was it too soon? Should he let her make the next move? She answered the question by crossing the room, kneeling in front of him and putting her hands in his.

"I'm so happy you're here, that you were willing to finally share these things with me. Can we start over, maybe take things a little slower?"

"Of course." He kissed her forehead and pushed the "how slow?" question to the back of his mind. He had another chance and this time he wasn't going to blow it.

"Thank you." She kissed him back, lightly on the mouth, and stood up. "Sit, enjoy the fire, I'll make some coffee. I have…um… There's something else we need to talk about."

He let her go, wondering what else she wanted to say but knowing they both needed a few minutes to process everything that had transpired. And it gave him a chance to look around, take in this new place that she had all but fallen in love with before she'd even seen it.

The living room was a good size but still cosy, with a nice fireplace and a bay window where she planned to put a Christmas tree. The wood floors looked to be original but in good shape. He recognized some of the furniture but most appeared to be new. No sign of that hideous black leather sofa. And there were plenty of feminine touches—a vase full of flowers on the mantel, framed photographs of her friends and her family, books neatly stacked on the coffee table.

He absently picked up the one from the top of the pile, thumbed the pages and realized it was filled with names. He flipped it shut. Baby names, according to the title. The book beneath it had a pregnant woman on the cover, her round, bare belly exposed between a short T-shirt and a pair of exercise pants. He set the first book down, picked up the second, read the inscription on the flyleaf.

For Claire and her baby. Congratulations! Love, Sam & Kristi.

Her *baby*? She didn't look pregnant, unless she wasn't far enough along to look pregnant, which could mean several things and he didn't like any of them.

His chest imploded, squeezing the air out of his lungs.

Was it his? The thought scared the hell out of him.

Someone else's? That idea sickened him.

Either way, he'd just sat here spilling guts while she neglected to tell him she was having a baby. That took "lying by omission" to a whole new level.

He was on his feet in the middle of the room, the

book still open in his hands, when she came in with the coffee. One look at her and he had his answer.

She set the cups on the table, hands shaking, the contents sloshing.

"You're having a baby?"

There was no color in her face now, and he didn't care. The anger and betrayal were as real as that night in the E.R. with Sherri, but this time they cut deeper, and the wound was salted with fear. By the time he found out about Sherri's pregnancy, there was no longer a baby. This was different. "Is it mine?"

Her nod was barely perceptible.

He closed the book with a snap. "You trick me into getting you knocked up, then you accuse me of lying?"

"Luke—"

"How the hell did this happen? I asked, remember? And you told me you were on the Pill."

"I was. It wasn't until the next morning that I realized I'd missed quite a few—"

"How many?"

"Almost a week."

"God, Claire. A week? And you kept having sex with me?" Some might call that irresponsible but for him? Irresponsible wasn't even close.

"No. I saw my doctor that day and she recommended using a diaphragm until the end of my cycle. So it was just that one night…"

"Oh, well, I feel so much better. Especially knowing you didn't trust me enough to say something at the time."

"I was afraid to. You had already told me about Sherri and how much you resented what she did, and you made a point of telling me you didn't ever want a family."

His gaze intensified. "So if I hadn't come here tonight, hadn't stumbled on this myself, when were you going to tell me? At least I assume you plan to go through with it since you're already picking out names."

"I…I'm not sure. I just found out a couple of days ago and I knew you'd freak out, but then you came here tonight and we talked and—"

He swung away and stared into the fire, unable to look at her. "And you thought a goddamned cup of coffee would make this easier to swallow?"

She didn't respond, and when he faced her again, she was chalk-white and shaking.

What should he do now? There were no good options that he could see, so the only thing he could do was get the hell out of here before he said or did something he would regret. "I can't do this, not tonight. I'll call you tomorrow."

He didn't slam the door on his way out, but the wreath rattled anyway.

Home sweet home.

Right now that seemed like the biggest lie of all.

Chapter 15

Stunned, Claire flipped the dead bolt shut and leaned against the front door. What was she going to do now?

"I think I'm going to be sick." She covered her mouth with her hand, turned and ran to the bathroom.

Several minutes later, still on her knees, she flushed the toilet and hauled herself to her feet. After she rinsed her mouth and dragged a cool, damp cloth across her face, she looked at herself in the mirror.

"So this is what death warmed over looks like."

And so much for morning sickness living up to its name. She'd felt a little off all day, but this was the first time she had actually thrown up and it was...she checked her watch...almost eight-thirty in the evening. She'd read in the book that morning sickness could happen anytime of day and that some women didn't have it at all, but she had assumed that if she was going to feel this way, it would start in the morning. The past few hours had felt just like a roller coaster, though. Those made her sick, too.

Now Luke knew the truth, had stormed out feeling angry and betrayed, and who could blame him? All because he'd found that stupid book before she'd had a chance to tell him herself. They had just smoothed things out, and now they were worse than ever. And she was sick, and tired, and looked like hell.

She went into the kitchen, put some soda crackers on a plate, poured herself a glass of water and carried them into the living room. Trying to ignore the light-headedness, she snuggled into an afghan and hoped the warmth of the fire would stop the shivering. She picked up a cracker and nibbled on the corner, then washed it down with a sip of water.

Luke said he would call tomorrow. Would he be calmer by then, or even angrier? Either way, they didn't have much more to say to one another. No matter how many times she apologized and tried to explain, he would never forgive or trust her again. And his not wanting a child didn't make her any less pregnant. When he was ready to talk, all she could do was hear him out. She at least owed him that, and then she would assure him she didn't expect anything from him.

Keeping her breathing shallow and even, she swallowed hard against the taste of bile in the back of her throat, bit off another piece of cracker and had another sip of water.

And she really needed to take better care of herself. No more skipping meals, although missing dinner tonight was hardly her fault. She could blame Donald for that, and Luke.

Chloe strolled into the room, looped around the coffee table and paused in front of Claire's chair before leaping onto her lap.

"I'm having a lousy night. Did you know I needed some attention?"

The cat arched her back, turned herself in two full circles, then did one complete revolution in the other direction before tucking her paws beneath herself and doing a side-wrap with her tail.

Claire laughed. "I know, I know. You're the one who's being needy." And that was okay. She didn't need anyone to take of her.

She yawned. She'd always believed everyone who said pregnant women had to eat for two, but who knew she'd also be sleeping for two?

"Come on, girl. Time for bed."

Luke sat in his truck for what felt like a long time, but when he pulled out his phone to make a call, it was only half past eight. He called Kate Bradshaw for an update.

"Luke. How's your friend?"

"She's fine." It was a rhetorical question and that was the only right answer. "Just checking on where we're at with Robinson."

"We're keeping him overnight. I was going to call but I figured you might, you know, be kind of busy."

Ha. She didn't know the half of it. "Good to know he's off the street. Call me when he's released tomorrow?"

"Will do," Kate said. "Have a nice night." Clearly she thought he was spending the night with Claire, and it was easier to let her believe that than set her straight.

After he disconnected, he poured himself a cup of

coffee from the thermos on the seat next to him. After Kate had called to tell him about Donald's arrest, he had stopped at his place to feed Rex, and while he was there he made the coffee and grabbed a warm jacket. If Donald had been released tonight, Luke would have spent the night here to keep an eye on Claire's place.

That wasn't necessary, and now his head was full of questions with no answers, problems with no solutions and accusations with nothing to refute them. He only knew one way handle situations like this and he didn't dare let himself go there. If he went back to that liquor store tonight, there'd be no way he could walk away.

One day at time just didn't cut it right now.

He wasn't a religious man but there were times when only a prayer would do. This was one of those times.

God, grant me the serenity to accept the things I cannot change, the courage to change the things I can and the wisdom to know the difference.

He rested his forehead on the steering wheel and recited the words again, and then he picked up his phone and called Norman.

Claire set her water and the plate of soda crackers on the nightstand and crawled into bed with her phone and the pregnancy book, intending to read everything she could about morning sickness. Before that she checked her voice mail. There was only one message, from Officer Bradshaw, letting her know Donald was being "detained" overnight. She liked the picture her imagination created of him in a jail cell. Served him right.

She also had two text messages, one from Sam and the other from Kristi.

Did you and Luke work things out? Is he spending the night? xoxo

That was from Kristi.
Sam's message was a little more graphic.

OMG, that man is hot! Hope he's heating things up for you. S.

She replied to both with the same message.

Things did not go well with Luke. TTY tomorrow. C.

She set the phone on the nightstand, picked up a cracker and opened the book to the table of contents.

Her phone rang.

"What happened?" Sam asked.

"He explained everything about the undercover operation, and I believed him."

"But you wouldn't forgive him?" Kristi asked. Apparently Sam had linked them with a conference call. "Why not?"

"Oh, I did. We talked and agreed to take things a little slower this time. And everything was okay until I went into the kitchen to make coffee and came back to find him looking at the pregnancy books you gave me."

"Oh, no!" Sam said.

"Where were they?" Kristi asked.

"On the coffee table."

"You should have told them they were mine," Sam said.

"There was no point. He'd already read the inscription. I knew he'd be angry, but I never imagined this."

"Sweetie, you had to expect he'd be shocked," Kristi said. "Even angry."

"Of course, but he accused me of deceiving him, and then he accused me of lying to him, and then he stormed out. Oh, and then I threw up."

"Oh, dear. I can relate to that," Sam commiserated. "How are you feeling now?"

"I'm okay. Exhausted, though. I'm already in bed."

"What do you think will happen with Luke?" Kristi asked.

Claire wished she knew. "Honestly, I'm not sure. Before he slammed out of here, he said he couldn't talk to me tonight. He said he'd call me tomorrow, but I'm not sure if there's much point. He doesn't want a family, so there's no possible way this is going to work."

"He said that?" Sam asked. "He definitely doesn't want kids?"

"Several times, and he isn't going to change his mind."

"I wouldn't be so sure," Kristi said. "The guy's crazy about you. You should have seen him when I answered the door tonight. He was so worried. If I hadn't opened it when I did, he might have broken it down."

Claire rolled her eyes at the ceiling. "Just what I need. Two break-ins in one day."

Sam laughed.

"Okay, you know I was exaggerating. What I'm saying is that I've seen guys in love, and this guy has it bad."

"Kristi's right. Give him time, give him space if he needs it, but don't slam the door just yet."

Luke had already slammed it, literally and figuratively. "I'll see what he has to say tomorrow, but I'm not counting on him having a change of heart.

"What about Donald?" Kristi asked. "Would you like us to come back and spend the night?"

"Just say the word," Sam added.

"He won't be released until tomorrow." She still had trouble wrapping her head around that.

"That's a relief," Kristi said.

Sam simply let out a whoop.

"I'll be fine here on my own. I love you guys."

"Will you call us tomorrow after you've talked to Luke?"

"I will, I promise."

Luke spent the first half of the night with a pot of coffee and the TV remote, and the second half lying in bed in the dark waiting to nod off. Sleep eluded him, and by dawn he knew this would be a lousy day. Maybe the lousiest on record.

That was confirmed when he threw on a load of laundry, a hose or a seal or something went on the washing machine, and water leaked all over the utility room floor. He was mopping up the mess when Kate called to let him know Stalker Don was out on bail. And then Norm called, insisting they meet for coffee.

Luke didn't want to see anyone, he really didn't want any more coffee and he sure as hell didn't need a lecture on the dangers of having a drink or having sex without a condom.

Norm wasn't taking no for answer and, as he always did, he managed to say exactly what Luke needed to hear. Luke had started out not wanting to hear any of those things, but Norm didn't give a rat's ass about that. And that, Luke thought wryly, was an exact quote.

He'd taken Norm's advice and called Claire, just as he'd said he would. She answered, and he didn't know whether to be surprised by that or not. He suggested they get together for coffee…what the hell, it wasn't like he was ever going to sleep again…and she had agreed.

He knew better than to suggest her place, this would be better done in public, someplace where they, well, mostly he would be on his best behavior. No chance of theatrics like the raised voice and door slamming he'd been guilty of last night. Claire had agreed to meet him and suggested a place near her office in Pioneer Square.

He arrived half an hour early and was nursing his second cup of coffee when, through the window, he caught a glimpse of her crossing the street. She would always be the one woman who would turn his head, not only because she was beautiful, but also because she had always been able to cut through his crap. Maybe if he'd paid more attention, he'd have figured out how to cut through hers.

Claire had tried on half a dozen outfits before she left for the office that morning, but as she went to meet Luke, she was having serious second thoughts. Instead of one of the suits she usually wore, she'd decided on dark jeans and a black turtleneck sweater under the cobalt-blue jacket she'd worn the first time they'd gone out. Marlie had been surprised to see her dressed so casually, but she had assured her that she didn't have any appointments that day. Technically true, since she had already rescheduled them.

Now, as she crossed the street to the coffee shop

where she, Sam and Kristi met for their weekly business meetings, she had second thoughts. She wanted to show Luke that she could be as cool and casual as he was, but she was more herself in a suit. More polished and professional, and a lot more confident. She should have gone with that.

Too late now, she thought as she opened the door and went in to face the music. She spotted him right away, and her heart did that skip-a-beat thing it always did. He was wearing his leather jacket, his helmet on the seat next to him. Now she really wished she'd worn a suit. Not that it would make her heart behave, but it might disguise its misbehavior.

He saw her, too, and his detached gaze suggested that although he could see her, he would rather not look at her.

She stopped at the counter and ordered a decaf latte, then reluctantly crossed the narrow space and joined Luke at the back corner table he'd chosen. He leaned back in his chair, watching her like she was a petty criminal. He had a lot of nerve.

She set her briefcase on the floor next to her chair, still not sure why she'd bothered to bring it but willing to acknowledge it was part of that professional facade she wished she'd gone with. Right now the only thing that gave her the upper hand was waiting for him to be the first to speak.

"How are you?"

"I'm fine."

"Did you hear Donald's out?"

"I got a call this morning." She should have known that Kate Bradshaw would call Luke, too.

"You should think about getting a security alarm."

One step ahead of you. "I have a company coming this afternoon to give me an estimate."

"That's good."

The barista set her latte on the table in front of her, table service being one of the perks of being a regular customer.

"Thank you," she said, not missing the young woman's appreciative assessment of Luke.

If he noticed, he didn't let on.

She sipped her drink and a few seconds of silence ticked into ten, twenty…

"I'm sorry about the way I behaved last night," he said, running a hand through his hair. He looked tired, she noticed, as though he hadn't slept well.

"I'm sorry you had to find out the way you did. Not that there was a good way to tell you."

"What happens now?" His question was so direct, it caught her by surprise.

"Nothing has to happen. I know how you feel about kids."

"So you're planning to go through with this?"

Go through with *this?* He couldn't even bring himself to say the words. *Pregnancy. Baby.*

She could be as direct as he was. "I am."

He leaned forward, forearms on the table, coffee cup cradled in both hands. "Last night, after two weeks of ignoring my messages, you let me back in your life. You said you wanted to take things slow. Since you knew you were pregnant and I didn't want kids, exactly how did you think that was going to work?"

How this worked was really up to him. "I'm not sure, Luke. Last night I was going to tell you myself, and I was prepared for you to be upset—"

"Upset? Jeez, Claire…" He seemed to catch himself, lowered his voice. "I get 'upset' when I get a flat tire or the damn washing machine breaks down. Getting a woman pregnant the first time I sleep with her, that freaks me out."

"You didn't 'get me' pregnant. That was my fault."

"It's mine, that makes me responsible."

It *is a baby,* she wanted to remind him.

"You should have said something as soon as you knew. I mean, there were options."

Now she was angry. "I'm very well aware of the options. I've already chosen one."

His expression finally registered the reality of the situation. "You really plan to go through with this?"

"I told you I do." She couldn't tell him this might be her only chance to have a baby. That had nothing to do with him, and he would never understand anyway. "That's my decision, which makes it my responsibility."

He looked bewildered. "Do you want to get married?"

"Is that a proposal?"

He shoved his cup away. "It's a question."

A dumb question, she thought. "And the answer is no. I don't."

He slowly reached into his pocket, pulled out a folded piece of paper and slid it across the table to her. "This is the best I can do right now."

She didn't have to unfold it to know it was a check, but she had to ask. "What's this for?"

He shrugged. "Whatever you and…whatever the two of you need."

He was offering money? This was his solution? Curiosity being what it was, she picked it up, opened it and was pretty sure she gasped. It was payable to her, in the amount of ten thousand dollars.

So this was it? Throw money at the problem and make it go away?

She refolded it, set it on the table and made a show of slowly sliding it back.

He watched with narrowed eyes. "What are you doing?"

"I'm not trying to land a husband, and I'm not looking for money."

"What do you want?"

"Nothing." Just as well, since he couldn't give it to her anyway.

"There has to be something."

Since she had nothing to lose, she told him. "I'll tell you what I want. It's all or nothing, Luke. With kids, there's no halfway. You're either in or you're out."

"But—"

She cut him off. "I have a home, money, a stable career. I'm perfectly capable of raising a child on my own and providing everything she or he needs."

The only thing worse than no father was a reluctant one. This was his loss, even though she couldn't bring herself to say it. She didn't want to hurt him, she just wanted him to go away and let her get on with her life. And she needed to take the first step.

She reached for her briefcase and stood up, actually grateful that Luke was at a loss for words.

"If you ever change your mind, you know where to find me." And she walked away from the one thing she wanted even more than a baby—the man who'd given her one.

Chapter 16

Luke spent the next four days alternating between anger, disappointment and relief. The only constants were the struggle to stay sober and the feeling that he was a bigger jerk now than he'd ever been. After Claire told him it was "all or nothing"—and since she didn't want financial support or marriage, he didn't have a clue what that meant—he had talked with Jason Wong and taken a leave of absence. One thing was certain. In his current state of mind, he was no good to anybody.

This morning, like every morning since Claire's ultimatum, he joined Norman at the coffee shop.

"How's it going?" Norm asked.

"Good."

"I didn't ask how you are, I asked how it's going."

Luke knew what the question was. "Somewhere on the road between step four and step ten, with a stopover at eight." Except the moral inventory wasn't so fearless, and while he figured he was more than willing to make amends, he still hadn't figured out what he'd done wrong.

"It is a journey, all right."

Luke rolled his eyes. "That's the best you've got?"

Norm laughed. "How are you sleeping these days?"

"Better."

"That's good. What are you doing to keep yourself busy now that you're not working?"

He shrugged, feeling a little a kid who'd forgotten to take out the trash. "Watching TV, taking Rex for a run. I fixed the washing machine."

"Driven past Claire's place?"

It was the first time Norm had mentioned her since Luke told him about the baby. Why would he ask if Luke was keeping an eye on her? And how the hell did he know he was? Norm was smiling, like he knew everything.

"A time or two." Every day. To make sure Donald wasn't hanging around.

"Do you love her?" Norm asked.

"I don't know. I'm pretty sure I've never been in love so it's hard to tell."

"Let's forget about the baby for a minute. Do you think about her very often?"

"All the time."

"Is that right? So when you're doing all this thinking, is it all about the sex?"

"Jeez, Norm. What kind of question is that?"

"Just answer it, and be honest."

Honestly, he did think about the sex, it was amazing, but more often she occupied his thoughts in other ways. "It's more about the things she's said, or how she takes her glasses off and cleans them on her sleeve, or watching her in the kitchen. She's a really good cook, did I mention that? Best lasagna I've ever had."

"Huh." Norm had sat quiet for a few moments, drinking his coffee and no doubt pondering his next question. "You think about her all the time and it's hardly ever about the sex. But you've had a lot of women, right?"

Luke had glanced around the coffee shop, hoping no one overheard.

"Just answer the question," Norm said.

"I've had my share."

"And you've felt this way about how many of them? All of them? Some of them? Say, half of them, maybe."

Luke didn't know where Norm was going with this, but there was only one honest answer.

"None of them."

"Huh. So she occupies every waking thought. Maybe even a dream or two, I'll bet, since you're sleeping okay. It's not just about the sex, and she's different from any other woman you've ever met. One of a kind." Norm paused to polish off his coffee. "Did you see that lightbulb come on?" he asked.

"Yeah, I did." Bright as a beacon.

"That, my friend, is love. Now the only question is, what are you going to do about it? Let it go because you're afraid you can't live up to your responsibilities? Or take a shot at being the luckiest man alive?"

"I always liked the sound of lucky."

"Then do it. You're going to make a great dad."

Luke still wasn't sure about that. He was just getting used to the idea of being in love. "Why didn't you ask me all these questions a couple of days ago?"

"Figured you weren't ready to answer them."

"What's different today?"

"Figured you were ready."

Damn. Norm was right, he was ready. He didn't know how long it would have taken to reach that conclusion on his own but now that he had, he needed to find a way to convince Claire.

"Any suggestions where to go from here?"

Norm pulled out his wallet and paid for their coffees. "Sorry, kid. You're on your own."

"I was afraid you were going to say that." But even as he said it, the plan started to form. Now he needed to make it work.

It took him nearly a week to work out the details, but the plan had finally come together. He didn't know if it was a good plan or if it was even going to work, but it was the only thing he could come up with. Now it was time to put it to the test.

"Come on, Rex. We're going for a ride."

He put the dog in the front seat with him, tossed the package on the dashboard and set off for Claire's. He hadn't seen her since the morning they'd met for coffee, but he'd finally figured out what she meant by in or out, all or nothing.

Although he was still on leave, he'd been relieved to hear from Kate Bradshaw that Claire's problems with Donald had been resolved. In exchange for not being charged for breaking into her home, he had signed an affidavit forfeiting any claim to Claire's book. There was also a restraining order in effect, but because the condo was sold and the book was no longer an issue, they didn't expect any more trouble. When questioned about his motive for wanting to steal the book, it had come out that he and his new girlfriend had been living the high life, and he was deep in debt to a couple of loan sharks. That was his problem, not Claire's.

Luke knew she'd be home because he had talked to her friends, Sam and Kristi, and they had helped him set this up. Claire thought they were dropping by to help with some decorating project. Instead she was getting him.

She was on the veranda sanding an old piece of furniture, and she didn't notice him pull up. Chloe sat in the bay window inside, not missing a trick.

"Rex, stay," he said as he got out. He grabbed the package off the dashboard, though, and tucked it under his arm.

She looked up from her work and saw him when he got to the gate.

He had hoped to see her smile, but she only looked surprised.

"I really must have been concentrating on what I was doing. I didn't hear your motorcycle pull up."

"I'm not on the bike."

"You have your truck?" She scanned the street for it.

"No. I sold it."

"Is that—?" She pointed to the shiny new SUV with Rex sitting in the front seat. "Is that yours?"

"It is." He opened the gate and walked toward her.

"You bought an SUV?" She set the sanding block on the top of an old dresser and came down the steps to meet him.

"Traded the truck and the Ducati for it."

"You sold your bike? Luke, you love that bike."

"As it turns out, there's something I love more."

"Is there? And what would that be?"

"You."

Her mouth softened into a smile and it was all he could do to resist kissing her.

"What made you change your mind?" she asked.

"You have to remember I'm not as smart as you are, so it took me a while to figure out what it means to be all-in."

"And now you know?"

"I do. Actually, I think I was close before. I really would have married you, supported you, if you'd let me. But I was missing a step."

"Which step was that?"

"Saying I love you."

"Is that what you're saying now?" Trust Claire to not make this easy.

"I'm saying I love you, Claire DeAngelo." There. He said it, and he meant it, and he would never forget the way she was looking at him right now.

She took his hand and laced her fingers with his. "I love you, too, Luke Devlin. I think I always have."

Yep, Norm was right. He was the luckiest man alive.

"There's more," he said.

"More than loving me and wanting to… I'm sorry, why exactly did you buy an SUV?"

"Because I'm all-in, Claire. I want to marry you and have a baby with you, and this has the highest safety rating of any vehicle on the market right now."

She laughed. "Usually when a guy asks a girl to marry him, he buys her a ring, not the safest SUV on the market."

"Oh, I'm not *asking* you to marry me right now. I just said I *want* to marry you. Besides, I thought we were taking things slow."

"Fair enough."

"I have something else for you, though."

"A pre-engagement present?"

"Sure." He gave her the package and watched her while she examined it.

"It's a book."

"I know what it is. Are you going to open it?"

"Of course I am. I'm just savoring the moment." She carefully unstuck the tape and removed the wrapping without a single rip.

"The Tale of Benjamin Bunny." The way she ran her hand over the cover was practically reverent. "And it's a first edition. Luke, where did you find it?"

"Online. I had it shipped by courier." He'd been worried it wouldn't arrive for him to give it to her today, but his luck had held. "When I helped you pack your books, you said you'd like to have a first edition someday."

"I can't believe you remembered. Thank you." She put her arms around his neck and kissed him, and he went from being the luckiest man alive to the happiest. "I love the book. And I love you."

He held her close, this incredible woman who had his child growing inside her, this amazing woman who knew all of his flaws and loved him anyway. He wanted this to last forever.

"Let's get Rex and go inside," she said.

Rex leapt out of the SUV and dashed through the gate, excited to see Claire, but when he caught sight of Chloe standing in the window, arched and hissing, the poor guy dropped to the ground and covered his nose.

Claire knelt, blocking his view of the window. "Come on inside, Rex. Would you like a treat?"

He bounded up the stairs to the front door.

"I'm glad you brought him. Rex and Chloe need to work out their differences," she said, standing and taking his hand again.

"Like we did?"

"Yes, like we did." She gazed up at the house, then back at him. "Now that the two of you are here, this house will finally feel like home."

Home sweet home. The phrase finally made sense to him. They climbed the front steps and went inside together. Someday he would carry her across this threshold, but for today this was enough.

Epilogue

Six months later...

Claire carried the cake, decorated with soft pink rose-buds and ribbons of pale green icing, into the dining room and set it in the center of the table. Luke had put in all the leaves to extend the table to accommodate everyone, and they would all be here soon.

"Now will you please sit down?" he asked. "Even if it's just for five minutes."

"If I sit down, I may never get up again." She had two months to go before the babies would be here, and her body had all the grace and proportions of a beached whale. But every day Luke told her that she was the most beautiful mother-to-be on the planet, and she was more than happy to have him as her mirror.

He guided her into her favorite armchair in the living room. "Don't move. I'll be right back with a decaf latte."

And so she sat with nothing to do but admire the vases of pink roses and baby's breath she'd scattered around the room. Today's baby shower was for Sam and AJ and their new baby daughter, Rose. Kristi and Nate and their family were coming, too.

Claire gently rubbed her bulging belly, feeling a foot here, an elbow there. Four months ago she and Luke had found out they were having twins, and while the surprise had worn off, the shock hadn't. Kristi, who was raising twin stepdaughters, said it would probably last until they left for college.

Luke, her devoted husband, set her cup on the side table.

"Thank you. I keep thinking how nice it will be to have real coffee again."

"It won't be long now." He sat on the arm of her chair and his hand joined hers in an exploration of her belly and the protruding baby appendages.

Car doors slammed outside, followed by the sound of voices and footsteps on the veranda. Claire got to her feet, excited to greet their friends, who were really their extended family at the door.

"So much for you having a rest."

She kissed his cheek, then ran her hand over the light stubble on his jaw. "The doctor says I'm healthy and the babies are healthy. We're all fine, and I can rest later."

She had wanted to throw this party for Sam, to celebrate the arrival of her new baby, but mostly she wanted to do it for herself. She had her dream home, complete with white picket fence, and the person who'd been the man of her dreams all her adult life shared it with her. And they would soon have the family she had always longed for. With so much love in one house, it would be a shame not to share it. She wasn't sure if Luke agreed with her or just humored her, but either way she loved him for it.

Luke helped her to her feet and together they greeted their friends.

Kristi and Nate trooped in with their five-year-old twin daughters, Molly and Martha, bouncing ahead of them and their teenage daughter, Jenna, straggling behind and tapping out a text message on her iPhone.

"Claire's living room is a gadget-free zone," Kristi reminded her.

Jenna rolled her eyes, stuck her phone in her pocket and hugged Claire.

"It's Luke's rule," Claire whispered to her, eliciting a laugh.

Behind them, Sam and AJ appeared in the doorway, with their four-year-old son, Will, between them and the baby carrier in AJ's hand.

"Oh, Sam. She's beautiful."

Sam gave her a warm hug. "See what you have to look forward to?"

"Times two," Kristi said.

"I can't wait."

Everyone shed coats and jackets, and while the children dashed out to the backyard and Jenna retreated to the dining room with her phone, the grown-ups settled into the living room.

Sam answered questions about how well the baby was sleeping and AJ told them about the last checkup with the pediatrician and how much weight she'd gained.

Then it was Claire's turn to share the news of her last prenatal exam and Luke told everyone he thought the doctor should have told her to take things easy.

That made everyone laugh, and then Kristi took Nate's hand. "While we're on the subject of babies…"

"Omigosh! You're pregnant, too?" Sam hugged her. "Congratulations!"

"More babies!" Claire said, clapping her hands together. "I'd hug you, too, but I can't get up."

"A baby," Nate said, grinning widely and accepting hearty handshakes from the other dads. "One set of twins is plenty."

One set of twins is perfect, Claire thought.

"If the three of us plan to keep this up," Sam said, "we'll have to come up with a schedule so we're not all on maternity leave at the same time."

Claire joined in the laughter as she gazed around the room at her friends, then up at her husband who sat next to her, one arm around her shoulder. She had to be the luckiest woman alive.

"Ready Set Sold is in the business of creating homes for families," she told them. "I'd say we're managing just fine."

"Home sweet homes," Luke said, seeking out her hand and giving it a squeeze. "That could be your company slogan."

She laced her fingers with his. "It's perfect," she said. Everything was perfect.

* * * * *

As an only child, **Pamela Stone** spent her summers at her grandparent's house in the country. She would while away long hot afternoons reading romance or creating her own fantasies and imaginary friends. These days, she loves to travel. From Hawaii to California, to Florida to the Caribbean, if there's a beach, she's there. She has combined her romantic nature and love of the ocean to become the author of great beach reads.

Also by Pamela Stone

Last Resort: Marriage

Visit the Author Profile page at Harlequin.com.

SECOND CHANCE DAD

Pamela Stone

I'd like to again thank my editor, Johanna, for believing in my writing and helping bring this book to life. My family for their patience and support. My critique partners, Linda and Juliet, without whom this book might have never gotten written. I'd also like to thank my fans for buying my first book and giving me the confidence to put myself out there again!

Chapter 1

Something was badly amiss in the Texas public school system: Hanna Rosser's straight-A son did not participate in fistfights.

Hanna pulled into the parents' parking lot of Marble Falls Elementary and tried to keep her cool as a motorcycle roared into the spot she'd been eyeing. Calmly she parked her white Volvo SUV two spaces down and tried not to notice how the tight denim hugged the guy's long legs as he slid off the macho contraption and headed up the sidewalk, unbuckling his helmet.

Trade the helmet for a Stetson and the Harley for a stallion and he'd epitomize the phrase *long, tall Texan.* Six feet and some change, dirty cowboy boots and a swagger that said he couldn't care less what anyone else thought.

Slinging the helmet by the leather strap, he jabbed

his fingers through his disheveled hair and then opened the heavy glass door. He stepped back, allowing her to precede him into the hall. For each of his long strides Hanna made two, her heels tapping on the shiny waxed tile in her rush toward the office.

Ashton's first day in a public school and he'd been involved in a fistfight? This couldn't be happening.

She reached for the metal handle of the office door, and again, Mr. Tight Jeans leaned around and held it open for her. Deep dimples bracketed his mouth. "After you, ma'am." His voice held the same interesting mix of smooth and tough as his jeans.

Leading the way into the office, she wondered if this man's bully son was the one who'd taken a swing at Ashton. Fighting hadn't been an issue in Ashton's private school back in Dallas. She'd certainly brought him up to know better than to strike another child.

The secretary stood and nodded. "Ms. Rosser. Vince."

Vince? Hanna glanced at him from the corner of her eye as he flashed those killer dimples at the little redhead behind the desk. This guy was on a first-name basis? Oh yeah, undoubtedly his son had been picking on the new sixth-grader.

"Please take a seat. We're just waiting on one more parent, and then Principal Montgomery will see you."

Vince stood until Hanna sat, and then folded his long, lanky frame into a matching wooden chair, placing his black-and-silver helmet on the one between them with a clunk. She inched farther away as Vince crossed one leg over the other, his giant cowboy boot further staking his claim on the center chair.

Please God, don't let Ashton's asthma have flared up.

Was her baby boy okay? Richard would have a hemorrhage if any harm had come to his son.

A photocopier occupied one corner of the office, copying, collating and stapling, the noise adding to her nervousness and humiliation during the excruciating wait to go before the principal. The entire experience made her feel as guilty as if she'd been the one called to the office instead of her child.

"So who is the other parent?" Vince asked the secretary.

"William Baer." She shuffled papers on her desk and looked up as the door creaked and a stocky male entered the office. Even sporting a company emblem on the breast pocket, Mr. Baer's navy golf shirt and tan Dockers looked more respectable than Vince's denim ensemble.

Vince stood and shook his hand. "Hey, Will."

"Vince."

Hanna smoothed her skirt as she stood, uncomfortable with the way Mr. Baer's gaze roamed up and down her frame.

He extended his hand. "William Baer, ma'am. I don't believe I've had the pleasure."

Accepting the overly zealous handshake, she almost choked on his sweet aftershave. "Hanna Rosser. We just moved to the area this weekend."

"Well, I must say, you're a most welcome asset to Marble Falls."

Vince cleared his throat and for the first time actually seemed to notice Hanna's appearance. Without comment, he turned his attention back to the secretary. "So, what's the problem?"

She punched a button on the phone and within moments Principal Montgomery stepped out. Hanna had met the woman literally six hours earlier when she'd enrolled Ashton. Approximately forty, tiny, rather attractive in a no-nonsense sort of way. Short blond hair tucked behind her ears, black slacks and a bright-red blazer. "Please, step into my office."

Both men stood, allowing Hanna to walk between them before entering.

Principal Montgomery nodded to each as they entered. "Ms. Rosser. Mr. Baer. Mr. Keegan."

Hanna did a double-take at the girl sitting between Ashton and the other boy, as if separating the boys so they wouldn't throw more punches.

Hanna rushed to Ashton, scanning him for any injuries. She gasped and ran her finger over the caked blood at the corner of his split lip. Jerking away, Ashton scowled and glanced at the other two kids.

Taking the hint, Hanna pulled her hand back, still assessing the damage. One shirtsleeve had been half ripped from the seam, Ashton's lip was swollen and his dark hair was a mess, but he held the ice pack in his hand, not to his lip. At least, his breathing wasn't labored, and there was no wheezing.

Afraid she'd embarrass him further, Hanna resisted the urge to pick the sprigs of grass out of his dark curls.

Taking a stance behind Ashton, Hanna watched the men as they waited for the case to be presented and Principal Montgomery to deliver her verdict.

"Who wants to speak first?" the principal asked the children.

Mr. Baer turned to the pudgy boy. "Billy, did you start this?"

"No way. I was just minding my own business."

"So who hit who?" Mr. Baer demanded.

Billy shrugged and looked sheepish.

Hanna couldn't imagine that Ashton had hit him at all, much less first. "Did you strike this boy?"

Ashton mimicked Billy's sheepish shrug. "Not first."

"So who threw the first punch?" Principal Montgomery asked.

Ashton cut his eyes sideways at the girl while Billy shuffled his dirty sneakers.

Mr. Tight Jean's gaze landed on the girl with the falling-down ponytail and grungy jeans. "You're unusually quiet, Mackenzie."

The girl stood and placed her hands on her slim hips. She had a good three inches on either boy. "He asked for it."

"Nuh-uh." Billy leaned into her face. "You hit me first. I don't hit no girls, not unless they punch me first."

Ashton stood to the side while the other two faced off.

"Mackenzie, did you hit Billy?" Vince asked.

"He's a yellow-bellied scum reptile, Dad. He's always picking on people who won't fight back just so's he feels tough."

Hanna stared at father and daughter. Both tall and slender with the same sandy-blond hair, Mackenzie's only a shade lighter than her father's. Even their honey-tanned complexions matched.

Mackenzie's left eye sported a darkening bruise, but her father didn't seem overly concerned. Hooking his thumbs in his pockets, Vince raised an eyebrow at Mackenzie. "Was Billy picking on you?" The guy's eyes were the same blue-denim color of his jeans as he matched stares with his rebellious daughter.

She didn't back down. "He knows better than to mess with me, but he figured Ashton was fair game showing up in church clothes and all." She flipped her bedraggled hair behind her shoulder and glared at Billy. "Didn't count on getting whipped by no girl when you picked on my friend, though, did ya?"

With a bruise on his chin, the remains of dried blood in his nose, on his upper lip and down the front of his dirty white T-shirt, Billy had obviously taken the worst of the beating. But he too held his ice pack in his hand instead of to his bruised face.

"Billy?" his father asked, but Hanna couldn't decide whether his perplexed expression had more to do with his boy hitting a girl or being bested by one.

"It weren't no fair fight. Two against one. They ganged up on me."

Glancing at Ashton, Hanna was stunned that her son's bruised lip actually snarled as he took his spot beside Mackenzie, toe to toe with Billy. "Don't mess with me if you don't want to fight."

"Ashton!" What had happened to her mild-mannered son? "Sit down."

William turned to Vince. "So what are we going to do about this?"

Vince slanted a grin and jabbed his fingers through his sandy hair, only tousling it more than it already was from the helmet. "Maybe you should warn your boy not to tangle with my daughter."

Was he insane? Holding her breath, Hanna waited for the other shoe to drop. Her friend's son in Dallas had once had charges filed against him for hitting another boy on the soccer field, and they'd ended up in court. The boy had received forty hours' community service. Just the kind of ammunition her ex could use in court to make his case that Ashton would be better off in Dallas with him and his new girlfriend.

Instead of the anger she'd expected, William Baer simply rubbed his forehead and grinned.

Both men were morons to make a joke out of this.

The principal motioned for the kids to sit as she remained behind her desk. "Totally unacceptable behavior. Billy and Mackenzie, you two are in this office way too frequently. Ashton, as you're new here, I'm going to withhold judgment. But you're starting out on shaky ground. You're all assigned to ISS for the remainder of the week. Tomorrow morning you will report to the office, collect your assignments and proceed to the library. In addition, I expect a five-page report from each of you by Friday on how you're going to learn that violence doesn't solve problems and how to get along. There will be no more incidents. Understood?"

"Yes, ma'am," Ashton said, but he flashed Mackenzie a conspiratorial grin.

Billy shuffled his feet. "I promise."

Mackenzie returned Ashton's grin. "Okay. As long as you make Bully Baer sit at a different table."

The early-spring wind popped the flag and clanged the cable against the flagpole in front of the school as Hanna shuffled Ashton toward the SUV. She couldn't believe he'd actually gotten into trouble, much less a fistfight. At least nobody had mentioned involving the police. She folded the form she'd received explaining In School Suspension and the possible consequences if this did not resolve the behavior issue.

Now that the divorce was finalized, she was fighting

to regain control of her own life. She hadn't expected her control of Ashton to be tested so quickly.

Vince and Mackenzie stood on the sidewalk beside the macho motorcycle, both holding helmets. Was he actually going to drive his daughter home on that unsafe vehicle?

Ashton waved goodbye to Mackenzie, but Hanna pointedly ignored Vince Keegan. With any luck, Ashton's friendship with Mackenzie would run its course quickly. Hanna had hoped he'd pick his friends more wisely.

He carefully placed his backpack in the backseat and buckled his seat belt. "Sorry, Mom."

Staring in the rearview mirror at those deep-brown eyes, she wanted to reach back and ruffle his curls the way she did when he was little. "I'm sorry you had such a horrible first day."

"It wasn't that bad, just some of the boys kept messing with me. Walking by my desk and knocking my pencil off. No real biggy. Morning recess was okay. I was talking to Ms. Jones. But at lunch, I didn't have anybody to sit with so I found a seat at one end of a table when Billy and these other guys crowded me. Billy knocked my milk over into my plate. He said he was sorry, but his grin was all full of meanness and the other boys laughed like it was a big joke."

"I'm so sorry, sweetie." Hanna stopped at a four-way intersection and looked back at Ashton.

He shrugged. "That wasn't so bad, either. But then at afternoon recess Billy kept calling me names, and Ms. Jones wasn't noticing since she was talking to another teacher." Visibly brightening, Ashton continued. "So I'm standing there wondering what to do, and Mackenzie swoops in like Wonder Woman. She shoves Billy and tells him to back off. He shoves back, and I don't know who hit who, but I couldn't just stand there like a wuss and let a girl fight my battle, you know? So Billy grabbed Mackenzie's ponytail, and I socked him in the nose." Ashton's eyes sparkled with pure male elation. "Blood spurted out like a fountain, just like in the movies. It was cool. He swung back and busted my lip against my tooth, but it didn't hurt much."

"Ashton, I do understand. But this behavior cannot continue. You should resolve your problems with your words and not with your fists. No exceptions. No excuses. Okay?" She didn't mention that his lawyer father would twist such incidents to seal his argument that Ashton belonged in Dallas. "Your asthma didn't flare?"

"No, Mom. Anyway, I had my inhaler."

As they pulled away from the intersection, Ashton pointed to the Super Wal-Mart. "I need some new clothes before tomorrow."

Snapping her gaping mouth shut, Hanna wondered who this boy was and what he had done with her son. "You want to buy clothes at Wal-Mart?" She hadn't been in a Wal-Mart in fifteen years. To her knowledge, Ashton had never set foot inside one.

"Yeah. Mackenzie said they have jeans. I want the kind that looks like you've been playing in them already. And she said you can buy three-packs of T-shirts."

Oh—my—God. "We can get you some jeans and shirts at the mall this weekend."

"No!" He looked frightened, almost horrified at the thought of waiting four more days. "I have to have Wal-Mart clothes tomorrow or Bully Baer will smear me all over the playground."

Wal-Mart. She cringed at Ashton's ruined polo shirt. She hadn't thought twice about paying fifty dollars for that shirt at the Galleria last summer. Only three days living back in Marble Falls and she was already considering updating her son's designer wardrobe at Wal-Mart? Would Bluebonnet Books ever generate enough profit that she could again afford to buy her son designer clothes?

Chapter 2

Punching Billy Baer! Vince followed Kenzie's little red electric bicycle into the garage and parked the Harley next to it. They both slid off and placed their helmets on the respective seats. It amused him that she mimicked everything he did. He tugged on her ponytail as she adjusted her backpack. She wrapped her arm around his waist, he wrapped his around her shoulders, and they headed across the backyard playing their game of trying to see who could put their foot in front of the other one as they walked.

He watched her small sneaker jab in front of his boot in the tall grass and figured he'd better mow tonight or old Mrs. Haythorn would be over here cutting the lawn for him.

Boo stretched his paws out in front of him and yawned from his afternoon nap, his rear end straight up in the air and tail wagging in excitement as they climbed the three stone steps onto the back porch. Kenzie turned Vince loose and squatted, throwing her arms around the gigantic red beast. "Hey there, Boo. You should've been at school today. Bully Baer was a total dweeb again."

She giggled as Boo's long pink tongue lolled out and licked her neck in unconditional adoration.

Vince headed into the kitchen, closely followed by Kenzie with Boo trotting along behind. The screen door slammed shut behind them, and the dog sat his butt on the floor and waited patiently while she tossed her backpack on the chair and handed him a doggie biscuit out of the daisy-painted canister on the bar.

The mutt stretched out full-length on the cool vinyl and made short order of the biscuit. Kenzie grabbed two sodas from the fridge and gave one to Vince on her way to the pantry.

Vince popped the top and dodged Boo's flapping tail. If he'd realized he was allowing Kenzie to adopt a horse seven years ago, he might have been more insistent on one of the smaller pups. But she'd tossed a fit at the animal shelter for the red puppy with the huge feet. It had reminded her of her favorite TV show at the time, *Clifford*. Part Irish Setter and part Great Dane, Boo was a bottomless pit. Girl and dog were inseparable, leaving Vince to justify why half his grocery bill went for dog food.

"So, who's the new kid?"

Rummaging through the pantry, Kenzie retrieved a package of cookies and plunked it and her soda on the bar. She hoisted herself onto the bar stool and waved a cookie. "Ashton and his mom just moved here from some fancy park in Dallas. His dad lives there with his new, very hot girlfriend."

"Highland Park?"

Kenzie nodded. "Yeah, I think so."

"Highland Park is a ritzy, old-money neighborhood, not a park." Vince grinned. "But what does his absentee dad and very hot girlfriend have to do with why you got in a fight over the kid?"

She took a drink and her blue eyes lit with mischief. "I couldn't just stand by and let Billy pick on him. Then I'd have been no better than Bully Baer."

Although Vince was proud she was willing and able to stand up for herself, and evidently others as well, he wasn't sure that noble motive was entirely the root of this incident. "You used this new kid as an excuse to punch Billy Baer."

Kenzie washed her cookie down with strawberry soda. "Stupid bullies tick me off."

"Agreed. But next time you might give the new kid a chance to fight his own battle, or Billy and his gang of misfits will peg him for a sissy and continue to make his life miserable." Vince tossed his empty can in the recycling bin and grabbed the pickup's keys off the counter. "I've got to run over and check on the crew working on the Andersons' dock before they skip out early and we miss our deliverable. Want to go with?"

"Come on, Boo." She sealed the package of cookies, jammed her pink ball cap with the ridiculous logo Pink Is The New Black on her head backward and picked up the soda. "We need to stop for dog food."

"Woof," Boo chimed in, trotting out the door behind her.

Out of dog food already?

* * *

After checking on the progress of the Andersons' dock, Vince pulled into the crowded Wal-Mart parking lot. He loaded a fifty-pound bag of dog food, two boxes of breakfast cereal and other odds and ends into the cart and headed across the store for new socks for Kenzie. Where they disappeared to once inside the dryer was a mystery, but he'd never done a load of laundry and had the socks come out even. There had to be a huge cosmic black hole somewhere full of all sizes and colors of mismatched socks.

Of course, they didn't make it past the video-gaming department without her spotting a game she couldn't live without. "Dad, they have Wii NASCAR. Can we get it?"

"Forty bucks? You got that much saved from your allowance?" He flipped the game over and checked the rating.

"I have eighteen. Come on. You'll play it as much as me, you know you will. If we get it, you can deduct the other two dollars for my half from my allowance this week."

Her keen rationalization always suckered him into helping fund her plans. He tossed the game in the cart. "Fine, but don't try to hit me up for the full ten dollars when you only get eight Friday."

"Thanks, Dad." She gave him a hug and headed toward the girls' department. "I'm going to wipe you off the track when we get home."

"In your dreams." He should count himself lucky that she had only asked for one game this trip. "No games until all your homework is done. And you get me called up in front of Principal Montgomery one more time and the Wii goes in the closet until school's out. It's been years, but I distinctly remember graduating sixth grade. I've got no desire to go back."

"It's okay, you're cool. You still like to play games. And you slowing down in your old age is what gives me the edge so I can win."

Picking through the bins, she selected a plastic bag of assorted socks plus a new purple-striped sleep shirt and Vince herded her in the general direction of the checkout. His day had started at 5:00 a.m., and he still had to get home, unload the groceries, throw something together for dinner, make sure Kenzie did her homework and took her bath, and only then could he get time to work up the bid for the two docks on Lake Travis. He grinned. And now there was NASCAR to work into the schedule.

"Ashton! Hey!" Kenzie called out, making a ninety-degree turn into the boys' department.

"Hey." The kid Kenzie had defended at school today stood in the boys' jeans section grinning at her. His mom didn't look nearly as pleased.

"Can you make Mom understand that these faded jeans are way cooler than those dark-blue ones?" he asked.

Kenzie held the offensive jeans in front of her. "Geesh, these things are so stiff they can stand up even when you aren't wearing them."

Vince ventured a grin at the mom. She looked even more uptight here than she had at school. Chocolate-brown eyes and lashes, complexion like melted vanilla ice cream. He'd seen some bow-shaped mouths, but hers was classic. A pair of designer sunglasses perched on top of her dark curls. If he tugged one of those soft little ringlets, it'd probably spring right back into place.

She offered a half grin and took the jeans out of Kenzie's hand. "These are nice. Tailored."

"And Bully Baer will call me a nerd," Ashton said.

"It's not my fault if Billy Baer has no taste," Ashton's mother defended in a gravelly, Demi-Moorish voice. "I won't have you going to school in sloppy, faded clothes."

Vince leaned on his cart, staying out of the fight as he followed the woman's quick perusal of his daughter's faded jeans and pink ball cap. She dismissed Kenzie's casual style, picked through a rack of three-button golf shirts and selected a banana-yellow-and-white-striped number.

This boy was going to get the crap beat out of him tomorrow.

With a mutinous scowl, Ashton slunk into the dressing room, the jeans and golf shirt grasped in a tight fist.

Undeterred by the mom's ruling, Kenzie plowed through a shelf of faded jeans as if she could override her if she found just the right pair.

"Vince?" Hanna's sultry pronunciation of his name sounded sexy as hell. She stared at him as if she'd rather be anywhere else than standing in the boys' department at Wal-Mart. "I'm sorry, I don't believe we've actually been introduced."

"Pardon my manners." He grinned and extended his right hand, hoping to at least get along, seeing as how their kids seemed to have hit it off. "Keegan. Vince Keegan. Nice to meet you."

"Hanna Rosser." There was a definite wariness as she brushed his hand with those long, delicate fingers.

He gave her right hand a gentle squeeze, avoiding

the huge emerald solitaire. "Kenzie tells me you and Ashton just moved to town."

"Last week. And it's *back* to town. I grew up here."

She didn't sound too happy about that. "Right. And you and your mom are opening a bookstore in the old souvenir shop just off 281."

"How come I'm not surprised you know that?" She pulled her hand away, then adjusted the shoulder strap on her neat little purse. Judging from those woven *C*s on the fabric, he'd take bets it wasn't the fifty-dollar-knockoff variety. Her left hand was bare, with a conspicuous pale circle around her ring finger.

"Small-town grapevine. Can't beat it. When do you open for business?"

"Next week. Mom's been overseeing the renovation the past couple of months while I handled the ordering and—" she appeared to have lost her train of thought "—wrapped up some things in Dallas." Frowning at the video game in his cart, she didn't even look up. "We're including a large children's section. Mackenzie might find some books she'd enjoy."

Wow. He'd totally bombed as a father just because he allowed his daughter to play video games? What did Ms. Rosser have in her cart? He hooked his thumbs in his pockets and looked around, but there were no other carts in sight. How could anyone come to Wal-Mart and manage to leave without at least a dozen items? "Maybe I'll bring her by."

Ashton shuffled out, looking like a striped banana stuffed in dark jeans, his turned-down mouth showing he was almost as unhappy as he'd been earlier sitting in front of Principal Montgomery's desk. "Mom."

Kenzie handed him the faded pair she'd selected and a dull green T-shirt.

Clutching the ensemble, Ashton looked to his mother for approval. "No way, Ashton."

"Might help him fit in," Vince said, pitying the kid.

Hanna tugged at one of her short curls and the little wrinkle between her brows deepened. "I believe I know how to dress my own son."

Maybe the woman could have the kid's shirt monogrammed to match the beige initials on the collar of her starched white blouse.

Vince leaned in and whispered. "Faded jeans, fourteen ninety-nine. Green T-shirt, five bucks. Boy's self-confidence, priceless." Even the faint whiff of Hanna's perfume smelled expensive.

Her big brown eyes scorched through him, then focused on her son's face. She blew out a deep breath. "Try them on."

Clutching the faded jeans like a trophy, Ashton raced back into the dressing room.

"So anything with a decent brand is still taboo in Marble Falls?"

"There are plenty of people around here who have a taste for expensive clothes, but they aren't exactly the rage on sixth-grade playgrounds."

Ashton bounded out of the dressing room almost as quickly as he'd entered, wearing the jeans, the T-shirt and a wide grin. "They're cool."

"They'll be more comfortable once you get them broke in." Kenzie tugged the green shirttail out of his waistband.

Judging by those ever-deepening frown lines between Hanna Rosser's eyebrows, she wasn't any more impressed with Ashton's new fashion statement than she was with Vince and Kenzie's intervention. "Do you know how hard your father works so you can wear nice clothes?"

Called that one right. Time to escape before he ticked her off even worse. Vince jerked his head toward the checkout. "We'd better get moving, Kenzie. Boo's in the truck. Later, Ashton. Ms. Rosser."

"Mr. Keegan."

Kenzie dragged him back through the grocery section for fresh strawberries and by the time they finally worked their way to the checkout, Ms. Rosser stood at the next register, a small box of caramel chocolates on top of the faded jeans and shirt, and her nose buried in one of those entertainment rags they always stocked at the checkout to siphon more money out of people's wallets.

It was fascinating how young she looked with her attention riveted on some bizarre story in a tabloid.

They'd both checked out before Hanna noticed Vince. She clutched her two plastic bags, the rolled-up tabloid sticking out the top of one.

"So, do you think Elvis weighs four hundred pounds and works behind the counter at the Memphis KFC?" he asked.

She glanced down at the bag and her cheeks turned the most adorable shade of pink. "They must have stuck it in my bag by accident."

She shifted the bags to her other hand, fished her sunglasses off the top of her head and shoved them on her nose. As she adjusted her shoulder bag, her blouse gaped apart, giving him a glimpse of sexy pink lace against creamy breast.

He gulped and looked up, catching her eye as she noted the direction of his stare. *Shit!* What did he say now? *Nice bra there, Hanna.* "Let me know if you spot Elvis."

Chapter 3

Hanna wiped her damp forehead with the back of her hand and grabbed a handful of mystery novels from the cardboard box. Smiling, she arranged them on the shelf she'd just polished. Bluebonnet Books was just what she needed to take her mind off the fiasco her life had become. Books had always been her escape. When Hanna was young, her mother had installed floor-to-ceiling bookcases in Hanna's bedroom beside the padded window seat where she'd read to her. Books about faraway places and people with exciting lives. The stories had given Hanna a yearning for life outside of small-town Texas.

"I thought you were going to put those in the front display window to draw in folks strolling down the sidewalk. That author's on the *New York Times* best-seller list."

Taking a deep breath, Hanna straightened the books on the shelf, whether they needed straightening or not. "I plan to put some up front, too, Mom. Doesn't hurt to have a few copies in both places so they're easy to find."

"I'm sure you know what's best," Mom said. "We also need a display of the latest romances on an end cap. Mrs. Haythorn reads a romance a day. Oh, and Mr. Miller always used to lend those adventure books to Daddy after he'd read them, so make sure they're at eye level. His knees are bad."

Toting the box to the front of Bluebonnet Books, Hanna dropped it on the wood floor, which was scarred and aged from years of various businesses that had opened their doors there. Hopefully the bookstore wouldn't suffer a fate similar to the other shops. She glanced through the large plate-glass window as Darryl and Mary Wortham strolled by arm in arm, as much in love as they had been when Hanna went off to college. How could she have been gone fifteen years and returned to find everything the same? She took a breath and considered the wisdom of going into business with her mother. True, the combined funds helped. She'd never have pulled it off without her mother overseeing the renovation and being in the store to receive shipments while Hanna was still in Dallas battling Richard in divorce court. And it would be good to have two of them to switch off managing the store until they could afford to hire additional help. Plus Norma Creed needed something to keep her busy and out of everyone else's business.

But after only one week officially back in town, Hanna already doubted the wisdom of spending twenty-four hours a day, seven days a week with her passive-aggressive mother. Not that she didn't love her mom, but living under her roof again after fifteen years away put Mom smack in the middle of every aspect of Hanna's life. That wasn't good in the best of situations, and right now Hanna was still trying to recover from Richard's heart-breaking betrayal and the bitter divorce.

In a few months, she hoped the store would start turning enough of a profit that she and Ashton could find their own place.

Scooping up a couple of books, she turned as a small red motorized bicycle putted up to the curb—with her son riding behind *that girl.*

"Ashton!" Her heart leaped into her throat as she dropped the books and raced out of the shop. "What are you doing on that thing?"

He slid off from behind Mackenzie and removed the red helmet, grinning as if he'd just descended from an amusement-park roller coaster. "You don't have to pick me up anymore, Mom. I got a ride."

No way! "You are not ever to get on that thing again. You could be killed."

Mackenzie threw her leg over and stood beside Ashton, removing her own helmet. What was left of her ponytail hung in tangles. "We had on helmets."

"He did not have permission to get on a motorized bicycle. That thing is small and hard to see and dangerous."

"I know how to ride it and watch for cars and stop at lights and stuff," Mackenzie said. "I'm a good driver. I took a class and got all the questions right."

"Why are you two even out of school?" Hanna checked her watch. Oh my God. She'd been so busy stocking the shelves for next week's opening she'd forgotten to pick up her son. "Both of you hear this very clearly. I won't have Ashton riding on that thing. End of subject."

Ashton stood on the sidewalk shuffling his new white sneakers. "But, Mom."

"No *but Moms*. Do you understand?"

"Yes, ma'am."

Hanna stepped aside so Dave Barkley, carrying two plastic bags, could pass on the narrow sidewalk. Mrs. Barkley had probably given him a list of groceries to bring home from their corner grocery store. All the men in town gathered each afternoon in the old wooden chairs out front of Dave's store to shoot the breeze. Hanna returned his nod and waited until he climbed into his truck. "Mackenzie, I don't know how things work at your house, but we have rules in this family. The first rule is to ask permission before doing new things. The next time you would like Ashton to do something, he has to check with me first or he won't be allowed to run around with you. If your parents let you risk your life, that's their business, but Ashton's safety is my responsibility. Do I need to spell this out?"

The girl set her jaw, took the extra helmet from Ashton and strapped it on the bike's back bar. "Why don't you just lock him in his room until he's, like, eighteen? It'd be about as much fun as you let him have. At least nobody'd pick on him, huh?" She jammed her helmet on her head, straddled the motorized monstrosity and sped away from the curb.

Ashton squared his shoulders and glared. "Now you've chased off the only friend I have. You treat me like a baby. You dress me like a wuss. You don't want me to have any fun, ever! And now tomorrow, when

Bully Baer picks on me, Kenzie probably won't even be on my side. Why do you hate me?" He slung his backpack over his shoulder and stomped past his grandmother and into the store.

"Ashton, come back here!"

Norma Creed stood in the doorway of the shop worrying the lace collar on her prim pink blouse and staring after Mackenzie. "You're wise to restrict Ashton's association with that wild child. You have to keep him safe."

"Mom, I fully realize that." She followed her mother back into the shop. "Where did Ashton go?"

Norma looked around the vacant bookstore. "You don't think he took off out the back after her, do you?"

Wonderful! Hanna walked through the narrow store, looking each way until she reached the back door into the alley where Ashton was kicking up a cloud of dirt and gravel. "What are you doing?"

"I hate stupid glowing white shoes." He jabbed his new sneakers in the dirt. "Why couldn't you buy me blue or gray? I hate it here. I don't have any friends and it's all your fault. It's worse than Dallas," he accused, spinning around and stirring up dust like a Texas dirt devil.

His unhappiness jabbed through her heart like a rusty knife. "Honey, I want you to have friends, but I have to make sure you don't get hurt and that bike is dangerous."

"I don't care. It'd be better to get hurt than to get made fun of," he said, looking away.

"Slow down before you start wheezing." She reached out and touched his shoulder, but he spun farther away. Sandy stains ran down his cheeks where the dust had turned his tears to mud. "Ashton, I love you. I just…"

He turned and raced down the alley. "I'm going home."

Norma stood silently in the door, wearing her motherly wisdom like a halo, and once again, Hanna felt like the child who had performed below expectations. "Mom, can you lock up?"

Her mother touched Hanna's shoulder. "Why don't you lock up and let me go after him? He'll calm down walking the few blocks. Take time to calm yourself before confronting him again."

Hanna resented her mother stepping in and playing the good cop when Ashton was angry at Hanna, but it probably wasn't a bad idea. "Okay, but I won't be long."

Collecting her purse from the office, Norma marched across the street to her blue Chevy, which was nestled against the curb between two tall pickups. The only time there was any real traffic was on spring weekends, when tourists descended on Hill Country to see the wildflowers.

Turning out lights and locking the back door, Hanna stopped short at the sight of Vince Keegan standing inside the shop. "Do you need something?"

For once, he didn't smile. "It's time you and I had a little chat."

"If it's all the same to you, I'm not up for any more confrontations today."

"Lady, when someone upsets my kid enough that she calls me crying, I want to know why. And when you start telling people, especially my daughter, that I'm a bad parent, then Mackenzie's the least of your problems."

"Your daughter is out of control." The more congenial approach would have been to offer him a cup of coffee and calmly explain that his darling daughter was a bad influence on her son, but Hanna's temper won out over her manners.

His legs were slightly spread and his eyes narrowed. "Out of control? She's the most in-control kid in town."

"From what I can see, Mr. Keegan, she does whatever she wants and has no respect for authority."

"Really?" He hooked his thumbs in his front pockets.

"Need I remind you that your little hellion got Ashton into a fistfight and placed in ISS? She inserted herself in the middle of buying him clothes, completely overriding my wishes. And now she brings him home on the back of some kind of dangerous motorbike without even asking permission. This is only day two! I'm biting my nails in anticipation of what she'll do the rest of the week."

"My little hellion kept your little prep from getting his ass kicked on the playground yesterday. And best I can figure, that was her goal again with the clothes advice." Vince leaned forward and maintained eye contact, grinding his teeth. "Today she gave him a lift home because he was afraid Billy would show up before you got there to pick him up. What exactly do you take issue with?"

"Why would any sane parent buy a sixth-grader a motorcycle?"

"It's an electric bicycle, and I bought it for her twelfth birthday so she could get where she needed to be while I was working. Unlike you, I realize I can't be everywhere at once."

"Just please ask Mackenzie to stay away from Ashton. I can't do anything about your poor judgment, but I won't put my son at risk."

His jaw ticked. "She and I took a class before she was allowed to ride it, and she only rides the side streets where any regular bicycle would go." He glanced around the store and let out a long sigh. "Why in hell am I defending myself? Since you don't seem to mind condemning my parenting style, how about we discuss yours?"

"Excuse me?" She stared at his wide shoulders. Why was it that good-looking and cocky were directly proportionate in men?

"Maybe you should reexamine your theory that keeping Ashton under your wing is the best way to protect him." His voice remained soft and mellow, but his words bit. "Maybe consider what's going to happen when something goes wrong and you aren't Johnny-on-the-spot to stand between him and danger. Might consider teaching him to take care of himself and make his own decisions."

Not hard to see where Mackenzie inherited her disrespect for authority. "So I should let him wear ratty clothes and race around town like a delinquent in training, fighting with other children?"

Vince's denim-colored eyes narrowed, but he still didn't raise his voice. "The most important thing to teach kids is judgment and how to make intelligent decisions. If you lock them in a protective bubble, when they do escape they have no idea how to function or protect themselves in the real world."

"Do not insult my son's ability to think for himself."

"He's giving it his best shot, but you're dictating how you want him to dress and act. Kids should fit in with their peers, feel like they belong. You're making Ash-

ton a laughingstock trying to dress him like a miniature yuppie instead of a regular kid."

Blood pumped through her veins and she took a step
toward him. What did this irresponsible father know
about how to dress? He was wearing old jeans and a
navy T-shirt, blue plaid flannel flapping in the breeze
and a Keegan's Docks cap topping off his faded outfit.
Clothes that fitted his self-assurance and tight body
like a glove. "You justify letting Mackenzie run wild
as teaching her to make wise decisions? Might I ask
what her mother thinks of this approach?"

His features stiffened. "Mackenzie doesn't have a
mother."

Crap. Leave it to Hanna to put her foot in her mouth.
Had Mackenzie's mother deserted them? Died? "I'm
sorry."

He didn't even acknowledge her apology. "I can't be
with Kenzie every minute, so I teach her how to handle
herself." He came closer, bringing them nose to nose
and continued to speak in a deep, controlled tone. "Kid
gets invited to a party. All the other kids are swimming,
but one kid's parents didn't teach him to swim because
they were afraid he might drown. He wants to be part
of the fun. Guess which kid is most at risk?"

"If the child didn't know how to swim, a responsible parent wouldn't let him go to a swimming party
to begin with."

"Yeah, that's the way to raise a well-adjusted kid.
That really helps him grow up and fit in, make friends."
His jaw set. "You have any further issue with Mackenzie, you take it up with me." He sauntered out of Bluebonnet Books and onto the sidewalk, the bell on the
door clanging in his wake.

She vibrated with anger as she locked the front door and made her way home.

Hanna found Ashton sitting cross-legged on the living-room sofa, his nose buried in his homework while her mom rattled around in the kitchen.

Giving Ashton's shoulder a gentle squeeze, Hanna put her purse on the credenza and left him to finish his work. "Need any help, Mom?"

Norma turned from the fridge. "You can wash your hands and peel the carrots."

Hanna bit her tongue. Like she was six and needed to be told to wash her hands? "Thanks for stepping in and calming Ashton down." Hanna dug the carrot peeler out of the drawer. "What do you know about Vince and Mackenzie Keegan?"

Norma ripped apart a head of lettuce. "Mackenzie is Belinda Maguire's girl. Since Belinda was killed, her father just lets her run wild. Spoils her rotten. Even in church, which is the only time I've ever seen her in a dress, she still manages to look like a tomboy."

"Belinda Maguire? I remember her from school."

"They were living in Austin. Huge pileup on I-35. Both Belinda and their older child were killed, but if I remember right, Mackenzie wasn't in the car. She was a toddler."

Putting her hand over her mouth, Hanna tried to imagine what Vince had gone through. Such a tragic loss. And then to be faced with the awesome responsibility of raising a small daughter alone. She'd think after losing a wife and child Vince would be even more protective than Hanna.

After getting the carrots on to cook, she took a break

and joined Ashton in the living room. "I'm sorry if I overreacted this afternoon, but you frightened me."

He stuck the paper between the pages of the book and closed it. "You embarrassed me in front of my friend. It's bad enough that all the other kids think I'm a sissy, but now Kenzie knows I am."

"I'm afraid Mackenzie is going to get you hurt." The loneliness in his eyes made her weep inside. "Ashton, I'll try to do better if you'll exercise more caution."

He shrugged. "It doesn't matter anymore."

Hanna hesitated in front of the Keegans' porch and looked down the street of manicured lawns and homey little houses that could have come straight out of an episode of *The Andy Griffith Show*. She allowed the fading pink-and-purple brushstrokes of the Marble Falls sunset to calm her nerves. Hanna the mother wanted to turn around and leave. What if this girl pulled another dangerous stunt and Ashton got caught in the crossfire? But whether she approved of Mackenzie Keegan or not, she was the only ally Ashton had in his new environment, and that was worth something. Hanna the still-insecure child knew firsthand what it felt like not to have a friend.

She clapped the brass knocker and waited. On the second rap, the porch light flashed on and the door swung open. But instead of a twelve-year-old girl, she faced a navy blue T-shirt stretched to the max attempting to cover a muscled six-pack. No denim jacket or loose flannel shirt for camouflage tonight.

Vince cocked his head. "Ms. Rosser."

"Please call me Hanna." She focused on his face. "I come in peace."

"Then you might want to come in off the porch." Standing back, Vince motioned for her to enter.

She stepped inside the room and whirled around as a massive reddish dog came up from behind and nuzzled her hand. She jerked her hand away and jumped sideways into a solid chest.

Vince's arm encircled her waist and he grabbed the dog's collar with the other hand. She fought to breathe as Vince leaned around and captured her gaze. "He's harmless."

The dog, maybe. Heart pounding, she stared into Vince's intense blue eyes and something inside her flipped. Hormones surging into high gear, she eased away from him. She wasn't sure whether to be more fearful of man or beast.

Vince retained his grasp on the dog's collar. "Come on, Boo. Let the lady settle in before you slobber all over her."

"I…uh." Eyeing the dog, she stood in the center of the living room and prayed for her voice to return. She didn't even trust dogs behind fences, and this one was too close and too big. "I came to apologize to Mackenzie for jumping on her today."

Vince turned the dog loose. "Lie down, Boo."

Obediently, the dog walked a couple of feet away and stretched out in front of the rustic stone fireplace. But his ears remained perked, and his black eyes focused on Hanna as if waiting for Vince to leave the room so he could pounce.

"Kenzie is at my in-laws' house for dinner."

"Oh." She was alone with Vince Keegan. On his turf! This had been a bad idea to begin with. "I'm sorry for not calling first. I just thought…" Trying not to look at the dog in case he might interpret that as an invitation to come closer, and avoiding Vince's gaze because, well, just because, Hanna scanned her surroundings. Framed family photos on the mantel, including a family shot of Vince with one hand resting on the shoulder of a small brown-haired boy as they posed beside a woman holding a lacy pink bundle of frills and blond curls.

Quickly looking away, Hanna focused on a soft beige leather sectional sofa. A large wooden coffee table with drawers and shelves under it, scattered with books, magazines and a crystal vase of silk daisies. A white king lay on its side in the center of a chessboard along with various other pieces and the rest off to the side. "You play chess?"

Vince narrowed his eyes. "Surprised?"

She adjusted her purse on her shoulder and clasped her hands together, not sure what to do with them. "Oh, no. I mean, my father played chess."

"Would you like to sit down? We could discuss the kids and figure out how not to be at each other's throats."

Sit? Okay. Sitting was good. She eased down on the end cushion of the sofa and placed her purse on the wood floor.

"Coffee is made or I have iced tea."

Boo stood and she held her breath. Vince could not leave her alone in this room with that animal. "No, nothing for me. I can't stay but a minute. I left Ashton doing his homework and my mom cleaning the kitchen. I have to get back soon and make sure Ashton brushes his teeth and gets his bath. His bedtime is nine o'clock." She clamped her mouth shut in an attempt to stop babbling.

Vince shoved the chessboard and vase of daisies

aside and sat on the edge of the coffee table, only a foot from her face, his knee bumping hers. *Breathe, Hanna, breathe.* Deep dimples bracketed his full lips. "So my daughter isn't the only one in the family who makes you jumpy?"

The room closed in on her. The man was hogging all the oxygen. "I don't like dogs."

His dimples deepened as he rested his elbows on his knees and leaned closer. "I wasn't talking about Boo."

Instinctively she started to lean back from his nearness, but caught herself and held her ground. She gulped at his muscled forearms and large hands. "Look, Mr. Keegan…"

"Vince."

"I…we need to come to an understanding about Mackenzie and Ashton. I am glad he has a friend, but I insist on maintaining more control over what he does. I can't risk him getting hurt."

"He's going into middle school next year. If your goal is to keep him safe and out of fistfights, I'm not sure overprotecting him is going to work in your favor."

"I can see the wisdom in that. But I do not condone fighting."

"Me neither, unless the other kid throws the first punch. In which case, Kenzie will defend herself."

Hanna twisted her hands in her lap. "She should tell a teacher."

"And then the kid would pick on her the next day and the next because he'll take her as weak, looking for someone else to fight her battles." Vince's eyes narrowed. "Give Ashton a chance to fit in. To be like the other kids. He might come out with a black eye or busted lip, but that'll heal and his self-esteem will be stronger for having not backed down."

The intense raw masculine aura that surrounded Vince Keegan consumed her. She pictured Ashton earlier, sitting in the living room, so alone and desperate for a friend. He could benefit from some of this man's confidence. But too much physical activity caused his asthma to flare up. Richard might lack the down-to-earth, take-care-of-himself attitude Vince had, but he made up for it in polished courtroom expertise. If he learned about yesterday's fight, he'd have one more reason to yank Ashton out of school and re-enroll him in the private school in Dallas.

Hoping to keep Vince from noticing her shaking hands, Hanna stuck them beneath her thighs, sandwiching them between the cushions. "How about this? I'll loosen up on Ashton if you'll meet me halfway and make Mackenzie understand that Ashton has to ask permission before trying new things."

"Okay, and about the bike." Vince took a deep breath. "I realize you don't want me or anyone telling you how to raise your son. But Kenzie said Billy Baer and his group of misfits always wait for Ashton after school and torment him. Riding home with Kenzie saves him from getting into a fight."

Hanna closed her eyes. "Why wouldn't he tell me something like that?"

"Because he's trying his damnedest not to be a sissy! Not to run to his mommy to solve all his problems."

"Maybe I'll ask Mom to pick him up on days I can't."

"Oh yeah, his nana picking him up in a blue Chevy sedan every day is going to make him not look like a sissy. There's just a couple of blocks between Bluebonnet Books and the school. Give him some space to handle this himself."

"I want him to fit in, have friends. I guess as long as they're only on neighborhood streets and come straight home. I certainly don't want Billy Baer tormenting him."

"Fair enough." He grinned. "Now that we've resolved that, do you want to talk about what it is about me that makes you so skittish?"

Chapter 4

Hanna broke down a box and tossed it onto the growing stack, turning as the bell over the door clanged.
A lady in jeans and a loose white blouse entered the
shop, closely followed by an uncharacteristically doc-
ile Mackenzie.

The woman ran her hand through her short salt-and-
pepper hair, actually more salt-and-cinnamon, and adjusted her enormous hobo-style purse on her arm. She
was probably one of those perpetually prepared women
who could produce anything from that monster purse
from a wet wipe to a Swiss Army knife.

Eyeing Hanna, she extended her hand. "You must
be Hanna Rosser."

Hanna smiled and shook her hand. Tiny brown freck-
les dotted every exposed inch of the woman.

"I'm Claire Maguire, Kenzie's grandmother." She

turned to Mackenzie. "Don't you have something to say to Ms. Rosser?"

One corner of Mackenzie's mouth turned up, but the other maintained her scowl. "I won't make Ashton do anything without asking your permission first."

Claire cleared her throat and arched an eyebrow.

Mackenzie yanked off her pink cap and twisted it. "I'm sorry."

The apology was obviously coerced, but it was a start. Hanna extended her hand. "Apology accepted. And I apologize for getting so angry yesterday. Can we start fresh?"

Again Mackenzie shrugged. "Okay."

Claire patted Mackenzie's shoulder. "That wasn't so hard, was it?"

"I guess not." She looked around the store. "Is Ash here?"

Ash? Nobody had ever called her son that. "He's at home with his nana doing his homework."

"While it's still light out?"

Hanna raised an eyebrow.

"I mean, why waste time indoors when everyone else is playing? I do my homework after dinner." Mackenzie looked at her grandmother. "I mean, that way Daddy is home to help." She grinned as if proud of her conjured-up excuse. "Can I wait outside now?"

Claire nodded, and Mackenzie dashed for the door, adjusting her pink cap back into place.

"Vince seldom has to help Mackenzie with her homework," Claire said with a grin. "He dotes on her, but she's a smart girl."

"I'm sure she is, a tad precocious maybe, but I can see the intelligence."

"Sharp like her daddy and book-smart like her mom. She whizzes through school with very little effort and maintains As and Bs." Claire picked up a copy of *Charlotte's Web* and thumbed through it. "Vince is a good son. I'm not sure how I'd have survived without him and Kenzie in our lives."

Son? Vince was her son-in-law. The woman's daughter had been gone nine years. Hanna wasn't sure what to say. "I was sorry to hear about Belinda."

"Thank you. Do you remember her?"

"We were only a year apart in high school. She was a sweet girl."

"Her family was the world to her." Claire swiped her hand across her freckled cheek. "I'd better get Kenzie home. Vince insisted she come by and apologize."

Really? "I want Mackenzie and Ashton to be friends. It's just that Vince and I have very different parenting styles."

"Vince is an excellent father."

Being his daughter's best buddy didn't qualify him as an excellent dad, but Hanna did envy the close relationship he had with Mackenzie. Richard had always been too busy earning a living to have time to bond with Ashton.

"I'm sure he is, but—" Hanna caught herself. "We just have different approaches."

Possibly because the kids were in ISS, the rest of the week progressed without serious incident. Each afternoon when Hanna picked Ashton up at school, he had some story about Mackenzie's escapades, escapades that typically involved him.

Friday afternoon was no different, except they had

to drive two hours to Waco to meet Richard so Ashton could spend the weekend with his father.

Ashton tossed his backpack on the floorboard and buckled his seat belt. "You should have been at school today, Mom. The teacher left the library to go to the restroom and Billy started being a jerk, called me a nerd, and then Kenzie called him a scum reptile. I thought they were going to get into it, but Kenzie didn't want to get expelled so she ripped a sheet of notebook paper out of her binder, wadded it up and threw it at him instead. World War *Three* broke out and we were winning, but then she saw Ms. James coming."

Geez. "Ashton."

He laughed. "Dumb Bully Baer was so busy pummeling us with paper wads that he didn't notice we'd stopped. So it looked like it'd snowed around our table when Ms. James came in, and paper was just flying one way so Bully Baer got in trouble, not us. And the best part was that he was really ticked that he'd wadded up his report and threw it, too, so when he was picking up the paper he had to unwad each one to find his report, then he had to copy it over."

The tendons in Hanna's neck threatened to snap. "Not getting caught is not the same as not misbehaving. You two were just as guilty."

Ashton huffed and glared at her. "Mom, you are so lame. You're never fun."

"There are many ways to have fun without misbehaving." Well, okay, that did sound lame. "Have you made any other new friends besides Mackenzie?"

Ashton let out a deep, exasperated breath. "Bully Baer, does he count? Why do you hate Kenzie? She's cool."

Mischievous and undisciplined was now cool? Following basic classroom rules and good behavior was lame? She'd hoped Ashton would avoid buying into the whole rebellious game. And he had, until he'd moved to Marble Falls. "I just think that next week when you're out of ISS, you might meet some other nice kids to hang around with. It's good to have more than one friend."

"Kenzie is the only one I have since you made me move to dumb Marble Falls." Ashton flipped down the DVD screen and snapped his headphones on. "Let me know when we get there."

Great. The first weekend Ashton was spending with Richard in Dallas and the boy was going to leave angry at her. Just peachy. Wonderful start to an already stressful weekend.

Hanna drove in silence while Ashton sat in the backseat, headphones isolating him from further conversation. He laughed at the movie, but didn't even acknowledge her. Waco was approximately halfway between Marble Falls and Dallas and where she'd arranged to meet Richard. This was the first time Ashton would be so far away from her since the divorce. What if he had an asthma attack? Would Richard know what to do? She wouldn't relax until she had Ashton back with her.

Richard's silver Lexus sat in the McDonald's parking lot, but he wasn't alone. That college student who had broken up Hanna's marriage sat in the passenger seat, her hair twisted and stuck to the back of her head with one of those huge finger clips, blond sprigs sprouting out at odd angles. She stared straight ahead and avoided looking at Hanna. Good! The little home wrecker *should* feel guilty.

Hanna gulped as Richard opened his door and came around to collect Ashton's suitcase. As always, Richard was dressed to the height of style. Gray slacks she'd bought him last Christmas and a white button-down. Both starched and pressed, courtesy of the Highland Park Cleaners. Short brown hair freshly trimmed every third Tuesday at five-thirty. Every detail attended to.

This whole situation was surreal. What had happened to their family? How had they gotten to this point? She glanced at the little blonde in the front seat. Hanna's stomach threatened her with nausea. Suddenly this girl had Hanna's family and Hanna was the outsider.

At least Hanna had primary custody. For now. She could take Ashton anywhere in Texas as long as she contributed half the expense of his transportation for designated visits with his dad.

But what if Richard didn't bring Ashton back Sunday afternoon as agreed upon? When she'd announced her intention to move home to Marble Falls to be close to her mother, Richard had insisted that Ashton would be better off remaining in Dallas with him. He'd argued that the divorce had been hard enough on their son and it would only make it harder if they uprooted him from the home and school he was accustomed to.

What if Ashton decided he missed Dallas and didn't want to come back to Marble Falls? Especially given that Hanna didn't seem to be at the top of his favorite-person list at the moment. In a couple of weeks, Ashton would be twelve and the judge would probably go along with his wishes.

Engulfing Ashton's slender shoulders in a tight hug, she breathed in his playground scent and forced back her tears. "You have fun with Daddy, and I'll see you Sunday. Do you have your inhaler?"

Rolling his eyes, he dug the tube out of his pocket and held it up as proof. "I have it, Mom."

She managed a cheery smile and prayed it reached her voice. "I love you."

"See you in two days." Ashton gave her a quick squeeze then crawled into the backseat of the Lexus and switched on his Game Boy. Was he trying not to cry, too, or was he just angry? Was this what they had to look forward to every other week for the next six years? A hundred and fifty more weekends!

Richard closed the car door and turned to Hanna. "Don't look like I'm torturing you. You just can't let him go without making him feel guilty for leaving you, can you?"

Her jaw dropped, but Richard only smirked. "You aren't totally innocent in all this, you know."

Snapping her mouth closed, she glared at him. "You're blaming me? I honored my vows, fulfilled my duties, took care of the home and family, remember?" She took a deep breath. "Ashton has an extra inhaler in his bag and the doctor's info is on a card in the side pocket just in case."

"I'm still his father, Hanna. He'll be fine."

She crawled back into her car and slammed the door before he could notice her shaking. Maybe their marriage hadn't been the most passionate, but she wasn't the one who'd strayed, and she'd be damned if she'd take the blame.

The Lexus purred to life, and Hanna waited to start her own car until Richard had pulled out of the lot and out of sight. She stared up at the giant yellow M and blinked back tears. Families and small kids inside the window gorged on chicken nuggets slathered in ketchup while others climbed in and out of the colorful playground tubes. Okay, so Ashton was too old to enjoy crawling through tubes, but he still liked McDonald's burgers.

At the thought of food, her stomach growled and she swiped the tears out of her eyes, took her sunglasses off the top of her head and put them on. Nostalgia wasn't going to buy her anything tonight. She started the car and pulled into the drive-through lane behind a dirty white pickup with ladders sticking out of the bed. A person had to eat and who wouldn't feel better after a bag of hot, salty fries?

On the drive home, she tried to think about anything rather than the fact that for every mile she drove one direction, Richard was driving one in the other and Ashton was two miles farther from her.

This was insane! Ashton was almost twelve years old and he'd been away from her before. Summer band camp. Weeks with his grandparents. But never a weekend with that other woman while Hanna was over two hundred miles away. It made Hanna's blood boil to think about that home-wrecking co-ed taking care of her child. It wasn't insulting enough that she'd stolen Hanna's husband, now she had her son. And the three of them would spend the weekend in Hanna's house! The Highland Park house she'd loved and spent years and a fortune remodeling and decorating.

Bluebonnet Books. Grand opening Monday. Think about all the things that had to be done this weekend. She needed this time to take care of all the final details. Ashton would be fine. It wasn't as if he was a baby. He was perfectly capable of making himself a sandwich even if the woman was helpless. And he'd be comfortable in his old room.

Books. Coffee. Pastries. Her life was certainly in a big mess, maybe the bookstore could be successful enough to take her mind off the fiasco Richard had made of all their lives. Other than an occasional call from her friend Tiffany, there was nothing left of her life in Highland Park.

Sleep at least was sound once Hanna got home. She woke up early Saturday morning ready to plow into all the last-minute details at Bluebonnet Books. If she kept busy, maybe she wouldn't think about that girl in *her* house with *her* husband and son.

She left a note for her mother, who was still snoring like the little engine that could in the next bedroom, and walked to the bookstore. A late-April chill filled the air as the sun crept over the trees, turning the sky to pink and orange. Today Hanna was relieved her mother wasn't an early riser. She relished the sanity time.

By nine-thirty, when her mother strolled through the front door, cell phone to her ear, the rich aroma of coffee filled Bluebonnet Books. Hanna had arranged copies of the latest magazines on the front rack. She quickly replaced the entertainment magazine she'd been thumbing through.

Norma Creed's eagle eyes glanced at that exact spot in the display. She put her hand over the phone. "I can't believe you're planning to sell those gossip rags in our wonderful community bookstore. They're nothing but trash."

Hanna fought to keep a straight face, at least until

her mother talked her way to the back office to stow her purse. Norma was the ringleader of the town gossip grapevine. The woman knew everyone's little secrets and, although she professed to hate gossips, delighted in sharing whatever she knew with anybody she ran across. That was just one of the reasons Hanna had taken the first road out of Marble Falls as soon as her high-school diploma was in her hand. Thanks to good grades and a college fund, she'd headed for SMU and a degree in English and never looked back.

So much for her great escape.

Her mother's cell phone rang again as she reentered the room. Hanna listened to a five-minute ramble about some poor woman whose husband was evidently having trouble making babies. It seemed that the only change in the grapevine in the fifteen years Hanna had been absent was that it had become turbo-charged thanks to cell phones.

Norma hung up, poured herself a cup of coffee and selected a Danish from the small box Hanna had picked up on the way in. "So, have you heard from Ashton this morning?"

Thanks, Mom. I really needed to be reminded. "Ashton is fine. He has my cell number if he needs anything."

"I was just concerned, as I know you are. How was Richard? Did you two talk?"

"Richard had his new girlfriend with him. I wasn't in the mood to stand around a parking lot and chat." Hanna picked up the empty boxes and toted them to the back. It was going to be a long day.

About the time Norma settled into organizing the tourism and travel section and Hanna thought she might get a moment of peace, who should pull up to the curb on her red bike and slink into the store but Mackenzie Keegan. Helmet in hand, she spotted Hanna. "I was just wondering if Ash is around."

Hanna stood and stretched. "Good morning, Mackenzie. Ashton is spending the weekend with his father. He won't be home until late tomorrow evening."

Shrugging, Mackenzie selected a comic book off the shelf and studied the front cover. "I knew that. But I thought maybe he'd come home early." Mackenzie placed the comic book precisely where she'd picked it up, even straightening the arrangement. "Yeah, well, he wasn't too thrilled with going so I just figured he might've gotten out of it."

Sudden warmth bubbled up inside Hanna. "Dallas is four hours away. Unless something unforeseen happens, he'll spend the entire weekend. But just for the record, I wasn't too happy he left either. I miss him."

Mackenzie jabbed the helmet on her head and buckled the strap. "I figured. So, just tell him to call my cell if he gets back early."

Hanna's day brightened. Not that she wanted to deprive Ashton of time with his father, but it was certainly a boost to know he hadn't been eager to go. She poured another cup of coffee and hummed as she arranged the children's section to accommodate the little wooden table and benches that had arrived.

She opened an adorable book of bedtime stories and "Twinkle, Twinkle, Little Star" chimed from one of those tiny embedded music boxes. Putting thoughts of Ashton out of her mind, she snapped the book shut just as the bell on the front door clanged again. She hoped they'd have this many patrons next week when the store actually opened.

"May I help you?" she asked, standing up from behind the low bookshelf and coming nose to shoulder with Vince Keegan's Henley T-shirt.

His blue eyes twinkled as he noted the tiny children's book in her hand. "Kenzie said she stopped by. I wanted to make sure she was on good behavior."

Hanna carefully placed the book back on the shelf and gave her heart a second to stop fluttering. Why did she let his presence do that to her? "She did stop by. Looked bored."

He cocked an eyebrow. "Now there's a dangerous combination. Kenzie and boredom."

"The town should be put on alert, I'm sure."

Hanna was still grinning as Norma came out of the back room, wiping her hands down the front of her navy knit slacks and leaving streaks of dust. "Did I hear someone come in?"

"Good morning, Norma." Vince twisted his cap in his hands and turned back to Hanna. "Kenzie tells me Ashton's in Dallas this weekend. I thought maybe I could persuade you to join me for lunch at the Falls Diner."

To discuss the kids? Hanna blinked. Lunch with a friend? Lunch as a—gulp—date? He didn't elaborate. Just lunch.

Remembering the scene the other night at his house when Vince's knees bumped hers still made her break out in a sweat.

Although her feminine ego was pleased by his invitation, she just wasn't ready. Her heart still felt numb toward anything that remotely resembled romance. Besides, half the town gathered at the Falls Diner every day for lunch.

What happened at the bustling little diner did *not* stay at the diner. As in any other small town, the locals gathered at the local eatery as much for the daily gossip as for the food and wonderful selection of homemade desserts.

She watched her mom frown and move to a closer shelf to rearrange the books.

Nodding toward the coffee area in the front of the shop, Hanna led him out of her mom's earshot. "With Bluebonnet Books so close to opening, I just can't spare the time."

"Fair enough." Tilting his head, he grinned, flashing those deep dimples. "Maybe another time."

She smiled. When was the last time a sexy guy had unexpectedly asked her out? A sexy guy with just a touch of mischievousness that if she wasn't careful could suck her in.

For a long moment, he just stood there then pulled a card out of his pocket and handed it to her. "I realized after you left in such a hurry the other night that we didn't exchange numbers. Just in case."

Phone numbers? She paused. Not a bad idea, given the kids and all. She grabbed a brochure for the bookstore out of the rack and scribbled her cell number on the front. "Here you go."

Vince folded the brochure and slid it into the front pocket of his jeans. "Thanks. And Kenzie mentioned a comic book she wanted."

Hanna grinned. "Let me get it."

She rang up the comic book and took the money from Vince. Their fingers brushed as he took the bag from her and tingles shot up her arm. She quickly pulled her hand back, rubbing it down her blouse. He'd been a gentleman and not stopped her from leaving the other night. But she reacted to his slightest touch and the worst thing she could do was send out sexual signals she was not ready to follow through on.

He slung the bag by the handle as he backed toward the door. "See ya."

"See ya." Hanna stared at his denim-covered ass as he left the shop. The guy did know how to fill out a pair of jeans. "Hmph. What was that all about?"

Norma walked up and followed the direction of Hanna's gaze. "Heartache in faded denim, if you're asking me."

Chapter 5

Monday afternoon, as Vince was unloading tools from the truck, Kenzie's bike pulled into the drive. Ashton jumped off from behind her and removed his helmet. "I hate Bully Baer!"

"Your mother is going to hate me if you didn't tell her where you are. Does she know you're over here?" Vince asked.

Ashton shook his head.

Vince handed him his cell phone.

Kenzie took off her helmet and looped the chinstrap over the handlebars, but she was too angry to pet Boo as he ambled up. "We were playing softball at recess and Ash was the last one picked. Bully Baer had a hissy fit when he had to have Ash on his stupid team."

Rolling his eyes, Ashton fidgeted with the phone. "Yeah, like I was thrilled to be on the 'moron' team."

He kneeled down and buried his fingers in the dog's silky red mane, letting him slobber all over his face.

"Dad, they just kept poking fun at him. Every time he was up to bat they made cracks like he wasn't even on their team."

"It doesn't help that my mom gave me a stupid, sissy name like Ashton."

Vince grimaced. "I grew up with Vincent so don't complain to me."

Ashton looked up. "I guess that would suck about as much as Ashton, but at least Vince is cool."

"Now, maybe. About the third fight I got into over it, I went home ready to fight my dad for naming me Vincent in the first place. He told me it was a classy name and if I acted ashamed of it, the other kids would continue to torment me. But if I acted proud of it, like it was a cooler name than theirs, then the other kids would back down."

"Did that work?" Ashton asked, scratching Boo behind the ears. The dog's tongue lolled out in complete euphoria.

"Not always, but it helped. I actually started liking it by high school."

"Yeah, but you were probably never a wuss. I suck at sports." Ashton stood and jabbed his sneaker in the dirt on the drive. "I missed that fly ball."

"The sun was in your eyes. Anybody would've missed," Kenzie said, fisting her right hand.

Boo looked from Kenzie to Ashton as if giving his support.

Ashton did not look convinced. "I suck."

Evidently softball wasn't part of the prep-school curriculum. "Have you ever even played softball before?"

Shaking his head, Ashton looked more miserable by the second. "I played soccer one season, but I sucked at that, too. Mom says it's okay. Some people just aren't athletic and that I could beat them at chess or spelling and that they probably couldn't play the saxophone."

Yeah, not exactly going to make the boy feel manly. "Kenzie, go grab our gloves and let's toss a few around."

"I gotta go," Ashton said, giving Boo a goodbye pat and holding out Vince's phone without using it.

"Nobody is born knowing how to catch a ball. You gotta learn, practice. Now's as good a time as any."

Ashton smirked, but flipped the phone open. "I guess so."

The first few balls, Ashton ducked rather than trying to catch them. Vince finally got him past that, and left Kenzie to toss him a few while he finished unloading the truck to make room for a load of lumber he needed to pick up the next day.

Ashton's catching skills improved fast. How to hold a bat and actually make contact with the ball proved to be more of a challenge. But with Kenzie's help and about twenty strikes, Ashton finally knocked the ball down the baseline. It didn't even make it to first base, but it was a hit and enough to give Ashton cause to jump around as if he'd just won the World Series.

"Do it again." Vince straightened up the garage and kept an eye on the kids as Boo watched from the sidelines. Vince did not need Ashton to get hurt and bring Hanna down on his case.

He laid his tool belt on the bench. Actually there could be worse things. Hanna was impressive when she got all self-righteous and mother hennish.

Vince grinned at the sound of wood cracking against the ball and Ashton's "Woohoo!" If these two kept this up for a while, maybe by next year Ashton would be able to hold his own on the diamond.

Billy Baer and two of his buddies pedaled up the drive and spun their bikes sideways. "Mackenzie, you're wasting your time on the nerd."

Shit! Not what Ashton needed.

"The only time I'm wasting is any time you're around." Kenzie tossed the ball to Ashton, and Vince could see the concentration and focus but nervousness won out and he missed.

Billy guffawed. "You suck worse than a girl."

"If girls suck so bad, then why do I always get picked before you?" Kenzie boasted.

Vince put his hands in his pockets and turned to Billy. "So, you any good? Maybe you could show Ashton?"

"Dad! We don't want Bully Baer here."

Vince removed his cap, stuck it on Ashton's curly hair and took the ball from Kenzie. "Come on, Billy, let's hit a few."

Laying his bike down, Billy eyed Vince suspiciously. "Sure. Why not? I can hit better with my eyes closed than the nerd can."

Vince threw a couple of balls and allowed Billy to hit them. "Good job," Vince said as the ball sailed past the makeshift second-base sycamore tree.

Billy's smug expression grew as one of the other boys retrieved the ball and tossed it back to Vince. He let Bully Baer hit one more and his two buddies clicked fists. "See, nerd. That's how it's done."

Kenzie paced with Boo dogging her heels and Ashton looked downright miserable. Vince put a slight spin on the next throw and Billy barely made contact. The ball fouled off to the right just missing the mailbox—uh, first base.

"No fair, you didn't throw it right. One more time."

Kenzie tossed the ball back to Vince.

Adding more spin, Vince curved it directly over "home plate" and Billy swung, missing the ball as it curled to the left and bounced down the drive.

"What was that?"

"A strike, you idiot," Kenzie yelled.

"Mackenzie." Vince shut her down with a raised eyebrow. He'd probably hear about that tonight, but at least she hushed.

"Throw me another one," Billy demanded.

Vince threw him another curveball. Billy missed and flung the bat on the driveway. "You're cheating."

"Just your basic curveball. Watch any pitcher worth his salt."

"I can't hit those! They're stupid."

The shorter kid who'd ridden up with him shrugged. "Even I can throw a curveball and I'm just learning to pitch."

Billy's face turned as red as his bike.

"Here, try another one," Vince offered. "A little practice and you'll get into the swing."

Ashton grinned for the first time since Billy Baer and his team of misfits had arrived. "Yeah, even you weren't born knowing everything."

Vince tossed the ball to the kid who claimed to know how to throw a curveball. "So you're a pitcher? How about you toss some balls and let the others take turns hitting? Everybody can benefit from practice."

As they took positions, Billy shoved past Ashton. "At least I can hit most of them."

"At least my belly doesn't jiggle like a bowl of Jell-O when I run," Ashton returned.

Vince narrowed an eye. Not exactly a manly chide, but Ashton was standing up for himself. For a minute, Vince wondered if he was going to have to pull them apart, but they both took note of him and let it drop.

"What's going on here?" a female voice asked from behind his shoulder.

Hanna Rosser. He recognized that husky voice without even turning around. No woman in nine years had captured his attention the way she had. Not since Belinda… "A friendly little game of baseball."

"And what are you doing?"

"Refereeing." Vince snagged the ball Ashton fouled and tossed it back to the pitcher.

"Since when does a friendly game of baseball require a ref?"

He glanced her way. "Since Bully Baer joined the competition."

Today was the day Bluebonnet Books opened, and Hanna sported a white skirt and lacy turquoise blouse. Her dark curls glistened in the sunlight.

"So, was the grand opening grand?"

She shrugged, drawing his gaze to the curves beneath her blouse. "Not as much as I'd like. We've had a steady stream, but no big rush. Thought I'd take a break and check on Ashton."

The breeze molded her skirt to her legs, and Vince

nearly groaned out loud. Long legs. Tight little ass. Those few inches of added height she had over most of the women he'd dated fueled all sorts of imaginative ideas. *Okay, Keegan. Focus on the daughter you have to raise, not lusting after her friend's mom.*

Hanna flinched as the ball bounced haphazardly off the front stoop—third base—and hit Ashton in the leg.

Vince grabbed her arm as she took a step toward her son. Her skin felt as soft as it looked. "He'll let you know if he's hurt."

Slow down. Give this time to see where it goes. She'd just come off a divorce and was probably gun shy.

Standing back, she monitored Ashton's movements until he lifted the bat to his shoulder. "This game is extremely physical."

"You ain't seen nothing yet. Next week we're tackling football."

She jerked around, anger flashing in her eyes.

Vince winked. "Kidding."

Wood cracked and Ashton's ball popped high into the trees. Billy Baer raced down the street in pursuit.

"Look, Mom!"

"Way to go, Ashton."

"Run!" Kenzie jumped up and down and squealed.

Ashton flew around the makeshift bases whooping like a hyena. Mailbox, sycamore tree, front step and back to the drive. "Safe!"

Both Ashton and Kenzie bounced up and down like kangaroos until Ashton slowed down, wheezing.

Hanna took a step toward her son, but Ashton shook his head and straightened.

After his breathing settled, she let out an audible sigh and turned back to Vince.

"Asthma?" Vince asked. That would explain a little of her overprotective streak.

"It's improved a lot from when he was small." Hanna smiled. "Thanks for this. He sounded beaten down when he called earlier."

A thank-you? From Hanna? "You're welcome. It's a kick actually to have a boy to teach things to." For a quick second, thoughts of what it'd been like to teach his own son made him pause. Funny that no matter how hard he tried, he couldn't picture Matt at fourteen. He winced at the memory. His son would remain eternally five.

Hanna turned around. "It seems you spend a lot of time teaching Mackenzie things. She's not jealous of you working with another kid?"

"Kenzie can hold her own. A little friendly competition is healthy."

Billy puffed back into the yard and tossed the ball to Kenzie. "We gotta go."

"Good," Kenzie said in her typical "dislike for Bully Baer" tone.

He gathered his posse and the three of them mounted their bikes and sped off around the corner.

"Sore loser." Kenzie led Ashton and Boo into the house as if they'd just won a championship.

"So you're okay with sports?"

"I'm okay with Ashton smiling, and that hasn't happened much since this whole divorce debacle." Hanna raised one eyebrow. "Just as long as he doesn't overdo. He keeps an inhaler in his pocket."

"I'll keep an eye on him when he's here." Vince said as Boo ambled out the front door, displaying a dog biscuit like a trophy. The kids followed behind with sodas.

"So, Dad. You think Ash could tag along this weekend if we get to tube down the Guadalupe?"

"Mom, can I? It'd be awesome."

"That is a big *if,*" Vince said to Kenzie.

Shifting from one foot to the other, Hanna glanced from the kids to Vince. "It's April. Probably too cold to go tubing."

He tugged Kenzie's ponytail. "The temperature is supposed to be close to ninety, but the weather has to hold out and it still may be chilly in the water."

"We did it last year and it was a blast because it wasn't crowded. Remember?" Kenzie grinned. "We had a picnic at the bottom of the float, then swam. Ash has never been tubing."

"Maybe this summer when it's warmer," Hanna offered.

Was her concern really for the cold water, or was it entrusting Ashton into Vince's care? Vince offhandedly said, "You could come with."

Kenzie cocked her head and stared at him as if he'd suddenly sprouted pointy ears, but she and Ashton both turned to Hanna.

"Please, Mom. Tubing and swimming and a picnic. Come on."

She squeezed Ashton's shoulder and glanced nervously at Vince. "We don't want to intrude on the Keegans' trip."

"No intrusion at all." The idea of spending the day with Hanna Rosser, in wet swimsuits no less, had already kicked his imagination into overdrive. He wasn't sure it was the smartest thing to do, but damned if she wasn't the most interesting thing to come along in years.

"So…? Cool. We're going tubing!" Kenzie high-fived Ashton.

Ashton stared at his mother as if daring her to ruin the adventure.

Hanna glanced at Vince. "We're going tubing."

Chapter 6

In spite of having been coerced into tubing down the Guadalupe, Hanna awoke with unfamiliar excitement at the thought of the day ahead. And if she were honest with herself, the man who'd instigated this adventure had more than a little something to do with that.

Just a fun day on the river. It had been a rough few months for Ashton and he'd had his life turned topsy-turvy by the divorce. Today would be a good escape. A fun adventure. Nothing in Dallas could match the friendship he'd found here. He smiled more with Mackenzie than with any friend he'd ever had.

The sun was barely up when Hanna and Ashton piled their stuff into the bed of Vince's red pickup. No magnetic Keegan's Docks signs on the doors today. However, the Keegan's Docks cap Ashton had worn home from the ball game earlier in the week had become a permanent accessory. It was the first thing he donned when he got home from school and the last thing he removed before his bath.

The pink-and-orange sunrise faded into a clear blue sky while they grabbed a quick bag of fresh-baked goodies at a local bakery. The early-morning breeze cut through her thin cotton T-shirt, but the sun should warm it up before they hit the river.

Back in the truck the kids chattered nonstop, eliminating any awkward silence. With Ashton and Mackenzie around, Vince would play the role of doting father, not tentative suitor. It should be a relaxed day for them all.

The two-hour drive passed in no time. As they cruised into Gruene, the small community was just waking up. The pickup bounced across the gravel parking area as Vince pulled around and came to a stop under a huge pecan tree. "Pile out. Let's float!"

Mackenzie knew the drill and jumped into her sidekick role, hauling their paraphernalia down to the water. Vince didn't even have to tell her what to do. Father and daughter made quite a team. Ashton took his lead from Mackenzie, although he bounced around like a jumping bean while helping. Hanna just stood to the side, clutching Ashton's blue life jacket and feeling useless.

Vince noted the life jacket and narrowed an eye. "He does know how to swim, right?"

"Of course he knows how to swim." She hadn't forgotten Vince's analogy when they'd first argued over the kids. "But he isn't a very strong swimmer."

"It's shallow and he'll be on the tube. I'll watch him."

Holding the vest to herself, she closed her eyes, weighing Ashton's safety against the need not to embarrass him. The only other person with a vest on the rafting tour was a little girl who appeared to be about three.

Reluctantly Hanna tossed the vest into the truck. "Don't let them get too far away from you."

Vince slammed the tailgate and locked down the cover. "You got it."

"How much do I owe you for the tickets?"

Walking backward toward the river, he flashed a grin. "I'll settle for a smile."

She rolled her eyes. Okay, so she'd deal with repaying him later. This was not a date, and she didn't want him to think she expected him to pay her and Ashton's way, especially when they'd horned in on the Keegans' outing.

"Pictures." Hanna pulled her camera out of her purse.

The young college-age guide took the camera from her and motioned for her to join Vince and the kids. "You don't want to be left out."

Hanna eased in behind Ashton and smiled. The guide assumed they were a family, but then why shouldn't he?

The guide handed her back the camera and covered the rules for the group of about fifteen, then they were set. Each group stayed together to some extent.

Vince zipped Hanna's camera into the waterproof bag along with Ashton's inhaler and his T-shirt. They had a fifth tube tied to Vince's with water bottles, towels and a few supplies sealed up for the trip. Vince called out, "Kids, stay together and don't drift off. It's not deep in most places, but grab the tube if you flip."

Hanna sucked in her breath and diverted her gaze, but she kept sneaking peeks at Vince's long, muscled torso. Sandy hair covered his chest, then narrowed to a thin line, running down his stomach and disappearing beneath his dark swim trunks. Not that her ex was bad on the eyes, but Vince had at least a half foot on Richard's five foot nine inches and from her vantage point, all those inches were in his chest. Okay, so maybe a couple were exhibited in those long legs. Where Richard's legs were shorter and thicker, Vince had runner's legs.

She and the kids started out with T-shirts over their swimsuits. The water was like ice cubes when Hanna waded in. River rocks poked into her bare feet as she awkwardly plopped into the tube, but as soon as her body adjusted, the water felt invigorating.

Mackenzie shed her T-shirt before they got started. Following her lead, Ashton tossed his to Mackenzie, and she piled them on the extra tube. They both jammed their caps on their heads backwards.

Hanna scrubbed her hands over the chill bumps, but kept her wet T-shirt on. It'd warm up as soon as they floated out from beneath the trees and into the center of the river.

She'd enjoyed rafting on her high school senior trip, but she'd only had to worry about herself, not her son. She'd assumed she'd be more nervous with Ashton along. Maybe it had to do with the way Vince, in his laid-back way, always gave the impression that he was in control.

A couple of groups floated past, but there was no rush to get anywhere. The day was theirs and she loved the kids' laughter. Water had soaked through her T-shirt and in spite of the sun, goose bumps speckled her arms. The other three river rats in her party looked perfectly comfortable as both kids decided to kick water on Vince. He returned the challenge, and Hanna gave up on the T-shirt. She wasn't entirely comfortable with

Vince seeing her in a bathing suit, even if she had worn her conservative navy-blue one-piece. But it was insane to ruin the day by freezing.

She eased the dripping T-shirt over her head and Vince paddled over and took it from her, then tossed it on top of the others. His perusal warmed her body even more than shedding the icy cotton shirt had.

"Having fun?"

She glanced up at the tree canopy overhanging the river. "I'd forgotten how beautiful the river is."

"Yeah, we try to come once in the spring and once in the fall when school is in session. Fewer crowds."

She returned his grin. "Good plan. The one time I came was mid-July and you couldn't see the water for the tubes."

His warm chuckle engulfed her. "Kids are having fun."

The giggles validated his remark. Hanna dipped her hands in the water and let the drops trickle through her fingers.

Ashton's scream and a splash brought her straight up, almost tipping her own inner tube over. Mackenzie's head was visible between the two tubes, but if Ashton was above water, he was hidden by the tubes. She caught a glimpse of Vince and stopped herself before she bolted into the water. Vince's body was tense and his eyes glued to the scene, but he hadn't made a move toward them.

Hanna turned just as Ashton's head popped up, then both kids stood. The water barely reached their waists, but even though he'd flipped in a shallow spot in the river, Ashton could have hit his head on a rock. He shoved the hair out of his face, and she thought he was crying before she realized he was actually laughing.

"That was cool. I flipped twice."

Mackenzie bent double, guffawing. "All I could see were flying arms and legs."

"Happy to give you something to laugh at there, Kenzie." Ashton dumped the water out of his Keegan's Docks cap and tugged it over his curls.

Still laughing, both hoisted themselves back into the tubes. "You looked like an octopus."

Releasing her breath, Hanna glanced at Vince.

He winked. "Resilient little critters, kids."

"Ash, grab hold of my rope." Mackenzie paddled closer and tossed him her tow rope. "This way we don't have to work so hard to stay together."

The tension eased out of Hanna's body and she just drifted with the water. Everyone who floated past seemed happy and the kids were never out of Vince's sight. She needed this escape as much as Ashton did.

It probably took them an extra half hour to reach the park area where they were to have a picnic, but Hanna didn't care. She wrapped her towel around her waist and quickly discarded the idea of putting on her wet T-shirt.

Exhausted from the float, they wolfed down hot dogs cooked on a rusty outdoor grill provided by the tour company. They tasted better than dinner at the Mansion on Turtle Creek. Orange Cheeto dust stuck to Hanna's fingertips as her napkin blew away. Ashton caught it and tossed it in the trash can, so Hanna settled for licking the orange dust off her fingertips.

Vince laughed. "Want another hot dog?"

She popped her pinky finger out of her mouth and

hoped she wasn't blushing. "No, I filled up on cheese chips."

Vince's cell phone chimed, and Hanna turned away to give him privacy.

"Vince." There was a slight pause. "Hey, Grayson. Okay, let me see if they can spare Gutierrez on the Barkley dock for the day. I'll send him your way."

Grayson? Had to be Grayson Maguire, Belinda's twin brother. Not exactly an everyday name.

Vince hung up, made another brief call and called Grayson back. "Gray, he's on his way." She could hear rambling over the phone, but Vince didn't seem too interested. "Everything else okay? Listen, I'm kind of busy. I'll talk to you Monday." He laughed. "Yeah, or see you at the folks' tomorrow. Thanks again. I owe you."

The folks? The Maguires?

"Mom, can we swim before the van leaves?" Ashton begged. "Please. I finished two hot dogs."

Tossing her paper plate into the trash can, Hanna nodded. "Sure, I'll come down there and watch."

Ashton raced after Kenzie. "Wait up. I'm right behind you."

"Last one in is a dead fish," Vince said, yanking his T-shirt off, tossing it and his cell phone on the riverbank and charging ahead of them and into the water.

Hanna sat on the cool grass and watched Vince hoist Mackenzie up on his shoulders then toss her unceremoniously into the water. He repeated the act for Ashton, who raised his arms and pointed them over his head as Vince bent and dumped him into the river. Just hearing Ashton squeal and laugh, seeing him energized, warmed Hanna's soul. She didn't remember him ever laughing so much. She snapped a few pictures as both kids piled on Vince and tried to push him under. They did finally succeed, but he took them both with him.

After fifteen minutes of frolicking, Vince dropped down on the riverbank beside Hanna. "You could have joined us."

"I'm too full."

"Yeah, cheese chips. You were just afraid I'd get the best of you."

"Right. That was it." She refused to stare at the droplets of water dripping off his hair and onto his chest. The guy did have a certain irresistible, Southern charm. "Did you and Belinda bring the kids here?"

He skimmed water off his arms and pulled on the T-shirt. "No. They weren't old enough. We did Sea World and the circus. Made a trip to South Padre Island. Belinda always enjoyed the beach."

"Richard isn't the outdoors type. We took Ashton to New York summer before last. Caught a play and a couple of museums."

"Man, I loved New York. Spent a summer studying there between my junior and senior years. Incredible energy."

"New York?" Now that was something she wouldn't have guessed. "What was your major?"

He stretched out on his back. "Engineering. Actually I was taking classes across the Hudson in Jersey. I had landed an internship with a company in Austin that designs bridges and they worked with the college and arranged the summer in New York. We studied some of the city's bridge designs."

And now he was designing boat docks and decks. "Did you finish your master's?"

"Bachelor's, but never got a chance to go beyond that. Best-laid plans."

The damp cotton stretched across his wide chest and pulled tight with each breath. And those legs poking out from the long black swim trunks were equally impressive.

"What happened?" Norma had mentioned that he and Belinda had met at the University of Texas.

Vince closed his eyes against the bright sun, or against more questions and rubbed the stubble on his chin. "Life."

Which was more interesting, the sun glistening off the water as the kids splashed or watching Vince's chest rise and fall? He bent one knee and adjusted his position, but his breathing remained even.

Ashton struggled to dunk Mackenzie, but it didn't appear there was much danger of that. If she were a regular girl, Hanna would've put a stop to it, but Mackenzie had already pushed him under before Hanna could react.

Hanna's gaze drifted from the kids back to Vince. He had promised to keep an eye on Ashton, yet he was napping? Leaning forward, she frowned, then noticed that his eyes were half-open.

"They're fine, Hanna."

Insane. How the heck did he know what she was thinking?

The tour vans were packing up to haul everyone back to Gruene, and Hanna motioned for the kids to come to shore. "You two need to get out and dry off."

"Mom," Ashton wailed. "Just five more minutes?"

Propping up on his elbows, Vince appeared as reluctant as the kids to leave. Yet he didn't override her command. "Come on, Kenzie. Out."

To Hanna's amazement, Mackenzie didn't even put up a fuss, just hopped out of the river and snuggled into the towel her father wrapped around her dripping shoulders. Ashton looked as bemused as Hanna, but followed his friend's lead. It seemed that the trick to getting her son to mind was simply getting Kenzie to mind.

After showers at the bath hut and changing into shorts, they piled their wet paraphernalia into Vince's pickup and set out to explore the historic riverside community of Gruene. The small town looked like a postcard with antique stores and restaurants lining the main street. Hanna snapped pictures of the kids with the water tower in the background and one of Vince and the kids eating ice cream in front of the old dance hall.

"Hey, kids. I want a few pictures in the bluebonnets over there."

"Geesh." Ashton groaned. "More pictures?"

"Come on, Ash. They won't stop pestering us until we cooperate."

After a few shots of the kids, Vince grabbed her camera. "Get in the shot with them."

Hanna waded into the small patch of bluebonnets behind the children and put a hand on each kid's shoulder. Ashton let him take a picture, then picked his way out of the flowers and reached for the camera. "My turn to take pictures. You get in the shot."

Hanna sucked in a breath as Vince squatted down between her and Kenzie, his knee bumping against Hanna's. Kenzie perched on his knee and Vince put his hand on Hanna's shoulder.

"Smile, Mom."

Both she and Vince had been seeing that the kids had a good time, but the sun was beginning to set and Hanna's one hot dog was no longer enough. "Anybody up for dinner?"

"Grist Mill!" Mackenzie yelled. "It's my favorite and we can eat outside."

"Grist Mill!" Ashton mimicked although he'd never been to Gruene before today and couldn't have any idea if he even liked the food.

Vince swept one arm elaborately and led them all across the street. "Grist Mill, it is."

Mackenzie didn't give anyone else a chance to answer when the hostess asked whether they wanted outside or in. "Outside, where we can see the river."

As the hostess led the way, the kids trooped along behind her. Hanna's breath caught at the feel of Vince's hand on the small of her back, ushering her toward the table. Just a gentlemanly gesture. A very intimate, masculine, gentlemanly gesture.

Hanna hadn't been to Gruene since high school and she'd never eaten in the old mill converted into an open-air restaurant. Rustic and quaint, it sprawled down the hillside toward the river with small decks and tables nestled into the trees.

Mackenzie raced over to a corner table, one of the few that actually offered a view through the trees to the river. A group of late-afternoon tubers floated by, laughing and waving.

Ashton leaned over the wooden rail and waved back. "This is sooo cool."

Hanna slid along the bench on one side, but Ashton took his seat beside Mackenzie on the other bench.

Vince joined Hanna and leaned back against the rail as the waitress placed the menus in front of them.

With all the spring pollen, Ashton was beginning to wheeze. Unsure whether she'd embarrass him or not, Hanna used a hand gesture to simulate the inhaler.

Reluctantly Ashton pulled it out and took a quick breath, then shoved it back into his pocket.

Kenzie just grinned like it wasn't anything out of the ordinary. Hanna hoped that was a sign that he'd used it in front of her before when he'd needed it.

The sun set as they were finishing their meals, and the kids raced over into the trees where there were more picnic tables. Ashton stopped to rub a black-and-white cat that was more intent on bathing his paws than on the horde of restaurant patrons watching him.

Hanna turned to Vince. His skin was a shade darker from today's adventure and his hair a shade lighter. The whole effect with the sunset colors made those blue eyes twinkle. "Amazing what one day away can do."

Vince twirled the saltshaker on the table. "Yeah, getting away from the rat race is good for the soul."

"So, will you get angry if I ask you a personal question?"

He shrugged. "Shoot."

The waitress refilled their iced-tea glasses and cleared away the dishes.

"How do you do it? I'm scared to death every time Ashton is out of my sight. Part of that is because of his asthma, but also something might happen that I could have prevented. How do you stand giving Mackenzie all that freedom? How do you resist locking her up so she won't get hurt?"

He grinned. "First off, if she's doing something she

shouldn't and I don't catch her, somebody else will and let me know."

Hanna shook her head and sighed. "Ahh, the notorious small-town grapevine."

Vince raised an eyebrow then he ran one hand through his hair. "After Belinda and Matt were killed, I wanted to. God, I wanted to. My parents smothered us. We were at their house every weekend and some evenings for dinner. They're workaholics and their answer was to hire a nanny to watch Kenzie while I worked sixty-hour weeks. I tried to make Austin work, for a few months."

Hanna studied his profile as he watched the kids.

"But my in-laws loved Kenzie, too, and me. They'd lost their only daughter and my three-year-old little girl had lost her mother. She and her grandparents needed one another to fill that void. I wanted to be a bigger part of my daughter's life and Corporate America didn't allow time for that. So moving to Marble Falls and starting a business made sense on a lot of levels. I figured the best way to give Kenzie a happy life and at the same time to keep her safe was to spend time with her and to teach her to think for herself. Maybe if I'd done more of that in my marriage, my wife and son would still be alive."

"I'm sorry about your loss." Hanna felt tears well up at the back of her eyes. "You love the Maguires very much."

"I do." Vince took a long drink of iced tea and forced a smile. "They're family. Good folks."

Good folks. They'd filled the void from the loss of their daughter not only with Mackenzie, but also with Vince. And it appeared to be mutual.

"Vince, just so you understand, I'm still struggling with how to be a single parent. I've worried since Ashton was a toddler and we almost lost him to a serious asthma attack, but now I'm solely responsible for his safety. Richard loves Ashton, too, but he believes he'd be better off in Dallas. I can't give him fuel for that argument. Your tactics won't work in my favor."

Ashton wove his way through the picnic tables toward them, the black-and-white cat cradled in his arms. "Look, Mom. Isn't he beautiful? Touch him, feel how soft."

Cats and asthma, not a good mix. Yet she didn't want to ruin the day for Ashton. She ran one hand down the cat's tail. It wrapped around her hand and slid through as the cat purred like a Weed Eater. "Yes, he is. Now go put him back in the trees before you start wheezing."

That earned her a glare from Mackenzie, but Ashton turned and eased his way back into the more open area of the rambling restaurant, carrying the cat like a precious bundle.

She felt Vince's stare. "Don't tell me. He needs a pet."

"There are breeds of dogs that are supposed to be safe for asthma sufferers."

"He has allergies." Hanna set her jaw and crumpled her napkin. "I realize he's lonely and a pet might be a good idea, but we're living in my mom's house and no way am I going to add one more stress factor to the mix."

Vince leaned around and she thought for a second he might touch her, but instead he picked up his glass. "He can stop by and play with Boo anytime. Maybe that'll help."

The way he looked at her warmed her heart, even though her common sense argued that she was on the rebound. Feeling undesirable. "It would—help, that is."

His intense gaze burned into hers, but she couldn't break away. "You look relaxed. Happy. Beautiful."

So did he. But she couldn't very well say that. "I appreciate you letting us crash your father-daughter adventure. Today's been magical for Ashton. He so needed an escape. We both did. As good as my mom is to us and as much as I love her, sometimes..."

He shook the ice in his glass and drained the last drop. "I love my mom, too, but if I had to live with her one of us would kill the other within a week. Tops."

"But you're close to them."

"Yeah, they're in Austin. And they idolize Kenzie. They're taking her to Disney World over spring break. My brother owns a large animal clinic a couple of hundred miles south, so we only see him two or three times a year."

"I'm an only kid," Hanna said. "Siblings would be good. Mom just has me and Ashton to fret over."

"Brothers mostly look for any excuse to pound each other senseless those first few years. Leo is still a self-absorbed ass most of the time. Has more sympathy for animals than people, but I haven't been tempted to take a swing at him in...I don't know, a month or two."

"Leo?"

"My parents have a strange take on baby names. Leonardo and Vincent. What's up with that?" Vince kicked back and laughed. "In middle school, we got it in our heads to take them to court for cruel and unusual punishment."

Hanna smiled. "How'd that work out for you?"

"We knew a lot of lawyers, but we couldn't come up with one strong enough to go up against our mother. A good mom, but a force to be reckoned with in the courtroom."

"Your mom is an attorney?"

He nodded. "My mom is a hell of an attorney."

Mackenzie and Ashton returned, sans the cat, and sat down. Ashton slurped the last drop of his pop through the straw. "We don't have cool places to eat like this in Dallas."

"Dallas does not sound like my kinda place," Mackenzie chimed in. "No way I could wear a dumb uniform and look like every other kid, including dweebs like Bully Baer, every day. I'd wear striped sneakers or something so as to *not* be like them."

Probably very little danger that Mackenzie would not distinguish herself in any situation. If not with her trend-setting attire, with her outgoing personality.

The lights around the restaurant came on, and Ashton's eyes sparkled. "Can we come back this summer? We can do everything exactly like we did today."

"We'll see. I don't want to impose on Mom by expecting her to run the bookstore alone all the time." Hanna wasn't sure what the summer would bring, she was so busy trying to get through the now. Bookstore. Single-parenting. Living with Mom. The Keegans.

As they made their way out of the restaurant, the old dance hall was lit and a few couples danced as the jukebox crooned George Strait. The music filtered through the screen windows and created an ambiance of a gentler, more carefree time in Hanna's life.

Vince put his hand on the small of her back. "Ever been dancing in the Gruene Dance Hall?"

Hanna fought a blush at the warmth of the gesture. "Are kids allowed inside?"

"They'll be fine as long as they're with us. Looks like a sedate sort of crowd. No band tonight."

They wandered in and took a seat watching the couples as they stomped and swayed to the Texas two-step.

Ashton grabbed Mackenzie's hand. "Come on."

Mackenzie watched him dancing the two-step a few minutes, then held up her hands and grinned at Vince, nodding toward Ashton. "Who'd a thunk it?" She started mimicking Ashton's steps. "How do I look?"

A little awkward on the steps, but she seemed to be feeling the music as they strutted.

"Lookin' good," Vince said, then took Hanna's hand and pulled her to her feet. "I don't know about you, but I'm not about to let a couple of sixth-graders show me up." He fell into step beside Ashton. "Is this right? Show me again."

Delighted, Ashton assumed the role of instructor for the other three. Hanna hadn't country-danced in years, but she'd made sure that Ashton took lessons in all styles of dance. She'd always loved to dance, to lose her inhibitions and let the music move her. Tonight, Ashton's lessons were paying off as he beamed from ear to ear, leading Mackenzie and Vince through the steps.

Surprisingly, given Vince's lankiness, he demonstrated decent rhythm as he followed Ashton's direction. Hanna wasn't so much trying to two-step as she was just feeling the music and letting her body move. She missed a step and realized she was watching Vince more than she was Ashton. Pure symmetry.

After a bit, the adults sat and contented themselves with watching the kids. Hanna relaxed into the old wooden straight-back chair and turned to find Vince staring at her. He flashed those deep dimples and sauntered over to the jukebox before stopping by the bar for four sodas.

Hanna was so parched from dancing that she gulped hers down even faster than the kids did. Mackenzie and Ashton didn't sit, just finished their drinks and hit the little section of dance floor closest to Hanna and Vince that they'd been monopolizing.

When the Bellamy Brothers catchy tune "If I Said You Had a Beautiful Body, Would You Hold It Against Me?" cranked up, Vince tilted his head toward the dance floor and winked at Hanna. "This is more my speed. Whatta you say?"

Hold her body against Vince Keegan's long, tight, sexy frame? Probably not Hanna's wisest move.

Vince tugged her to her feet. "You can't come to the country's oldest dance hall and just sit. Where's the fun in that?"

"Come on, Mom. It's not hard at all," Ashton said, wiggling his little butt.

Placing her right hand on Vince's shoulder and her left around his waist, she tried to relax. When she was younger dancing had come naturally. But now? With Vince? "Song's sorta cheesy, don't you think?"

He covered her hand and held it flat against his shoulder. "I don't know. Seemed to serve the purpose." She didn't resist the pressure of his left hand secure against her waist. The melody filled her body and she allowed the rhythm to take control and flow through her. She leaned her head back to study Vince as he buried his long fingers in her hair. She leaned into the caress then nuzzled her head against his shoulder.

God, her bruised ego craved the attention of this attractive male. She needed to feel attractive, desirable to the opposite sex.

She closed her eyes and drifted around the scarred wood floor in Vince's arms. The same dance floor where thousands of others had danced for over a century. But dancing with Vince was so different from dancing with Richard. Richard knew the steps, but Vince just moved to the rhythm and…to the lyrics. Even being five foot eight, she felt small and feminine within his arms. His heart beat against hers as they moved as one.

Everything about Vince was different from Richard. His casual approach. His subtle come-on. Okay, not so subtle given his choice in music.

"Daddy, dance with me now," Mackenzie demanded. "Let's trade partners."

The spell shattered and Hanna eased out of Vince's arms. He seemed nonplussed as he took Mackenzie's hands and flashed a smile, then spun her around and through the few couples on the floor.

Oblivious to what was going on, Ashton happily grabbed Hanna's hands. "I haven't ever, ever had this much fun."

Hanna held Ashton's hand and tried to follow his steps, but her gaze followed Vince as he twirled his giggling young daughter.

By the time they walked to the truck, Ashton was yawning at every other step. He wasn't accustomed to so much physical activity and it was ten o'clock, his bedtime. Vince took Hanna's hand and steadied her as she climbed into the tall pickup. The kids buckled into the backseat and were both asleep before they even got out of town.

Vince was quiet most of the two-hour drive as they let the kids sleep, but every time Hanna dared a glance his way, he was looking back at her. Like those tentatively exchanged glances across the high-school lunch-room, only not so tentative. It was way too soon after her divorce and too early in this friendship to be thinking these thoughts. She should not be fantasizing about Vince Keegan's long, lean body against hers. And that dimple-bracketed mouth conjured up all sorts of interesting ideas.

She stared out at the stars, so much brighter out here away from artificial city lights. The air-conditioned cab, quiet and intimate, cocooned them in the night as they drove toward home. Kids sleeping peacefully in the back. Handsome guy driving. Oh yeah, way too much like a family.

Yet, pulling into town, Hanna wished it wasn't over. Her life of late was anything but romantic and peaceful. Vince swung the pickup into her mother's drive, and Hanna smiled. "Thanks again for a fantastic day. Ashton had such a wonderful time."

He leaned forward and wrapped a curl around his finger. "So did I."

Staring into his eyes, her breath caught in her throat.

He slid his hand down her cheek and behind her neck, urging her closer. Closing her eyes to keep from drowning in the depths of his deep-blue ones, she gravitated toward his warmth, waiting, wanting.

After an eternity, his lips touched hers. Warm and gentle as he deepened the caress.

The taste and pressure of his lips moving over hers

spun time away. As though she were being pulled, she tilted her head for a better angle. Scooting close, she adjusted her position to feel his heat and touched her tongue to his lips. His hand increased the pressure on her waist, urging her closer as he opened his mouth to hers, exploring and spinning her senses into a hot frenzy for more, faster, hotter.

His ten-o'clock shadow scratched her palm before she slid her hand around his neck to hold him close. She squeezed her legs together and tried to squelch the building warmth. Her tongue met his, acquainting itself with his.

The kids stirred in the backseat and Ashton sat up, rubbing the sleep from his eyes. "Are we there?"

Hanna shot backwards, away from Vince's magnetic pull and toward reality. If Ashton had witnessed the kiss, he wasn't letting on. "We're home."

Chapter 7

Hanna couldn't get last night's kiss off her mind. Even as she walked to Bluebonnet Books on Sunday, she inhaled the scent of someone grilling outside and tasted Vince's kiss, felt his sexy mouth on hers. And whether she wanted to admit it or not, it left her aching for more.

She wasn't a teenager and rebound romances were always a mistake, but that didn't cool the warmth inside her. She glanced up each time someone came through the door wondering if it might be Kenzie come to see Ashton, perhaps with her father in tow. But Vince was probably with his family today. And it was too soon after Richard's betrayal for Hanna to rush into anything.

By Thursday, she'd convinced herself that the kiss had meant a lot less to Vince. Kenzie had brought Ashton home each afternoon on her bike right on time. But no sign of her father. Which was probably for the best.

Hanna finished checking out the last of a group of tourists and glanced at the clock. Ashton should have been here fifteen minutes ago. She watched the second hand on the clock slowly tick another few minutes, but still no red electric bike.

No need to panic or assume the worst. Except she did. Were the kids hurt? Had some sicko grabbed them after school? When Hanna was growing up here, crime was practically unheard of. But nowadays, even small towns had their share of perverts.

Maybe they'd gotten into trouble again and had to stay after school. But the school would have called, wouldn't they?

Okay, deep breath. Maybe they'd gone to Mackenzie's to play the Wii or practice softball. At one time she'd have felt confident that Ashton would call, but since meeting Kenzie, he'd become rebellious. A moody pre-teen had replaced her quiet, levelheaded, straight-A student.

She didn't have Mackenzie's cell number. She did *not* want to call Vince. It was best if she extinguished whatever spark she felt before it got started. Yet she had no choice. She needed to know Ashton was safe, and calling Vince would be easier than driving over there and having to face him.

Once the store started showing a profit, she'd get Ashton a cell phone. But for now, she had to watch every penny. Reluctantly she dialed Vince's number, her worry for Ashton outweighing her need to avoid talking to Vince.

"Vince," he yelled over pounding and the loud zing of nail guns.

"It's Hanna!" she yelled in return. "Do you know

where Mackenzie and Ashton are? They didn't show up here after school."

"Just a second." Heavy bootsteps on wood and the sound of the nail guns subsided. "The kids haven't shown up?"

Her heart plummeted. They obviously weren't with him. "No."

"Let me try Kenzie's cell. I'll call you right back."

Hanna continued to watch the second hand on the clock. It circled four and a half times before her cell rang. "They're out on the lake fishing. I told them to get home."

"On the lake? In a boat?" What next? "God, if it's not one thing it's ten with that girl. Mackenzie may be allowed to run amuck, but Ashton has to be where he's supposed to be when he's supposed to be there."

"Hanna, stop. They didn't ask my permission either. They should be at the bookstore in fifteen minutes or so. You need to calm down." The line went silent.

Hanna stared at the dead phone. He'd hung up on her? Her hands shook as she slid the phone back into her pocket. Ashton knew better than this. He knew the rules. But because Mackenzie didn't have rules, Ashton didn't think he had to follow his either.

Vince no more than got out of the truck at Bluebonnet Books than Kenzie flew out the door. "She's really, really ticked off this time."

Vince tossed his ball cap on the seat and slammed the door. "Did Ashton ask if he could go fishing?"

"I don't know. I just asked if he wanted to and he did."

"Well, you know better than to go out in that boat

without telling me and you didn't, so I'm figuring Ashton didn't ask either."

Kenzie looked down. "Sorry."

"We'll take that up at home."

Luckily there were no customers in the bookstore when Vince marched Kenzie in. Ashton sat in one of the chairs in the little coffee section, looking as if he'd lost his last friend. Which, if Hanna had her way after this, might not be far off the mark.

When Hanna saw them enter, she walked up from the rear of the shop. "Mr. Keegan."

They were back to surnames? It was like Saturday hadn't happened. Like she'd never let him kiss her. "Ms. Rosser." Vince looked between the three angry faces. "Someone want to fill me in?"

"Did I not make it clear enough that Ashton was not to try new things without first asking permission?"

Vince forced his fists to unclench. "And I thought I made that clear to Kenzie. Obviously not." He pegged Kenzie with a glare.

Ashton stared at his sneakers and Kenzie tugged at her ball cap.

Hanna looked as if she was going to blow a gasket as she turned her attack from him to her son. "You're grounded, young man."

Ashton sneered. "For how long? I go to Dad's for spring break this weekend, and you can't ground me from that. It's in the court papers. Besides, Saturday is my birthday."

"Maybe next time you'll remember to ask permission."

"He's not a baby," Mackenzie interjected, yanking her pink cap off.

"Mackenzie." Vince shut her down.

She jammed her cap back on her head and stood, sullen but quiet, to the side.

Ashton jumped to his feet and kicked the chair. "I didn't ask because I knew you'd say no. You always say no. You don't know how to say yes to anything. I'm tired of you treating me like a baby! I hate everybody calling me a nerd! I hate it here! Why do you keep ruining my life?" He grabbed his backpack off the chair and slammed out the door, the bell clanging in his wake.

Kenzie grabbed her helmet and started after him, but Vince took the helmet out of her hand. "Make sure Ashton's okay, then meet me at home. I'll put your bike in the truck."

An eerie quiet engulfed the store in the absence of the kids. "Where's Norma today?"

"It's her bridge day. Then she's stopping to make a deposit at the bank, and she and a certain teller she knows will gossip for at least half an hour." She looked up at the ceiling and blinked, returning to the issue at hand. "Vince, I can't tolerate this!"

"Settle down. I very clearly told Kenzie the rules."

Clasping her hands, Hanna dropped down in the chair Ashton had vacated. "How am I supposed to keep him safe if he won't mind? I've never been a single parent. My whole life is upside-down and I'm expected just to know instinctively how to raise an adolescent boy. I don't understand guys. They're weird."

"Women are a little weird from our perspective, too, you know." Vince squatted down in front of her and attempted to capture her gaze. "Is something else going on?"

She scrubbed her hands down her face. "Ashton

emailed his father pictures of the tubing trip. Richard called this morning demanding to know who you were. You and Mackenzie are in most of the pictures. As you can imagine, Ashton was excited to tell his dad about all the fun he had, and evidently your name came up. A lot. So now Richard thinks you and I are…"

Vince couldn't hide a grin. "The guy fooled around while you were married, then divorced you for a younger woman. What the hell business is it of his who I am or what you and I are to each other? Tell him to f— mind his own business."

As she shook her head, Hanna's lips curved up. "That is exactly what I told him. But he feels it's his business if another man is spending time with his son."

"Male ego." Vince figured the guy was probably having second thoughts now that he could no longer control Hanna. "It has nothing to do with Ashton and everything to do with you. It's fine that he's moved on, but he sure as hell doesn't want another man to have you."

"That at least gives me some pleasure." She wiped her eyes.

Vince just wanted to hold her and make all the hurt go away. He took his thumb and wiped the remaining moisture from beneath her eyes. "You're a beautiful woman, Hanna Creed Rosser. Your ex is a moron."

Hanna stood and paced away from him, toward the back of the store. "A moron with a twenty-three-year-old blond law student who looks up to him like he's a king."

Slowly Vince approached Hanna as she straightened a shelf of knickknacks, putting them back in the exact same places they were before she started.

The corners of her bow-shaped mouth turned down.

"Thanks for the lovely compliment, Vince. But...that kiss Saturday night was...a mistake."

"I don't see it that way." He moved in closer and wrapped a silky brunette curl around his finger. "As hard as I've tried to stay away this week, not to rush things, I couldn't stop thinking about you. We have something here and you know it."

She leaned her face into his caress. "Yeah, but we're at different places."

Moving closer, he brought his lips to within a hair-breadth of hers. "I think we're at the exact same place. I've just been here a little longer."

Her gorgeous brown eyes searched his for a long moment, then fluttered closed. "Convince me."

He followed her as she backed up against the wall, then cupped her face and took her mouth for a slow, sensuous kiss. "We're both single parents." His lips traveled down her jaw to nuzzle her neck, just where it curved into her shoulder.

She sighed. "Um-hmm." Her tongue touched her lips and her eyes remained closed, her long lashes dark against her creamy complexion.

"Both our lives center around our kids and they get along." He slipped a hand behind her neck and nibbled her ear, breathing in her faint perfume. His other hand glided lower to her bottom.

"True." Her husky voice sounded breathless as she arched her back and pressed against him.

"But as much as we love our kids, we both need adult companionship." He adjusted his position so they were touching full-length and covered her mouth again, deepening the kiss.

She tilted her head back and threaded her fingers

through the hair at the nape of his neck. "You're a romantic sort. Direct and to the point."

He slid one hand beneath her shirt and up her torso to cup her breast. "Gotta be specific about what you want or you end up with a green tie with a dopey-looking Santa on it for Christmas."

A smile curved her lips and her eyes slowly opened. "Or a new vacuum with all those snazzy attachments that nobody uses. Figuratively speaking, of course."

Vince winced. "Hope he slept on the figurative sofa that night."

Her smile faded. "Vince, that Southern charm of yours is quite disarming, but I'm not ready for this. The timing just…isn't right."

"At this stage, I'm not suggesting we get married and live happily ever after."

She eased out from between him and the wall. "No. You just need a bed partner."

"You know it's more than that."

"I've only been divorced a month. I am not rushing into another mistake. I can't put Ashton through more drama."

"Hanna, at the risk of sounding crass, spring break is next week. Both kids will be out of town. I'll take you anywhere you want to go."

"And at least three people will call my mother to get the scoop before we're even out of the city limits. When I stopped by for cinnamon rolls this morning, Mrs. Barkley commented that your truck spends a lot of time parked at the bookstore."

"We'll be discreet," he said.

She laughed. "That might be a tad difficult since I

live with the queen of the grapevine." She ran her palm
down his cheek. "I can't put myself through that."

Vince tried not to grit his teeth. He understood not
being ready. Hell, it had taken him nine years to be open
to another relationship. How could he expect her to be
there straight out of a messy divorce? Yet something
felt right with Hanna that he hadn't felt in way too long.
"The last thing I want to do is add to your stress." The
woman was wound so tight she was about to snap. "I'll
back off. I won't pressure you."

"Thank you." It was some consolation that at least
she didn't look quite as relieved as he'd anticipated.

"I'm sorry the kids upset you today. And I'm sorry
for interfering with the way you're raising Ashton. Once
again I'll try to make it clear to Kenzie that Ashton
had better get your permission before they do anything
else."

Hanna rubbed her forehead. "I appreciate your support. And I realize Ashton is testing his boundaries,
testing me and I'm overreacting, taking it out on you.
There's anger buried inside Ashton and it's beginning
to erupt." Tears swamped her big brown eyes and that
tough gravelly voice cracked. "And what scares me is
that, if asked, Ashton very well might choose to move
back to Dallas with his father."

"I can't imagine. I was forced into single parenthood,
but it was just me and Kenzie and we had to figure it
out together. Nobody was trying to take her away from
me." He twisted a soft curl around his finger. There was
a lot of anger and hurt buried in Hanna, too.

Vince left Hanna locking up the shop and loaded
Kenzie's bike into the truck bed. His daughter could
use a lesson in respect.

The kitchen light was on when he got to the house, but Boo was outside. "What's up, boy?" The mutt nuzzled his hand and loped along behind him into the house.

Vince dropped onto a bar stool and watched Kenzie flounce around the kitchen, giving the dog a rawhide bone, grabbing a soda. "You want one?"

"Yeah." He took the soda she handed him. "Now sit down and let's talk."

Popping the top on her can, Kenzie flipped her ponytail behind her shoulder and took the aggressive approach. "Dad, you see what she does to him. He's not in kindergarten."

"It's not your place or mine to dictate how someone else raises their child. Hanna is doing what she feels is in Ashton's best interest whether you agree or not. And in this case, I happen to agree with her. He should have asked permission before he went fishing. And so should you."

"Sure, and have her tell him he couldn't go. I even told her we had on life jackets and she still went off on us."

Boo took his rawhide and moved a safe distance away. He flopped down in the hall to chew the treat, but his eyes followed every gesture they made.

"Hanna's his mother. She has the right to tell him he can't go."

"Just because she's his mother, that gives her the right to ruin his life?"

"Your attitude needs adjusting. Since you aren't showing that you can be responsible, the bike is off limits until after spring break. One more outburst and

I'll call Gran and Pop and cancel the Disney trip for next week."

Kenzie swallowed and her eyes got watery, but she didn't respond.

What they said about disciplining your kid hurting you more than them had never seemed quite so profound, but he'd be damned if he was going to raise a brat. "Mackenzie, I don't let other people tell me how to raise you. I make the best choices I know how to make, whether they turn out to be the right ones or not. Ms. Rosser does the same. I respect that and I expect you to do the same."

She sniffed. "Yes, sir."

"Now finish your drink and get started on your homework. I've got to make a couple of calls, then I'll start dinner."

Dinner was unusually quiet, and afterwards Kenzie returned to the living room and her homework without being told. Vince was in the middle of loading the dishwasher when Boo's ears perked and he let out a low growl from deep in his throat.

Vince dried his hands and opened the back door to find Ashton, loaded down with a backpack and a little blue overnight bag. "Hello, Mr. Keegan."

"Ashton."

"I was wondering if it'd be okay if I stayed here, at least until Saturday when my dad comes to get me."

Crap. Vince stood back and motioned him in off the dark porch. "You have a home."

Boo plodded over and sniffed Ashton's suitcase as if he expected to find a treat.

Ashton rubbed Boo's head, but didn't seem to get too much relief out of petting the dog. "My home used to be in Highland Park, but now my dad has that girl living there. I go there every other weekend, but last time he worked all day Saturday and she looked at me like she'd never seen a kid before. Then on Sunday we had to go to church, have lunch with my grandparents and then drive and meet Mom in Waco." Misery was etched in frown lines on his forehead and around his downturned mouth.

"What about your new home here? Marble Falls is pretty cool."

"Living with Nana?" He snorted. "She's totally in my business all the time. I just have this little room and only half my stuff. Mom acts all weird and mad at everything. I didn't have many friends in Dallas, but now they're always busy when I'm there, and Mom screws up the one friend I made here." Ashton tried to act tough, but his dark eyelashes were damp and spiky. "So I just need to stay here until Saturday, if that's okay."

Kenzie slipped quietly into the kitchen. "It's okay if he stays here, right, Dad? It's just two nights."

"Homework, Mackenzie."

"But…" Scowling, she turned and stomped back to the living room.

"Sit down, Ashton. You need a bottle of water or anything?"

"No, thanks. Just a place to stay." The kid deposited his stuff beside the chair and sat. "I can sleep on the sofa."

"Does your mom know where you are?"

"No, she was in the shower when I left."

Vince sat across from him. "Divorce sucks, huh?"

"It sucks green pond scum," Ashton said without

even a smirk. "Parents don't care what they do to the kid, they're so busy hating each other."

"I don't know your dad, so I'm not going to speak for him. But your mom is more worried about you and making you happy than anything else right now. You're her whole life. Divorce sucks for her, too."

"Mom says we're living in Nana's home and we have to conform, but I hate it there. I love her, but living with her is not fun."

"You and your mom will get your own place eventually. This is just temporary. Running away from things you don't like isn't going to make them go away."

"You don't know how much it sucks there."

Vince kicked back from the bar and tried to figure out whether to approach him as a kid or an adult. "When Kenzie's mom and brother were killed, it was just the two of us left. We were both upset and lost and confused. She was only three, but we stuck together. It took a while, and we still just take one day at a time and figure out what works for us. Good or bad, we're a team and we stick together. So are you and your mom. Don't you think she might be worried about where you are?"

"You could call her and tell her I'm staying over. She listens to you."

Yeah, right. "She'd listen to you, if you'd talk to her. Gotta face your problems and be involved in the solution or other people end up making decisions you don't like."

One corner of Ashton's mouth turned up. "So you're telling me to man up?"

"Pretty much. You're old enough and smart enough to do that."

"I'd look more like a man if Mom would let me get

a real haircut. She keeps taking me to a salon. Think I might tag along next time you go to your barber?"

"That's just one more thing you need to take up with your mom. She'd skin me alive if I took you for a haircut without her permission."

"So you're scared of her, too?"

"Well, yeah." Vince grinned and picked up the suitcase. "Ready to give it a shot?"

Vince kept his hand on Ashton's shoulder for moral support and had his finger on the bell when the door burst open and Hanna almost ran them down.

Car keys in hand, no makeup and wild wet corkscrew curls that smelled like shampoo. Old sweatpants and a T-shirt, but no bra.

Staring at him, she blinked, then looked down and her gaze landed on Ashton. She grabbed him by the shoulders and Vince wasn't sure whether her intent was to shake the boy or kiss him. "Where have you been? I got out of the shower and went in to see how the homework was coming and you were gone."

Ashton leaned away from her, but they were both teary-eyed. The kid didn't respond.

Straightening, Hanna stepped fully out on the porch, closed the door and faced Vince. "What's going on here?"

This was between mother and son, and Vince's intent was to deliver the boy and stay the hell out of it. "Ashton, you going to tell your mom?"

Ashton shrugged, and Hanna finally noticed the blue suitcase and backpack. "You ran away from home?"

"Oh come on, Mom. Don't act so surprised." He shoved past her, lugging his suitcase and backpack.

"Thank goodness I'm going to Dad's for a week." The door slammed behind him.

Hanna put her hands on her hips and stared up at the sky. "What next? I can't take this anymore. I don't know what to do."

It took all Vince's willpower not to pull her into his arms. Instead he squeezed her shoulder. "Just one day at a time."

Chapter 8

Hanna held two pitchers of lemonade high over her head and plastered herself flat against the door frame as three twelve-year-old boys raced out into the yard. It was still five minutes until two, but already six kids from Ashton's class had arrived. In spite of a forecast of possible storms, Saturday had dawned with only scattered clouds for Ashton's birthday party.

She'd debated whether to cancel the party entirely after Ashton's recent disobedience, but hadn't had the heart. Seeing his beaming face as the other kids arrived, she was happy she hadn't. At least he was settling in here. Whether Kenzie's friends or Ashton's, they'd showed up.

She inhaled the sweet scent of the freshly mowed lawn and listened to the squeals of the kids playing dodgeball against the back fence.

"Dad!" Ashton yelled, tossing the ball to another boy and heading toward the patio where Hanna was setting up the refreshments. The fragrance of Richard's cologne preceded him, even before she turned and saw him coming out the sliding glass door.

"Happy birthday, kiddo." Richard gave Ashton's shoulder a squeeze and handed him a huge, beautiful package wrapped in bright-blue foil paper and tied with a shiny silver bow.

"Oh, wow!" Ashton shook it and held it up to his ear as if he expected it to whisper what was inside. "Can I open it now?"

"We'll open presents later," Hanna said, reaching to take the package. "Let me put that in the house with the others."

"Here, let me get it. It's heavy." Richard touched Hanna's shoulder, then retrieved the present from Ashton.

She flinched at his touch before she caught herself. At least he hadn't brought Phoebe, the new girlfriend. "Thanks. I'm glad you could make the party."

Richard grinned at her, then hauled the gift back inside. They'd agreed to spend special occasions together as a family, for Ashton's sake. It had sounded like a good plan, but this was the first shared event to come up. Maybe it would get easier, but being around him made her jumpy. This was her world, not his. In the years they were together, he'd spent only rare occasions in Marble Falls. Before her father had died three years ago, her parents had typically driven to Dallas for designated holidays. Richard spent so much time at the office, it had just worked out better that way.

"Ashton, the doorbell rang. Better see who it is," Hanna said.

"Let him play. I'll get it," Richard offered, altering his route and heading toward the front door.

The idea was for Ashton to greet his own guests, but Hanna didn't argue. Whatever kept the peace today.

She dumped a bag of chips into a bowl and glanced through the glass door as she heard Vince's deep voice.

Hanna dropped the whole bag in the bowl and bolted into the small living room in time to see Richard extend his hand to Vince. "Richard Rosser, Hanna's—Ashton's father."

"Vince Keegan." Vince shook his hand, but his dimples flashed as he exchanged a knowing glance with Hanna.

Fidgeting by her father's side, Kenzie looked Richard up and down, then smiled at Hanna. "Hi, Ms. Rosser. Thanks for having me."

"Hi, Kenzie." Hanna blinked at Kenzie in the cute little purple short set, with even a matching bow on her ponytail. Okay. So this must be a twin Mackenzie? "Your hair looks so pretty today. Did you do it yourself?"

Mackenzie crossed her eyes and nodded toward Vince. "I always do it myself. See, he's an engineer and he engineers a ponytail so tight my eyes are on either side of my head."

Vince smirked. "When I put it up, it doesn't fall down, now does it?"

Kenzie smirked at him, then, having fulfilled her mannerly obligation, darted into the yard with the others.

Richard laughed then switched his attention back to Vince. "Have you always lived in Marble Falls?"

"Austin."

Oh, yeah, here came the subtle interrogation. Leave it to Richard.

Richard's gaze quickly took in Vince's faded jeans and white button-down. "Austin. You're not by chance related to Madeline Grant Keegan are you?"

"Guilty." Vince grinned. "My mom."

Well, that slowed Richard down. Hanna'd never seen him look quite so stunned. "At last year's state conference, she gave a hell of a keynote on family law."

"Yeah. Don't mess with Mom."

The hair on the back of Hanna's neck stood up. Having these two men in the same room might not feel awkward to them, but it sure as heck did to her.

Ashton rushed into the living room. "Vince, we're choosing teams for a softball game. Mom bought me equipment for the party. You have to pitch. We decided it's fair as long as you pitch for both teams."

Richard glanced at Vince then took a step toward the back door. "I can pitch a few balls."

Without missing a beat, Ashton grabbed Vince's arm. "Thanks, Dad, but Vince knows how to throw curveballs."

Closing her eyes a second, Hanna prayed Vince would just follow Ashton out and let her deal with Richard. When she opened her eyes, Vince was staring at her.

"Sounds like I've been drafted," he said, rolling up his sleeves and following Ashton.

If looks could kill, Vince would be annihilated by Richard's menacing glare. Without saying a word to her ex-husband, Hanna grabbed the plastic cups and tray of cookies and carted them out to the patio table.

Richard followed her outside, slammed closed the ice chest one of the kids had left open and watched the game, hands on hips.

She deposited the stuff on the table and turned to make sure he wasn't going to do anything to ruin Ashton's birthday. She didn't need the two men getting into a macho turf war over who threw the best curveball.

As she turned, Richard grabbed her arm. "Don't try to tell me nothing's going on between you and the cowboy."

She sucked in a breath. "It's not my plan to tell you anything."

He stuffed his hands in his navy blue Dockers and narrowed his eyes at her. She held his stare. No way in hell was she discussing Vince Keegan with her ex-husband. Let him think whatever he wanted.

Slowly he dropped the stare and surveyed the ball game being laid out. "This is how you're raising our son?"

A backyard party certainly hadn't been the norm up until this year. It couldn't compare to trips to the planetarium, laser tag or the gaming arcade that had cost more than she currently cleared in two weeks. But it had been what Ashton had requested and it fit her budget. "Ashton is settling in nicely here. He's made friends. Experienced new things."

She started to turn away, but Richard captured her hand. Obviously he was looking for anything to make his case that Ashton belonged in Dallas. "And education? How's that going? Is he in honors classes? He said he isn't in band. How are his grades?"

Gently she pulled her hand out of his grasp. "There's more to education than just the right schools. There's…"

Hanna risked a glance outside at Vince, then turned and found Richard waiting on her to finish her thought. "I mean, Ashton has come a long way. His three-week report was all A's. Marble Falls has been good for him."

Her gaze was drawn back to Vince and this time that intense blue gaze bored into hers.

Bully Baer put the bat on his shoulder. "You gonna pitch or what?"

Turning his attention back to the game, Vince wound up and threw a curveball over home plate.

Billy missed and put the bat back on his shoulder. "Toss me another one."

"Why? You can't hit worth a flip anyway," Kenzie taunted from second base. Her ponytail was loose and the hair ribbon, no longer in a bow, hung down her back as she flashed her father a wide smile.

Ashton was covering first base. He bent at the waist, spat on his hands and wiped his palms on his jeans. "Let's play ball."

It wasn't his improved athletic skills that touched Hanna, it was his confidence. His assurance. She grabbed her camera off the table and snapped a couple of pictures. His happiness and well-being were all that mattered.

Richard leaned over. "So that's the infamous Mackenzie that I hear all these exaggerated tales about."

"I assure you, tales about Mackenzie require no exaggeration."

Billy made contact with the third ball and it bounced down the first-base line. Ashton rushed to grab it, but Billy raced past first and on toward second. Huffing, Ashton rescued the ball and tossed it to Kenzie, but Billy was halfway to third.

Kenzie tossed the ball to Vince in the pitcher's box and Billy froze on third.

"You'll never make it home, Bully Baer," Kenzie taunted.

As Hanna fidgeted with the refreshment table, Richard frowned. "What if I paid Ashton's tuition? Could you afford a place in Dallas? Put Ashton back in private school? Be closer so I could see him more?"

"Don't start this. We've already uprooted him once this year. I'm not doing it again."

He took her hand and stilled her so she had no choice but to look at him. "I'm no longer first in my own son's life. I can't believe I let this happen."

Not exactly her perception. "Richard, you didn't 'let' it happen, you had an affair. You demanded a divorce. You were the one who was unfaithful, yet you're acting angry as though it was my fault."

Dropping her hand, he looked away. "I felt like an ass, but I couldn't accept that I was to blame, so I lashed out at you. The 'If you'd only been more attentive' defense."

She watched the other team take the field and Ashton's team line up to bat. Clouds were rolling in, but she hoped they'd hold off for a couple of more hours.

Turning back to Richard, she tried to sort out what she was hearing. "You couldn't have just been honest and said that you'd found someone else?"

Now he wanted to have his cake and eat it, too. He wanted his new young girlfriend, but he wanted Ashton and Hanna close by so he could be a part of Ashton's life.

Squeezing her shoulder, Richard shrugged. "I handled the situation badly. I admit it. But look around.

You're too classy for this nowhere town. Ashton doesn't belong here. What if I help you get a bookstore started in Dallas? You'd generate more business than here."

Of all the nerve. "I love my little bookstore here in Marble Falls. And frankly, I have no desire to disrupt my life to make yours easier. You made your choice. Pardon me if I don't really give a shit whether you get to see Ashton."

"What? Now I don't even get to see Dad?"

She hadn't realized Ashton had walked up. How much had he overheard?

"First you moved me to Marble Falls away from him, and now I don't get to see him at all?" Ashton's voice rose with each syllable.

"Ashton…"

"All you two do is yell and fight. You don't care about me at all, just yourselves. Well, fine. I hate you both!"

Ashton's shrill voice silenced the yard. Mackenzie pushed her way through the other kids to her friend and Vince followed.

"You're ruining my life. I was happy in Dallas before the divorce. You said nothing would change, but then you moved me here and said it'd be cool. I was miserable until we met the Keegans and then you tried to forbid me from playing with Kenzie. And you said not to worry, that I could always see Dad, and now you even lied about that."

"Son, calm down," Richard said, reaching for Ashton's shoulder.

"Just leave me alone! I hate you for divorcing us for another woman. And I hate not having a home. And I hate my whole stupid life." Jerking away, Ashton took off down the hall and slammed his bedroom door.

"Ashton!" Hanna raced after him, but he was leaning against the door, preventing her from opening it.

"Go away! I don't want to talk to you."

Hanna's insides were wound so tightly, she wasn't even sure how she could move. "Okay. We can talk later when you aren't so angry."

She turned back toward the living room and found a roomful of little eyes on her. What now? She tried to smile, but her eyes were full of tears.

"Okay, teams." Vince motioned toward the patio door. "Everyone back outside. There are drinks in the cooler and snacks on the table. Five-minute break then get back to the game. Hopefully Ashton will be out shortly."

Hanna flashed him a grateful look.

Mackenzie's eyes were as round as half dollars. She looked at Hanna. "Let me talk to him. Maybe he still likes me okay."

Hanna nodded and Kenzie disappeared down the hall. Vince herded the other kids back toward the yard and closed them outside. Hanna exchanged looks with Vince. If Ashton would listen to anyone, it was Vince's daughter.

"I'll take care of him." Richard took a step.

Vince touched his shoulder. "Might want to let him simmer down a little first. Don't think you're going to get too far right now."

Richard spun on him. "Don't tell me how to handle my son. *My* son. And *my* wife, who, no doubt, you've been sleeping with."

Hanna couldn't just let that one pass. "Ex-wife. And

whatever does or does not happen between Vince and me is not your concern."

"It certainly is my concern when it involves my son being subjected to his mother's sordid affair with his friend's father." It took a lot to make Richard lose his cool, but Vince had managed it without even breaking a sweat.

The front door opened and Hanna's mother walked in. She looked between the three angry faces and froze. "Uh, Anne Haythorn volunteered to watch the shop for a couple hours so I could come home and see Ashton blow out his candles. Did I miss it?"

Hanna shook her head. "No, Mom. We haven't brought out the cake yet."

"I obviously missed something."

The men didn't even acknowledge Norma, but continued to glare at one another. Richard looked angry enough, but Vince could halt an entire room given his current stance. Jaw set, hands in his jeans pockets.

"I'm going to see about Ashton and Mackenzie." She left them standing in the living room and knocked on Ashton's bedroom door. Not a sound. "Ashton." Nada. She opened the door and peeped inside, but the window was wide open, curtain rustling as the wind picked up.

She raced back into the living room. "They're gone!"

Chapter 9

Vince blinked and bolted down the hall. Hanna wasn't sure whether he thought she might have overlooked them hiding under the bed.

Thunder rumbled in the distance and the clouds overhead rolled across the sky. That spring storm the weatherman had predicted was moving in. Naturally, this would be the one time a weatherman was right.

Hanna raced after Vince as he ran for the pickup, digging his keys out of his pocket. "Where are you going?"

"Checking to see if the boat's missing. When Kenzie needs to escape, that's her method of choice."

"Oh my God. The wind is picking up and the bottom is going to fall out of those clouds. Surely they wouldn't go out on the lake."

She grabbed his arm and turned, yelling over her shoulder. "Mom, can you get the other kids home safely?"

"I've got it. Just find Ashton," Norma said.

Vince pulled away from Hanna and got in the pickup, but she jumped in beside him, and Richard pushed her over to the center and joined them.

"If anything happens to Ashton…" Richard started.

Hanna glared. "You're right in the middle of this whole insanity, Richard. Don't start making threats."

How much of a head start did the kids have? How much time had they wasted arguing?

Vince took out his cell and dialed. "Kenzie's not answering." He dialed a second number and looked out at the sheet of rain as the clouds opened up. "Hey, Gray, where are you? The kids are missing." Vince paused to listen. "Okay. Can you swing by the house and see if there's any sign of them? Then maybe Bluebonnet Books."

Vince nodded. "Yeah, I'm headed to the folks' house to see if Kenzie's boat is missing." Heavy raindrops pelted the cab but didn't slow Vince down.

Hanna glanced at Richard sitting helplessly beside her. The wipers swished at high speed and still couldn't keep the windshield clear enough to see.

Vince pulled up to the Maguires' dock and got out. The red bicycle. Hanna's stomach plummeted. No kids. And no boat.

"Dammit!" Vince looked out across the lake. Heavy clouds hung low across the choppy water, limiting visibility. "I don't see them."

Bolting out the driver's door, Hanna yelled, "Wouldn't the Maguires have stopped them?"

"They're in Fredericksburg at my brother-in-law's for the week, watching his kids."

Hanna stared across the lake. "I don't think they'd take the boat out in this."

"This moved in so fast, they probably didn't think how bad it was going to get. Even ten minutes ago it didn't look like this." He pulled out the cell again. "Hey, Sheriff, this is Vince Keegan. We've got a problem."

An old rattletrap pickup pulled up beside them, and Gray rolled down the window. "They'd been there. House is unlocked and Boo's gone."

"We wasted too much time," Hanna said, climbing back into the truck cab.

"Two twelve-year-old kids and a big dog. My daughter's small runabout is missing, and I'm figuring she and Ashton took it out on the lake. They were upset." Vince slid behind the wheel and closed the door. He pushed his wet hair back, listening to the sheriff. "Okay. Headed downriver. If you get any reports, you have my cell."

Gray waved. "I'll wait here in case they circle back."

Funny how Vince and Gray anticipated each other's thoughts. Richard hadn't opened his mouth since Hanna had shut him down.

"Where are we going?" Hanna asked as Vince pulled the truck back onto the highway.

"If they're on the water, the wind and waves will take them in this direction. Just watch the lake."

Hanna closed her eyes a second and offered up a prayer for their safety. This could not be happening.

As Vince crept along the lake road, Hanna and Richard kept their eyes peeled for anything on the water, but they could be only twenty feet away in this rain and she wasn't sure they'd see them.

The shrill ringing of Vince's cell phone broke the sound of the rain, and he pulled over to answer it. "Yeah. Okay. How long?" He'd already started moving again and turned up a side road along a cliff. "We're close. See you in a minute."

The truck bumped down a gravel road and Vince squinted through the struggling wipers. "Somebody re- ported two kids in a boat floating downstream. Watch the water and the shore."

"Look," Hanna screamed. "Isn't that Boo?"

Pulling the truck off the road, Vince slammed it into Park, jumped out and grabbed the huge dog in a hug. "Where are they, boy? Come on."

Ignoring the rain, Hanna raced after Vince as he ran after the dog. Hopefully there would be two wet but alive kids waiting.

"Quiet." Vince put out his hand and stopped Hanna. "Listen."

Richard raced up beside Hanna, but remained quiet.

"Help! Down here. Anybody!" The voice was faint, but obviously Mackenzie's.

"Mackenzie, where are you?" Vince yelled.

Two voices joined in the noise. "Down here. Look over the ledge. Right below the tree."

Vince lay down on his belly and eased out far enough to see over the granite ledge. "Are you both okay?"

"I am. Ash can't walk on his ankle. We tried to climb out and he slipped."

"Just stay where you are. I'll come to you." He went back to the truck and moved it closer, circling around so the back of the truck faced the cliff. He dug a rope out of the bed and tied it securely to the trailer hitch. Toss- ing the other end over the ledge, he looked at Hanna and

Richard. "It's only about a ten foot drop, but it's straight up. I need one of you to get behind the wheel and the other to stand close to the ledge and relay whatever I tell you. When I say pull up, keep your foot on the brake and creep forward as slowly as you can."

Richard jumped behind the wheel. Hanna moved closer to the edge. *Please help Ashton not be hurt.* "I'm here, Ashton. It's going to be okay. You'll be out of there in a minute."

She hoped the two of them would hold it together, but Hanna couldn't even breathe. She held on to the limb of a tree and leaned over so she could see.

Vince grabbed the rope and walked his way down the ledge, holding the rope.

He wrapped the bedraggled little girl in a quick hug and then pulled Ashton into the mix and hugged him. "You okay?"

"Yeah, just my ankle hurts."

"Okay. Hang tight. Kenzie, you're first. I'm going to tie the rope around your waist, but I want you to hold it and walk your way up like you learned in Girl Scouts. Can you do that?"

There were a few grunts and groans as she made her way up, but soon she scrambled over the edge, then stretched out flat on her belly and peered down at Vince and Ashton. "I made it. But Ash can't walk up with his ankle."

Hanna tried to squelch her panic.

Boo sat beside Mackenzie and licked her face. Hanna rubbed the rain out of her eyes and looked down at Vince. His hair was plastered to his head, water dripping over his forehead.

"Toss the rope back down and stand back. I'm going

to tie the rope around my waist, and Ashton is going to hang on to my chest while I walk up. With the extra weight, I need Richard to pull the truck forward very slowly when I say."

Mackenzie untied the rope, dropped it back over and wrapped her arms around Boo.

Hanna's silky pantsuit was muddy and wet, but who cared?

"Tell Richard to put the truck in Drive and ease forward. You and Kenzie stand back in case the rope snaps."

Hanna relayed the message and pulled Mackenzie back.

Mackenzie nodded. "It's not that far down. Dad will get him up."

"He sure will," Hanna said. "Everything is going to be fine."

Don't cry. That'll embarrass Ashton. Hanna swiped at her tears, and realized tough little Mackenzie was doing the same as she leaned back against Hanna.

Inch by infinitely slow inch the rope creaked and popped as it strained against the cliff. She could hear Vince talking softly to Ashton, but she wasn't sure what he was saying. It didn't matter. They were in this together, and if there was anyone on Earth she trusted in a situation like this, it was Vince.

Hanna focused on the rope and the voices grew louder.

"Almost there. Now as I get to the top, you need to just lean back with me until you feel the ground. Okay?"

Slowly Ashton appeared, and Hanna rushed to him and wrapped her arms around his waist, pulling him onto level ground. She couldn't do anything but sit there in the mud and rock him in her arms like an infant. He clung to her, too emotional to remember to be embarrassed.

Vince hoisted himself up beside Ashton as two police cruisers and an ambulance arrived in a kaleidoscope of flashing lights and screaming sirens.

The emergency lights reflecting off the cloud of heavy fog left the cliff side eerie and mysterious. The situation turned chaotic.

Both kids' clothes were muddy and ripped. Kenzie's hair ribbon just a droopy remnant of the pretty bow. But they were safe.

Mackenzie clung to her father, much like Ashton clung to Hanna. Or was it the parents clinging to the kids? Boo couldn't decide who to lick, and even Hanna got a slobbery tongue up her neck. Having never been comfortable with animals, it was amazing how much love she felt for the stinky wet dog as she wrapped her arms around him. He'd led them to the kids.

Richard, the medics and two officers buzzed around them. Richard ran his hand through Ashton's hair. When a medic asked to examine him, Ashton realized he had an audience and released his hold on Hanna, but he sat beside her as the guy examined his ankle.

"Where are your shoes?" Hanna asked as the medics removed Ashton's dripping sock and exposed a purple-and-red ankle twice the size it should be.

"At the bottom of the lake with the boat. I couldn't swim with them on." He winced as the medic gently rotated his foot.

"Life jackets. Did you have on life jackets?" Hanna demanded.

Vince stood, bringing Mackenzie with him to her

feet. He didn't even bother to push back his wet hair. His white shirt was stained and half the buttons were missing or unbuttoned.

"Yeah, we had on life jackets. They're down on the ledge. I can go down and get them," Mackenzie offered.

"No." Vince gave her a nudge. "Wait in the truck. There's a blanket behind the seat."

Boo padded along behind Mackenzie, and Vince squatted down beside Ashton. "You were trying to climb the ledge?"

Vince rested a hand on Hanna's shoulder. His quiet strength felt warm and reassuring. Amazing how much a simple touch could soothe her stress.

Ashton winced as the doctor gently rotated his foot. "We thought we could climb up, and Kenzie probably could have, but she wouldn't leave me. It was slippery and my foot got stuck in a crack between two rocks, so when I fell, it didn't. Then she held me up and I wiggled it out. Is it broken?"

The young medic grinned at Ashton. "I don't feel any broken bones, but we'll need an X-ray when we get you to the hospital. Feel like a ride in an ambulance? If you want, we could even turn on the siren."

Not wanting to let Ashton out of her sight, Hanna climbed into the ambulance with him. There was only room for one parent so Richard reluctantly got back in the pickup with Vince, Mackenzie and the dog.

Once they were on their way to the hospital, Vince called Gray to get him to let everyone know they were safe. The pickup cab was quiet. Richard focused straight ahead on the ambulance. Kenzie huddled in the back-seat, wrapped in a blanket and hugging Boo. Vince had never been this upset with her, but he kept it to himself, for now. At least he'd get a chance to deal with her later. He'd never been so frightened. His heart was just beginning to settle back to a normal rhythm.

Gray and Norma arrived at the hospital at the same time as the rest of them.

Norma kissed her grandson on his muddy cheek before they wheeled him into the emergency room.

Gray engulfed Kenzie in a bear hug. Richard's clothes were wet, but in good shape compared to Kenzie's and Vince's muddy, soaked attire. Hanna paced back and forth in front of the emergency room's swinging door, oblivious to the swipe of mud down one cheek and her soggy curls. Her pastel-blue pants and blouse would never come clean.

The air-conditioning and his wet clothes left chill bumps, but Vince couldn't leave until he knew Ashton was okay. The medic tried to check Kenzie out, but she insisted she was fine. The girl had scaled the granite ledge like a pro, so Vince didn't see a need to put her through an exam.

Grayson put a hand on Vince's shoulder. "You found them. Everything is okay."

Letting out a breath, the reality of how close they'd come to losing the kids began to register.

As Kenzie paced by, Vince grasped her arm. "Why the hell did you take the boat out in a storm? Don't you have any common sense?"

Her eyes were full of tears and she looked like a drowned cat, but at the moment, he wanted to shake her as much as hug her.

"Ash was mad because his parents are morons, and

we just wanted to get away from all the adults that keep ruining our lives so we took the boat."

"You didn't answer your cell."

Her lip quivered. "Ashton didn't want me to, but when the wind kicked up and the waves were tossing us around, I pulled it out to call you, but the boat rocked and I grabbed to hold on and dropped the phone overboard. Then things got scary. The motor wasn't powerful enough against the wind, and we were going backwards more than forwards and waves were coming in the boat. Then the motor died, and I couldn't get it started so we just drifted. I tried to paddle, but the waves were bigger than the ones at Galveston." She sniffed. "I couldn't do anything and then one wave came over the side and we had lots of water in the bottom of the boat. It sunk and we floated until we could reach the bank."

"I still can't understand how you did not notice the storm moving in." His stomach churned from just the thought of what could have happened.

"Because I was so mad at Ms. Rosser."

"Mad or not, you have to use good judgment."

"I know." Tears trickled down her dirty cheeks leaving mud tracks. "Daddy, I'm so sorry. I was so scared and I didn't know what to do."

Grabbing her, he swung her up—something he hadn't done in years—and held her tight.

She wrapped her legs around his waist and her arms around his neck, burying her head in his shoulder.

Her heart beat against his. He couldn't stand being angry at her, but neither could he let her think what she did was okay. "I love you, Kenzie. Next time, think about what you're doing first."

Her arms squeezed his neck so tightly he could barely breathe. "I love you, too, Daddy. I'm so, so sorry. Is Ash going to be all right?"

"I doubt he'll even spend the night in the hospital."

Grayson patted his back, and Vince loosened his daughter's hold, letting her slide to the floor.

Kenzie scrubbed her wet face, only smearing the mud more. "I want something to drink."

Vince handed her a couple of dollars and then looked across to where Hanna and Richard stood together.

"She's just a kid, Vince," Gray said as he watched Kenzie disappear down the hall.

"And I was too hard on her?" He massaged his temples. "God, man. I almost lost her, too."

Gray motioned toward a couple chairs and sat down. "I know. And I know how devastating just the thought of what could have happened is right now, but the kids are safe."

"Yeah, but Hanna won't ever forgive me for this one. She's told me all along that I was too lax."

"I'm not so sure Hanna blames you." Gray looked across the room, then back at Vince. "You gonna tell me what's going on or do I get to guess?"

This wasn't the time to get into that with his brother-in-law. "Nothing."

"Uh-huh." Gray stared at him. He wasn't buying a word of it.

Kenzie returned with a soft drink and eyed Vince warily. He held out his arms, and she leaned back against him, taking his hands and hugging them across her belly.

"It's okay, Kenzie. Everything's going to be fine."

Squeezing her tight, he wondered how much longer she'd let him do that before she grew too old for hugs.

A nurse came through the swinging doors, and Hanna, Richard and Norma followed her down the hall.

Vince left Kenzie with Gray and went to the men's room. He looked in the mirror and scrubbed his hands up and down his face only to realize they were still shaking. He tried to wash some of the caked mud off his face and hands to at least be a little more presentable.

Kenzie met him at the door, anxious to go check on Ashton. He gave the Rossers a few minutes of family time then went to the receptionist's station. "Is Ashton Rosser allowed to have visitors?"

She checked the computer. "He's just waiting to be released. Emergency room four, just down this hall on the right."

Holding Kenzie's hand, he led the way down the hall and knocked on the door. "Ashton, up to a couple of more visitors?"

The kid was propped up in bed, his ankle elevated on two pillows. "Hey, Vince. Come on in."

Kenzie was sheepish, so Vince walked in ahead and gave the ankle a once-over. "That's some injury you've got there, pal."

"Isn't it cool? It's purple and red and even a green stripe right there. They stitched this up here where the rock ripped the skin. I got to watch. The doc said the scar won't be too bad."

"No biggie. Girls love guys with scars."

Ashton wrinkled his nose. "You think? I can't practice baseball for a week or two."

Kenzie eased up beside Vince, grasped his hand and

looked at Ashton's trophy ankle. "I'm sorry I almost got you drowned."

"If it'd just been me, then I'd have drowned. We didn't drown because you made me wear my life jacket and because Boo swam to shore and climbed out and got Mom and Vince."

"So you're really okay?"

"Sure. Look at my foot. It's like twice the size of the other one." He beamed as if having a sprained ankle somehow gave him passage into coolness.

"May not be so fun when the painkillers wear off," Richard said.

Hanna met Vince's eyes and offered a tentative grin, but she remained on the other side of the bed beside Richard.

This was a family deal, and he wasn't family. "Kenzie, we should get you home and into dry clothes."

Hanna stepped around the bed. "May I talk to you a minute first?"

Here it comes. Vince left Kenzie sitting on the corner of Ashton's bed expounding about their experience and followed Hanna into the hall and to the window at the end of the corridor where it was quiet. He stared out at the pouring rain and waited. Waited for Hanna to yell about how his lazy parenting style had almost cost her Ashton. Or for her to tell him that she wanted him and Kenzie out of her life.

When Hanna actually touched Vince's shoulder, he jumped. "She's just a child, Vince. It wasn't Kenzie's fault. Or yours."

"I shouldn't have given a twelve-year-old so much freedom."

"And if you hadn't taught her to think for herself,

we might be planning two funerals right now instead of just dealing with a sprained ankle and sunken boat." She eased around beside him and caught his attention. Tears glistened on her lashes. "Look at me."

He shoved his hands into his pockets and turned back to the window. Away from her hurt. "If I'd have been stricter with her, she'd have known better than to take the boat out. I gave a kid credit for having adult judgment."

"Mackenzie is a little tenacious, but this little debacle was instigated entirely by Ashton." Hanna flicked a tiny crust of mud off Vince's neck. "Kenzie's ability to think under pressure probably saved both their lives."

"But I gave her too much leeway to do so. Not so smart."

Hanna shrugged. "Agreed. There should be a happy medium."

He stared out the window at the dark clouds and rain, and then turned. He had to see her. Placing both palms on the windowsill behind him, he leaned his weight on them and stared into that gorgeous, muddy face. Even on the rafting trip, Hanna had maintained a classy, together look. He grinned at the mud stains on her expensive outfit and the smudge on the right side of her nose. "Yeah. I'm gonna work on that."

There were still tears in her eyes, but she returned his grin. "All we've heard since we walked into Ashton's room is how you hoisted him up that cliff. If you weren't his hero before, you sealed it this afternoon."

It had been nine years since he'd felt this helpless. His common sense still told him he was raising Kenzie right, but the emotional dad who'd almost lost a child wasn't buying it. "I'm not a hero."

"Maybe not. I still don't agree with the amount of leeway you give Kenzie. But Vince, without her ability to think on her feet and your fast actions, I'm not sure we'd have found them."

He tilted his head and tried to read her. "Is Ashton still going home with his dad tonight?"

"Sounds that way. As long as the doctor releases him in time."

Vince ran a thumb under her eye to dry the tear and only succeeded in smearing the mud. "And your little boy is hurt and you don't want to be apart from him?"

The corner of her bow-shaped mouth turned up. "You know me too well." She massaged her forehead. "God, I need a break. I need a couple of days of total freedom from single parenting and meddling mothers and controlling ex-husbands. I need to get a grip. I need sleep."

"With ya there. After today, I just want to crawl in bed and sort it all out. Or not think about fatherhood at all. I don't know."

Her dark, sad eyes glistened with unshed tears. She stared at him a good two minutes. "Spring break is next week."

He nodded.

"Convince me we'll be discreet."

Chapter 10

Tuesday morning, Hanna pulled her Volvo into the small parking lot across from the San Antonio River Walk hotel where she and Vince had arranged to meet. She hadn't actually seen him since Saturday evening when he'd left the hospital, and they'd only found time for a couple of phone calls to plan their getaway.

What if he'd backed out?

She glanced at her cell phone for the umpteenth time, but there were no missed calls or text messages. Not from Vince and not from Ashton.

Vince had spent Sunday in Austin, replacing Kenzie's cell phone and driving her and his parents to the airport for their flight to Disney.

Hanna had spent extralong hours at the shop Sunday and Monday, putting everything in order so her mother couldn't complain about her neglecting her duties. Hanna was in her mid-thirties and really shouldn't let her mother stress her out like this. She and Vince were only going to be gone two days and one night, but she wanted to minimize the flack.

As much as she hated to admit it, her mom was better at knowing what the customers wanted than she was anyway. Mom knew the locals' favorite writers, and when new books were hitting the shelf. She was a wealth of information on local history and activities for the tourists. Hanna's strong point was keeping the financial end of things straight. Boring accountant, divorced single mom. How depressing was that?

She glanced at the hotel. Surrounded by more opulent high rises, it was a quaint little four-story brick building nestled in the towering hundred-year-old live oaks. A splashing fountain added a welcoming touch to the circular brick courtyard. Hanna smiled. The hotel had the same classy, weathered appeal as Vince. Vince. What was she going to do if Vince wasn't inside waiting for her? He might have changed his mind, decided that two days away wasn't worth the risk of the kids finding out.

Steeling herself against further panic, Hanna grabbed her overnight case and locked the car. He wouldn't do that to her.

She shouldered her purse and slid her sunglasses on top of her head to keep the wind from blowing her hair in her face. Pulling her little roller bag behind her, she started toward the hotel entrance.

This escape had disaster written all over it. What if they ran into someone from Marble Falls? She stopped. She should just get back in the car and drive as fast and far away as she could. She took another step forward. This escape might just save her sanity.

The heavy glass door swung open as she approached and refreshing air cooled her face. She looked around the plush lobby. Beautiful silk flower arrangements and leather sofas you could bury into. A polished wood reservation desk. Small but classy.

As she recognized Vince slowly walking toward her, she let out her breath. No man had ever looked as good as he looked to her in his familiar faded jeans and black shirt. That lazy smile and the crinkles at the corners of those denim-colored eyes. He kissed her cheek. "I planned to play the Southern gentleman and at least meet you at the car."

Shivering in the air-conditioned room, she released her roll-along bag and wrapped her arms around him, tilting her face up for a real kiss. "You have two whole days to practice."

He encased her in a full bear hug, then, keeping an arm around her, grabbed the handle of her bag, escorting her toward the elevators.

The clerk behind the counter smiled as they passed, and welcomed her to San Antonio. People roamed about the lobby and a young man and woman herded two small, swimsuit-clad preschoolers toward the pool.

Riding up in the elevator, Hanna's stomach fluttered like springtime butterflies in the Hill Country. She glanced at Vince standing beside her and sucked in her breath. She'd never in her life done anything this spontaneous and irresponsible.

But never before had she been this emotionally drained and in need of something for herself. Something that she wasn't doing for her husband. Or for her son. Or for her mother. Or because it was the proper and expected thing for her to do.

She turned as Vince touched her shoulder and the elevator doors glided silently open. She tried to still the butterflies. She'd never spent the night in a hotel with any man other than Richard. And they'd been married.

Vince inserted the card key and stood back for her to enter.

Grasping her small yellow purse, Hanna stepped into the room, and, in spite of the balcony and view of the river, her gaze landed on the king-size bed piled with assorted pillows and shams. This was far from a bargain-priced room.

Vince hoisted her bag up beside his leather duffel on the bureau. Averting her eyes from the bed, she opened the French doors onto the balcony and stepped out.

Two wrought-iron chairs and a round table decorated the semi-circular balcony. Trees reached as tall as their third-floor balcony, giving it a cozy, natural feel. Hanna leaned over the wrought-iron rail and waved at the water taxi that putted by on the river below. A couple strolling arm-in-arm along the sidewalk waved back along with the people on the boat.

Vince stepped up behind her and placed both hands on her shoulders. "What do you think? Good enough for a getaway?"

"Perfect. All the times we drove through town when I was a kid, we never came down to the river."

"You grew up an hour and a half from the River Walk and never came here? Now that is amazing."

"Mom didn't like the humidity on the water."

Vince wrapped his arms around her stomach and nuzzled her neck. "Humid or not, it's one of the most romantic destinations in Texas."

"Romance. Not Mom's strong suit. Or I don't think it was anyway."

Turning her head, Hanna met Vince's lips. "Just for tonight. Let's pretend we don't have mothers." She tilted her head, stared into his eyes, then covered his lips with hers. "Or kids or ex-husbands."

He sucked her bottom lip into his mouth. "Right there with you."

Hanna felt the slight trepidation in his kiss. Was he as nervous as she was about this? He wound one dark curl around his finger and stared at her mouth. "Ready to experience the Mercado? Make lunch an adventure."

"Uh, sure." That husky voice of his was sexy as hell. She'd heard of bedroom eyes, but he had a bedroom voice.

"You said you wanted a Southern gentleman," he drawled as he took her hand and looked wistfully at the king-size bed.

She smiled. There was always tonight. Before she changed her mind and decided just to go for it, Vince led her out of the room and locked the door with the bed safely behind them.

It was late morning as they strolled through the Mercado Mexican market to see what goodies they could find to snack on as they shopped. It felt good to stretch her legs and not to worry about whether Ashton was entertained. They bought some trinkets for the kids and grabbed sodas and a paper container of nachos to tide them over until dinner.

The Mercado was crowded, but it was exciting to wander through and check out all the vendors, food and clothes. Hanna enjoyed the feel of her hand in Vince's as they browsed and people-watched. She wasn't interested in buying so much as just checking things out.

They tried on hats in one store and Vince even modeled a sombrero. By the time they finished their tour, they were both tired, so they bought two passes for the river taxis.

Holding Hanna's arm as she stepped into the flat boat, Vince tried to put sex out of his mind. But the sway of her jeans-clad bottom as she walked in front of him and selected a spot on one of the benches wasn't working in his favor.

She was tall for a woman and slender, but there was nothing fragile about Hanna Creed Rosser. She hid her strength beneath classic clothing and that gravelly voice, but it was there. Hanna bounced back from adversity with the same determination as her sexy dark curls bounced back when pulled.

She could take care of herself. Which was why he was flattered by her eagerness to escape responsibility for a couple of days with him. They both needed this.

Hanna seemed content to lean back against his arm and just take it all in as they made their way down the various forks in the river, passing other hotels, outdoor restaurants and expensive shops. "See anywhere you want to check out, just speak up."

Nodding, she pointed to a pigeon perched on the beams under a bridge as they cruised beneath it. The taxi driver, an older Hispanic gentleman wearing a black-and-white-striped shirt, tossed out tidbits of San Antonio history as they toured different areas of the river.

Vince moved to the bench opposite Hanna and pulled

out his camera. When he lined her up on the screen, he found that she had her own camera, taking his picture as he took hers. "Trying to be funny, woman?" After a few shots he moved back beside her and another passenger reached for Vince's camera. "Allow me."

They snuggled close for another shot.

The chime of Vince's cell phone interrupted the tour and he glanced at the readout. "Hey, Kenzie. Having fun?"

"Oh, Dad, it's a blast. Not as much fun as when you came with us before, but we spent today at the water park and yesterday we rode every roller coaster at Disney—Space Mountain twice. And you should see the pool at the hotel!"

"Cool. You minding Gram and Pop?"

"Yeah, they're having fun, too. Sorry you're missing Pop's purple-flowered swim trunks. Whoa. I had to put on my sunglasses."

"Don't forget the sunscreen, okay? Remember last time."

"I know. Gram slathered it all over me twice already. I feel like a greased pig. Gotta go. Pop just came back with hot dogs."

"Love you, Kenzie. Be good." He slid the phone back into his pocket.

"Sounds like she's having a good trip."

"She has my parents wrapped around her finger. Leo and I never got away with half of what she does."

"And I thought Ashton's grandparents spoiled him. But they mostly buy him things. They're quiet people. Not sure they'd survive spring break in an amusement park full of hyper kids. I just wish Ashton would call. I'd like to hear his voice, you know?"

"So call him. Bet he'd like to hear your voice, too."

The corners of her mouth turned down. "He's with his dad, and I don't want to interfere. We'll talk when he gets home."

So much for not thinking about the kids. Then again, Vince could call Kenzie whenever he wanted. He didn't have to share custody or worry about the ex factor.

Hanna pointed across the river. "Look at all those shops. I'll bet I couldn't afford a thing down here anymore."

Vince motioned to the driver and gave Hanna a kiss. She didn't look nearly as excited as she was trying to sound. Vince took her hand and helped her out of the boat. "Browsing is free."

"True."

In the second shop, Hanna pushed her sunglasses up on top of her head and eyed a bright floral sundress. She looked at some other items, but came back to finger the fabric and check the price tag.

"Try it on." His blood pumped just picturing how she'd look in that feminine little number.

"Nah, I have no place to wear a sundress these days."

"Doesn't cost anything to dream." He leaned around and whispered in her ear. "Do it for me."

With a grin, she selected her size, handed Vince her purse and allowed the saleslady to show her to a dressing room.

He watched the people stroll by as he waited, but when Hanna came out, he couldn't see anything but her. The bodice clung to her like a second skin, the deep V showing off enough cleavage to make his mouth water. Not that she was busty, but she had nice curves. The saleslady picked up a pair of sandals with bright-colored straps and held them up for her approval.

"The heels are too high. I'd look like the jolly floral giant."

Vince took the shoe. "I like 'em. They sorta look like rainbows."

"They are cute."

The saleslady asked Hanna's size and selected a box from beneath the display.

While Hanna sat on a padded bench to try them on, her cell rang. She grabbed her phone as the saleslady buckled the strap on the second shoe. "Tiffany, what a surprise." Her face lit up and she continued to listen as she stood and checked out her reflection in the floor-length mirror. The full skirt moved seductively as she turned for a side view. "Really. They were having lunch at the club? I'm so happy Richard took time off to spend time with him. Ashton needs that reassurance right now."

She became even more animated as the conversation progressed. God, she looked amazing. The dress, the smile, the way those ridiculously high heels made her legs look endless. Maybe she'd be okay with skipping dinner and just hopping a taxi back to the hotel? No, he'd told himself. This trip was for her, and he wasn't going to blow it by rushing things.

"Oh, I miss you all desperately. Just the other day I was thinking about that bread at Kirby's and their wonderful salad."

Vince handed the saleslady his credit card. "Just put the jeans and sneakers in the bag."

"Oh my gosh, you're kidding. Did she really?" Hanna's laughter filled the shop. "So what did he do? Did she get the car?"

The saleslady collected a pair of scissors from the counter and touched Hanna's arm, then gently cut the tags off the dress.

Hanna jerked around, saw the credit card and mouthed at him. "You can't buy this. It's outrageous."

He flashed his best grin and ignored her protest.

"A Jag! Oh man, he must have realized how bad he screwed up to spring for a convertible."

Vince signed the credit receipt and took the bag, winking at the clerk. "Thanks."

The wistfulness for her old life was clear in every syllable. It was painted across Hanna's face like a mural. He thought back to the house he'd sold in Austin before moving Kenzie to Marble Falls. A house he'd hoped would make his young wife happy. He'd stretched their resources to buy the place, but he'd been making good money and along with Belinda's teacher's salary, they'd managed.

Although Austin's lifestyle was more laid-back and centered on music than Dallas's country-club culture, Marble Falls had still been an adjustment. It had taken a while even though he'd made the move willingly. But returning to Marble Falls and into the house with her mother probably wasn't a life Hanna would have chosen if there were other options.

He placed his hand on the curve of her back and felt her slim waist beneath the silky fabric. Why did he feel the urge to protect her? The woman would resist him at every step if he even hinted that was his intent.

She took her purse from him and met his eyes. "Listen, Tiffany, I've gotta run. Thanks for reporting in on

Ashton. I try not to worry, but it's hard, especially with his sprained ankle. Please don't be a stranger. I love keeping up on the latest. Not as good as being there, but it helps."

Vince slipped his arm around Hanna as they walked out of the store and down the River Walk. "You miss Big D, don't you?"

"I miss my life in Dallas terribly. My house. My friends. Most of the women I ran around with stopped calling after the divorce. I guess Richard got the friends in an unwritten codicil to the divorce decree, huh?"

Ouch. With friends like that… At least she didn't mention missing her ex-husband. "I miss Austin every so often. But a weekend there usually takes care of that."

The corner of her mouth turned up. "Nice place, but you wouldn't want to live there?"

"Not anymore. It was a great place to grow up and UT was a trip." He turned and walked backwards so he could look at her. The dress left her shoulders bare and her legs. Those heels should be sold in one of those sexy, how-to-seduce-a-guy stores.

She fished her sunglasses from the tangle of curls on top of her head and slid them back on her nose. "At least you chose to move to Marble Falls."

After dinner at a small outside table beside the river, they decided against the river taxi in lieu of walking off the heavy enchiladas and margaritas.

Hanna rubbed her stomach and stared at Vince. "That was an amazing dinner, but I probably gained at least three pounds."

He swung the shopping bag in one hand and took her hand with the other. "You can't come to San Antonio without eating Mexican food, though. Trust me, in a week your mouth will start watering and you'll lie in bed dreaming about salty chips and salsa."

Replaying the day, Hanna had no doubt that it was Vince and not just the amazing cuisine that had drawn Hanna in. Her relaxed state had more to do with him than the slushy margaritas they'd consumed with dinner. She dropped his hand and slid her arm around his waist. "Thanks for this."

The sun had set and the River Walk came alive. Tiny white lights twinkled in the trees along the sidewalk and neon flashed from restaurants. Old-fashioned streetlamps illuminated the arched stone bridge that spanned the river. The walkways had become crowded with slower-paced tourists.

Strolling in rhythm to the music of a floating mariachi band on one of the taxis, Hanna couldn't keep from dancing. A small band set up outside a steakhouse cranked out country music. The music, conversation and river taxis' engines melded and overloaded her senses. Hanna had never been anywhere like this.

Vince set the shopping bag against the stone wall and silently pulled her into his arms and into the crowd of country dancers. There were a few others dancing and she willingly melted against him. Being in his arms felt about as right as anything had in years. She buried her fingers in the little curls at the nape of his neck, damp from the humidity. The sexy little sundress made her feel pretty and feminine. And heels. She actually had on three-inch heels for the first time in fourteen years. And even wearing them, she felt small and feminine in Vince's arms.

As the song changed, he fell into the Texas two-step and Hanna tried to follow. He had the steps down to an art. He was good, amazingly good to have just learned a couple of weeks ago in Gruene. Suddenly she froze; a lump lodged in her throat as reality set in. Tears swamped her eyes. "You already knew how to dance the other night? Yet, you let Ashton teach you because you knew how much he needed that."

Hanna's heart melted into a puddle at her feet. Vince had let Ashton "teach" him because he'd realized that the boy needed to feel good about knowing something others didn't. That might not have been a huge deal to any other kid, but to her son, who was struggling in every aspect of his life, it had been a wonderful boost to his ego.

She rested her cheek against Vince's shoulder and felt his heart beat against hers, completely forgetting the steps. As much as she'd tried to resist getting emotionally involved, he'd drawn her in. She'd never met a man like him.

Thunder rumbled off in the distance. "Vince."

"Hmm?" he said, resting his chin on top of her head.

"We should go back to the room."

Chapter 11

Vince pulled back and smiled that lazy smile of his. The next moment he was kissing her, his lips hot and full of seductive promise.

He collected her shopping bag and flagged a water taxi as a flash of light illuminated the sky.

Hanna snuggled into the crook of his arm as they chugged along beneath the twinkling lights. The boat's vibration had nothing on the bubbling anticipation she felt in her heart.

Which was ridiculous. She was a thirty-four-year-old divorced woman, not some virgin on her wedding night. Yet she felt jittery and her palms were sweating.

Lightning flashed across the night sky and a deep rumble of thunder chased it down the river. The air felt heavy with the smell of rain. Wind rustled the trees that draped over the river and she buried into Vince's warmth.

She was ready to get to the room and off this water. But the boat continued slowly along, stopping to pick up and let off riders. Their hotel must be the final stop.

"Spring in Texas," Vince said as the water taxi finally glided up to their hotel. He handed the driver a folded bill and took Hanna's arm to steady her as she stepped out of the boat. Huge drops of rain spattered the sidewalk as they raced into the hotel lobby.

Except for the rain pelting the windows, the lobby was as quiet as if they were isolated, alone. The rest of the world didn't exist.

Vince's shirt clung to his skin, outlining his sculptured chest. She shivered at the goose bumps on her damp skin from the air-conditioned lobby.

Vince scrubbed his hands up and down her arms and their gazes met. The hunger in his eyes matched hers as he took her hand and headed for the elevator.

As soon as the elevator doors shut, Hanna turned and wrapped her arms around his neck, pulling him closer for a kiss. With a rough groan, he covered her lips with his, sliding his hand down her back to cup her bottom. They couldn't get to the room fast enough, and he handed her the shopping bag while he dug the key card out of his wallet and opened the door.

Happiness and nervousness merged and frothed up inside her. This romantic little getaway was totally out of character for her, yet it seemed so right. Almost as if she was just now discovering her true character.

She dropped the bag beside her yellow duffel and reached to remove the wet dress, but Vince was already behind her, his hands at her shoulders. He bent his head to kiss the sensitive skin below her ear. His warm lips felt exquisite against her chilled skin as he slid his fingers beneath the straps and eased the fabric down her arms. Stepping out of the dress, she shivered in only her bra and panties.

She heard his boots hit the floor beside her dress and then the rustle of his shirt joining them. Leaning her head back against his chest, she craved the touch of his skin. The heat from his chest seared into her back.

They'd not bothered to turn on the light, but the drapes over the patio doors were open, and the lightning flashed through the glass like a strobe.

Hanna turned to stare as Vince stepped back and reached for the snap on his jeans. With a smile, she brushed his hands away and took over the task, enjoying the warmth in his touch as he leaned forward and stole her breath away with another kiss. One hand cupped each side of her face as he deepened the assault.

She slid the zipper down and pushed the jeans over his lean hips, exposing tighty whiteys that were more tight than decent at the moment. Running her hands up his chest while he stepped out of the soft denim, her heart raced. His skin burned beneath her fingers as she tilted her face up, starved for another kiss, desperate for his body against hers.

There was only a second of shyness before Vince waltzed her to the bed and pulled the blanket over them. "Come here."

She snuggled against him, reveling in his hot flesh as he rolled her beneath him and covered her mouth, his kisses deep and greedy. Large hands cupped her satin-clad bottom and held her tight against his long, masculine body. "Warming up?"

She rubbed her hands up his back and thrust them through his rain-dampened hair. "You tell me." Even in the dark, his eyes bored into hers. She relaxed into the soft pillows, enjoying his weight. Enjoying his closeness. And, whoa, those full lips and insane kisses.

Rain peppered the French doors, accompanied by a bright flash of lightning and then thunder so intense the windows rattled.

But the intensity of the storm held nothing to the passion of the man in her arms.

As he slid her panties off, her hands explored his buttocks and legs, taking his tighty whiteys with them. Oh yeah, there was something to be said for a man who didn't earn his living behind a desk. She thought of Richard for a brief second, then Vince was touching her, caressing her, making her forget…forget…whatever it was she'd been thinking about.

Rubbing her hands down his arms as he rose, she sighed as his muscles flexed and tightened. He rolled away and the bedside drawer creaked open, then she heard the tear of cellophane. She giggled.

He'd told her not to worry about anything. That he'd take care of all the details.

Welcoming him back into her arms, Hanna ran her hands down his shoulder blades, thrilled at how well his body fitted against hers.

Vince groaned and moved lower, kissing her right breast and sliding one hand down her abdomen and between her thighs. His tongue circled her nipple and drew it into his mouth.

Instinctively she arched her back as his fingers penetrated her, sighing in contentment.

"You have a gorgeous body." He kneaded her breast and kissed his way down her stomach. Lightning flashed through the window and she smiled. She had a beautiful body? Vince was an Adonis.

He adjusted his position and brought his lips back to hers. Hanna couldn't get close enough fast enough.

Wrapping her legs around his hips, she slanted her mouth over his and almost purred in ecstasy as they came together.

He seemed to enjoy her participation as they moved in unison, the thunder and lightning barely noticeable compared to the tempest that exploded between them.

It had been years since she'd felt as totally feminine and desirable as she felt in Vince's arms.

Slowly she drifted back to earth and relaxed against him. Smiling in contentment, she ran a hand down his chest, letting the hairs thread through her fingers. "So, what are we going to do if it's still raining tomorrow?"

"What are you worried about? You have a car. I'm down here on the bike." His lips trailed kisses around her jaw and he gently nipped with his teeth. "Still, an excellent excuse not to leave the room all day."

Vince woke sometime during the night with his right arm tingling. Hanna lay snuggled against him, one bare leg thrown across his, an arm across his chest and her head nestled into his shoulder. Pretty comfy, except his arm was numb. He eased her head up, her dark curls tickling his left hand, then slid his right hand from beneath her and placed her head on the pillow.

She was like a cuddly kitten. Playful and fun, yet there were claws waiting beneath the surface if he got out of line. He hadn't been sure what to expect from this trip. More reluctance, maybe.

He picked up one curl and watched it corkscrew

around his finger. She worried about the gossip grape-vine, yet she hadn't let that sway her from this trip. Obviously Marble Falls wasn't where she wanted to be, but that's where she'd landed to pick up the pieces after her divorce. And since she'd opened Bluebonnet Books, he could only surmise she planned to stay.

The storm from the night before had settled into a spring rain, and he perhaps had settled into a relation-ship of sorts. At least, he wanted more than just a hot and heavy trip down the river. It had been nine years since Belinda's death, maybe it was time to move on. He was tired of not having a woman in his life.

He rolled over on his back and closed his eyes. Had he been looking for more from a relationship than a temporary good time? Mrs. Haythorn and even Han-na's mother had hinted for years that he was looking for a mother for Kenzie, or should be. They'd even kept him apprised of any newly single women in town. And twice lately Mrs. Haythorn had brought up how attrac-tive Hanna was. But he had Kenzie under control, and adding a stepmom into that mix could go over like a lead brick. No, what he only now realized was that he was looking for a partner.

He rolled over and watched Hanna rub her eyes and stretch. The sheet fell to her waist, and he trailed a finger from her belly button upwards and palmed her breast. Maybe they could stay all week.

One dark eye opened and she smiled. "Exactly what do you have in mind this early?"

Rolling her on top of him, he started a slow seduc-tion of her lips. Soft, dark curls surrounded her face, brushed against her neck and forehead, and into her eyes. Hanna had no clue how disheveled and cute she looked as she leaned down for another kiss. "The sun isn't even up."

He massaged her back and adjusted her against him. "But I am."

The sky was still gray when Vince crawled out of bed, took a quick shower and put the coffeepot on. Leaving Hanna snuggled beneath the covers, he slipped into his jeans and T-shirt and padded barefoot to the elevator. They needed sustenance. Once downstairs, he loaded a tray with croissants, bacon and glasses of juice from the buffet breakfast.

By the time he returned, Hanna was coming out of the bathroom looking sexy as hell in nothing but a hot little yellow negligée. How was a guy supposed to concentrate on breakfast? He placed the tray on the bed and tossed beside it a worn copy of a celebrity rag that someone had left downstairs.

Picking up the magazine, she cocked an eyebrow.

He shrugged. "Thought there might be something in there about Elvis."

Laughing, she dropped it on the nightstand. "You think it's funny that the town gossip's daughter reads tabloids?"

"Sort of."

"I guess the apple doesn't fall far from the tree after all." She didn't look too upset by the discovery.

He leaned in and gave her a quick kiss. "It's charming."

She wrinkled her nose and filled two cups with coffee. "We could eat on that little table by the window."

"Or we could crawl back in bed and eat here." He winked.

Setting the coffee on the nightstand, she eyed him suspiciously. "Vince, I'm really hungry."

He shucked his jeans and propped the pillows up against the headboard. "Me, too."

Without further argument, she joined him. "Breakfast in bed, huh? Always seemed awkward and messy, but hey, this is my time to live dangerously."

Vince wondered if he needed to go down for another tray as they devoured every last crumb he'd brought up. He reached into the bedside drawer and handed her a small box of caramel chocolates. "Dessert."

Licking her lips before she even got the crinkly cellophane off, she opened the shiny gold box. "Chocolate for breakfast! Don't tell my mom."

"After all this, it's the chocolate you're worried about keeping from her?"

Selecting a rich chocolate morsel, she placed it between his lips. "Oh, she had you figured out way before this trip."

He fed her a chocolate in return. "She did, did she?"

"Um-hmm," Hanna said, setting the box on the nightstand and licking a dribble of sticky caramel off her bottom lip. "That was amazing," She looked out at the rain. "I dread going home today."

He took both cups and set them aside. "You worry too much, woman."

"I probably haven't worried enough the past two days. Facing my mother won't be pleasant, and I hope she's all we have to deal with."

He leaned back against the pillows and she curled into his side, resting her head against his chest.

"Your mother and her grapevine of gossips can only make you as miserable as you allow them to."

"I'm just a bored housewife who couldn't even manage to keep my marriage together. Unlike you—the loving husband who lost a wife and child. They're sympathetic toward the horror you went through."

A lump blocked Vince's throat and the nine-year-old nightmare resurfaced. She couldn't know how much guilt he'd felt—still felt—over the accident. He stood and paced over to the window to stare out at the drizzle. "You don't have the market cornered on guilt."

"Vince, they died in a car accident. There was nothing you could have done to prevent that." Hanna stayed in bed, but her voice penetrated his soul.

"Right! Hell, I was at work. Couldn't have been my fault."

"Vince, I'm sorry." Hanna bolted off the bed and came up behind him. "Bringing that up was totally insensitive of me. I didn't think. I can't imagine how devastating losing your wife and son must have been."

He walked back, sat on the edge of the bed and pulled on his jeans, needing to feel less vulnerable, less…exposed. "Belinda was my best friend. But…when she told me she was pregnant, I thought my life was over. I acted like an ass."

Sitting beside him on the bed, Hanna didn't speak. He expected her disgust, but she just waited. He'd never opened up about this to anyone and he wasn't sure he was ready to now. Hell, he could go to his grave and still not be ready.

"See, I had a plan for my life. I was going to get my Masters in Engineering and Design, and the world was going to be my playground. I was going to design these masterpiece bridges, work all over the world and people were going to stand in awe." He huffed. "A wife and kid didn't fit into my plan, at least not until I had my career together. I figured maybe when I was forty."

Hanna slid her hand down his cheek. "Vince, having a dream is nothing to feel guilty about. Having it taken from you hurts."

"Belinda knew my dream, knew I wasn't ready to get married. Told me to go on with my life. Said her family would be there for her and that she didn't need anything from me. Left campus and headed home to Marble Falls."

Hanna shook her head. "I'm sure you aren't the only guy who wasn't thrilled with that kind of news."

"I stalked around my apartment for a day or two, just wanting her and the baby to…go away…not to exist. Then I went to Marble Falls and met her folks. Apologized to Belinda for acting like a jerk and asked her to marry me."

Hanna touched his arm but didn't comment.

God, he couldn't do this. But when she looked at him like that, he couldn't stop. He needed her to know the truth. "I honored my commitment. When we got married, I was in it one hundred percent. I had a wife and a baby and I did everything I was supposed to do, plus I worked on my Masters at night. We gave the marriage our all. She wanted a home, I worked overtime and bought her a house. She wanted a second child and we had Kenzie. She wanted a perfect family picture on the Christmas card, no problem."

Hanna wrapped the sheet around his bare shoulders and offered him the warmth of her body. "But?"

"Belinda was a hell of a woman. I think I loved her from the day we met. Growing up with four brothers, she understood me too well. I couldn't get away with anything with her." He grinned, remembering the way she'd always had his number. "We thought alike. There were no bullshit games. Yet she could be totally feminine when she decided to be. The only problem was that I wasn't ready to be married. Then, about the time it penetrated my thick skull that being married to my best friend was a pretty sweet deal, they were gone. Ironic, huh?"

"Not your fault."

"After all, wasn't that what I'd wanted in the beginning?" He forced his fingers to unfist. "She hated freeways. She was a small-town girl and Austin traffic freaked her out. I knew that. She didn't even like to ride with me on I-35, much less drive. So that day I was supposed to get home and take Matt to soccer, but I got tied up at the office. She called, and I told her that I couldn't get there and that she could take him, knowing full well that the only way to get him there on time was I-35 in rush-hour traffic. She left Kenzie with a neighbor and…" His eyes stung and he couldn't even say the words.

Hanna pulled the sheet fully around them both. "You had no way of knowing." She kissed his cheek and hugged him tight. "Things happen. Nobody could blame you."

Except himself and he knew he was at fault. He could have taken the work home and done it after soccer. He could have done it the next day. He could have told Belinda that it was just practice and to blow it off. "Instead of belittling her fear, I should have taught her to drive on freeways and in traffic. Then they'd both be alive."

He felt tears against his bare shoulder, and Hanna rubbed her cheek. "It's time to forgive yourself. Don't beat yourself up over hindsight." Through his blurry vision, her liquid brown eyes stared into his. She blotted the corner of his eye with the sheet. "You are a good guy and a loving father. You never intended anyone any harm."

Rubbing Hanna's back, Vince buried his face in her soft hair and felt his body tremble. "I didn't protect my family. For whatever reason, God left me one last chance. To be a good father to Kenzie. That won't make it up to Belinda, but it's something."

As Hanna held him and let him cry, he realized he'd never felt as close to another human being. At least not in nine years. But facing his own vulnerability scared the shit out of him. "I've gotta get outta here."

He lifted her away and yanked his T-shirt over his head. Shoving his feet into his cowboy boots, all he could think of was getting out of that room before he broke down completely and made a bigger fool of himself.

"Vince, wait!"

But he couldn't face her, not right now.

Chapter 12

Hanna's heart shattered for Vince. Would he ever not blame himself? It finally registered why he was so insistent on teaching Kenzie to take care of herself. It was his way of protecting her. Of making sure that what happened to her mother didn't happen to her.

Hanna crawled off the bed and wandered to the balcony doors. Could she help him? Could anyone heal that hurt? At loose ends, she showered and dressed, straightened the room. The drizzle had subsided into a fog as she stepped out onto the balcony for the third time to see if Vince was walking the river. The water taxis glided by on their endless loop, but no sign of Vince. She wanted to give him space to deal with his emotions, yet she wanted him to come back. She needed to hold him.

She considered going down to the lobby, but wanted

to make sure she was here when he returned. She picked up her camera and scrolled through the pictures from the day before. He appeared so happy and carefree on the surface. But it just proved you never really knew someone. He'd been living with this guilt for nine years. How could anyone get over losing a spouse and child?

Laying the camera on the table, she thumbed through the entertainment rag, but not even the insane headlines warranted a smile.

The room door clicked quietly shut. She turned from the balcony and her gaze met Vince's. His navy T-shirt was damp and stuck to his chest. His hair curled over his forehead from the humidity.

Holding back from rushing to wrap him in her arms, she slowly walked toward him. "You okay?"

"Yeah." Shrugging, he stuffed his hands in his pockets. "Chilled."

"Hop in the shower and I'll make another pot of coffee."

"Thanks." He dug dry clothes out of his bag and headed into the bathroom. By the time he padded barefoot out of the steamy bathroom, dressed in jeans and a gray plaid flannel, she handed him a fresh cup of coffee.

Curling his long fingers around the cup, he took a sip. "I'm sorry for unloading on you."

She poured herself a cup and tried to find the right words for what she wanted to say. "My divorce pales in comparison to what you went through. But we all live with regrets. We all have things we wish we'd done differently if only we'd known."

"Richard screwed around on you. Not sure how that translates into you being the guilty party."

"Men aren't the only ones who get caught up in their

roles and responsibilities in a relationship. I should have put more energy into my marriage and not put it all into Ashton, the house, charities, all those things that I thought equated to a perfect life. Then maybe my husband wouldn't have needed another woman."

"That's crap. If a guy wants to screw around, he does. He may blame the wife, but most likely that's just because he feels guilty and has to transfer it to someone rather than himself."

She grinned. "I can't believe you said that. I mean, it's so obvious to women that men don't handle guilt well, but I had no idea that you realized it."

"Oh, we realize it. We just don't typically admit it." He winked. "You caught me on an uncharacteristically vulnerable day."

"Men." Hanna grinned. "See, I had a dream too, Vince. Richard and I had a beautiful home and two expensive cars. Ashton was in private school. We had tons of friends. Membership in the country club. I thought we had the life we both dreamed of. The life I left Marble Falls for, you know? Like you, I wanted something different than what I grew up with."

"Did he give you an excuse as to why he started running around?"

"Said he'd fallen in love with someone else who fulfilled him as a man. Failed to mention that she was a twenty-three-year-old law student interning in his office and the daughter of one of the firm's founders."

Vince leaned forward and touched her face. "So returning home to Marble Falls signifies the end of your fantasy? Not just the failed marriage, but all those things you'd dreamed about and obtained before he yanked it all out from under you?"

"Pretty much. But at least I got to live it for thirteen years. And now I'm going to make this bookstore work and start over. It's never too late. When I was a little girl Mom always bought me books or took me to the library. We both loved to escape into a good book. She and I would talk about opening our own bookstore, but she knew my dream didn't involve spending my life in Marble Falls. She wanted me to be happy. Like you said, dreams change." She sniffed. "Vince, you should finish your Masters. Take Mackenzie and work abroad. It'd be a fantastic experience for both of you."

He rolled the coffee cup between his hands. "I'm finally content with my life. Kenzie is a kick. My in-laws are supportive and all-around good folks. They give her all the love and family she lost when Belinda and Matt died. My parents are an hour away and spoil her rotten. My business is successful. Life is good." He winked. "Your purse is vibrating."

"Oh, crap! I put my phone on vibrate yesterday after Tiffany called." She jumped up and dug her phone out of her purse. "Hello."

"Where the hell are you?" Richard barked. "You didn't answer your phone all damn night. Your mother wouldn't tell me a thing."

A million horrible thoughts filled Hanna's mind. "Richard, what's wrong? Why have you been calling me all night?"

"We spent the night in the emergency room. The pain medication they prescribed for Ashton reacted with his asthma meds and he couldn't breathe. You didn't tell me he was allergic to pain meds."

Oh, God. She knew something like this was bound to happen. "Is he okay?"

"They put him on oxygen." Richard didn't elaborate further.

"But how is he right now? I can be there in a few hours."

"He's home and resting, Hanna. It was last night that you could've shed some light on what we should do." Richard sounded like a petulant child.

All Hanna could think about was getting to Ashton, making sure he was okay. "I'll be there as soon as I can."

"No. This is my week with him. You and the cowboy enjoy whatever it is you're doing. Phoebe and I handled things." The connection clicked off in her ear.

She stared at the phone and tried to get a grip. Richard knew she was with Vince? Was Ashton really okay? And even if he wasn't, unless Richard wanted her there, she had no right. Her baby had been struggling to breathe and had had to rely on a woman he hardly knew and a father who'd seldom had to deal with his asthma. Hanna had always been the one to watch out for him and nurse him through.

Vince touched her shoulder. "What's wrong?"

Turning to him, she was stunned that he was even in the room. "I have no business being here with you. What kind of mother doesn't hear her phone when her son is in the emergency room?" She darted around the suite, gathering the rest of her belongings. Stuffing her new sundress and shoes into the bag, she spotted her bra from the night before under the edge of the bed. As she stooped to retrieve it, Vince grabbed her arm.

"Slow down. Is Ashton okay?"

"He's fine now, but he wasn't last night and they couldn't reach me."

Vince leaned down and looked into her eyes. "Okay, but he's out of danger now. You're overreacting a little, don't you think?"

"I'd have never forgiven myself if Ashton hadn't made it because I turned my phone down so it wouldn't interrupt my romantic getaway. What kind of self-absorbed mother does that? We can't just decide not to have responsibilities. Who am I kidding? We have responsibilities, Vince. We're parents 24/7 whether the kids are actually with us or not." She jerked away, stomped into the bathroom and stuffed her cosmetics and toothbrush into her bag.

When she came out, he grasped both her shoulders. "Nobody said we weren't responsible parents. We're entitled to a break. That doesn't make you a bad mother or me a bad father."

She felt like a bad mother. Ashton was the one thing that she'd done right and even that was going down the tubes since the divorce. He was always angry at her. Thought she was screwing up his life. But the one thing he'd never complained about was her being there to help when he couldn't breathe, and now she'd even failed at that. Zipping the case shut, she tried to calm down enough so Vince didn't think she was a raving lunatic.

Shouldering her purse, she turned to him. "Vince, this was a mistake. I can't pretend to be someone I'm not."

He shoved his hands into his pockets and didn't say a word, didn't try to stop her.

By the time she got to her car, she was crying and shaking so hard she couldn't drive. She tossed her bag in and leaned her head against the steering wheel.

There wasn't one single thing in her life that she hadn't messed up.

Hanna sat in the car until she'd calmed down enough to drive. She had so many thoughts bouncing around in her mind, she probably shouldn't have been behind the wheel at all, but she couldn't sit here in this parking lot.

Just outside of Marble Falls, she stopped for gas and made a side trip to the ladies' room. She washed her face and dried it with a paper towel, then brushed on a touch of blush, eye shadow and lip gloss. Mom already didn't approve of this little getaway. The last thing she needed was for Norma to realize she'd been crying.

Feeling slightly refreshed, she drove the last few miles into town and parked across the street from Bluebonnet Books. She found her mother checking out one lone customer, a man buying three books.

"Did Richard get hold of you last night?" The cash register rang as Norma closed the drawer.

"I talked to him this morning. Ashton's okay." Hanna blew out a breath and smiled as the gentleman, with a camera around his neck and his new map of the Hill Country in hand, closed the door behind him. "Sorry to put you on the spot with Richard last night, Mom."

Mom shrugged. "It happens. It just upset me that Ashton was sick and we couldn't reach you. I'd have called your hotel, but I didn't know where you were staying."

"It was my fault for putting my phone on vibrate. I meant to turn the ringer back on, but I forgot."

"I guess Vince can be rather distracting."

That was an understatement. Hanna's emotions surrounding Vince were too raw to verbalize, especially with her mother. "Everything run okay here?"

Norma narrowed one eye as if weighing the wisdom of pushing the point. "We've been busy with the lunch-hour rush. Anne Haythorn stopped in and helped out for a bit. She said she was sorry to miss you. But that woman keeps close tabs on every move Vince makes. I'm sure she was just fishing to see if you and Vince were out of town together."

"Mom! Don't start." Hanna gritted her teeth and headed for the minuscule office to put away her purse.

Norma leaned against the doorjamb and sighed. "Sweetie, I just don't want you to rush into something too soon. Your pride has been bruised, and I'm afraid you're on the rebound and are going to be hurt again."

Hanna knew her mother's concern was genuine, yet she also knew she would keep questioning until she knew every detail. "I know, Mom. If it makes you feel any better, I ended it. It's too soon for me to consider a relationship."

Mom poured two cups of coffee. "I think that's wise."

Taking one of the cups, Hanna knew she'd made the right choice by breaking things off. "San Antonio was lovely though."

Norma shivered. "With all that humidity?"

Here she went again with her dislike of San Antonio. "Has to be more than humidity to turn you against such a beautiful, romantic city. Have you ever been?"

Norma gripped her cup. "Once. A long time ago."

"With Daddy?"

"No, not with your father." Norma gulped down half her coffee. "It was nothing. A long time ago. Way before you were born."

"Another guy?" Hanna wasn't sure how much she really wanted to know. Her mother talked about everyone else, but seldom about herself. Especially not about the past.

"I may need something stronger than this if we're going to talk about all that."

Hanna's stomach knotted. "Did you love Daddy?"

"Yes, I loved your father." Mom pushed the cup back. "But he wasn't the love of my life. The man I went to San Antonio with, the man I first gave my heart to, died in Vietnam. After that I never had the desire to return to San Antonio."

"You didn't know Daddy then?"

"I knew him. After Brad was killed, your dad started calling me. They were friends and I think Daddy wanted us to help each other grieve for Brad. It took him two years to convince me to marry him, but I finally gave in. Not the life I'd envisioned, but I've never regretted it. Your daddy gave me a good life, probably better than what I had planned." Norma smiled. "And he gave me you."

Hanna's eyes filled with tears, and she stood up and wrapped her arms around her mom. "Thanks for that. I guess that's just the way life goes. Best-laid plans…"

Norma patted Hanna's back. "I'm going to enjoy having you close by to share things with."

Maybe her mother was finally starting to see her as an adult. "It's nice to be close again. Get to know each other as women."

Pulling back, Mom laughed. "Yes, it is. But you'll always be my little girl."

Hanna's heart warmed. Just like Ashton would always be her beautiful baby boy. "I know."

"So, it didn't work out well with Vince?"

Not an easy question to answer, but her mom had

shared an extremely personal experience. "It worked out too well. It scares me how easily Vince drew me in. I don't think I realized how vulnerable I am right now. My emotions are all over the place. The last thing I need is to rush into a possible second mistake while I'm still raw from Richard."

"Richard is a good father." Mom shrugged. "No matter what happened between the two of you, he loves Ashton."

"Yes, he does. But Vince is giving Ashton self-confidence, guy confidence. I know I can't do that, and Richard doesn't even realize Ashton doesn't have it."

"So you're interested in Vince for what he does for Ashton's self-esteem?"

Hanna closed her eyes and thought back to the attentive lover and sexy body she'd just spent twenty-four hours with. It would be so easy if Vince's attentiveness to Ashton was all there was. "Getting to know Vince was an extremely pleasant surprise. He's not at all what I expected when I met him. But it'd be awkward, unfair to ask him to continue to mentor Ashton since I told him I couldn't keep seeing him."

"Ashton will be okay."

Maybe, but Hanna knew how important Vince and Mackenzie had become in Ashton's life. And now she'd cost him his new hero. It was just one more thing her angry preteen would hold against her.

Chapter 13

Hanna idled the engine and squinted to focus through the rain-streaked windshield. She didn't want to miss Ashton when he came out of school. The spring storm had rolled in a couple of hours ago, and she didn't trust him not to get on the back of Kenzie's bike and head home on the slick streets. Good judgment had not been in abundance of late where her son was concerned.

Or herself.

She caught sight of Ashton and Kenzie as they raced from the bike rack, pushing the electric bicycle. By the time Hanna jumped out to wave them down, they were already down the sidewalk and Vince was loading the bike into the bed of his pickup. The kids piled into the cab, and Hanna crawled back into her car, unseen. At least they weren't on that bike in this weather.

What a madhouse. Shaking the rain off her arms,

she cranked up the defrost and looked for a break in the bumper-to-bumper SUVs. Parents and kids dashed through the downpour in between cars. Just as Hanna spotted a gap in the line of cars, her cell phone chimed.

She put the car back in Park and fished the phone out of her purse. "Mackenzie?"

"Hey, Mom, it's Ashton. I'll be at Kenzie's. Vince is going to do his paperwork while we're doing homework. Then he said if we were done early enough and it was okay with you, he'd spring for pizza before he brings me home."

"Ashton, you don't want to impose on Mr. Keegan." Since she'd decided not to see Vince anymore, she wasn't sure about him continuing to be such a big part of Ashton's daily activities. Ashton was attached enough as it was.

"Please, Mom. He offered. I didn't ask."

"Please!" Kenzie pleaded in the background.

Hanna didn't have the heart to say no. This was the first day back in school after spring break and they probably wanted to catch up. "Okay, but tell Vince to let me know if it'd make it easier if I picked you up. I do not want us putting him out."

Vince followed the kids into the house and grinned as Boo's tail started wagging. The silly dog was getting as attached to Ashton as he was to Kenzie. "Kenzie, go get on dry clothes. And toss Ashton that navy-blue sweatsuit. It should fit well enough while I dry his clothes."

While the kids were getting dry, Vince changed his shirt and jeans. That rain was chilly. He put on a pot of coffee and heated milk for hot chocolate for the kids. They could all use a warm-up.

"Put your wet clothes in the dryer." He nodded toward the laundry room, then tossed Boo a biscuit.

Kenzie started the dryer and came back out. "Summer softball signup is tomorrow."

"I know." Kenzie had been playing every summer since she was five.

She dug a bag of cookies out of the pantry and grinned at Ashton. "So you're still not going to sign up?"

"Nobody would want me on their team." Ashton took a cookie in one hand and rubbed Boo with the other.

"So who cares? Sign up anyway."

"Nah, I don't think so. Everybody else has been playing for years and I'm still learning."

Vince set the two cups of hot chocolate on the bar in front of them. "Do you want to play?"

Ashton shrugged. "I'm not good enough. The guys would make fun of me."

"Can't succeed if you don't put yourself out there." Vince poured himself a cup of coffee. He'd never met a kid with such low self-confidence, especially when it came to sports.

"Mom probably wouldn't let me anyway with my asthma. And I'd have to change the weeks I'm at Dad's."

"If you want to play, my dad can talk to your mom," Kenzie volunteered.

"Ashton can ask his mom," Vince said. After San Antonio, he wasn't about to challenge Hanna on how to raise her son again. "You've come a long way on your batting, Ashton. Kenzie and I practice almost every night during the season. You're welcome to come over and join us."

"You think I could get good enough?"

Vince took a sip of coffee. "The only sure way to fail is—"

"To not even try." Kenzie finished the sentence for him. "He says that a lot," she explained to Ashton.

"Okay, busted." Vince laughed. "Now jump on that homework and let me get a couple of bids out. My stomach's growling, and I can already taste that pizza. Are we going to order in or go out?"

"Order in so I have time to beat Ash on Wii NAS-CAR."

"In your dreams," Ashton said, opening his backpack.

A loud clap of thunder vibrated the windows, and Vince decided staying in was definitely the best plan. "Give it your best shots. I'll take down the winner."

"Not!" Kenzie laughed.

Vince went into his office and booted up the laptop, but he could hear the kids talking and laughing. Kenzie was not going to let Ashton off the hook on the baseball deal. She had plenty of friends, but he'd never known her to take to a kid quite like she had to Ashton. It was strange because she typically didn't have much patience with kids who weren't like her. Even when they weren't together, she was talking about some funny thing Ashton said or did.

Vince minimized the spreadsheet he was working on and opened his picture folder. Hanna on the Guadalupe River. Hanna and the kids in the field of bluebonnets. Hanna and him on the river taxi in San Antonio.

Hell, it wasn't just his daughter who had an obsession with the Rossers.

Hanna's decision to work through her post-divorce issues and figure out where her life was going made perfect, rational sense. The flawless rhythm of her body in unison with his had just as much merit. How could something that felt that right be wrong? What they'd shared on that trip had been too intense, physically and emotionally, not to give it a chance.

She owed it to herself to get her head straight before jumping into another relationship—he'd never deny her that. But there was a niggling fear that maybe he'd frightened her by coming clean about his past with Belinda. It sure as hell had frightened him. God, he'd never gone into that crap with anyone else, and it was way too early in the relationship to have gone there with Hanna. She likely thought he was a total jackass.

Probably because his brain was still in a San Antonio hotel room, the kids finished their assignments before he was done with his proposal. They plugged in the Wii and he was serenaded with the sounds of race cars and cheering as they got into the competition.

"If you'd just use your instincts and play instead of analyzing how the game works, you might actually win." Evidently Kenzie had won the first race.

"Games are really pretty simple," Ashton explained. "It's just a program that reacts to how you move."

"Yeah, yeah, yeah. Next race. Quit thinking and drive, Ash! I've almost got a full lap on you."

It was almost eight by the time they finished their pizza and Vince drove Ashton home. Hanna opened the door when they pulled up and Vince got out. He hadn't actually seen her since she'd run out of the hotel room.

Her hair was kinky from the humidity and she looked comfortable in a pair of faded jeans and a huge white blouse. No makeup. No jewelry. No logical reason his libido was kicking up, but he couldn't stop staring at her. In his defense, she didn't break eye contact, either.

"Mom, here's a paper on softball sign-ups tomorrow."

She blinked her beautiful dark eyes, and took the paper from Ashton. "Oh, honey, I don't know about all that running with your asthma."

"I want to do it. Vince said the only way I can fail is by not trying at all. And I can practice every day with him and Kenzie. I'm getting better."

Here it came again. She was going to jump down his throat about encouraging Ashton. She glanced back at Vince. "Ashton, go take your shower. Let me talk to Vince a minute."

Oh, yeah. This wasn't going to be pretty.

Ashton went inside, but turned. "Thanks for the pizza. Kenzie said you'd have to talk to her."

Now he was getting "I told you so" from the kid? "You're welcome, Ashton."

Hanna stepped out on the covered porch with Vince and closed the door. The rain dripped off the roof and splattered in a puddle behind the bushes. "Softball and asthma aren't a good mix."

"It's important to him. How about if I promise to be at all his games to keep an eye on him?"

"Vince, I'm not sure what to say here. You aren't obligated to look out for Ashton."

He tilted his head. "I'm not doing it under any obligation. He's a good kid and my daughter's friend and, no offense, but he needs a guy around."

She took a deep breath and reached one hand out and let the next drop of rain land on her palm, then turned her hand to let it drip off. Anything to avoid looking at him probably. "Yes, but how can we handle this after…"

Shoving his hands in his pockets so he didn't touch her, he leaned around and captured her gaze. "We're friends. That hasn't changed. We have kids to raise. It's a small town. I don't want us to feel uncomfortable around each other every time we're together. Truce?"

The corners of her mouth turned up. "We can try."

"What happened in those two days was pretty cool. Too cool to let it ruin a good friendship."

"It was more than cool." She smiled, but nibbled her lip. "And I do value your friendship."

He winked. "I'll try not to picture you naked if you'll try not to picture me naked. Deal?"

"Oh, that helps keep things casual." She laughed. "It was childish of me to run away like that. I'm sorry."

"And softball?"

"Let me think about that one."

Hanna finally gave in and signed Ashton up for softball. He assured her that he was going to give it his all and that he'd use his inhaler anytime he needed it no matter who was watching. What convinced her was that he admitted he knew he might fail, but he wanted to take the risk. How could she deny him that chance when he was just beginning to fit in?

On Thursday, when the kids arrived at the bookstore, Kenzie went straight to the bathroom. Ashton dropped his backpack in one of the chairs by the coffee center. "Is it okay if Kenzie stays here and we do homework together? Then when Vince gets off, we're going to her house to toss a few balls."

"Sure. Offer her a cookie and a soft drink when she comes out." She hugged his shoulders. "Just keep the noise level down."

By the time Hanna had helped a couple of regular customers pick out some of the latest romance novels, Kenzie still hadn't returned from the bathroom.

Hanna checked the ladies out at the register and put their books into a bag. Ashton was working away on his homework. Something was up or Kenzie would be out by now. As soon as the women left, Hanna walked to the back of the shop and knocked on the restroom door. "Kenzie, are you okay?"

Nothing. Not a sound.

"Kenzie?"

Finally a very weak "Yeah" came from inside.

"Are you sick?"

"Not exactly. My stomach hurts way down low."

Hanna nibbled her lip. Twelve years old. Stomach cramps. Oh, dear. "Are you bleeding?"

"Yes. I'm not sure what to do."

"Hold on. Let me get you something."

Hanna went to her office, pulled a sanitary pad from her purse and returned to the bathroom. "Open the door."

Slowly it opened, and Kenzie looked up at her. Her face was pale and she'd been crying.

Hanna handed her the pad. "Everything's fine. Take your time and I'll drive you home. Okay?"

Kenzie nodded and closed the door.

Hanna filled her mother in and told Ashton that Kenzie wasn't feeling well. She gathered up Kenzie's backpack and asked Ashton to put her bike in the office until Vince could come by and pick it up. Then she called Vince and told him what was happening.

His voice sounded shaky. "Is she okay? Do I need to come get her?"

"No, I'll get her home. You might want to stop and grab a few supplies. Do you know what to buy?" Hanna figured the way Kenzie looked, she shouldn't put her through stopping by the store on the way home.

There was total quiet for a few seconds. Vince at a loss for words: that was one thing she'd never expected. "Maybe I should meet you at the house and you can make me a list."

"Okay." Hanna wasn't sure whether he just needed to see his daughter and make sure she was being taken care of or whether he was in shock. "She'll get through this, Vince. We all do."

Hanna led Mackenzie to the car and placed the backpack on the backseat. "You feeling any better? Maybe an aspirin would help."

She shrugged. "I don't think so. I'm not sure what 'better' is supposed to feel like."

Mackenzie crawled into the car and buckled her seat belt, but leaned against the window as if the cool glass helped.

Hanna drove the short distance to the house, and Mackenzie darted into the bathroom and closed the door.

The shower started and Hanna heard the pickup door slam. Vince bolted into the kitchen. "Is she scared?"

On impulse she gave him a hug. "A little. Want me to run to the drugstore?"

He glanced down the hall at the closed bathroom

door. "Maybe you should stay here and just make me that list."

Wow, he really *was* feeling out of his comfort zone. Hanna quickly jotted down a few items. "You could also pick up some ginger ale and whatever kind of soup or comfort food she likes. She might be queasy tonight."

"You sure you're okay here?"

"I'm fine. Mackenzie will be fine." She pushed him toward the door.

Hanna dug through her purse and pulled out another pad. She knocked on the bathroom door. "Kenzie, I'm leaving this right here by the door. I'm here if you need me."

The shower stopped. "Thanks." Hanna moved away from the door, but Mackenzie stuck her head out. "Where's my dad?"

"He ran to the store to get what you need."

"Does he know what happened?"

Hanna grinned. "Of course he knows. He was married to your mom for years. I'm sure this isn't the first time he's had to make an emergency run. Can I get you a nightgown?"

Mackenzie nodded. "Second drawer on the right. I'd like the blue one with the butterflies."

So far so good. Surprisingly the room was neat and organized. The walls were bright yellow and the spread sported a white daisy pattern. Hanna located the gown and fresh panties easily enough. She handed the items through the crack in the door and went to the kitchen for a glass of water. By the time she returned with a daisy-painted glass of ice water, Mackenzie was snuggled under the covers, her knees drawn up to her tummy. She looked so young to be going through this. Her face was pale and her blond hair spread across the pillow, still damp from the shower.

Hmmm, how to approach her. "Feel better?"

Mackenzie nodded.

At least she wasn't belligerent about Hanna being here. "I'm not sure what to say. Do you have any questions?"

The girl actually met her eyes. "The nurse talked to us and gave us all a pamphlet in health class. And I can ask Dad or Grandma."

"Okay. But if you think of something, I'd be happy to try to answer. You hungry?"

Kenzie puffed out her cheeks. "My stomach hurts bad enough already."

"Try to relax. That always helps me. I'll be in the kitchen."

Hanna actually felt sorry for Kenzie, although she didn't seem like the same feisty girl who typically kept things stirred up.

Hanna's stomach growled, and she figured Vince would be hungry, too, since it was almost dinnertime. She rummaged in the fridge and made a turkey-and-cheese sandwich. She grinned. Even the plates had a daisy pattern that matched the canister set.

Gravel crunched as the pickup pulled in. She grabbed a soda out of the fridge and placed it on the bar beside the sandwich.

When Vince walked through the door, he put the bag on the counter and looked around. "Everything okay?"

"She's resting. The thought of food makes her nauseous and she doesn't want to discuss it."

He pulled the Midol out. "You think this would help?"

"You could call her doctor and ask, but I don't see that half a tablet could hurt."

"Me, either." He took out a knife and split one tablet. "I'll go check on her."

The door was open and Hanna could hear the conversation almost as if they were in the room with her.

"Hey, punkin', how you feeling?"

"Like crap."

Leave it to Mackenzie to put things into perspective.

"Here, see if this helps."

The bed springs squeaked and Hanna heard a slurp of water. "So, are you okay, Dad?"

Short pause. "No, but we'll get through this like we have everything else. It's just nature."

"Nature sucks green pond scum."

He laughed. "You rest. Hanna and I'll be in the kitchen. Yell if you need anything."

"Can you turn on my new CD? Then maybe I can whip you at NASCAR later."

"In your dreams. Ain't gonna happen in this lifetime."

Rascal Flats filtered through the air and the bedroom door clicked shut. Vince walked back into the kitchen. "Isn't she sort of young for this? I thought I'd ask my mother-in-law to talk to her this summer, but I figured that might even be rushing things. Geesh. She's barely twelve."

Hanna watched as he paced the room. Instinctively she reached out and wrapped her arms around his waist. She'd never seen anyone who looked more like they needed a hug. Her body trembled the instant it touched his. San Antonio. River taxis. Intimate hotel rooms and rainstorms. She felt his heart rate accelerate as if they were sharing the same wavelength.

She pulled back before she gave in to the temptation to kiss him. "Next we'll see how you handle Mackenzie dating."

"Yeah, let's not talk about that right now."

All Hanna could think about was how homey and intimate the little kitchen felt. How she should not be nearly as sexually aware of the man in front of her as she was. She needed to get out of here.

She nodded toward the bar. "I made you a sandwich."

"I appreciate all you've done today."

What was she supposed to do with her hands? "Not half as much as you do for Ashton."

That blue stare bored into her and held her captive.

"I need to go."

"Don't." Before she could take a step, his hand reached out and he pulled her to him. His lips touched hers, demanding and receiving. His tongue exploring and enticing.

Pressing her body into his embrace, she rubbed her hands up his back and tangled them around his neck. The short hair at the nape of his neck tickled her fingertips, but she could do little more than groan in satisfaction at the familiar scent of shampoo and sweat.

"Hanna," he whispered against her lips as he cupped her butt and held her tight against him. "I don't want to be your friend."

Chapter 14

That evening Hanna scrolled through the pictures from both the tubing trip and the San Antonio trip, as she'd gotten in the habit of doing before bedtime.

Her body still tingled with sensation from Vince's touch, his kisses. Who was she kidding? Vince was right. She didn't want to be friends either, at least not "just" friends. She shut down the laptop and crawled into bed, imagining Vince's hands on her body and his mouth on hers.

She snuggled under the covers and closed her eyes, but her mind was too awake to sleep. Could they make this relationship work? It was too soon. And she was taking a huge risk. And it might not work out. And... her cell phone chimed.

She glanced at the display and grinned. "Hey."

"Hey," Vince said. "Kenzie's finally asleep."

"She having a hard time?"

"She's miserable. Stomach hurts, back hurts, head hurts and she's irritable as a hornet. I called her doctor, and she said to give her a full tablet every four hours if she needed it. She also wants to see her next week."

"That's probably a good idea."

The guy sounded exhausted.

"She decided she'd rather suck on a Popsicle than eat her Grandma's vegetable soup. And it's her favorite."

"So are you going to keep her home tomorrow?"

"Unless she does a major turnaround, I don't see her going to school. Maybe she'll at least feel like doing her homework. My mother-in-law is going to pick up her assignments, and Kenzie will probably go home with her for the day."

"Next month will be easier, I bet."

She heard the bed springs creak. "I sure as hell hope so. If this is what I'm in for every month, I'm clueless. She never falls apart."

Poor guy. He'd dealt with diapers, being a single parent, school and probably all the childhood illnesses, but this was more than he'd bargained for.

"Ashton asked what was wrong with Mackenzie," she said. "I guess I pulled the same trick you did. Couldn't figure out the right words. I'm stuttering, and he says, 'So, is it that girl cycle thing?'"

"And you just answered yes?"

"Yep." Hanna grinned at how well they could read each other. It was nice to have another parent who understood kids and wasn't afraid to admit when he didn't have all the answers. God, she'd just like to hold him. Sleep in his arms. "Vince."

"Yeah?"

"I…I miss you tonight." If she wasn't careful, she could fall in love with this man.

"I miss you, too. We'll make this work. Sweet dreams."

Bluebonnet Books was getting busier each day, which was a good thing. With any luck, it was more than the novelty of a new shop in town and everyone would continue to stop by. Even if each patron only purchased one item, it could add up.

Hanna was getting ready to lock up when the front-door bell jingled. "Mrs. Maguire. Nice to see you. How is Kenzie today?"

"Much better this afternoon. Her father got home early." There was a slight hesitation, but she nodded. "We do appreciate your helping out yesterday, but don't worry about Kenzie. We can take care of her."

We? As in "the family"? "I was glad I could be there for Kenzie and Vince."

"Vince has handled things for the past nine years better than most men would've. He did sound a little out of his element when he called me last night."

The woman's tone was friendly enough, but her message came across crystal-clear. *You're not family. Vince called me.* The last thing Hanna intended was to threaten Vince's ex-mother-in-law's role in his and Kenzie's lives, but obviously her handling of the situation had done just that.

"I'm glad to hear that Mackenzie is better. Can I help you with anything?"

"Kenzie likes adventure books."

Hanna showed her to the children's section and the appropriate shelf. "Just sing out if you have any questions."

* * *

"Are you sure this is smart?" Hanna asked as Vince closed the garage door at his house and helped her out of the truck.

"Not sure about smart." He backed her against the truck and covered her mouth with his. "But you gotta admit it sure feels right."

That it did. "And you don't think Mrs. Haythorn will notice me walking into your house with you at 6:00 p.m.? People are getting home from work now."

He laughed and pulled her close against his side. "Keep your head down until we get inside the house. Even if she does spot us, she won't know who you are. It'll give her something new to ponder."

Hanna followed him across the lawn and tried to figure out just how much of this they could possibly hope to keep from burning up the phone lines. "And she'll call my mom to ponder it with her. 'Oh my, who is Vince Keegan sleeping with now? Is it Donna Martin's daughter, Kim? Or perhaps some new victim?'"

"Kim? How the hell do you know about Kim? Oh yeah, you live with the town gossip. What other interesting incidents of impropriety have I had?"

Hanna bumped him with her hip. "They must not have been that interesting if you don't even remember. But I'll see what I can dig up for you when I get home."

He flashed those deep dimples. "Just want to make sure I didn't miss anything good."

"Mrs. Haythorn will be positively gleeful when she discovers it's me sleeping with you. My mom told the ladies at church about Mrs. Haythorn's daughter having a bun in the oven and having to get married."

"Seriously? A bun in the oven?" He dropped his bag

on the chair and checked the messages on his machine. A couple from Gray and an invitation to dinner Sunday at "the folks."

Why did it make her uneasy to think about how much a part of the Maguire family Vince remained after nine years?

Hanna wasn't ready to expose their new relationship by having a dinner out, so Vince pulled bacon and eggs out of the fridge.

"The man is good in bed *and* he cooks."

He placed the bacon in the skillet and then bowed. "Thank you, on both counts. My mother-in-law is not a fan of McDonald's and was afraid Kenzie might become malnourished. She had us over almost every night and finally took it upon herself to teach me to cook. I make a mean beef stew with all fresh vegetables and corn bread that can warm you up on a cold night. I suck at pies, though."

Hanna was torn between admiring Vince for remaining so close to Belinda's family and letting it make her uncomfortable. How would they react when the news hit town that he had a new girlfriend?

They hadn't even gotten dinner cooked when someone knocked on the back door. Vince set the plate of bacon on the table and opened the door. Boo bounded inside, tail wagging and tongue lolling out as Vince bent and scratched him behind the ears.

Grayson Maguire followed the dog into the room. Not quite as tall as Vince, but similar style of dress. Tight, faded jeans, work boots and a ball cap, only his cap and dark-green button-down sported a Maguire Landscaping logo. "I had a job in town and thought I'd drop him off. Since Kenzie was in the house instead of playing with him, Boo decided to dig up the flowers Mom just planted." He eyed Hanna and shuffled from one foot to the other.

"Great, guess I get the opportunity to replant, courtesy of Boo?"

Gray rubbed the dog's head as Boo ambled back his way. "No permanent damage."

Vince glanced from Grayson to Hanna. "Oh, do you know Hanna Rosser? Hanna, Grayson Maguire, my brother-in-law and salvation when I need a day or two's break from work. We trade out."

Gray removed his cap and extended his hand. "Hi, Hanna. Nice to see you back in town." Dark, straight hair and nervous gray eyes that seemed to want to look anywhere rather than at her.

"It's been a long time." She shook his hand. He obviously wasn't comfortable with her being here, but she didn't know what else to do except be friendly.

"Years. Not since graduation." Glancing around the kitchen, he backed toward the door. "Well, don't let me interrupt your dinner. I need to get back over to the folks."

"Tell Mom thanks for keeping Kenzie." Vince shook his head as Gray tugged his cap back on and practically bolted out the door. "Can't say that I've seen him that nervous since some hot little redhead came on to him one night at dinner."

"He was always quiet. Not as outgoing as his three older brothers."

"Yep, still is."

"I don't think Grayson was thrilled with finding me here."

Vince cracked eggs into the sizzling skillet and

tossed the shells in the garbage. "Nah, don't take it personally. Gray's just got trust issues when it comes to contemporary women."

Hanna grinned, opening drawers until she located the silverware. "Wants a woman like his mom? Stay-at-home wife, dinner-on-the-table-at-six sort of woman?"

"Claire Maguire is a hard act to follow." Vince scooped the scrambled eggs into a bowl and grabbed the toast out of the toaster.

"I'm sure." She placed napkins and silverware on the table. Claire and Wayne Maguire were the grassroots of the community. Steadfast, good, upstanding citizens. Even Hanna's mother was hesitant to gossip about any of the Maguire brood.

Claire was everything Hanna no longer had the luxury of being. Hanna didn't have a husband to take care of her and pay the bills so that she could stay home and take care of Ashton and the house. Another adjustment to her new status in life.

After dinner, the dog stretched out on his back on the rug in front of the cold fireplace, all four paws in the air. Hanna and Vince settled in on the sofa to watch a movie, but she couldn't help worrying that the neighbors somehow knew she was here. Vince's answer to that was to wait until the lights were out in every house before taking her home. That might have worked, except her mother and Ashton would be home from dinner and the movie in a couple of hours. "I have to be home by ten or I turn into a pumpkin, so…"

Boo's ears perked up and he rolled to his feet at the sound of a second knock at the back door. Hanna narrowed her eyes at Vince. "Doesn't anyone come to the front door around here?"

With a sigh, he stood, straightened his shirt and headed into the kitchen. "Salesmen, sometimes."

Hanna recognized Mrs. Haythorn's Southern drawl and stayed discreetly out of sight in the living room.

"I saw Kenzie leave with Claire this afternoon. Just noticed your lights on. Thought you might like a piece of homemade apple pie."

"Appreciate it," Vince said. "But you didn't have to do that."

"Figured you might be hungry. I mowed your side yard. Out mowing mine anyway this morning before it got hot."

"You're a sweetheart, but you don't need to mow my lawn, Mrs. Haythorn."

"No problem at all. Ran out of gas or I'd have gotten the front, too. My granddaughter is spending the day tomorrow. Thought I'd see if Kenzie wanted to come over and bake cookies."

"She's spending the day at her grandmother's. She'll be sorry she missed seeing Molly."

"Molly will be disappointed. Was that Grayson Maguire dropping off Boo earlier?"

"That was Gray."

"Sweet man. He needs a good wife, too."

"Gray will figure it out. You take care now, okay?"

The back door shut and the deadbolt clicked into place before Hanna let out her breath.

Vince padded barefoot back into the room. "That woman needs a life."

Boo flopped back down on his rug as if disgruntled with the interruption of his nap.

Hanna rubbed her forehead. "Wow, she's persistent. She knew someone was here, you know?"

"Yeah, kept trying to lean around me to see who was in here."

"So is Molly Mrs. Haythorn's granddaughter?" Hanna tried to piece together the lives of the townsfolk since she'd been gone.

"Yeah, thirteen-year-old Molly, not to be confused with her eighteen-year-old sister, Candace, who I recently learned from you was already in the oven when her scandalous parents married. I was shocked!"

"Oh yeah, because we know that never happens." Hanna giggled, but it really wasn't funny. Her mother's little network of friends would have a heyday with her and Vince being here alone. In small towns, people didn't do that sort of thing until after marriage. At least, not unless they wanted to be the main topic of conversation.

Tugging her to her feet, Vince ran his hands beneath her shirt and up her sides, then cupped her breasts through her satin bra. "Just so you know, I intend to continue to see you and to hell with the grapevine if they don't approve."

Stretching her arms over her head, Hanna let him pull the shirt off. She wasn't ready to admit how much she wanted to spend every waking minute with this man. Correction, not just the waking minutes. "Yeah, you just wait until I find out all the things they've said about you. You might not be so cocky then."

"I've never set out to burn up the airwaves, but I'm not going to change my life just because your mother and her friends disapprove. I'm too old and I've been through too damn much. And I don't plan to let you get too caught up in it, either."

His shirt landed on the floor on top of hers. Then her bra. He pulled her tightly against him and started a seductive dance—bare chest to breasts, jeans to jeans. She hardly noticed the lack of music as she moved her hips with his and reveled at the touch of his calloused hands exploring her naked torso. The rub of his stubble as he nuzzled her breast and took her nipple into his mouth. His moist lips returned to hers and demanded attention as he hooked his thumbs into her waistband and slowed their moves to a sway.

Working their jeans off and adding them to the clothing pile, he opened his mouth across hers, exploring and melding her to him. He eased her down on the sofa and buried his hands in her hair, holding her face firm for a kiss.

"I tried not to worry about the grapevine when I was in high school. But every little thing made its way back to my mother before I even got home."

He backed away and stared at her. "So what did you do that warranted gossiping? Come on, you can't drop a bomb like that and not give details."

Hanna squealed as he tickled under her arms.

"I'm relentless until you give up every dirty little detail."

"Okay, okay." She tried to stop laughing long enough to catch her breath. "One night I went skinny-dipping in the lake with Freddie Smith. Old Man Thompson saw us and told Old Lady Thompson, who told Mrs. Haythorn, who couldn't wait to call Mom because of the whole Mom-spilling-the-beans-about-the-bun-in-the-oven thing, and Mrs. Haythorn had to get even. So by the time the story wound its way through the grape-vine and I got home, my mother thought Freddie and I were going at it on the bank like rabbits. We just swam! Kissed a little. Why do old men fish at night anyway? That's asinine."

Vince's hand roamed over her belly and lower. "So I'm messing around with a wild child! Good to know. Skinny-dipping. Maybe we should give that a try."

Her breath caught in her throat as she enjoyed his ministrations. "Oh come on, I'm sure you were wilder than I ever thought about being."

"No, I was studious. Had my eye on that engineering degree." His fingers kept up their ceaseless exploration. "I partied on occasion, but I was a good boy."

His stubble scratched her neck as he nuzzled lower toward her left breast. She cradled his head. "Oh you are very good."

Chapter 15

Hanna woke up early and dressed. Still in her euphoria from the night before in Vince's arms, she left her mom and Ashton sleeping. She stuck a note on the fridge to let them know that she was opening the shop and there was no need for them to hurry this morning. She couldn't wipe the silly smile off her face at just the thought of making out with Vince. They were really going to give this thing between them a shot and suddenly all was right with the world.

The sky had just enough wispy clouds to make it pretty, and Hanna breathed in the fresh scents from the newly mown grass and spring flower beds. What a great day.

She stopped by the Barkley's corner store for a box of Mrs. Barkley's croissants on her way in. Nothing in the store had changed from the recently mopped well-worn beige vinyl floor to the tan metal shelves stocked with breakfast cereal. Hanna grinned at the red soda machine in the corner. Just as Dave had mentioned, the variety included those old-fashioned chocolate sodas she'd loved as a kid.

Mrs. Barkley handed her the box of croissants and her change. "Say hello to Norma for me." As they'd operated for forty-plus years, Mrs. Barkley got up before the sun came up every day and opened the store. She took care of the morning baking and Mr. Barkley ran the afternoon shift and closed up each night. The only difference in the woman was considerably more gray hairs than when Hanna had last seen her.

"Thanks, Mrs. Barkley. I will. Have a nice day."

Hanna had the coffee brewing and had already given in to the temptation of the heavenly aroma of fresh bread by the time her mother arrived.

Norma glided into the shop, wearing one of her dozen or so pairs of black slacks and today's blouse, a deep royal blue. Yep, it was Saturday. Always blue on Saturday. Her salt-and-pepper curls framed her narrow face like a helmet and with all that hairspray, they were probably about as soft.

"Morning, Mom. Is Ashton still asleep?"

"I cooked him breakfast, and he was sitting in front of the TV when I left. Said he'd be by in a little while."

Hanna was still getting used to her son being old enough to stay alone. "Croissants are on the counter."

"Anne Haythorn rang this morning. Seems she suspects her neighbor has a new lady friend."

"Oh, really?" Hanna grabbed some Hill Country brochures to refill the plastic rack and tried not to snap at her mother. True, they were from different generations.

Yet her grandmother hadn't been a gossip, so that wasn't enough to sell Hanna on that excuse.

"She went over last night to take him a piece of pie, and he told her Kenzie was at her grandmother's house, but she could hear someone in the next room. And somebody was in the truck with him when he pulled in earlier that day."

Hanna slammed the stack of brochures on the counter. "Mom, I'm not trying to stir up the rumor mill, but I am going to live my life."

Norma shoved her glasses up on her nose and turned to face her daughter. "You have a son to think about, Hanna. How is this going to affect him?"

"Ashton likes Vince and vice versa."

"And if this relationship doesn't work out?" Norma paused for a breath. "That boy has been through enough."

Very true. "Mom, I don't want to argue about this. I enjoy Vince's company. And for now, that's enough reason for me to continue seeing him."

The bell on the front door jingled, and Anne Haythorn waltzed in. Her gray hair was cut in the latest style, in Hanna's opinion a tad too young for her, but who was she to judge?

"Good morning, Norma. Do you have that book I ordered for Molly? I was hoping it had come in before she arrives this afternoon." She turned her beaming smile on Hanna. "Hi, Hanna. I see a lot of that boy of yours at the Keegans."

"He and Kenzie are friends." Hanna pasted on her sweetest smile and walked over to the small coffee area. "Hot coffee? Croissant?"

"I guess I can spare a few minutes."

"There's sugar and creamer by the side. I'll just run and see if I can help Mom find that book."

Bluebonnet Books got incredibly busy as the spring tourists wandered in. Lots of people out for weekend excursions to see the wildflowers, and Norma managed to sell something to almost everyone who entered.

Ashton strolled in just before lunch with Kenzie in tow. Both kids had on faded jeans, T-shirts and backwards ball caps. "Mom, is it okay if we go to McDonald's for lunch?"

Hanna smiled at them. Neither she nor her mother had time to take off and make lunch for him. "Just a sec and I'll get you some cash."

She handed him the money and straightened a curl that had fallen across his forehead. "Be careful and watch for cars."

Ashton stuffed the money in his pocket. "We're walking today. Kenzie's bike has a flat. And if we have room after McDonald's, we may stop by Mr. Barkley's store for a chocolate soda."

A chocolate soda. Wow, kids still liked those? At least they were walking, with all the tourists adding to the traffic. "Have fun."

She was so busy when Vince called to ask her to lunch, she had to take the call while ringing out a customer. He waited until she was done, and Norma took over the register. Hanna eased her way back to the office for a minute's privacy. "I'm way too busy to take a lunch break today. Not that busy is a bad thing."

"No kidding. Kids tell you they were going to McDonald's?"

Hanna grinned. "They actually stopped by and asked permission for once. But you and I having lunch in public? Not such a good idea. Anyway, before we take this to the Falls Diner, we need to tell Kenzie and Ashton."

The line was quiet a minute. "Agreed. So we tell them after work tonight. Then I'll grab a bucket of fried chicken and some fishing gear and we'll pick you two up at seven."

Hanna frowned. "You don't waste any time do you? Think they might need an evening to adjust before we all go out?"

"They'll get used to the idea. Fishing will help. I don't think it'll surprise either of them too much anyway. See you tonight."

Vince hung up and dialed Gray. He wasn't happy about being turned down for lunch, but he did want to tell Kenzie before someone else did. God, last night with Hanna had been hot, but with Ashton at home, Hanna had left early. Alone time was going to be a challenge.

"Hey, bro. Got time to meet me at Mariah's shop and give me a lift home? I need to drop the Harley off for a tune-up. Might be a free lunch in it for you."

More like brothers than brothers-in-law, Vince and Gray covered each other's businesses when they needed time away. And since it was a pretty equal trade-off, they never worried about money. Still, it wouldn't hurt to buy the guy lunch. Plus Vince was a little worried about Gray's reaction about seeing his brother-in-law with Hanna.

Vince parked the truck in the garage and straddled the Harley, ignoring the helmet on the shelf. He wanted the wind in his face today. Wanted to feel the power of the bike. Life was good. He and Hanna were both on the same page, at least enough to want to give this a shot. Kenzie was feeling better, and he had a date tonight.

When he pulled his Harley into the shop, his gaze landed on Mariah Calabrezie's jeans-covered rear end as she bent over a bike she was working on. Wiping her hands on a greasy rag, she straightened and flashed him a grin. Petite, pixie-faced, she looked like anything but a top-notch grease monkey.

"Hey, Vince. Harley got a problem?"

Vince put the kickstand down and got off. "Just came back from a short road trip. Engine's cutting out, idling rough."

Gray then pulled into the parking lot, but remained in the truck.

Mariah stared at the truck a second, but didn't comment. "May be a couple days before I can get to it. Springtime. Everyone wants to hit the road. Probably just needs a little TLC."

"No rush. You've got my cell number."

She nodded. "I'll call you after I get a chance to look at it."

He headed toward Gray's old, faded, green-and-white pickup. "What do you think about Mariah?"

"Thought you were hooking up with Hanna Rosser."

"Wasn't talking about me."

The truck door squeaked open and Gray flashed him a go-to-hell look. "Me and the biker lady? What are you smoking?"

"Mariah Calabrezie is the best damn mechanic this side of the Red River. This lady can make a bike hum like June bugs around a porch light."

Gray glanced at Mariah, but didn't seem too impressed. "Not the kind of woman to bring home for Mom's Sunday pot roast."

Vince was in a great mood and it seemed that a woman might be just what Grayson needed, as well. "So what is your type? Donna Reed?"

Gray ground the starter, but it took at least thirty seconds for the engine to kick in. "Lay off. There's nothing wrong with an old-fashioned woman who believes in the important things in life. The whole world is screwed up."

Vince raised an eyebrow and razzed him. "So you don't think a woman should work?"

Gray dropped the truck into first and growled. "Just saying that I don't understand why there aren't any women left who want to stay home and have babies. What happened to home and family?"

"Here's your problem." Suddenly all the pieces fell into place. "You have superwoman as a mom. How can any woman compare? Gardens, cooks, keeps the house clean, babysits the grandkids, mows the yard, there for everybody when they need her." Vince pointed toward the Falls Diner. "Lunch?"

Gray whipped the truck into the parking lot.

"Hell, I'm not sure I'd have ever gotten my act together after Belinda was killed without her support," Vince admitted.

"Exactly my point." Gray wedged the truck in between a Lexus and an F150 with a rack and ladders in the bed.

"You might want to whittle your requirements down to a more realistic list," Vince suggested.

"You keep hounding me like this and I'm going to order the biggest meal on the menu *and* dessert. So tell me about Hanna Rosser. Things looked pretty chummy last night. And that chicken-eatin' grin has been plastered on your face since I pulled into the bike shop."

Vince cocked his head and wondered if Gray was as cool with this as he was acting. "Why don't you tell me what you think about Hanna?"

"She's a good person. I knew her in school." Gripping the wheel, Gray turned and stared at him. "Belinda's been dead a long time, Vince. You've got a life to live."

"Could say the same about you." Vince wasn't sure to what extent losing his twin had contributed to Gray's hang-ups about women.

"I miss her every damn day. She was my best friend." Gray flashed those white teeth. "But she'd kick our asses if she thought we weren't getting on with our lives."

"You got that right." For the first time in nine years Vince was actually beginning to realize that by his complete devotion to Kenzie and their life here, he'd closed himself off from some interesting possibilities. "When are you going to find a woman so I don't have to kick your ass for your sister?"

"When I'm damn good and ready. You buying me lunch?"

Vince slammed the pickup door and matched his stride to Gray's. "How about the secretary at the school? She asks about you almost every time I'm there." And that was more often than he'd have liked of late.

Gray shook his head. "Divorced. Two kids."

Vince snapped his finger. "Kim Martin. She's looking for somebody to be a daddy to her little girl. She'd love to stay home and have your babies."

Gray opened the door and walked into the diner. "I'm hungry. You hungry? Meat loaf smells good. I'm thinking banana cream pie."

At least they got to finish their first course, but Vince had taken only two bites out of his pie when his cell phone rang. He glanced at the display.

"Hey, Ken—"

"Bully Baer's telling everybody that you're doing it with Ms. Rosser."

Vince dropped his fork onto the plate. "Kenzie, calm down."

"I know you broke up, so why's he being such a jerk and telling people that? I told him…"

Shit. "Kenzie, slow down a minute."

Silence. Frightening silence. "Are you and Ms. Rosser doing it?"

How was he supposed to handle this over the phone? He should have told her sooner. "Are you at McDonald's? Is Ashton still with you?"

A pause, then Ashton's gasp. "It's true?"

"Stay there and I'll pick you up."

"I don't want to stay here. And I don't want to talk to you. You told me it was over. You lied."

The phone went dead.

Now even the kids were being hurt by the town grapevine!

"We gotta go."

Without asking what was up, Gray started shoveling in bites of banana cream pie. Vince did the same with his coconut cream. "William Baer's boy told the kids about me and Hanna."

"That kid's a pain." Gray finished his pie and pushed in his chair.

Vince handed the waitress a couple bills, probably twice the cost of lunch, and followed Gray toward the truck. He dialed Hanna's phone. "We got a problem. Kids are upset. Billy Baer was at McDonald's and told them that you and I are sleeping together. Kenzie hung up on me. I don't know where they are."

Grayson made good time getting to the house. Vince really wasn't sure where Kenzie would go, but he needed his truck to find her.

"Back door's open," Gray said.

Vince bolted out of the truck. "You coming in?"

Gray shook his head. "This is between you and Kenzie."

"Yeah."

Vince didn't even get in the door before Kenzie pounced, hands on her hips. "So did Bully Baer lie? Or did you?"

Deep breath. "Hanna and I are dating."

Her blue eyes flashed. "You couldn't have just told us? You had to let that dweeb know before we did? He said you're—"

"Stop right there. This just happened. We planned to tell you tonight." Geez, it even sounded like a flimsy excuse to him.

Kenzie stomped up and huffed. "Well that's not soon enough." She pushed past him and flounced down on the sofa, arms crossed over her chest.

Vince squatted down in front of her, but she wouldn't even look at him. Tears glistened in her blue eyes. "Mackenzie, I did not lie to you." He bent his head and tried to capture her gaze. "When I told you Hanna and

I weren't seeing each other, that was the truth. Things changed."

"Why do you need her anyway?" She sniffed and turned to face him. Instead of belligerence, he saw a hurt little girl.

"You're not a child anymore, Kenzie. In a few years you'll be going off to college. Probably get married and start your own life, and I want the best life possible for you. I want all your dreams to come true." He waited and let that register. "But where does that leave me?"

She shrugged.

"No matter where each of our lives lead, nothing can lessen what we have. You'll always be my little girl and nobody can come between us."

"But why Ash's mom?"

"I enjoy her company. Would you rather me date somebody who had a kid you didn't like?"

At least she finally uncrossed her arms. "No, but she's sort of a pain."

"She's been through a lot just like Ashton has. She's entitled to a little time to adjust before you start making judgments."

"What happens when you break up? It'll make it hard for me and Ash to be friends. Have you thought about that? I like hanging out with him."

"And I like hanging out with Hanna. So let's give this a try. It could work out well for all of us."

"I'm not so sure about that."

Vince checked the tackle box to make sure they weren't forgetting anything.

Kenzie jammed her pink cap on backwards and grabbed the fishing poles. "It'll be a hoot to watch Ashton fish, but tell me again why his mom's going? She doesn't seem like the fishing type."

"Because I want her to." Vince tossed the tackle box and a blanket into the truck bed and slammed the tailgate.

Kenzie smirked, then clapped her hands at the dog. "Come on Boo. Let's go."

Vince started the truck and Boo leaped into the backseat. "Just so we're straight, Kenzie. I expect you to be nice to Hanna. Show some respect."

"Whatever."

Hanna wasn't surprised that Ashton didn't have the least issue with the dating situation. His only concern was Billy Baer and how Kenzie was taking it. When Vince and Kenzie pulled up, he bolted into the truck and rubbed Boo's head. "Hey, boy."

Vince held the door for Hanna, and grinned at the boy and the dog's slobbery greeting.

Wearing jeans and a black T-shirt, Vince looked even more sexy than usual. She wondered if he'd kiss her hello, but he didn't. She was glad they were thinking alike, that maybe it was best to take it slow, give the kids time to adjust.

"Hi, Mackenzie," Hanna said, hoping to get some feel for how tonight was going to work.

"Hi," Mackenzie replied, then turned her attention to Ashton and began rattling off a thousand details about fishing.

Vince slid into the cab and leaned forward for a kiss. "You ever fish?"

Taken by surprise, she touched her tongue to her lip and narrowed her eyes. "Not since I was young and

Daddy took me. Let's just say that I was not a natural at the sport."

After a quick stop by the sporting goods store for licenses and a run to KFC for a bucket of chicken, they were off to the lake.

Mackenzie grabbed the chicken and staked out the concrete picnic table closest to the water. Ashton took the blanket and Hanna grabbed the drinks while Vince brought up the rear hauling the fishing gear. Boo didn't even slow down at the table, just headed straight for the water's edge to sniff around.

Please let this evening be a success. Hanna knew Mackenzie had a lot of pull with her father and she was the best friend Ashton had ever had. Hanna wanted to get along.

"Dinner first." Vince stopped Kenzie in her tracks as she started toward the water.

"Dad, can't we fish a few minutes, then eat?"

"Chicken's hot and you might want to eat before you get fish guts on your hands."

"Good point," Ashton said.

Hanna had never seen Ashton wolf down his food so fast. But Kenzie still beat him. She handed Boo the last bite of chicken, tossed her empty plate into the garbage and grabbed a rod and reel. "I'll be over there on the dock."

"Stay in sight."

"Wait up!" Ashton tossed his plate and looked at the other three rods. "Which one do I use?"

"The green one."

Ashton took off after Mackenzie and Boo, trying to run and hold the rod up.

"Ashton's okay with this?"

Hanna shrugged and watched a boat with two fisherman putt across the mirror-smooth lake toward the docks on the opposite shore, leaving a narrow wake behind. "Thought it was kind of cool. What about Kenzie?"

"Kenzie will get a grip."

Hanna certainly hoped so, but she wasn't sure. "And let's hope Bully Baer stays out of her path until after she does."

"No kidding." Vince smiled at Hanna. "What else is wrong?"

She gulped. He could read her way too well. She hadn't even told her mother this. "Ashton told me that Richard's law-student girlfriend is pregnant."

Vince didn't seem to grasp the gravity of that. "Good. Maybe he'll be preoccupied with the new baby and not have time to pressure you about Ashton."

"Evidently Ashton has known for a month or two and they asked him to keep it quiet because she's due in August."

"Which means she was pregnant when he asked for a divorce?"

"Yeah." Her voice cracked. She wasn't sure why the confirmation had hit her so hard. "I'd guessed she might be pregnant when Richard asked for a divorce, but he denied it."

Vince ran his palm down her cheek.

She swiped an escaped tear. "God, I hate him right now. Why do men think with their… Why can't they use their brains?"

"I'm sorry. That's gotta hurt." He ran a thumb under her eye.

"No, I'm sorry. I didn't mean to throw you into the

scumbag category with my ex. It just seems so sleazy. This girl is so young, she was still living at home with her parents. She's only ten years older than Ashton. How sick is that!"

Vince looked at the kids, then back at Hanna. "What does Ashton think about a baby brother or sister?"

"That's how Ashton slipped and told me. He went with them shopping for baby furniture during spring break. They're redecorating the bedroom that was my office with new pink baby furniture." She felt like bursting into tears. "It's so stupid, but that room was mine. It's not logical to feel this violated over a dumb room."

He slid an arm around her. "There's nothing stupid about it. It was your room. Your home."

"Winnie the Pooh is going to be living in my cherry-wood study. And I'm living with my mother and sleeping in the stupid white canopy bed I got when I was eight."

"Well, I could suggest a solution for the bed issue, but you might surmise that I was rushing things." He stood and tugged her to her feet. "Come on. Fishing soothes the soul."

She knew he was kidding about moving in, but the idea of the four of them sharing a house, of her sleeping in Vince's arms each night didn't frighten her nearly as much as it should have.

Vince tied a lure onto the line and demonstrated how to cast. When Hanna took the fishing rod from him and gave it a try, the lure dropped to the ground at her feet, not even close to landing in the lake. "Fishing's not really my thing."

Mackenzie rolled her eyes, but Vince was facing Hanna and didn't notice. Hanna was tempted to stick her tongue out, but instead put more determination into the next cast and at least landed it in the water with a tiny splash. Mackenzie didn't seem to notice, as she and Ashton were giggling about something.

Hanna frowned when Vince's line sailed past hers and landed in the middle of the lake. "That's what you expect me to do?"

He laid down his fishing rod, slipped one arm around her back and put his hand over hers on the handle. "I've got confidence in you. Try this."

Backing into his chest, she held the fishing rod and moved her arm with his, enjoying the unison of their body movement. She released the button on the reel and the line soared out over the lake. The lure dropped into the water with a gentle splash.

"I caught one." Mackenzie bounced from one sneaker to the other as she reeled in the fish.

Reluctantly Hanna felt the absence of Vince's warmth as he turned toward Mackenzie. She had to confess that she was impressed when instead of waiting for Vince to do it, Mackenzie removed the fish from the hook and held it up for Ashton's approval. Not a glimpse of squeamishness.

"Whoa! Look at that one. He's got to be at least a five-pounder," Ashton assured her.

Hanna studied the tiny fish. They'd be lucky if it weighed a pound.

"Unless you plan to catch a bunch more and treat everyone to a fish fry, you might want to toss him back now." Vince nodded toward the water.

"You don't eat them?" Hanna stared at him in bemusement as Mackenzie gently knelt down and released the fish.

"Sometimes, but mostly we just fish for fun and let them go."

"It doesn't hurt them?"

"Nah, they just get harder to catch next time. Just adds challenge to the game."

"You're an interesting man, Mr. Keegan."

He flashed those dimples and dug his ringing cell phone out of his jeans. "Hey, Claire."

Hanna cast her line and tried not to eavesdrop.

"No use in Greg driving all the way up from Fredericksburg. And like you said, Gray is a master at the lawn, but when it comes to anything mechanical he's useless. I'll drop by tomorrow sometime and take a look." He paused. "Have you ever known me to turn down a home-cooked meal?" He laughed. "Yeah, tell the guys they're off the hook this time. See you around noon."

It was dusk when they wrapped up the adventure. On another evening Hanna would have put the fishing rod aside and just enjoyed the breathtaking sunset and sounds of frogs croaking and water lapping against the shore, but tonight she wasn't about to give Mackenzie any reason to think she couldn't hold her own. She kept casting that silly rod until the rest of them started packing up.

"So where are we going tomorrow?" Ashton tossed his rod into the pickup bed with the others.

"We're staying home and doing homework. You two aren't out of school yet," Hanna stated. Vince obviously had plans with the Maguires and Hanna didn't want him to feel as if he had to entertain them every evening.

Both kids groaned as they piled back into the pickup for the short trip home.

Vince held Hanna's arm and gave it a squeeze as she climbed into the tall truck. She felt a warm rush when he winked before closing her door.

"But tomorrow's Sunday. What if we get our homework done early?" Kenzie asked. "Then we could go see the new movie that started yesterday."

"I got most of mine done at school anyway," Ashton chimed in. "So I vote for the movie."

"You heard your mom. Sunday is a school night."

"Then maybe Ash could come to our house in the afternoon and we could do homework and play the Wii?"

The fact that she wasn't mentioned in that invite did not go unnoticed by Hanna. "Not tomorrow. Ashton takes his grades very seriously."

Ashton sat up straight. "I take the Wii seriously, too, and last time she beat me, so I have to prove she's not better than me."

"I am better than you." Mackenzie punched Ashton. "You need to work on your swing and quit wasting all your energy trying to figure out how the game works."

"Oh, you are going to pay for that. I'm going to beat you so bad."

Vince turned onto the road and shook his head. "No Wii until all homework is done and we give permission." He high-fived Hanna. "Parents rule. *Ah-ah-ah-ah-ah!*" He sounded very much like the Count on *Sesame Street.*

Kenzie frowned. "Great. Your mom is wearing off on my dad. What's up with that?"

Ashton groaned. "That sucks green pond scum."

Chapter 16

If members of the grapevine had any doubts, they wouldn't in five minutes. During the Monday lunch hour at Falls Dinner, Vince put a possessive hand on Hanna's back. If they were going to do this, they might as well put it out in the open and squelch speculation. In nine years in Marble Falls, he'd dated, even dated in "public," but had never brought anyone to Falls Diner at lunch when the entire town was likely to be there.

He felt Hanna take a deep breath. As she glanced up at him, he smiled. "They won't have nearly as much to gossip about if we're not sneaking around."

She nodded and led the way into the café.

Vince's mouth watered at the aroma of home-cooking permeating the bustling café. He took off his cap and escorted Hanna to a seat at a booth next to the counter.

The waitress grinned as she placed their menus on the Formica-topped table. "Hanna Creed. I wondered how long it'd take you to wander through here."

Vince tried not to laugh at the blank expression on Hanna's face. She had no idea what the woman's name was. "Hey, Penny. What's the special today?" he asked, hoping to help Hanna out.

"Chicken-fried steak and homemade mashed potatoes."

Hanna grinned. "Penny Jones. It's been a long time."

Penny laughed and patted Hanna's hand. "Dave Barkley told me you'd moved back. I wondered when you'd get around to stopping by and saying hello. Lots of people leave and return, but I figured you would be the last person to move back."

"I should have kept in touch." Hanna tried to not take Penny's remark personally, but she was right. She and Penny had been friends; but at eighteen, while Penny had been planning a wedding, Hanna had been counting down the days until she could trade in small-town U.S.A. for an exciting life in the big city.

Penny placed napkin-rolled flatware on the table. "My daughter said your boy and Kenzie had become fast friends." She looked between Vince and Hanna as if wondering if it was only the kids who'd gotten close.

Vince was fascinated by Hanna's baffled expression. She moved her glass to the other side of her place mat, then back. "They are. Kenzie has done wonders helping Ashton adjust."

"And how are you adjusting to living back in Marble Falls? I'm sure we must seem pretty boring after living in Dallas."

Hanna's gaze shifted to Vince. "I'm settling in quite

nicely, thanks. And that chicken-fried steak sounds wonderful. Do you have baby carrots?"

"We do." Penny didn't even write the order down, just turned and grinned at Vince.

"I'll have the same, plus a glass of iced tea."

"Make that two," Hanna said.

As Penny bustled off to place their order, skillfully dodging another waitress balancing a tray of desserts, Vince chuckled. "Well, it's all but official now."

"Oh my gosh, I sure hope we know what we're doing here." Hanna's cheeks blushed an adorable rosy pink.

"Now that you mention it, there is one thing I'm trying to figure out. How the hell are we going to get any time alone with two kids?" Vince wasn't willing to have Hanna sleep over with Kenzie in the house any more than she was willing with Ashton in town. Spring break only came once a year and that wasn't going to cut it. "Does Ashton go to his dad's this weekend?"

She sat back and smiled as Penny placed two glasses of iced tea on the table. "We swapped weekends, so Ashton isn't going until the weekend after. It's Richard's birthday and he wants Ashton there."

"Is it getting any easier to let him go?" Vince took a drink of tea. He knew it had torn her up in the beginning.

Her jaw set as she squeezed lemon into her iced tea. "How would you handle another man interfering with raising Mackenzie?"

"I'd have to kill him."

Hanna took a drink and chuckled. "No, you wouldn't. If anything went wrong, Mackenzie would cause a ruckus…be in his face so fast he'd never want to have any part of raising her again."

He laughed. "True. But you might underestimate Ashton. He can stand up for himself."

"I hope so. He's a smart kid, just keeps his emotions buried."

Probably way too buried for his own good. "Kenzie doesn't bury anything, except maybe the bodies."

"A person knows where she stands with that girl."

"Just like her mother." He quirked an eyebrow. "Thanks for making the effort to get along with her. She can be a challenge."

Hanna twirled a dark curl around her finger. "I'm hoping she'll come around. And if she does, maybe I'll have fewer issues with Ashton."

"Ashton will settle in."

The waitress plunked their food in front of them, and Hanna picked up her fork and focused those dark eyes on him. "Are you really so sure of everything?"

Jake Watson clapped Vince on the shoulder as he and Dave Barkley walked by on their way to a table. "How goes it, Vince? Keeping out of trouble?"

"Where's the fun in that?" Vince asked the older men.

Jake tipped his worn, straw cowboy hat at Hanna. "Ma'am." He rolled the rim of the hat in his hand and cocked a crooked grin at Dave. "The boy might have a point there."

Dave didn't seem to hear Jake's remark. "Aren't you Norma Creed's girl? The one that scooted out of here for Dallas when you was still wet behind the ears? Heard you were back."

Hanna swallowed her bite of chicken-fried steak and nodded at Dave. "That's right, Mr. Barkley. I used to buy candy and pop at your grocery store."

Dave beamed. "You were fond of those chocolate sodas, weren't ya?"

"Wow, I can't believe you remember that. Couldn't get full of them." Her eyes sparkled.

"I've still got some cold ones in the chest. You just stop on by."

Vince frowned at the older man. "You trying to make time with my lunch date there, Dave?"

"Smart boy shouldn't turn his back on ol' Dave with a beautiful lady around." Jake winked at Vince, then shuffled off toward the table where the waitress had placed their menus.

"Small towns." Hanna shook her head as Claire Maguire suddenly bustled through the front door, a huge turquoise-and-silver hobo purse hanging off her right arm.

"Hello, Vince." Claire hugged Vince's shoulder. Her smile faded into a wrinkled brow. "Hanna."

"Mrs. Maguire."

The older woman flashed a motherly grin at Vince. "I ran in for some groceries. Thought I'd pick up a big apple pie for dinner. You and Kenzie are coming over tonight, right?"

"Sure."

"And the monthly family BBQ on Sunday? James and Jen are coming in from Austin with the kids."

Vince glanced at Hanna. He'd rather spend the day with her and Ashton, but he hated to hurt Claire's feelings. Besides Kenzie would be ticked if she missed seeing her cousins.

Claire stared at him, then across the table at Hanna. "You're welcome to bring guests."

"Um, that's up to Hanna." He didn't know how not to

put her on the spot, but he was pretty sure she'd rather not go. "Do we have anything planned Sunday?"

Hanna put down her fork. "No. It's up to you."

"Then it's settled. We'll expect you around noon." Claire hugged Vince, waved at Hanna and walked over to the counter to order her pie.

Hanna did not look pleased. "I'm sorry about that," Vince said.

Both eyebrows rose and she blew out a breath. "It's okay. I'd sort of hoped we could put that off until we were a little further along."

"They're nice folks and there'll be a crowd. Gray for one, and you like him. The kids will have fun fishing and swimming."

Hanna forked a carrot. "Yeah."

Hanna wasn't looking forward to the afternoon at the Maguire house, but at least she'd get to spend time with Vince. Still, it was going to be awkward at best. Ashton was certainly psyched. He had his swimsuit and towel packed. He'd called Mackenzie to remind her to bring him a fishing rod and the life jacket for the boat Mackenzie kept at her grandparents' dock. The Keegans were becoming his personal social directors.

The quick kiss from Vince when he picked them up was about as close to intimacy as the day presented. Vince unloaded a huge chest of iced-down sodas from the truck, and Kenzie and Ashton hauled it around back to the deck. Hanna picked up the spinach salad she'd made and followed Vince up the walk. The flower bed overflowed with bright multicolored impatiens—red, purple, white and pink. The one closest to the porch sported a bunch of daisies. Perfect picture of a family home.

A group of boys tossed a Frisbee across the manicured front yard. "Hey, Uncle Vince!" one yelled, tossing him the fluorescent-orange disk.

Vince snagged it out of the air and tossed it back. "Hey, guys. This is Hanna."

"Hey, Hanna," one said, spinning and tossing the Frisbee to one of the others from behind his back.

Hanna stepped onto the porch of the ranch-style home. A couple of men waved from two of the rockers on the porch that extended the full length of the house. "Vince, you need to get out back before Wayne burns the burgers."

Vince grinned. "And you guys weren't man enough to keep him away from the grill?"

"Supervising the grill is your job."

"Yeah, yeah." Vince held the door open for Hanna.

Hanna set the spinach salad on the dining table already laden with a host of other dishes. The house was full of women, all working together like ants in a colony. Everyone moved around the huge, country-style kitchen, dodging as drawers and cabinet doors were opened, balancing dishes as they zigzagged about the room.

"Everyone, this is my friend Hanna Rosser." Vince flashed a grin and hugged a couple of the women.

"Remember Hanna Creed?" Grayson arrived just behind them. "She was a year younger than me and Belinda in school."

Hanna smiled at the tiny white-haired woman by his side. Gray took the dish out of the older woman's hand and placed it on the sideboard. "Hanna, this is our grandmother."

Shaking the frail hand, Hanna smiled. "Nice to meet you. That peach cobbler smells wonderful."

The large sprawling house oozed with the four Maguire boys and their families. Hanna was introduced to so many people, she couldn't keep track of them. Belinda's three older brothers were all tall and dark-haired. All were married and had kids, although she wasn't sure who had how many and which kids belonged to which family. Some of the women who introduced themselves to her or to whom she was introduced, didn't even appear to be family members. But like the other women, they all seemed to be used to the routine of the Maguire kitchen.

Vince left her to the crowd and made his way to the grill on the back deck. The Maguire's manicured lawn sloped gently down to the wooden boat dock, crowded with people, yet tranquil and oozing family camaraderie. Hanna watched as Vince's father-in-law clapped him on the back and handed him the tongs for the grill. Kids fished off the dock while others pedaled around the lake in two paddleboats. An older boy glided up to the deck on a Jet Ski.

The routine appeared to be that the men kept an eye on the kids and manned the large smoker and grill while the women hung out in the kitchen and caught up on family happenings.

Other than that, Hanna wasn't exactly sure how the kitchen organization worked. Everyone else obviously felt right at home as they pulled dishes out of the various cabinets and flatware out of drawers. One woman peeled potatoes and another buttered and wrapped corn in foil for the grill. It was like a well-orchestrated, chaotic play as each woman took care of business. Every time Hanna tried to help, someone else was already on top of it.

Wandering into the homey family room, Hanna browsed the pictures on the mantel. Belinda in a pep-squad uniform. A family portrait when the four boys and Belinda were in high school. A framed snapshot of Vince, Belinda and the kids at Sea World. Wedding portraits, including Vince and Belinda's.

"He's a good man. One of us," Grandma said from behind her shoulder. "He and Belinda were an interesting match. Good parents."

Hanna smiled, her gaze landing back on Vince's wedding portrait. Belinda was holding a bouquet of yellow and white daisies. "Belinda carried daisies at her wedding."

"From the time she was little, Belinda loved the yellow and white daisies that grew in my yard." Her grandmother said. "Always picking a bouquet and bringing them inside." Grandma kissed her finger and touched it to the photo. "I think they represented her happy, sunny personality."

Hanna's heart hit bottom as she smiled at the older woman, then glanced back at the pictures, many of which showed Vince. The reality of how much of Belinda was infused into every aspect of Vince's life stung. This was the Vince etched in Claire Maguire's mind.

Hanna ran a finger down the smooth silver picture frame of Vince's past. She smiled at Belinda's diminutive grandmother when what she really felt like doing was having a good cry. "Vince is a good guy."

Grandma nodded. "Rather attentive to that boy of yours, too."

"He is." Hanna turned away from the pictures and faced her. "And Ashton is one of his biggest fans." Which probably wasn't good. As fond as Vince was of Ashton, Hanna would never penetrate the strong hold Belinda's memory still had on him. And she wasn't willing to play second fiddle.

Scrutinizing her, Grandma looked back at the pictures on the mantel. Hanna waited for her to speak, but she just shook her head and wandered out of the room as quietly as she'd wandered in.

Uncomfortable, Hanna returned to the kitchen and finally found a job helping haul paper plates, plastic dinnerware and huge bowls of food out to the picnic tables on the patio and lawn.

Hanna smiled at Ashton tossing a Frisbee with Mackenzie and another boy. She could only wish she was doing half as well with the women. They smiled and were genuinely friendly, but they all were in sync with the family dynamics. At any given time at least three conversations were fighting for air space around Hanna, leaving her at loose ends. Not that it seemed intentional, but she was odd man out.

Vince and three other men were sitting on lawn chairs beside the grill, laughing and carrying on.

This family obviously felt that Vince Keegan was one of them, and from what she'd observed, he shared that sentiment.

She leaned against the deck railing to check on Ashton and Grayson came up beside her. "Hey, Hanna."

"Quite an impressive operation you have here," she said.

"You look overwhelmed." Without the ball cap Gray

usually wore, he looked more like the boy she remembered from high school. Dark-brown hair and smoky eyes, chiseled features. Not bad at all.

"Want me to track down Vince to save you from the insanity? They're almost too much for me and most of 'em are family." He flashed white teeth and pointed to a scrawny kid in a lime-green swimsuit who jumped and snagged a Frisbee. "That one belongs to my cousin Charlie—or my other cousin Dan. I'm never sure."

She laughed. "So you're not exactly a family guy?"

"I love 'em all, one at a time." He raised a dark eyebrow. "But all at once?"

"I can relate." At Grayson's age, it was funny he wasn't married. He could have been through a bad divorce, but then again, she might just be equating his loneliness to her recent situation.

Ashton and Mackenzie sat on the edge of the dock, dangling their feet in the water and fishing with the boy they'd been tossing the Frisbee with earlier.

Hanna studied Vince and the other guys and how they laughed and joked. Grilling ribs, hot dogs and hamburgers. Taking turns carousing with the kids. Vince was just as much a part of this family as if he'd been born into it.

Loaded down with yet more food, Claire Maguire approached the kitchen door. Hanna rushed to hold it open for her. "Here, let me take one of those bowls."

Claire continued to balance the food. "I've got it, but thanks for getting the door."

Not giving his mother any choice, Gray reached for the bowl of green beans. Claire smiled and relinquished her hold. "Thanks, sweetie."

Again, Hanna was left at loose ends. Gritting her

teeth, she went back inside and offered to help one of the sisters-in-law scoop potato salad into a serving dish.

Maybe after lunch she could find an excuse to escape.

But later, Ashton wanted to go swimming and refused to leave before getting wet. Vince took all four of their plates and tossed them into a plastic garbage sack, then started gathering up more trash. Hanna smiled at him and helped clear off the tables.

He gave her a quick kiss on the cheek. "I've got to help the guys clean up the grill. Relax and watch the kids." He had no clue how uncomfortable she was in Belinda's mother's home. And the Maguire home was truly a home full of love, just not for the new girlfriend of their late daughter's husband.

By the time the afternoon festivities finally wound down, Hanna was done. She'd tried to fit in and some of the other women were friendly enough, but Claire tended to stay in another room or talked to someone else. Trying to put herself in the woman's place, Hanna didn't push it. Claire Maguire was probably just as uncomfortable as Hanna was.

Vince didn't seem to notice Claire's reluctance to include Hanna. He pulled her into a game of Frisbee and on a boat ride around Lake Marble Falls with Mackenzie, Ashton and two of the nephews. Vince took it easy, just cruising around the lake on the pontoon boat. They stopped in a cove and let the kids swim. That part of the day was enjoyable at least. Hanna was so intent on watching the kids swim that when Vince sat beside her, she jumped.

"You having fun?"

She shrugged. "It's so peaceful out here. The kids love it."

Leaning around, he gave her a sweet kiss. "Sorry if I've ignored you today. I get so tangled up in everything going on, I forget you aren't used to all the chaos."

The chaos wasn't what bothered her. What Vince couldn't see was that Claire still considered him to be Belinda's husband. The woman was cordial, but the thought of accepting a new girlfriend into Vince's life was tearing Claire apart. Hanna received the nonverbal message Claire sent out loud and clear. The Maguires were his family in spirit if not in fact. And Hanna couldn't ask Vince to choose between her and his family. It was a no-win situation.

By the time Vince dropped her and Ashton off at home, she was drained. Vince kissed her, but she pulled back. "It's late and I need to get Ashton into bed."

He narrowed one eye. "Okay."

Ashton finished his shower and she'd just kissed him good-night when her cell phone rang. Assuming it was Vince, she didn't even look at the display. "Hey there."

"Hey," Richard's voice answered.

"Oh. Hi. I… Just a minute and I'll get the phone to Ashton before he goes to sleep. He just crawled into bed."

"I called to talk to you."

Still dressed for the cookout, Hanna's mood was about as rank as her sweaty shirt. "Okay."

"I've been doing a lot of thinking, Hanna. I made a serious mistake. There is no excuse for what I did to you and to our family. I love you. I always have. I love Ashton. What can I say to get you to come home?"

Chapter 17

Dropping onto the edge of the bed, Hanna could barely think. "Come home? After everything you've done? The things you said?"

"It was a moment of weakness. Phoebe came on to me. She looked up to me like you hadn't in years," Richard said.

Hanna honestly couldn't imagine how to respond.

"Are you still there? Please don't hang up."

She should hang up. She should throw the phone so far across the room that it would shatter into a million pieces. But right this minute, the thought of putting all the changes over the past few months behind her and going back into her world sounded almost tempting. "I'm here."

"Did Ashton tell you that Phoebe is pregnant?"

"Yes."

"Of course I'll support the baby, but Phoebe's moved home with her parents. It just isn't working. She doesn't know how to take care of herself, much less a baby or Ashton. She's excited about having a baby, but not about raising one. She's focused on finishing law school."

"Did she leave or did you ask her to leave?"

"She was too emotional to discuss things rationally so I talked to her father. He's a senior lawyer in the firm and it just seemed that it was best if we worked things out. I think Phoebe was relieved. She isn't ready to be married and have a twelve-year-old stepson."

Hanna felt a slow burn in her chest. "So it didn't work with her, and now you want me back? Well, screw you." She disconnected. What she wouldn't give for a good old-fashioned phone, one she could slam down. Punching the tiny green Off button didn't give her anger nearly enough release. She paced, grabbed her old rag doll off the shelf and flung it against the wall. "Damn him!"

The bedroom door opened and her mother peeped around. "Are you okay?"

"No! That was Richard."

"And?"

Hanna took a deep breath and let it out. Took another and finally stared at her mother. "He figured out that he doesn't want to raise his young girlfriend *and* the baby, so now he wants me to come home." She fought to steady her breathing. "How can he possibly think I'd just come back as if nothing had happened? As if he'd done nothing wrong?"

"So you prefer to stay in Marble Falls? Make Blue-bonnet Books work? Keep seeing Vince?"

"Two out of three maybe."

Norma came fully into the room and sat on the bed. "Not a good day?"

"What was I thinking?" Hanna scrubbed her face. "Men are too much work, and rushing into this thing with Vince is a mistake until I resolve my anger around Richard. At the moment, my feminine ego is still too bruised."

Hanna plopped down on the bed and Norma wrapped a motherly arm around her shoulders. "It'll all work out."

"Even if I decided to take on Vince's daughter, mother-in-law and the Marble Falls grapevine for his affections, I don't stand a chance in hell against a ghost."

Norma kissed the top of her head. "You always have a home here. Take all the time you need to figure things out."

Hanna's cell chimed again and this time she checked the display. "It's Vince." The phone bounced as she tossed it onto the bed unanswered. "I'm taking a long hot soak in the tub."

Vince didn't get too worked up about Hanna not answering her phone on Sunday night until she still didn't answer twice on Monday. But when she still hadn't returned his messages Tuesday morning, he swung by Bluebonnet Books to see what was up. Obviously she hadn't had much fun at the Maguires' barbecue, but that didn't explain why she was suddenly not talking to him.

As he entered the store, he spotted her sitting in a short blue chair designed for children, helping a mother and little boy in the children's section. She glanced up at him, but didn't leave her customers. He snagged the latest copy of *Field and Stream* off the rack and thumbed through it.

He didn't see Norma, so hoped that when Hanna finished with the customer, they could actually talk in private. The beauty of being self-employed meant he didn't have to punch a clock. So until she talked to him, he wasn't leaving.

Finally the lady selected some books for their trip to Houston. The boy was stepping high and smiling when they left, swinging the bag with his new books in one hand and holding his mom's hand with the other.

Vince waited for the door to click shut before he spoke. "Cute kid. Now, care to tell me what's wrong?"

Hanna twisted a curl and avoided his eyes. Not a positive sign.

"Hanna, talk to me. Did I do something wrong?"

"No." Those sad, dark eyes closed. "You did everything right, maybe too right."

"What the hell does that mean?"

"It means I've been divorced only a few months and you're Mr. Perfect. Your charm is quite disarming. I needed to feel desirable, like I wasn't a loser in the romance department, and you waltzed in with all that slow Southern cool and voilà."

His throat tightened. "We're back to that old time-table thing?"

"I have to get myself straight before I'm going to be in any shape to contribute to a relationship. There are things I've got to deal with on my own first."

What the hell wasn't she saying? Something had happened. "Was it the barbecue?"

"The Maguires are nice people. The bazillion of

them. They love you and Mackenzie, and that's fantastic."

"They'll love you, too."

"No, they won't. I don't belong there any more than I belong in a relationship right now. I don't know what I was thinking. Or maybe I just wasn't."

"Hanna, you know what they went through losing Belinda. What I went through." He'd opened his heart to this woman. Shared his darkest moments with her. Was that it? Did that scare her? "Give them time."

"You need to give *me* time. It took you nine years to get here. To work through your issues and be open to a relationship. It's just been a few months for me. My wounds are still bleeding. I have to figure out…"

Suddenly it hit him. "Richard back in the picture?"

"I would never go back to Richard."

"Really?"

"I have a son to think about. The last thing he needs is to start relying on you and then have you reject him like his father did. He couldn't handle that."

Vince's head spun. "First off, your son is stronger than you give him credit for. And second, the one being rejected here is me. You're throwing away a good thing on the offhand chance that it might not work out. And that makes zero sense."

Tossing the magazine on the rack, Vince was so angry he was almost vibrating. "If you ever get ready to tell me what's really going on here, you've got my number."

"Vince, I'm not trying to hurt you."

"Hurt me?" Turning, he was tempted to shake her— or kiss her—until she came to her senses, but who was he kidding? For whatever reason, she'd made up her mind. "I'm fine! Hell. That's just the way us country boys roll, right?"

He'd never been one for slamming doors, but he'd have liked nothing better than making the windows rattle when he left the bookstore. Of course, Hanna had one of those springs on the door that closed it slowly, and he would have had to break the contraption to get a resounding slam out of it. So he got in the truck and slammed that door instead.

Whatever the hell was eating Ms. Rosser, he could only hope it would pass in time. Maybe he'd rushed things. Whatever it was, he'd gotten one message loud and clear—she didn't want him in her life.

After work, he ran by the house to pick up Kenzie and treat her to pizza. He'd been on his own a long time and he refused to brood over Hanna Rosser.

But as he pulled into the drive, Mrs. Haythorn stood up from working in her flower bed. She waved, sprinting toward him before he even got out of the truck.

"Hi, Vincent. Hope you had a good day. Mackenzie's in the house. Said she had math homework. How is Hanna today?"

He did not need Mrs. H. fishing for any juicy details she could spread around town. "Hanna is fine. Was that Dave Barkley's red pickup I saw in your drive this morning after Mr. Haythorn left for work?"

"Well, uh, y-yes." She stammered and looked slightly off center at having the tables turned. "This old house has shifted and he's working on the doors."

The stammer in her voice was just what he was going for. Busybody. He was tired of everyone knowing his business. Maybe he had sold out by moving here.

Maybe it was time to consider a change. "Hope Dave takes care of everything for you."

Kenzie piled her plate with pizza from the buffet and slid into the red vinyl booth facing him. "So today when I dropped Ashton off, Ms. Rosser was in a tiff. She barked at him to get right on his homework and didn't even speak to me."

"Does she typically speak to you?"

Biting into a slice, Kenzie shrugged and swallowed. "Yeah, she's been offering me a cookie or brownie or whatever they have for the customers."

"Maybe it was a busy day."

"There was a plate of sugar cookies beside the coffeepot." Kenzie stared him in the eye. "Something's wrong or she and Ash would be here with us."

Great, he was being quizzed by a twelve-year-old. If Kenzie had picked up on it, the grapevine would, too. Who the hell cared? "We're not going to hang out with Hanna and Ashton for a while."

Kenzie narrowed one eye. "Uh-oh."

"Hanna just needs some time. No big deal." Like hell, but he wasn't about to tell Kenzie that.

"That's cool. It's always been just you and me, kid." She winked as she quoted his stock line every time life dealt them a blow.

He reached over and tweaked her nose. "Think you're pretty smart, don't you?"

"Grandma said that you should always put me first anyway. So this works out."

What? He'd always put Kenzie before anything and everything. "Why would she say that?"

Kenzie slurped her soda. "Oh, she always says that.

She thinks you're an awesome father because you always want what's best for me."

"Of course I want what's best for you, but why would you or Grandma ever think Hanna or anyone else would change that?"

"I don't. Just saying." She pushed her empty plate aside. "I need more pizza. Want me to bring you another slice of pepperoni?"

Vince ate so much he practically had pizza sauce coming out his ears as they headed toward the truck. Kenzie wrapped her arm around his waist and jabbed her left foot in front of his.

He returned the favor and they continued on their way as they always had. Just him and the kid. That wasn't so bad. It was simple. But one of these days he was going to end up alone. One lonely rocker on the damn front porch.

If there was ever a time he needed the Harley, it was now. First thing tomorrow he'd call Mariah and see if it was ready. Maybe after school finished next weekend he'd drop Kenzie at his folks and just take off somewhere. Anywhere. Hell, maybe he'd take her with him. Call it a graduation trip.

Women! How could he have been so wrong about Hanna? There was one element of relationships he did not miss and that was their total unpredictability.

He started the truck and turned to Kenzie. "When you grow up and get a boyfriend, if you have a problem with him, just tell him straight out what you think. We don't know how to fix things if you don't tell us what's wrong. Got that?"

The cutest little wrinkle formed between her eyes.

"Got it, Dad. Wow, you're really hung up on Ms. Rosser, huh?"

"No." The kid should not be this smart at twelve. "I just do not understand the workings of women's minds."

The corners of her mouth threatened a smile, but she held it in check admirably. "Gotcha. Trust me, I say what I think. If someone is too dense to get it, I spell it out in simpler language again and again until I get down to their level."

"You saying I'm dense?"

"Never."

Reaching over, he tugged her ponytail. "You are not going to play games like other women do or I'll have to take you down a peg or two."

Laughing, she buckled her seat belt. "Whatever guy tangles with me is going to know exactly where he stands."

First thing the next morning, Vince called Mariah and she promised to have the bike ready by close of business. The freedom of the road was sounding better and better.

On the way to one of his job sites, Vince stopped at a florist, then made a side trip and pulled into the cemetery. He hadn't been there in a couple of months and for some reason today he needed the sanity.

He parked under the sprawling pecan tree and squatted down to face Matt's headstone. "Hey, kid. Just wanted to check in. Been thinking about you a lot lately. Kenzie's been bringing another kid around to play ball and stuff and he reminds me of what you and I never had a chance to do. Hope you don't mind. Nah, you wouldn't mind. You'd be a couple years older than him, but you'd get along. I miss you, Matt."

He turned to Belinda's headstone and removed the bouquet of faded silk daisies he and Kenzie had brought for her thirty-fifth birthday back in February. He laid them aside and placed the bouquet of Texas wildflowers in the vase beside the monument.

He wasn't surprised to look up and see Gray's truck bounce through the gate. It wasn't the first time they'd bumped into each other here. Something about twins. At first Vince had kept the area clean, but since Grayson had returned from the navy and started the landscaping business, the gravesite had become his pet project.

Vince ran a hand over Belinda's headstone. "Hey there, babe. Our baby girl is growing into a beautiful young lady, in spite of me. You'd be proud of her. Me, I'm not sure I'm handling things so well, but what else is new, huh?"

The old truck rattled to a stop behind Vince's pickup, and Gray walked up and knelt down beside him. "She'd be okay with this, you know. With you finally finding someone."

Vince rubbed his forehead. "I know. Belinda isn't the problem. Hanna is."

Gray got that "I knew it" look on his face, plucked a dandelion and looked around for any other weeds that might have popped out since he last visited. "Remember the first time you spent a Sunday at the house before you and Belinda worked out the whole baby thing? You hardly opened your mouth to anyone except Dad and Belinda."

"That was different."

Gray shook his head. "Yeah, you had a genuine goal

in being there, but the chaos was pretty overwhelming, no?"

Vince closed his eyes. "And that was even before there were so many kids. You don't have to tell me that I sort of left Hanna hanging out to dry, but I was busy watching the kids, keeping Wayne from burning the burgers and generally doing what we do."

I didn't pay enough attention to her at the folks' house and she breaks it off? What's up with that? If that was what had her panties in a twist, she could have said something while we were there instead of stewing over it.

"Hanna wouldn't let one afternoon mess things up," Gray said, reading his thoughts. "I talked to her, but she said she didn't need babysitting."

There were still pieces missing. "There has to be something else."

"Look. You seem pretty serious about Hanna. Try talking to her."

First Mackenzie and now Gray. Was it that obvious? "Got shut down. She broke it off. I'm not into groveling." Hanna knew where to find him if she got over whatever bee was in her bonnet.

Gray straightened and tossed the dead daisies and weeds into the trash can beside the road. "Then I guess you'd just as soon spend your evenings playing video games with Kenzie."

Vince raised an eyebrow.

"You sure Kenzie isn't part of the problem? No jealousy? You two are tight and she might not like Hanna encroaching on her territory."

Vince winced. "Kenzie's not really happy. Not sure she totally understands. I mean, how do you tell a twelve-year-old that her old man needs a woman in his life?"

"Haven't had that sex talk yet, huh?"

"We're both sort of avoiding it. Can't you just hear that conversation? Kenzie will be grossed out."

"You might be amazed how much she already understands. Kids grow up fast these days."

Oh, God. "And I thought diapers stunk."

"You could ask Mom to talk to her."

"Thought about that. But Kenzie's my daughter. I'm working up to it." Vince grinned. "Want to assist?"

Gray turned ashen. "I'd love to, but I have to scrub the toilet that evening."

Pretty much the response he'd expected. "Some uncle you are."

Chapter 18

Vince had two crews working, and by the end of the day every last one of them was probably ready to quit. Today he wasn't taking any crap from anyone. They either did the job the way it was designed or they were damn well going to hear about it.

Gray pulled up to the site just as Vince was tearing into the foreman about not staying on top of the guy sawing the timbers. "You just cost me two hundred bucks. If he doesn't know how to read the damn plans, put someone else on the saw."

"The kid made a mistake."

"Then the kid is back to using a nail gun and if he can't handle that, he can try his luck sacking groceries."

Gray nodded toward the truck. "Ready to pick up the Harley?"

Vince glanced at his watch. "I thought you were going to meet me at the house."

"Hey, don't snap my head off. I had a job just down the street. But if you don't need a ride, I've got a cold beer with my name on it waiting at home."

Vince gritted his teeth. "No need to get all testy." He locked his pickup, took a deep breath and crawled into Gray's. "Sorry. Been a bad day."

Gray turned the key and waited for the engine to kick in. He pumped the gas a couple times and the engine finally caught. "Lighten up. It's not their fault your love life tanked."

Vince acknowledged this remark with an obscene hand gesture that only earned him a laugh from his brother-in-law.

Vince blew off steam. "I mean, what the hell happened? One day everything was going great, then out of the blue, Hanna said it's over. What changed?"

Gray shrugged as he stopped at an intersection to let an eighteen-wheeler pass.

"Not only do women expect us to understand what they say, they also seem to think we can read their minds." Vince was getting worked up all over again just thinking about it. "How the hell are we supposed to keep up?"

Gray cocked an eyebrow and shifted into third.

"What does she expect me to do? Does she think I'll come knocking at her door? Is it a game? Or maybe she really does just want me to disappear."

"Bullshit," Gray said.

Vince wanted to think it was just a temporary bump in the road, but he wasn't sure. "There was something between us and it was more than San Antonio and sex. We connect. She tried to walk away once and came back, so why is she doing it again?"

Gray gave him a sideways smirk as they started across the bridge.

"Should I call her, you think?" Vince stared straight ahead. "No way. That's what she wants me to do."

"So you're both hardheaded? That'll turn out well."

Vince glared at him. "I thought she'd call me when she worked through things with Richard, but now I wonder. She'll call." Vince stared out the window at the field of late-blooming pink buttercups, trying to convince himself. "Won't she?"

Gray pulled into the parking lot and held up both hands. "When did I suddenly become the expert? Look at my love life."

"What love life?"

Gray grimaced. "My point exactly."

Vince slid out of the truck and eyed Mariah's cute little figure. She was a couple of inches shorter than Hanna, not a single curl in her cropped brown hair. But the whole package fitted together nicely, right down to those tight jeans and tank top.

Gray, apparently, was oblivious.

Mariah looked up from a bike and flashed a pair of green eyes. "Bike's ready. Take it for a spin and see how it performs."

It was still too early for afternoon rush hour, not that rush hour in Marble Falls amounted to much. Heading away from town, he opened the bike up. The engine purred like a tiger. When he got back to the shop, Mariah was working on another bike and Gray was in the parking lot, leaning against the truck as if there wasn't a good-looking woman twenty feet away.

"Trust me, the woman has magic hands."

Gray shook his head. "You're the one who shares

with her the thrill of risking life and limb on a two-wheeled get-ya-killed."

Giving him a go-to-hell look, Vince went to pay Mariah. He should ask her out. He'd thought about it a time or two, but then he'd met Hanna. He wrote out the check. "You do have a way with a machine, Ms. Calabrezie."

Her smile was sweet. "We all have our quirks. Personally I find that engines make more sense than most people."

"You called that one right." He handed her the check and took the receipt. "Take care."

"So, did you ask her out?" Gray asked as Vince coasted to a stop beside the truck.

Why, when he looked at Mariah, did he only see what wasn't like Hanna Rosser? That should have been a good thing. "Just follow me home to drop off the bike."

"Figured she might be your type."

"She's a doll, but I've had about all the small-town gossip I can stomach this week. Austin is looking better and better."

Gray grinned and pulled out of the lot. They dropped off the bike and picked up Kenzie at the house, then headed back to the job site for Vince's pickup.

"Uncle Gray, you coming to my graduation next Friday?"

Kenzie had a special bond with her mother's twin and it made Vince both happy and sad. Belinda had adored Matt, but she'd doted on her baby girl.

Gray nudged Kenzie. "You sure your grades are good enough that they're actually going to let you graduate from elementary school?"

"I've got it," Kenzie said from her perch between the

two men. "I could sign you up for that show *Are You Smarter Than a Fifth Grader?* and maybe you'd have to eat a few of those words."

Vince offered to buy Gray dinner, but he declined, so Vince and Kenzie headed for Wal-Mart to pick up groceries and dog food. Vince wasn't in the mood to eat out. Maybe they'd grill hamburgers.

Kenzie made her way through the aisles doing what Kenzie was best at, tossing cookies and chips into the basket. Vince turned down an aisle and almost ran his shopping cart into Hanna's. Their gazes met for a split second before she looked away.

"Hello, Ms. Rosser." Kenzie tossed in a bag of Oreos and stood in front of Vince, facing Hanna. "Where's Ash?"

"He's home, doing his homework." Those sad, dark eyes looked up from Kenzie and focused on him. "Vince."

"Hanna."

His gut hurt. His body had an elemental reaction to hers. He wanted to drag her aside and make her admit that what they had was worth fighting for.

Instead, he stood motionless and watched her walk away. She'd ended it. She could make the first move to get it back. If she wanted it back.

Hanna held her head high and forced one foot in front of the other. If she didn't look into those denim-colored eyes, maybe she could resist the spell Vince had over her. Maybe she could not lie awake again tonight and wonder if she'd lost her ever-loving mind for ending it with him.

But they had rushed into a physical relationship too

soon. Before she'd had time to get her head together after the divorce.

The night before, when her thoughts had been in so much turmoil over Vince that she couldn't sleep, she'd tried to picture her life back in Dallas. As much as she'd loved her beautiful home, it was no longer what she wanted. There was more to it than her unwillingness to forgive Richard; her dreams had changed. She might not know yet what the future held, but she knew she had to make it happen on her own.

Vince hadn't called or stopped by, but that was what she'd needed, right? Time to regroup, to get to know who Hanna was after the divorce.

Who was she kidding? Time wasn't an issue. Vince had her so wrapped around his finger, she couldn't stop thinking about him. She just wasn't willing to play second fiddle to Belinda for the rest of her life. Or to the entire Maguire clan.

She tossed a bundle of leaf lettuce in the basket with the six-pack of underwear for Ashton and went in search of French bread for dinner. It really was amazing how much money she saved by shopping at Wal-Mart. The identical underwear would be twice as much at the department store in Dallas.

At the checkout counter she picked up one of those flashy, sensationalized star rags, but glanced at the headlines and put it back. Who really believed any of that crap? It was mean-spirited gossip, just like the kind in small towns, only on a worldwide scale.

Bluebonnet Books was quiet Thursday afternoon. Norma had taken off to meet her friends for lunch and their weekly bridge game. Customers were evidently staying in out of the rain, or at least they weren't into reading. Hanna was sitting behind the counter filling out an order when she heard the bell on the door jingle.

Vince looked incredibly serious, dressed in jeans and the same black button-down he'd worn in San Antonio. He closed the door against the dark clouds and brushed the rain off his arms.

As he turned, their eyes met, but he stayed in the front of the store. Placing both palms on the windowsill, he leaned his weight on them and crossed one ankle over the other. Those intense eyes bored a hole into her soul.

"Hi," she said. Anything to break the silence.

"Hi." He looked up, then back at her as if he wasn't sure what to say. "I talked to Claire this morning."

Hanna's breath caught in her throat. "About?"

"You. Us. The past. The future."

She wasn't sure what that meant. "To ask her permission?"

He shook his head. "First, I need you to tell me why you broke it off after the barbecue. No games, Hanna."

She closed her eyes. She couldn't do this. Slowly she opened her eyes and looked at him. Okay, he wanted honesty. "I know Belinda was a wonderful person. And I know that you all loved her very much. You will always be a part of the Maguire family. I'm just not sure there's any room left for me."

"Fair enough." He continued to lean on the windowsill. "Belinda's family has been very good to me. I owed it to Claire at least to hear it from me. No matter how much I loved Belinda, it's time to move past that."

She stared at him in disbelief. "Vince."

"Hear me out before you say anything." He cocked one eyebrow. "I took your advice. I've registered for a summer class to finish my master's. And I talked to my old boss about some opportunities here and maybe eventually abroad."

"Oh." Hanna nibbled at her lip. So this wasn't about getting back together? It was about him moving on? She'd waited too long to tell him she loved him. She blinked at the realization. She. Loved. Him. Fighting back tears, she mustered up fake enthusiasm. "I'm so proud of you for following your dream. Living abroad will be an amazing experience for Mackenzie."

He pushed off the windowsill and took a step forward.

Don't touch me. I can't handle that. If you don't touch me, maybe I won't break down completely until I get home. Maybe I won't beg for another chance.

He took a second step and wrapped a curl of her hair around his finger. "Dreams change. I thought I could just move on and put us behind me." He slid a hand behind her neck and drew her closer. "I never thought I'd be in love again. This all-out, don't-want-to-waste-a-day-without-you sort of love." He ran the back of his hand down her cheek. "Living abroad could be an awesome experience for Ashton, too. And us."

Her heart raced and she couldn't tear her eyes away.

Tilting his head, he smiled. "I love you. I want you with me."

She stared at his gorgeous, sexy mouth as it descended toward hers. She parted her lips and reacquainted herself with the taste and feel of Vince. Wrapping her arms around him, she pulled him as close as she could, craving his touch. She rested her palm against his face and studied every single inch of him.

"It'll take at least a couple of years to finish school and get some experience under my belt. Give you time to..."

"Shh." She put her finger to his lips, still moist from the kiss. She ran a hand down his clean-shaven cheek, enjoying the sheer masculine realness of it. "I don't need time. As hard as I've tried not to, I've thought about nothing but you since you walked out of here the other day. I love you, Vince Keegan."

She leaned back against the wall, watching him, waiting.

He groaned and placed his hands on either side of her head and leaned in, pressing all six feet, two inches of his body against hers. She ran her hands down his abs, around his waist and cupped his tight buttocks. Couldn't get enough of the feel of his hardness pressing into her softness. The taste of his mouth, his skin.

Pulling back just enough so she could draw a breath, she touched his face and stared into those blue eyes. "We can make an amazing life for us and the kids. Whether it's here, Austin or overseas."

He ran the back of his hand intimately down the side of her breast. "What about Bluebonnet Books?"

Tingles ran up her spine. "I love the bookstore, but Mom is ten times better than I am at knowing what people want and selling it to them. She's not good at the accounts, though. If the time comes, she and I can work something out."

"You're serious about this? I don't do well with male-female games."

She tightened her arms around him and nuzzled into his neck. "Oh, man. You're the one who better be serious, because I have no intentions of letting you go again."

Hanna's cell phone chimed and she fished it out of her pocket. "Hello."

"I'm sorry to disturb you, Ms. Rosser, but Ashton has been in a fight. We need you to come to the school."

Her heart stopped. "I'll be right there."

She hung up just as Vince's cell rang.

Hanna locked the store and put up the closed sign, then jumped into the truck with Vince. They covered the blocks to the school in no time, and Vince helped her out and they darted through the rain. He held the door open for her and they walked into the office together. William Baer already waited in front of the receptionist desk.

"Vince. Ms. Rosser."

Vince shook his hand. "Will."

Principal Montgomery stepped out and motioned for them to enter her office. All three kids sat in chairs in front of her desk. Kenzie's ponytail was falling down. Ashton had a black eye and Billy held a damp, bloody rag to his nose.

"Okay, students. One more time. Who threw the first punch?" the principal asked.

They all exchanged glances.

"I did." Ashton stood up. "He said that Kenzie's dad was having sex with my mom and that she was a ho."

"Well, they are," Billy said. "You're not supposed to hit a guy for telling the truth."

Kenzie jumped to her feet. "What my dad does is none of your business. And Ms. Rosser is not a ho. You say that again and I'll pound you into dog poop."

Hanna's mouth dropped open. Kenzie defending her?

William Baer glanced from Hanna to Vince, then

focused on his son. "Billy, you know better than to say things like that."

Hanna tried to stay calm. The way Mr. Baer had looked her up and down, he obviously believed the rumors. Probably where Billy had heard them to begin with.

Principal Montgomery stared at Ashton. "This school does not condone fighting. You were in the wrong for striking another child. Do you understand that if I suspend you, you won't be allowed to graduate with your class tomorrow?"

Vince stepped forward. "Excuse me, Mrs. Montgomery. But you can't really hold it against a boy for defending his mother. I would have thought that behavior would be rewarded, not punished."

Hanna felt a sick ache in her stomach. A straight-A kid and he was in danger of not graduating because of her.

William Baer clamped a hand on his son's shoulder. "Billy. I expect you to apologize to Ashton and to the other people in this room. Your remark was inappropriate."

Ashton held his head high and stared at Billy, waiting. Kenzie stood beside him, united with him.

"I'm sorry." Billy shuffled his feet. "I shouldn't have said it."

He started to sit back down, but his father turned him toward Vince and Hanna.

Obviously uncomfortable, Billy laid the bloody rag on the chair and stuffed his hands into his pockets. "I'm sorry. I didn't really mean it. It's just that Ash gets so riled up these days. I couldn't help myself."

"Apology accepted." Hanna turned to Ashton. "You should forgive Billy."

"Okay." Ashton took a step forward and shook Billy's hand. "Just no more remarks about my mom or Vince."

Principal Montgomery took a deep breath. "Well, we only have a half day tomorrow, then graduation. Surely we can let this one pass and get through tomorrow without further incident."

Hanna shook the woman's hand. "Thank you, Mrs. Montgomery. I appreciate your decision."

Hanna and Ashton walked out of the school with Vince and Kenzie. She wasn't sure what to say to the kids about the recent turn of events.

The rain had moved out, but water ran down the curbs along the parking lot and dripped from the overhanging trees.

Ashton looked around. "Where's the car?"

"I rode with Vince." She watched Ashton's face for a reaction. Would he put two and two together? He'd known they were no longer seeing each other.

"Does this mean we're going to be a family?" Mackenzie blurted out.

Vince exchanged looks with Hanna, waiting for her to answer.

"There is that possibility." She watched the kids closely. "How do you two feel about that? Kenzie?"

Kenzie widened her eyes at Ashton, then they both erupted into giggles.

"Cool," Kenzie said.

Ashton high-fived Kenzie. "They don't know how much trouble they're in."

* * * * *

**WE HOPE YOU ENJOYED
THIS BOOK FROM**

HARLEQUIN
SPECIAL
EDITION

Believe in love. Overcome obstacles. Find happiness.

Relate to finding comfort and strength in the
support of loved ones and enjoy the journey
no matter what life throws your way.

6 NEW BOOKS AVAILABLE EVERY MONTH!

HSEHALO2020

SPECIAL EXCERPT FROM

◆ HARLEQUIN
SPECIAL EDITION

*When Jed Dalloway started over, ranching a
mountain plot for his recluse boss is what saved him.
So when hometown girl April Reed offers a deal
to develop the land, Jed tells her no sale.
But his heart doesn't get the message...*

*Read on for a sneak preview of
the next book in* New York Times *bestselling author
Allison Leigh's Return to the Double C miniseries,*
A Promise to Keep.

"Don't look at me like that, April."

She raised her gaze to his. "Like what?"

His fingers tightened in her hair and her mouth ran dry. She swallowed. Moistened her lips.

She wasn't sure if she moved first. Or if it was him.

But then his mouth was on hers and like everything else about him, she felt engulfed by an inferno. Or maybe the burning was coming from inside her.

There was no way to know.

No reason to care.

Her hands slid up the granite chest, behind his neck, where his skin felt even hotter beneath her fingertips, and slipped through his thick hair, which was not hot, but instead felt cool and unexpectedly silky.

His arm around her tightened, his hand pressing her closer while his kiss deepened. Consuming. Exhilarating.

Her head was whirling, sounds roaring.

It was only a kiss.

But she was melting.

She was flying.

And then she realized the sounds weren't just inside her head.

Someone was laying on a horn.

She jerked back, her gaze skittering over Jed's as they both turned to peer through the curtain of white light shining over them.

"Mind getting at least one of these vehicles out of the way?" The shout was male and obviously amused.

"Oh for cryin'—" She exhaled. "That's my uncle Matthew," she told Jed, pushing him away. "And I'm sorry to say, but we are probably never going to live this down."

Don't miss
A Promise to Keep *by Allison Leigh,*
available March 2020 wherever
Harlequin Special Edition books and ebooks are sold.

Harlequin.com

Copyright © 2020 by Allison Lee Johnson

HSEEXP0220

HARLEQUIN

Heartfelt or suspenseful, inspiring or passionate, Harlequin has your happily-ever-after.

With new books published
every month, you are sure to find the
satisfying escape you know you deserve.

SIGN UP FOR THE HARLEQUIN NEWSLETTER

Be the first to hear about great new
reads and exciting offers!

Harlequin.com/newsletters

HNEWS2020

Love Harlequin romance?

DISCOVER.

Be the first to find out about promotions, news and exclusive content!

Facebook.com/HarlequinBooks

Twitter.com/HarlequinBooks

Instagram.com/HarlequinBooks

Pinterest.com/HarlequinBooks

ReaderService.com

EXPLORE.

Sign up for the Harlequin e-newsletter and download a free book from any series at **TryHarlequin.com**

CONNECT.

Join our Harlequin community to share your thoughts and connect with other romance readers! **Facebook.com/groups/HarlequinConnection**

HSOCIAL2020